EMPIRE'S HEIR

Marian L Thorpe

I0601972

Arboretum Press

EMPIRE'S HEIR

Arboretum Press
Guelph, ON, Canada

www.arboretumpress.com

ISBN (print): 978-1-7771783-8-3
ISBN (e-book): 978-1-7771783-7-6

Cover Design by Anthony O'Brien
www.bookcoverdesign.store

Epigraphs

Part I: from *The City*, by C.P. Cavafy. Translation © 1975, 1992 by Edmund Keeley and Philip Sherrard. Princeton University Press
Part II: *The Ides of March* by C.P Cavafy. Translation © 2006 by Aliki Barnstone. W. W. Norton
Part III: from *The God Abandons Antony*, by C.P. Cavafy. Translation © 1975, 1992 by Edmund Keeley and Philip Sherrard. Princeton University Press
All used under Fair Use Policy.

In memory of my father
Harry Joseph Thorpe
1916-2015

The Story So Far

To learn what happened in the previous books in this series (or have your memory jogged), please go to

http://bit.ly/LegacyMainEvents

The password for this site is: TheStorySoFar

The Characters of Empire's Heir

Characters in italics are deceased.

Character	Role
Alekos	Prince of Casil, soon to be Emperor of the East
Amlodd	A *scáeli* of Linrathe
Apulo	Cillian's body servant
Åsmund	*Prince of Varsland, murdered by his brother Fritjof in* Empire's Exile
Bernikë	Druisius's sister, a prostitute of the baths
Bjørn	Prince of Varsland, but also thought to be Sorley's son
Bruccius	Tutor to Alekos, advisor to Eudekia
Bryngyl	King of Varsland, Bjørn's brother
Callan	*The last Emperor of the West, Cillian's father,*
Cassia	A Casilani woman, daughter to Severa and Livius
Casyn	*The first Princip of Ésparias, Callan's brother,*
Cillian	*Comiádh* of the *Ti'ach na Cillian*; senior prince of Ésparias;
Colm	Lena & Cillian's teenage son, prince of Ésparias
Constyn	Faolyn & Suisan's son, prince of Ésparias
Dagney	*Scáeli and Lady of the Ti'ach with Perras,*
Dalphe	Bride candidate from Sylana
Daragh	Ruar's oldest son, heir presumptive to Linrathe
Debora	Sahira's chaperone
Decanius	Financial Comptroller of Casil, advisor to Eudekia
Dern	Commander of the Ésparian Fleet
Druisius (Druise)	Captain in the Ésparian army; Cillian's bodyguard
Elon	*King of Leste, who attempted to assassinate Callan in* Empire's Daughter
Elsë	Jordis's daughter
Eudekia	Empress of the East
Faolyn	*Princip* of Ésparias, son to General Talyn.
Faria	Dalphe's mother
Farry	Captain in the Ésparian army, old friend of Lena's
Flavian	*Decanius's father, Procurator of Qipërta,*

Character	Role
Fritjof	*King of Varsland in* Empire's Hostage & Empire's Exile
Garia	Gwenna's bodyguard
Gnaius	A physician of Casil
Gwenna	Lena & Cillian's adult daughter, princess of and heir to Ésparias
Hagen	*Eirën of Hagenstorp*
Hairle	Sorley's nephew
Hathus	Prince of the Boranoi, married to Eudekia
Helvi	Ruar's wife, a Marai earl's daughter
Iorlath	*Comiádh* of the *Ti'ach na Iorlath*
Irmgard	Widow of Åsmund; Bryngyl and Bjørn's mother
Jordis	*Konë of Hagenstorp*
Junia	Commander of the Horse Archers of Casil
Lairís	Sorley's niece
Lena	Captain, later Major, Ésparian army; Lady of the *Ti'ach na Cillian*
Letitia	A woman of Casil
Lianë	*Lena & Cillian's daughter, princess of Ésparias,*
Livius	Casilani Governor of Ésparias
Lynthe	Lieutenant in the Ésparian army; princess of Ésparias.
Marius	Druisius's brother, a merchant of Casil
Maya	Lena's lover in *Empire's Daughter*
Melis	Cassia's servant
Mhairi	Housekeeper at the *Ti'ach na Cillian*
Michan	Major in the Esparian army, Gwenna's superior
Mihae	*Headman of Sylana in* Empire's Exile
Nyle	Sorley's half-brother
Perras	*Comiádh* before Cillian, deceased
Philatos	*Emperor of Casil; Alekos's father*
Quintus	*Past advisor to Eudekia, uncle to Decanius*
Roel	Estate manager at the *Ti'ach na Cillian*
Rosale	Princess of Halachia, a client kingdom of Casil
Ruar	*Teannasach of Linrathe*
Sahira	Princess of Qipërta, a province of Casil
Severa	Wife to the Casilani governor of Ésparias

Character	Role
Shugo	Shepherd at Hagenstorp
Siusàn	Wife to Faolyn
Sorley	Lord Sorley of Gundarstorp, *Scáeli* to the *Ti'ach na Cillian*
Talyn	General of Ésparian army; mother of Faolyn & Lynthe
Teárdh	Lena's nephew, son of her sister Kira and a Marai man.
Timor	Sahira's uncle, brother to the King of Qipërta
Turlo	*General of the Ésparian army*
Vita	Marius's wife

Background characters with a historical counterpart

Archyte	Archytas
Adricius	Hadrian
Annaeus	Seneca
Catilius	Marcus Aurelius
Cotta	Julius Caesar
Lekandar	Alexander the Great
Mestrius	Plutarch
Serventius	Epictetus
Tullius	Cicero

Peritas, Colm's dog, has the same name as Alexander the Great's dog

Family trees for main and some supporting characters can be found at
http://bit.ly/AppendicesLegacy

The Vocabulary of Empire's Heir

The languages spoken in *Empire's Heir* are my inventions, but they are based on existing or historic languages. Pronunciations and grammar may not follow the conventions of those languages. Roughly, Casilan is based on Latin; Linrathan primarily from Gaelic, both Scottish and Irish, and Marái'sta from Scandinavian languages. The dialect of Sorham is an analogue of Norse Gaelic.

Word	Meaning	Language
amané	lover	Casilan
Athàir	father	Linrathan
cithar	cithara	Casilan
comiádh, comiádha	professor(s)	Linrathan
consor, consori	partner(s)	Esparian
dalta/daltai	student(s)	Linrathan
danta	saga	Linrathan
duíne	man	Linrathan
Eirën/ Eirënnen	male landholder(s)	Linrathan
fiscarius	financial comptroller	Casilan
fuádain	peregrine falcon	Linrathan
fuisce	whisky	Linrathan
gràhadh	beloved	Linrathan
idióta	idiot	Casilan
käresta/kärestan	beloved (f)/(m)	Linrathan
Konë	female landholder	Linrathan
ladhar	stringed instrument	Linrathan
leannan	dearest	Linrathan
li'ítho	marriage bracelets	Sorham
Magistere/magistera	high-ranking advisor(s)	Casilan
Mathàir	mother	Linrathan
mensores	surveyors	Casilan

Word	Meaning	Language
mo charaidh gràhadh	my beloved friend	Linrathan
mo charaidh	my friend	Linrathan
mo duíne gràhadh	my beloved man	Linrathan
mo duíne	my man	Linrathan
mo mhac	my son	Linrathan
mo nihéan gràhadh	my beloved daughter	Linrathan
mo nihéan treún	my brave daughter	Linrathan
mo nihéan	my daughter	Linrathan
mo Somhairle gràhadh	my beloved Sorley	Linrathan
mo	my	Linrathan
na (as in Ti'ach na Perras)	of	Linrathan
Princip(e)	leader, prince, princess	Casilan
scáeli/scáeli'en	bard(s), skald(s)	Linrathan
scrapta/scraptae	female prostitute(s)	Casilan
subura	marketplace	Casilan
Teannasach	chieftain; leader of Linrathe	Linrathan
Ti'ach/Ti'acha	school(s)	Linrathan
torp	farmstead & cottages	Linrathan
torpari	cottager, peasant	Linrathan
toscaire/toscairen	envoy(s)	Linrathan
weàn	young child	Linrathan
xache	board game	All

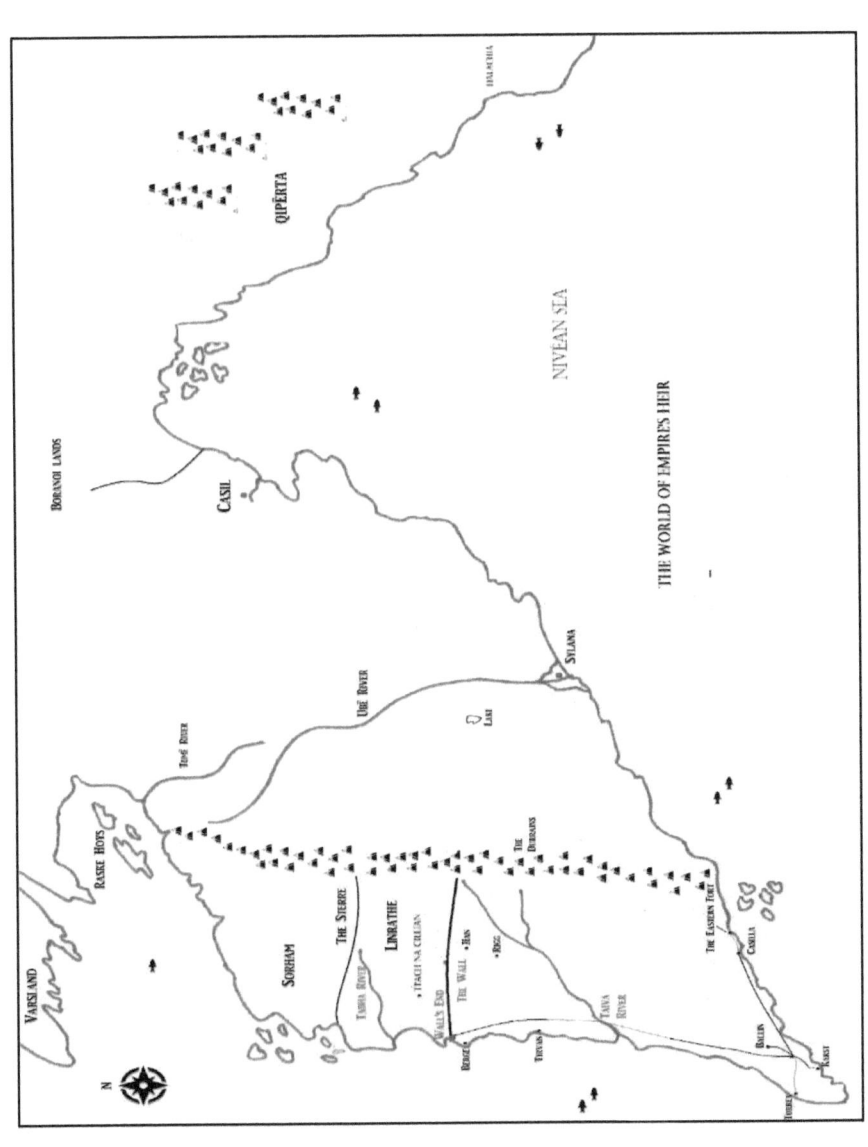

THE WORLD OF EMPIRE'S HEIR

Part I

... with what pleasure, what joy, you enter harbours you're seeing for the first time.
. .
C.P. Cavafy

Chapter 1

~DAUGHTER~

"GWENNA." RUAR SAT BACK IN HIS CHAIR. "I can't accept that."

He is your ally, not your adversary, I told myself, facing the *Teannasach* of Linrathe across the table. "The tariff on fleeces must be increased," I said firmly. "Ésparias has no shortage of sheep. We've dropped the fees on timber, after all."

"Timber benefits only some landholders. Fleeces bring money to almost everyone," Ruar countered. Beside him, his young son shifted a little. Bored, perhaps; we'd been renegotiating the border tariffs for two days.

I glanced down at the figures before me. I still had room to bargain. "A reduction in the tariff on salt fish would serve the coastal *torps*." I suggested a number. We needed timber, with all the new buildings being constructed, and salt fish for the ships going back and forth to Casil. The coarse wool of the hardy northern sheep was of limited value in the Eastern Empire.

"Is this fair, Daragh?" Ruar asked his son. In the tradition of Linrathe, the boy was there to listen and learn. This wasn't the first question the *Teannasach* had asked him over the last two days.

"I think it is," Daragh said. "If Ésparias does not want our fleeces, Varsland will. We will not lose revenue, *Athàir*."

"Nor will we," his father agreed. "I accept the new tariffs. Fairly done, Gwenna."

"Thank you." Tension seeped from me. My first independent negotiation was over, and I'd got the agreement I'd been directed to produce. Granted, this was a routine process, slight adjustments made every three years, but still—I'd done it. "The agreement will be ready to sign soon, will it not, Sorley?"

"I'll have two copies done in the morning," Sorley said from down the table, where, in his role as *scáeli*, he'd been recording the session. "Will that be soon enough for you, Ruar?"

"It will," the *Teannasach* said. "We'll leave tomorrow. I've still things to discuss with Cillian, but I shouldn't be away from home too long. Nor should we intrude here more than we must."

Sorley's lips tightened. "The needs of government go on. Government and Empires."

"And lives." Ruar put a hand on his son's shoulder as he spoke. "Loss comes to us all, and sometimes far too soon." His too would be a house of mourning before long; his wife, Helvi, was dying. She'd been ill for over a year, a wasting illness slowly killing her. An expected death now, unlike the sudden fever that, just over a week ago, had taken the little sister I had barely known.

We—Sorley and Druise and I—had returned home four summers past from our northern travels to my mother's announcement that she was pregnant. The baby, she told us, was due a few weeks after mid-winter. I'd been—what? Embarrassed, I suppose, although less so than I might have been before that summer and Druise's blunt words to me. He, I remembered, had been delighted.

But I had gone back to cadet school, and the next summer I'd only had two weeks of leave, and how well could one get to know a five-month-old baby? Lianë was sweet enough, her hair not the almost black of mine and

Colm's but a reddish-gold, and she gurgled and smiled contentedly in Mhairi's arms.

Except for the requisite three months in the company of my classmates, taking advanced lessons in diplomacy from my father, I'd been home fewer than eight full weeks in the last four years. Not much time to become more than fondly interested in Lianë. In the months of intense study, I hadn't been treated as a member of the family, but as another senior diplomatic cadet from Ésparias. Only in my private seminars with my father was the formality dropped, and we'd had things other than my baby sister to talk about. She hadn't been mentioned more than once or twice, and even then, still in the context of our discussions.

Ruar stood. "I'll see you both at dinner," he said. "Come, Daragh; let us find the *Comiádh*, and discover what you are to read and study." Daragh was twelve, and in the usual course of things he would have become a student of my father's this year. But there would be no students at the *Ti'ach na Cillian* until at least midwinter, because in a very few weeks, mourning a dead child or not, we were travelling to Casil to witness the investiture of Alekos, son of the abdicating Empress Eudekia, as the Emperor of the East. Alekos was twenty-one, and unmarried, and the invitation had been specific. I, heir to the leadership of Ésparias, must be present.

I hadn't needed six years of diplomatic training to decipher that message. Alekos needed a bride, and the Empress thought that bride might well be me.

I stood too, as protocol required. Further down the table Sorley hauled himself to his feet. I glanced over at him when we were alone. He looked exhausted.

"I need some wine." Fatigue roughened his voice. "You too, I should think?"

"Gladly," I replied. "Where? The hall? Ruar will be with my parents in their rooms."

"We could go to my teaching rooms." He hesitated. "But I'd rather be somewhere where I don't have to be the lord Sorley." There were still one or two students at the *Ti'ach*, awaiting their escorts. "Our rooms?"

"But—" Students weren't allowed in the annex. He smiled, wearily.

"You're not a student now, Gwenna. Come."

I matched his tired pace as we crossed the courtyard of the *Ti'ach*. We had been meeting in what had once been the mews and was now the armoury. A long table had been set up in the cool stone space, giving us privacy and freedom from interruption. In the hall, Sorley opened the door to the annex. I followed him up a flight of stairs and down another long corridor to its far end.

Inside their large sitting room, the shutters were open, allowing in light and breeze. Musical instruments hung on the walls, and bowls, mostly of Casilani glass in bright colours, stood on an array of shelves. The furniture was deep and comfortable. Sorley motioned me to a chair, taking a jug and cups from the sideboard. "Sit."

"This is beautiful," I said. He looked around.

"Much of this was sent to your father." He poured the wine. "From Eudekia, over the years."

"Does he come to look at it?"

"No. He's never been here."

Of course he hadn't. What had seemed so simple to me when I was fourteen no longer did. That the complex bonds among my parents and Druise and Sorley needed both deep trust and deeper love, I had understood. But I hadn't thought then about the ways their lives were also delineated: why my father would never see these rooms; why my mother never went, except in an emergency, to my father's library. Private spaces, hard to come by in a school, and harder when the true nature of two of the three relationships had to be hidden. Spaces in what they spoke of, too, even behind closed doors.

A price to be paid, for the love and the vision they shared.

Sorley handed me my wine before sinking into a chair opposite. There were hints of silver at his temples now. He was forty-three, I calculated, haggard with grief, despondent.

"Where's Druise?" I asked.

"Keeping an eye on Colm, I imagine."

My brother had been devastated, and so angry. He still was. He'd been a few weeks shy of eleven when Lianë was born, and he'd adored her from first sight. His only regret at leaving to go to the *Ti'ach na Iorlath* to begin his medical training a year later was leaving her. Well, maybe leaving his dog, too.

Druise had gone to tell him, and to bring him home, and with his usual thought for what mattered, he'd taken scruffy black-and-white Peritas with him. My mother had been furious over the puppy Sorley had bought for Colm on a whim; it had, I learned later, arrived on the same day she'd realized she was pregnant again. 'I do not need a puppy and a new baby,' she'd growled at Sorley, the day we arrived home.

"Is he out on the moors again?" Colm spent most of his time away from the *Ti'ach*, out on his horse, or sitting at Lianë's grave. He hadn't let me hug him, and at meals, if he was there at all, he was silent.

"I expect so," Sorley said. "If we weren't going to Wall's End so soon, I'd have suggested he went back to Iorlath. He needs something to do, some structure in his life. Having work to do helped me when my mother died when I was much the same age."

"*Athàir* hasn't assigned him translations, or essays?"

Sorley shook his head. "Not as far as I know."

Because *Athàir* is too upset, or because you and he have had no time together for him to tell you? I couldn't ask. My thoughts were interrupted by a gentle double rap at the door.

"That's your mother," Sorley said. "It's open," he called, a little louder.

"Don't get up," my mother said, seeing Sorley beginning to stand as she entered the room. "Gwenna!" she added, surprise evident in her voice. "I didn't think to find you here."

"I can leave." She'd want Sorley to herself.

"No, don't." She went to the sideboard, pouring herself wine. "Cillian and Ruar have gone to his study. The boy—his guard took him riding—is the same age Ruar was when I met him. I am getting old."

Sorley didn't say anything, so I didn't either. She'd been almost twenty-two when I was born, so she was forty this summer. There were lines on her face now, and she was thinner than I thought she should be. My strong mother, whose impossible arrow shot had killed the Marai king Fritjof, ending a battle and a war. I'd never seen her cry until this past week.

"Gwenna," she said, sitting. "You did well in the negotiations, I understand?"

"She did." Sorley almost smiled. "Are you surprised?"

"Not at all."

"Please," I said. "They were routine tariff agreements, and Ruar knew it." I still didn't understand why the *Teannasach* himself had come for such simple talks.

"He did," Sorley agreed, "but you were calm and reasoned throughout, and firm when you needed to be. A credit to your training."

"And of the right rank to negotiate with the *Teannasach* of Linrathe, when we were told he would be coming himself, not sending an envoy," I added. But my mother wasn't really listening.

"Sorley, you look terrible."

"I am weary." He was about to add more, when the door swung open.

"Lena," Druisius said. "Do you know where Colm is?"

"Weren't you with him?" Sorley asked.

"Not with him. Watching him, from a distance. But—"

"But what?" my mother said sharply.

"*Mathàir*," I said, "he's fourteen. He can take care of himself." She ignored me.

"He had taken flowers to the grave," Druise said. "As he has, every day. Then he sits, for a long time. He talks to her. He saw I watched him and shouted at me to go away. So I did."

Sorley pushed himself up and went to Druisius, putting a hand on his shoulder. "Come and sit, Druise. Is the dog with him?"

"Of course." Druisius let Sorley guide him into the room. His eyes fell on me. "Gwenna." Not Kitten, I noted. "What—"

"She's an adult," Sorley said, handing his partner a cup. "Drink that and sit down."

My mother was frowning, a look of controlled impatience and concern. But she waited, sitting on the edge of her chair, until Druise drank some wine. "You walked away," she said. "Then what?"

"I left him maybe ten minutes. I walked to the west. To where the hill rises, and back again," Druise said. "He and his horse were gone, when I came back." He straightened a little.

"Then he rode east, or south," my mother said. "Did you call the dog?"

"I whistled, three times."

"Where had he been, earlier?"

"Where he always goes. The high land at the end of the long pasture." Druise put his wine down. "The patrol had not seen him. I will send them out to search. I had not, in case he was here."

"No," I said. "I'll look for him. You stay here, Druise."

"I'll come," Sorley said.

"No. I will go, and yes, Druise, I'll take my bodyguard," I said, forestalling the objection I knew he'd make.

"He is so angry." My mother's voice caught. "So angry. Even Cillian cannot reach him; he tried, but it was Catilius he quoted, and Colm just swore at him and ran from the room. Sometimes I hate Catilius, too."

I found my bodyguard in the kitchen, drinking tea with Mhairi, and sent her to saddle our horses while I changed into riding clothes. I was fairly sure I knew where Colm had gone, and if the adults—if Sorley and Druise and my mother—were not exhausted and grieving, one of them should have guessed too.

The sun still hung high in the western sky, even with the day moving toward evening. I kicked my horse into a trot along the river path, slowing only for the cottages of the *torp*, and then urging him into a canter once we were past the buildings.

We arrived at Hagenstorp in less than an hour. I slid off my horse at the forge. "Wait here," I said to my bodyguard.

"My lady!" the smith greeted me. "Does your horse need shoeing?"

"No. But would you know where Shugo is?"

"The tops, with the flocks."

"Thank you." I went back to my horse.

"My lady?" the smith called. "I was sorry to hear of the little one's death."

"Thank you," I said again. I mounted, turning the horse's head north.

As I had guessed, Colm was with the shepherd, Peritas lying beside Shugo's sheepdog Meg. I left my horse with my bodyguard before walking across the cropped turf to where the two figures stood.

"My lady," Shugo said. Colm turned away.

"I've come to take my brother home," I said. "Where's your horse, Colm?"

"By the pool." Shugo jutted his chin. "You need to go, lad."

"Why?" Colm snapped, not looking at me.

"Because," I said, "we have the *Teannasach* and his son as our guests, and your presence is required at dinner."

"They shouldn't be here," he muttered. "They're intruding."

I put a hand on the shepherd's arm, mouthing, "Forgive me," before striding over to face my brother. "Colm, you are a prince of Ésparias. Act like it."

"I don't want to!" Tears glittered in his eyes.

"And do you think Daragh wants to do what he must, either? His mother is dying, but he's here, learning his role."

Colm sniffed, not replying. "Come," I said, more gently.

"Gwenna," he said, his voice breaking high. "Will you take me away?"

"Away?"

"To Wall's End. I don't want to be here another three weeks. I keep…" Tears overflowed. "I keep seeing her, hearing her. I want to go away." The dog whined and got up, coming to sit at his feet.

I considered. It wasn't a bad idea, and not just for Colm's benefit.

"All right," I said. "I will. But you must come with me now, and behave at dinner. And I hope your horse is rested, because we'll need to gallop."

"No," my mother said. Dinner was over, and Ruar and Daragh had retired to the annex. We were in my parents' sitting room, without Colm. I'd told him to leave this to me.

"*Mathàir*." I used my most reasonable voice. "Why not? Sorley told me earlier Colm needs something to do, some structure. He can spend the time with the fort's doctors, being useful and maybe learning something."

"I want him here."

"Sorley," I said, "offered me wine in his rooms, because he didn't want to be in public, where he had to be the lord Sorley. The other two students should be leaving tomorrow, and Ruar and Daragh too. If I take Colm away, then none of you have to be anything but yourselves."

"*Käresta*," my father said gently, "Gwenna is not wrong."

"Lena, consider what Gwenna is saying," Sorley said. "We have all been playing our roles in front of the students, and even with the *Teannasach*. In a few weeks there are different roles to be played, for all of us. A space where that isn't required would be welcome. For me, at least. I am tired."

Riding back from Hagenstorp, formulating my arguments in my mind, I'd thought again of the summer I'd spent travelling with Sorley and

Druisius when I was fourteen. A summer of secrets revealed, and the start of comprehending the depths of love among the four people I sat with tonight. 'See the man,' Sorley had said to me that summer, about my father.

But today the man I had seen clearly was Sorley: grieving, exhausted, bereft. He had, I realized, been doing his utmost best to hold everyone together: Druisius, his partner for almost twenty years; my mother, who was his closest friend, and my father, whom he loved. My father, who would not have left my mother's side except when work demanded this past week, and likely would not for some time. Sheltering her as best he could, as he had promised; there to hold her, comfort her. 'I felt extraneous in their lives,' Sorley had told me, of the months after my birth. I thought the same was true now.

"I can go too." Druise. Of course.

"No," Sorley said, almost under his breath.

"I want the Breccaith played for her," my mother said. "I know that's not what it's meant for. But do you remember, Sorley? 'For all we have loved, and all we have lost,' you said once, and that is what I want. You know the music now. Will you play it?" She turned to me. "And then you can take Colm to Wall's End."

The Breccaith. The traditional mourning ritual of Ésparias's army, midsummer and midwinter, for the fallen. "I could dance it, if you would like," I offered. I had learned it to honour my grandfather, Ésparias's last Emperor, dead in the battle that had nearly killed my father.

"Would you like that, *käresta*?" my father asked. His eyes on her were gentle, and full of both patience and sorrow.

"I think I would," she answered slowly. "For she was a sacrifice, wasn't she?"

My mother went to bed early; she often did, even before. Druise too got up to leave, another habit, one last check of doors and windows and night sounds before sleep. "I'll come with you," I said. "*Athàir?* Will you wait for me? There is something I'd like to talk to you about alone. It won't take long."

I walked out into the courtyard with Druise. Considering how much he had drunk tonight, he was remarkably steady, He stopped a few paces out on the flagstones, listening to the night. After a moment he nodded and turned as if to go back into the hall. "Druise," I began. He let me speak.

"It is true," he said, when I'd finished. "I worry for Sorley."

"I worry for you, too."

He shrugged. "Nothing can change what is." His words were just slightly slurred. He looked out into the darkness. "Sorley and I, we have ways to express the anger. But he needs more."

What do you need? I wondered. *Aurea*, he'd called her, golden one, for her hair. Even my parents had added it to her name, sometimes. Lianë Aurea.

"Kitten? Do not expect Cillian to agree."

I kissed his cheek, smelling the *fuisce* on him, and then I went back to my father.

Chapter 2

~FATHER~

TO ALWAYS BE THE SAME MAN, UNCHANGED BY PAIN, the loss of a child, in long illness. I put the book aside. Catilius's words brought no comfort but that of familiarity, the calm which comes from reading a well-known text again. Had he loved his children as I did mine? If so, his words had been written to convince himself, a bulwark against grief. I closed my eyes, seeing my dead child; our unexpected youngest, her red-gold hair as fine as strands of silk. I could almost feel her, standing beside me as she so often had, her face on my leg, Understanding, even at three, that I could not pick her up. *Unchanged by pain.* Was that possible?

I listened. The bedroom door was slightly ajar, but if Lena wept, I could not hear her. Her tears might come later, after Apulo had left me, or not at all. I expected not at all, tonight.

The door from the hall opened. Beads of moisture in Gwenna's hair caught the firelight. "Wine?" she asked.

"If you like." Handing me the cup, she sat across from me. I took a sip. Stronger than I would have allowed myself. "What is it, Gwenna? I should not leave your mother alone."

"Just that," she said. "Tomorrow night, should I stay with *Mathàir*? You need to sleep."

My jaw tightened, an involuntary reaction I should have been able to control. But weariness had its hold on me: weariness, and pain, and grief. And Gwenna was not wrong.

"My beloved daughter," I said, hearing the roughness in my voice. My only daughter, now. "It is for your mother to tell me when I may leave her.

As she will." Soon, I thought. I had seen a change in Lena today; she was calmer. A brittle calm: controlled and tenuous, and it would break into anger before long.

Gwenna flushed, the stain of red on her pale skin visible even in the firelight. "I'm worried about you." I put my wine down and held out my arms. She slipped off her chair to kneel beside me, resting her head on my shoulder. I kissed her temple, feeling the softness of her skin. She was so young for what might await her. "I'm worried for Sorley, too."

I stroked her damp hair. Subtly put, I thought. We had never spoken of Sorley, a tacit agreement.

"We have a few minutes, here and there, and for now that must suffice," I told her. "But your reasoning about taking Colm away is sound, and time without responsibility will help us all. As will the Breccaith, as difficult as it will be."

I heard her sniff, fighting tears. "What did *Mathàir* mean, about Lianë being a sacrifice?"

I could not deal with this tonight, not rationally. The dull ache in my leg had begun to pulse; it needed cannabium, and Apulo's hands. "I cannot speak of this, Gwenna."

She tensed, misunderstanding: I had not chosen my words well. "Not because you are too young," I added, "not this time. The implications of your mother's belief are difficult for me and for us all. I am still weighing my response."

"But—" She pulled away

"Do not ask me more."

She nodded. She knew, as all my students did, what the tone I had used meant. "Do you need help getting up?"

"No," I said, more gently. "Thank you, *mo nihéan*, but Sorley will have asked Apulo to come to me shortly. I will finish my wine and wait for him."

21

"Druise is drinking too much," she said as she stood.

I, alone of us, knew why, a confession made to me long ago. In Lianë, as in all our children, he had seen his atonement for a deed he regretted. He grieved her death honestly; he had loved her, but he grieved too this lost chance for redemption. "He is," I said. "We all have our ways to mourn."

Chapter 3

~DAUGHTER~

RUAR AND DARAGH LEFT AFTER BREAKFAST the next morning. I and my father accompanied them out into the courtyard, where their guard and their horses waited. The boy mounted, impatient to be away, but his father did not. He glanced around at the buildings, smiling slightly.

"I hope," he said to his son, "that you enjoy your time here as much as I did. You can have no better teachers."

"I am sure I will," Daragh said politely. "*Athàir*, can we go?"

"You may." Ruar gestured to the guard. "I will catch up with you. I am in no danger on the *Ti'ach's* land," he added, at the soldier's frown. "Druisius has seen to that." He turned to my father. "*Comiádh*, I intruded at a difficult time."

"There was work to be done," my father said, "work which could not wait. I too apologize for taking you from Helvi."

"*Athàir!*" Daragh's shout.

"He is eager to return to his mother," Ruar murmured.

"I'm sure he is," I said, feeling the inadequacy of the words. "I wish her strength. I wish you all strength, Ruar." I'd known him since early childhood, his days here coinciding with my first lessons from my father, learning my letters.

He acknowledged my words with a nod. "At least she is not in pain." Only resignation in his eyes. "So you are off to Casil for the first time. I was just about your age when Sorley took me."

"You were unimpressed," I said, remembering.

He smiled a little. "It's imposing. Huge, and so many stone buildings. The walls are like cliffs of brick. You'll see. But I belong to this land, Gwenna, among my people."

He held out a hand, and I stepped forward for his formal kiss. He was just a little shorter than I, but under my hand the muscles of his upper arm were defined and firm. Still a young man. "Go safely," I said.

The same farewell for my father; then Ruar mounted. He looked down at me. "Gwenna, you belong among your people too. Ésparias needs you more as Faolyn's advisor than as an Emperor's consort in Casil. I hope to see you again."

⌘⌘⌘⌘⌘

Finally we were alone as a family, the last of the students and her escort leaving not long after sunrise. We'd eaten breakfast—or at least some of us had—but no one had left the table. There was nothing that had to be done: no lessons, no diplomacy. Just a ceremony tonight, an honouring and a farewell.

"Cillian," Apulo said softly. "The day looks set to rain. If Gwenna is to dance tonight, should it be in this room? I will have the table moved, if so."

"That would be best," my father said. "Thank you, Apulo."

"Is there anything else needed? Do I sing again?" He had sung the parting song at Lianë's burial, after Sorley couldn't, his clear, pure voice laced with such sorrow. He too had loved her.

"No. The offering tonight is the music and the dance," my father said.

Apulo nodded. Without asking, he poured my father more tea, and then went away to the kitchen, the teapot in hand.

"Offering?" Colm said, his voice fierce. "To gods who may not exist?"

"There are gods," my father said. "Or at least one I can vouch for. I have felt his touch."

"The god of death." Colm knew the story. "Why did he want Lianë?"

No one spoke, and then, "She was the price demanded," my mother said.

"Demanded?" I asked. *A sacrifice*, she'd said the other night. "For what?"

"My life, Lena believes," my father answered.

"No," Sorley said, his voice strangled. "Lena, no."

"I said they would demand something from us all," my mother said. "Beyond the music you charmed the dark god with, beyond the supplication offered. Because that was only to one god, and not the one who asked for Cillian's life. An arrow guided is what must be paid for, and if not Cillian, then Lianë."

"You are wrong, Lena," Druise said. "I have killed many times. Sometimes only through luck, when I should have died. No sacrifice has been asked."

"You believe the *huntress* wanted Lianë?" The bronze statue stood in the courtyard, her shoulder shining where she was touched for luck or blessing by my mother and some of the female students. And by me, since childhood.

"Four times I asked her for help," my mother said. "Three times she gave it. The fourth time, she took her price for the death Sorley ransomed with his music."

"*Käresta*," my father said. "You are blinded by grief and exhaustion. Do not blame the gods; they do no wrong."

My mother, her face drawn, simply shook her head. "Do not quote Catilius at me." She pushed her chair back. "I am going for a ride. Alone." She did not kiss my father before leaving.

"I don't want there to be gods, if this is what they do," Colm said. "*Mathàir* speaks as if she knew Lianë was to be a sacrifice." He smashed a fist on the tabletop. "Why did you have her if that was her fate? She didn't deserve to be born just to die."

"She was born of love, Colm," my father said quietly. "As you were, and Gwenna. Not as a sacrifice. Your mother is distraught and looking for an explanation."

"Can I go riding too?" Colm asked.

"Where?" Druise, always the guard.

"I don't know. Away."

"If you wish to spend the day away from the *Ti'ach*," my father said, "you may. I would prefer you went to Hagenstorp and Shugo. But wherever you go, please be here tonight."

"Can I go alone?"

I'd asked the same of Sorley once, when I had difficult truths to absorb. I hadn't wanted someone I knew with me; they would have interfered, somehow, just by being there. "Why don't I ask my guard to accompany you?" I suggested. She would keep both silence and distance. I'd made that clear at Wall's End after Lynthe's promotion: if I had to be guarded, those were my requirements.

Colm's face relaxed a little. "Would she?"

"If I tell her to, yes. Druise, will that satisfy you?"

He grunted his agreement. I went to the kitchen to find my guard and tell her what her duties were today. "You are not leaving the *Ti'ach*?" she asked.

"No. If for some reason I must, Druisius will be with me." I could, to some extent, direct her, but she reported to Talyn, not to me, and ensuring my safety was her first obligation. But Druise would die for me, and she knew it. Not that I was in any danger here. Or anywhere, probably.

Chapter 4

~FATHER~

GWENNA LEFT TO FIND HER BODYGUARD. The woman knew her job, Druisius had reported. Nor did I believe there was any real danger here at the *Ti'ach*. I had my reasons for maintaining the guard, and not all were about a possible threat from the Marai.

Druisius's chair scraped on the flags as he stood. "I am going to train. I will be gone all morning." Sorley looked up at him. Druisius touched his shoulder for a moment. Neither smiled.

Fatigue purpled Sorley's eyes. I held out a hand. "Come here." He came, slowly, to sit beside me. "The baths?" I touched his hair, spiky and unkempt. He leant his head into my hand. When I kissed his temple, he said my name, helplessly.

"There is no one here," I said. "And I have done nothing to raise suspicion, not in a house of mourning." But I moved my hand from his head, years of caution precluding my wish to offer—and find—comfort. He reached out and took it, entwining his fingers with mine on the tabletop. I ran a thumb across his palm. I could find no physical desire, but what lay between us was far more than our rare nights together. A love which, in my many sleepless hours, when only the cat and long-dead philosophers kept me company, I had admitted I did not fully understand.

I heard Gwenna come back into the hall. "Mhairi might follow her," I said softly, and let my fingers slide from Sorley's.

"Druisius has gone to train the *torpari* boys, and your mother will be riding for some hours. Would you tell Apulo I—we—would welcome the baths?" I asked my daughter.

"Of course," she said. "Sorley? Can I use the table in your teaching room to write notes this morning?"

He nodded. "Go ahead."

We soaked for a long time, Apulo keeping the fire burning under the boiler, and the water hot. He'd helped me into the pool, as always, and then left us. We did not speak for some time, letting the heat do its work, relaxing the tight muscles of my back and leg. After a while I began to massage Sorley's neck with one hand: not with any skill, but the touch was as much for me as him. He sighed and slid closer. "Lena?"

"She is angry now," I said.

"We're all angry." Fresh bruises—bite marks—reddened his shoulders. We'd never spoken of them; we never would. Silence and secrets, for so many reasons. He leaned his head back. I stopped rubbing his neck, but I did not withdraw my arm. "I could offer sword practice." I caught the faintest trace of a forced amusement behind the fatigue and sorrow. Sorley's voice was a tool when he wanted it to be.

"Wear armour." He smiled, both of us remembering a day on a riverbank far away in both time and distance now, Lena directing rage and sorrow into sword strokes. He'd barely been able to defend himself.

"Cillian?" The amusement was gone. "What are you doing with your anger? And don't tell me it's not there."

"I am waiting for it to pass." As Catilius taught.

"Is that enough?"

"It has to be," I said. "What else can I do? I will write a poem for her, one day, and you can put it to music, but I cannot wield a sword, or throw a knife." Or express, in any physical way, the hollow ache inside me that frequently flashed into sharp pain. "But, yes, just now I resent my limitations."

"Do you want time alone when we are finished soaking?"

I had lain or sat awake in the dark for many hours in the last week, alert to Lena's restlessness and tears. To have no demands on me; to be undisturbed . . .

"No," I said. "Not yet. Time with you first."

Later, after Apulo had supported me out of the baths, and helped me dry and dress, we crossed the empty hall to my library. As soon as he had locked the door, Sorley came to me, to hold and be held. Under my hands, I felt the tremors running through his back. He'd always cried easily. I did not. I had held back tears for over twenty-five years, from when I was seven until a midwinter's night in exile: a constraint not easily lost. I stroked his head, letting my lips linger on his temple where his hair had silvered. He was no longer the young man—almost a boy—I had vowed to protect so long ago.

He stepped back a little. I brushed tears from his cheeks, not for the first time. "You shouldn't stand too long," he said.

"No." We moved apart. I went to my chair at the desk.

For a while we just sat, our fingers intertwined on the desktop. "She was so beautiful," he said, his voice low.

"So like her mother. Curious and active, but I would not, I believe, have taught her *xache* at four."

"No. But fearless. Cillian, why does Lena think—what she thinks?"

In truth, I did not know. Lena would not talk about it, although she was adamant in her belief. Which meant, logically, the anger growing in her would be aimed at me. I had given her cause enough, over the years. And not just her, but the man with me, too. That they had chosen to follow, or rather, to walk beside me on the dangerous path I was compelled to take still felt incomprehensible, sometimes.

"I'm worried about her," Sorley said. We rarely spoke of Lena, here in what was our private space, but today the exception was warranted.

"As am I." Should I say more? If Lena had not confided in Sorley, was there not disloyalty in mentioning my concern?

My leg ached, but only the scars. I shifted to ease it. "What did she say to you about being pregnant, after you returned from Sorham that summer?"

"To me? Nothing, except about the puppy. Why?"

"She was not happy about it. With reason. Gwenna was fourteen, and at cadet school; Colm was ten. She was free of most of the demands of children, and looking forward to more time to study, to finish her history. Another baby was not in her plans."

"But she loved Lianë," Sorley protested.

"Without a doubt. But I wonder if she cannot forget her first reluctance, and her grief is intensified by guilt."

"Should I speak to her?"

"If you do, she will know it was I who suggested it to you. I am expecting to be the target of her anger as it is. Perhaps we should not give her more cause?"

"I won't ask her directly," Sorley said. "But maybe she'll tell me, if I'm subtle about it."

"Perhaps she will." That Sorley was her confidant; that he knew things about Lena I did not, I had accepted long ago. Nor had he ever asked me to tell him what Druisius had confessed on the long nights when he sat with me as the desire for poppy had wracked both my body and my mind. 'You must trust me, yes?' Druisius had said, as blunt as he generally was. 'Trust me to give you the drug when it is time, and no sooner or later, and the right amount. To believe me when I say the illness will pass. So I have things to tell you.'

"Cillian?" Sorley sat straighter, freeing his hands from mine. "You felt the touch of a god. Could Lena be right?"

Darkness, and the smell of caves, and perhaps the sound of a river; an inexorable pull. The touch on my arm; to guide me, I had thought, but no. *Not yet*, the voice had said. *I accept the offering. Not yet.* And then music, song, a different tug upward, back to life.

"No," I said. "Not if there is justice among them. To demand further payment, when what was offered was accepted?"

"But gods are notoriously capricious, whatever Catilius may say about them. And even he was unsure, wasn't he?"

"I think not. But no doubt I interpret his words through my own experience. And," I admitted, "whatever Catilius or I think, Lena believes what she says just now. There is nothing I can do but listen." But she would say little to me; hurt, Lena retreated into herself. I had to let her take the lead.

He got up, coming around the desk to me. We kissed, without passion, his lips soft and familiar. He sighed. "Lena loves you," he said. "You love her." One finger touched my cheek. "You'll have an hour to yourself if I leave now. Do you want anything?"

"Tea, perhaps. Thank you, *mo Somhairle gràhadh.*"

Apulo brought tea, and then I was alone with my books and papers and my thoughts. Even the cat was elsewhere, hunting, or sleeping in a patch of sunshine. I picked up the book I had been reading, a history of the great general and emperor Lekandar. Alekos, the heir to the Eastern Empire, was named for him.

Alekos. I put the book down and pushed myself up, reaching for a box on the shelves. I could not retreat into history. I had a living daughter to consider.

I opened the box to take out Eudekia's letters. Four, on average, had arrived and been answered in each of the last nineteen years. I would read the last few years again, looking for insight from the subtle mind that had committed chosen thoughts to paper. She had married for politics, to placate a historic and possible enemy, to protect and expand the lands and city she held as regent for her son. She would choose a bride for him for the same reasons. Her last letters had spoken of unrest to the east of Casil, but one sentence had caught my attention. 'Alliances are not always easy, or in our Empire's best interest. We must consider not just the immediate future, but the security of our lands for our children's children, and beyond."

In our Empire's best interest. In a thought written as the Empress, using the imperial 'we', not simply as Eudekia. If this was, as I believed, a message, the questions it raised needed all my attention, not a mind clouded by grief and worry for those I loved.

I moved, trying to find a more comfortable position. A deep, pulsing pain had begun in my back. I leant forward, elbows on my desk, burying my face in my hands. I took a deep breath. Lianë was dead. Nothing could change that. Lena, and Colm too, needed me to comfort them, to share the sorrow, to make sense of her death. But I had no time to consider the caprices of gods, or even to let my grief and anger pass naturally. I had to push it away, to move past it. I inhaled again, resisting the downward pull, the desire to escape, to forget.

Gwenna would need all I knew of diplomacy, of nuance and subterfuge and its long, long history in Casil to guide her safely through what awaited her there. If I could. If I did not step off the ship to be arrested, for the second time in my life, for treason.

Chapter 5

~DAUGHTER~

LATE IN THE MORNING THE DOOR to Sorley's teaching rooms opened. "Gwenna," my mother said, "if you are here, then is Sorley with your father?"

"I assume so. *Athàir* asked for the baths to be heated after breakfast."

"Good," she said, pulling out a chair to sit. She looked calmer than earlier. "I'm sorry you had to hear what I said this morning."

I put down my pen. "Do you really believe it?"

"Sometimes," she answered. "There is always a balance, Gwenna, a price to be paid."

"What did you ask the huntress for? Three other times, you said. Guiding your arrow was one. What were the others?"

"For your life, twice. My horse threw me when I was carrying you. That was the first time. Then when Tyrvi took you, and you were out in a little boat in a storm."

"Not when *Athàir* was dying?"

She shook her head. "No. I thought . . . " She paused, rubbed a hand across her lips. "I thought I already knew her answer."

"That I heard what you said is of no matter," I said after a moment. "I wish Colm hadn't."

"So do I," she said. "I should have guarded my tongue. And you will have to deal with him, these next weeks. I'm sorry about that, but I'm also glad you're taking him away."

"He'll be better, away from the *Ti'ach*. And when we come back, he'll go straight back to school, or maybe he'll choose to stay with Ésparias's doctors, not Iorlath. Wasn't that always the plan?"

"It was." My mother rolled her shoulders before standing. "It's past midday. Come and eat."

Druise didn't appear for the midday meal; he'd be eating with the *torpari* boys he was training, Sorley said. A little less strain showed on his face.

"*Käresta?*" my father murmured, as my mother and I came to the table. She bent to kiss him. The hall, usually public space, was free of some of its restrictions, with only Mhairi and Apulo in the house.

"I'm better for my ride," she said. "You had the baths, and time with Sorley."

Mhairi and Apulo brought food from the kitchen, setting it on the table before taking their seats. Apulo, both aide and teacher, always ate with us; Mhairi, only when students weren't present. The subtle hierarchy of the *Ti'ach*, I mused, where to teach bestowed status, even though all my family had roles beyond that.

Sorley oversaw the lands and their management; Druisius taught weaponry and commanded the watches and patrols. My mother, Lady of the *Ti'ach,* could be found instructing pupils on the bow or secca, or teaching aspects of the *danta*, as well as her responsibilities for the well-being of the students. As for my father . . . He was firm about how he was to be addressed, even, I remembered, when both Ruar and my cousin Faolyn had been students here. *Comiádh*, not Prince. Only Casilani envoys on their occasional visits could use the Ésparian title.

I passed bread to Sorley, and cut a slice of soft sheep's cheese to spread on mine. *Athàir* would have to be Prince Cillian in Casil. To do otherwise would insult the Empress who had made him royalty, and myself the heir after Faolyn.

I had watched my father in his diplomatic work for many years now. I had learned from him, both formally and informally. He was capable, I knew, of consummate, subtle dissimulation, words, both said and unsaid, tools used with exquisite and precise skill. His face—unlike Sorley's, I thought in amusement—could hide his thoughts, or reveal them, as he chose.

Had he taught me well enough? Because in Casil, facing the Empress and her son, we had secrets to keep, he and I. Almost since the Eastern Empire had arrived to reclaim her lost province, the price paid for their support in the war against the Marai, he had been weaving another future for our western lands: he, and Sorley, and my mother, and Druisius too.

But only my father held every thread in the warp and woof of the carefully woven alliances. Everyone else saw only parts of the fabric of his plans. Everyone else except me. I was both heir to Ésparias, and heir to my father's sedition.

⌘⌘⌘⌘⌘

He'd begun to reveal his vision to me after the summer I'd spent travelling with Sorley and Druisius, just broadly at first. Nothing I would not have learned as his student. How history suggested that, one day, war or disease or internal strife would mean the Eastern Empire would again leave our lands. What might happen then? he'd asked, and over the course of a few days, thinking of what I already knew, I'd realized the answer: Ésparias and Varsland and Linrathe could return to being warring states, fighting each other for land and resources, or we could be an alliance, working for the common good of our peoples, bound by treaties and trade, education and marriage.

"What about Leste?" I'd asked.

"A possibility," he'd said. "But unlikely, for one reason. What does Leste not have, that Varsland and Ésparias and Linrathe do?"

It hadn't taken me long. We'd been playing *xache* just a few minutes earlier. "A leader. They only have a Casilani governor, don't they?"

"Correct. Their last king and his heirs were killed after Elon tried to assassinate the Emperor."

35

"How did he have the chance?"

"A lesson in never trusting too much, Gwenna. The King of Leste came into the council tent that day with a hidden knife, because two men my father thought loyal to him were not. Your mother—she was there—tells me the outcome could have been seen, had my father and his brothers been less distracted in the previous months by Leste's plans to invade. The signs were there, if subtle. A man who had wanted to be Emperor, but lost the election to Callan. A brother as loyal to that man as Callan's were to him. Enough to say they bore watching, except that in the repulsion of the invasion, every man—and woman, as you know—was needed; the Wall was secured by the minimum number of men, and there was no one to observe what the commanders in the north were doing."

I'd thought about it for a while. "Is anyone watching you?" I'd been proud of the question.

"Almost certainly," he'd said calmly. "What does that mean, Gwenna?"

"You could be in danger."

"Only I?"

"All of us," I'd said, slowly.

"And so? What responsibility do you have?"

Only a few weeks earlier, I demanded to know why our family had so many secrets. I thought I understood now.

"You know enough," he'd said gravely. "No more, until you are older."

"But you will tell me?"

"I may." He'd reached out then, taken my hand. "*Mo nihéan gràhadh*, you have been forced into a role not of my choosing, or your mother's. When we decided we could not fairly remove our children from the succession, it was to let you decide. The Empress changed that. I would wish you a different life, but it is not mine to give."

"I know," I'd said.

"One other thing," he'd replied. "As an adult, as the heir, you can choose to agree with my thinking, or not. If you decide not, you will have information that could destroy many people. An extraordinary power, Gwenna, and one that will affect not just others' lives, but yours. I will ask a promise of you, a vow, when you are adult, that you will never use what you learn to hurt anyone."

"I won't," I'd protested.

"So you believe now," he'd said mildly. "But I asked this of Sorley and Druisius, too, and even your mother. I will ask it of you when you are seventeen, before I tell you more."

⌘⌘⌘⌘⌘

Last year I had made the promise, and in the three months I spent at the *Ti'ach* with my classmates, almost every minute of our private seminars was spent on the intricacies of the relationships he'd so carefully built. How the schools spreading into Ésparias and Varsland were part of the plan; how trade in certain commodities was too, and how marriages—the only part I'd had any inkling about, at fourteen—underpinned it all. The last time we'd spoken of Lianë, I remembered sadly, it had been in that context.

Bryngyl, King of Varsland, thwarted in his attempt to gain me as a bride, had chosen not to wait to hear what other possibilities Ésparias might offer, and married instead the daughter of one of the earls who had sheltered him and had been his regents. His oldest child, a boy, was much the same age as Lianë. "That alliance must wait for another generation," my father had said. "Unless his wife dies, and then perhaps, he will look to Ésparias again. But even then his heirs would not be tied to both lands, so I would prefer to wait."

"Lianë will be the right age," I'd pointed out.

"She would be," he'd replied. "But I will ask no marriage nor partnership of any of my children except the one you want. Or none, if that is your preference. I promised your mother."

Not very long after, the summons had come from Casil. My marriage might have no part in my father's plans, but there was a good chance it did in the Empress Eudekia's.

⌘⌘⌘⌘⌘

I spent the rest of the afternoon packing, and thinking. and as the day wore on, I went to find Mhairi in the kitchen. I needed something to occupy myself. "Can I help?" I asked. I knew Apulo would be with my father now, helping him through the exercises and giving him the massage which kept him mobile. My mother often came then to give Mhairi a hand, but she hadn't today.

I sliced bread and ground mint and rue for the greens, mixing them with vinegar and olive oil. "Is Colm back?" I asked Mhairi, as I returned from the hall.

"Your mother went to fetch him," she answered. "They should be here soon."

"Are you attending tonight?" Apulo would be, and it only seemed right that Mhairi, who had been Lianë's nursemaid—and mine and Colm's too—should be present for this last memorial.

"I am." She bent to baste the chicken in its clay pot. Straightening, her face flushed, she added, "When you are away to Casil, I will put the *weàn's* clothes and toys in a chest, so your mother does not have to see them when she returns."

"That will be kind." Lianë's favourite toy, a wooden horse on wheels, had been buried with her. Impulsively I went to put my arms around Mhairi. "You will miss her too," I murmured.

"Aye," was all she said.

Chapter 6

~FATHER~

"YOUR BACK IS TOO TIGHT," APULO SAID. "You need cannabium."

"Not before the ritual." His tongue clicked his disapproval as his strong fingers worked around the scars. Pain flared. I breathed steadily, and it diffused and faded. His hands moved down my hip and onto my thigh, calming the throbbing ache. Half an hour, morning and night, every day. He began to sing softly; a Casilani song.

Then the oils, warmed and scented, rubbed into the scars themselves, and he was done. I sat up, slowly swinging my legs around. He helped me dress. "Should I shave you?" he asked, straightening from fastening my shoe.

"No. Not until tomorrow."

"The same as at her burial." Linrathan custom meant clean-shaven men let their beards grow between a death and a burial. Nor were hair or fingernails cut until the day after, a ritual for the living, to mark the return to the routines of life. The Breccaith required no such practice, but I wished it for myself. Because I would have so little time to mourn her, I thought, acknowledging my motives. I can do this, at least.

"Apulo," I said. "Thank you, my friend. You have taken on so much, this last week and more, and you have been grieving too."

He gave me a wan smile. "I would rather work than sit and think. I can sing when I work." His greatest solace, his pure, high voice; that he found joy in what had cost him so dearly was something I contemplated occasionally, wondering at its lessons and its parallels.

"Are you playing tonight?" He was straightening the room, putting the oils back in the cabinet. He could play several instruments: Sorley had taught him, years before.

"Only Sorley and Druisius. Their last gift, you see. Shall I walk with you?"

"No need." I made my way along the corridor and across the hall to our rooms. Lena was curled at one end of the wide seat, her head turned against its back. She opened her eyes as I came in.

"*Käresta*?" I sat beside her and held out an arm. She slid over, raising her face for a kiss. I held her. She felt less tense, but far too thin, the muscles of her shoulders and back wiry now.

"I'm worried about Colm," she said.

"He will be better away from here," I said gently.

"He wants to take the dog to Wall's End. I suppose we should let him."

"To Wall's End, yes. But not to Casil. Were it killed by other dogs, or under the wheels of a carriage—I would save Colm from that."

"Would you?" she said, suddenly angry. "And will you save Gwenna from what awaits her in Casil, too?"

"If I can." Were I allowed to; not a fear to be shared, not now.

"She will never be a piece in Eudekia's games, you said. I said it, too. Why are we allowing this, Cillian?" We. I had not expected that.

"Because to refuse is a defiance the Empress will not overlook. It is too dangerous."

⌘⌘⌘⌘⌘

Gwenna sank to the ground in the last movement of the dance, her head bowed. The notes of the *ladhar* faded into the night. She held the pose for a breath, and another, and a third, before she slowly rose. She had danced exquisitely to Sorley and Druisius's sorrowful music. I hadn't tried to stop my tears.

I held out my arms. Gwenna came to me, bending to accept my kiss on her cheek. "You have honoured Lianë," I told her. "Thank you." She went to Lena next, embracing both her and Colm, who had watched the dance from within the solace and support of his mother's arms.

Mhairi and Apulo brought us the cups of wine, and we drank to Lianë's memory—and it was done. Tomorrow Gwenna and Colm would leave us to mourn, and to what healing a few brief days could bring.

⌘⌘⌘⌘⌘

We breakfasted early. Gwenna wanted to reach the Wall by evening, and it was a considerable ride. I approved of her reasons: at the guardpost where the road crossed the border into Ésparias, they would get beds and food, but not the expressions of sympathy and carefully worded questions they would have to endure at a *torp*. Gwenna could deal with it, but she thought Colm could not, and I agreed.

As we finished our farewells in the grey morning, the sound of hooves on the track coming from the north made us turn. Jordis, *Konë* of Hagenstorp, dismounted, going straight to Lena. "I was told the children were leaving," she said, wrapping her arms around her, "so I came right away." Mhairi would have sent the message.

Lena accepted the embrace, but she did not give in to tears. "Thank you." She stepped back from Jordis's arms, straightening her shoulders. "There is much to do; we too must leave before long." We were meant to be at Wall's End soon, to give me time to recover before the voyage to Casil.

"Hagen will meet with you and Roel whenever you are ready," Jordis told Sorley.

Sorley had arranged for Jordis and Hagen to keep an eye on the *Ti'ach* while it was empty. Mhairi and Roel, her husband, needed no oversight, but were something to befall the house or lands—a fire, or disease among the sheep—decisions should be made by a landholder, not the *torpari*.

"We need to take the horses to be shoed," Sorley replied. "Tomorrow, I thought. I'll see him then." Life returning to its patterns, the demands of house and fields and animals not to be put off any longer. I too had preparations to make, and not just the letters outlining further study our students should be completing in our absence.

"And you are both going to Wall's End now?" Jordis asked Gwenna and Colm.

"I have reports to make, and there are discussions I should be part of," my daughter answered. Colm just nodded.

"Are you stopping at Heurlstorp?"

"I wasn't planning to. Is there something I can do for you?"

"Just a letter for Elsë, if you would." Jordis's daughter had married the factor of Heurlstorp's son last autumn. Her mother might be noble, but the girl was Marai-fathered, and by a man of no rank. A factor's son, in line to be his own father's replacement, had been a good match for her here in Linrathe.

"Of course." Jordis gave Gwenna the letter, and she tucked it into a saddlebag. "We must go." She swung up onto her horse, and with a smile turned onto the path out of the *Ti'ach*'s valley, Colm and the dog following.

We watched them ride up the hillside. "Do not stand too long," Apulo said softly from beside me.

"I'll walk, I think," I told him. "Druisius, would you accompany me? I would like to hear your plans for the guard."

He fell into slow step beside me as we crossed the flagged courtyard. Kept level and swept, and trapping warmth from the sun in the stone, it allowed me to be outdoors with little danger of slipping or falling. But conversation here could be overheard. "Shall we inspect the weapons?" I asked.

Inside the long mews building, Druisius closed the door. "What is it you want?"

"Sit." He pulled a chair out for me, then took one himself, lips pursed. "Listen to what I have to say, and then tell me if you have heard anything from Casil that could have bearing." I told him what the Empress's last letter had said, the words which concerned me and what I thought they could mean.

He crossed his arms. "You have not told the others?"

"No, nor will I. Lena is not—rational—just now, and Sorley could not hide his worry." He nodded.

"So," he said, "Have I heard anything? No. Nothing I have not reported. But how would she know your plans? Who has told her?"

I had given this much thought. "No one, I believe. But if you have the eyes to see, the information is there. The marriages. The schools being built, in Sorham and Varsland and Ésparias. The books I have requested, over the years. All this is not secret, and it makes a pattern."

"The letters, and your private notes? They are still in their hiding place?" Under the bathhouse, built the first year we were here, the hypocaust warmed its floor, and a larger chamber held the boiler in which the water was heated. The wall dividing the boiler room from the low warren of the hypocaust was hollow; on the hypocaust side, hidden from view, a wooden door gave access to the space inside. Or so Druisius had explained. I had never seen it.

"No. Apulo retrieved them for me. I gave them to Ruar."

Druisius grinned. "I wondered. The *Teannasach* negotiating border tariffs?"

"His reasons to be here were all plausible," I said. "And the Casilani may force a search of the *Ti'ach*, on the grounds that I and my family are Ésparian, but they would not dare raid Dun Ceànnar."

"They would find the other records." In two chests in my study, all the diaries I had kept since I was seven lay under false bottoms. I was not entirely happy with the idea of Casilani officials reading those from the first twenty-eight years, honest and revealing as they were not just of the work I had been doing as a *toscaire*, but of my inner doubts and turmoil. But that honesty, I hoped, would make them believe the diaries from the last eighteen years were equally truthful. In many ways, they were. But in other ways, they had been written to deceive. Anyone reading them should see only the concerns of a *Comiádh*, expanding education to include knowledge from Casil, lost to us for centuries, and his pleasure in bringing the light of reasoned thought to barbarian lands.

"You must tell the guard not to resist any Casilani search while we are gone," I told Druisius. "I want no one harmed."

He frowned. "No. The guard must argue, threaten a little. Or the Casilani will be suspicious."

"You know best," I conceded. "Do not give them their instructions until the morning we leave. I want no chance of rumour reaching Lena."

"If they come, a message should go to the *Teannasach*, yes?"

"Yes."

He sucked at a tooth. "You should tell Lena."

"Not now."

"What if you are arrested in Ésparias, before we even reach Casil?"

I leant forward. "Druisius, I hope I am being overly cautious. Eudekia may have meant to warn me, but there is another interpretation if I consider the words 'our children's children'. She may be doing no more than telling me that she sees the best road to a stable peace is for Gwenna and Alekos to marry."

"Or maybe both, yes?"

I raised an eyebrow. "You are suggesting she will forgive the treason if I agree to the marriage?"

"That is what negotiation is. Both sides give a little, make bargains. Do not tell me you had not thought of this."

"I had," I admitted. "But I will not agree, unless Gwenna truly wants to marry Alekos. Another reason no one else can know, Druisius. I want neither Lena nor Sorley attempting to dissuade me from what I may have to do."

Chapter 7

~DAUGHTER~

"I HAD BETTER GIVE YOU SOME IDEA of what to expect at Wall's End," I said to Colm, as we neared the fort. I explained the layout of the buildings, how the infirmary—where I expected he'd be spending his days—stood a distance from the headquarters. "You call the physicians by their rank," I told him, "even the Casilani ones. They are all officers, of course."

"Was Gnaius an officer?"

"Gnaius? I suppose so. I don't know."

"I remember him."

"You couldn't," I said. "He went back to Casil when you were still a baby."

"I was three," Colm said. "I asked *Mathàir*. And I do remember him, just a little. He came to see *Athàir*, before he left forever. If he hadn't gone, Gwenna, do you think he could have saved Lianë, the way he saved our father?"

"He would have had to have been at the *Ti'ach*," I pointed out. "And even then . . . " I thought back to what Sorley had told me. "Gnaius said his treatments were not why *Athàir* lived. He had told *Mathàir* and Sorley there was no hope."

"Sorley's music. I know. I don't believe it. How can music do that?"

Not music itself, I thought, but all it represented. But Colm was still speaking. "And if it can, then why bother being a physician?"

"Because you can't fix a broken arm with music," I said sharply. "Colm, what Gnaius meant was his treatments could do no more. What Sorley's music did was reach *Athàir*, reminding him he had reasons to live. Holding him to this world, *Mathàir* would say."

"And Lianë didn't have reasons to live?"

"I think," I said slowly, after a moment's thought, "she would not have understood death, to fight against it. For her it would be no different than going to sleep, an escape from the fever and pain, if there was any."

"But she never woke up." Tears roughened his voice. "I wish I'd been there. Maybe I could have done something."

The rain slowed to a fine drizzle, then stopped, clouds scudding rapidly eastward. I pushed my hood back. Skylarks trilled in the air above us. Half an hour would find us at Wall's End.

"I'm never having children," Colm said suddenly. "It hurts too much."

What to say? "You don't have to. If you still feel the same way when you're adult, then, well . . . " I broke off. "But you can't live your life without loving someone." I wasn't sure this was a conversation I wanted to have with my brother. "Colm, stop for a minute."

He reined his horse in and sat, waiting. "There are times," I said, "when we are not just ourselves. When the way we behave, or even think, must conform to our larger role, the one we play in the world." In my mind I could hear Sorley saying the same thing to me, four years before. "At Wall's End—in Ésparias—you cannot just be Colm. You haven't had to be the prince before, or at least not very often, but remember whose son you are, and behave accordingly. Can you do that?"

He looked up at the sky, or the singing lark, then south into the land he didn't know. The dog panted. "I can."

"Good." I hoped he could keep the promise. "Then let's ride."

As we rode up to the gates of Wall's End, the doors swung open. "Envoy," the guard greeted me. "Welcome back. Who's this with you?"

I explained. How many times would I need to do this? "Who is at the headquarters?"

"The *Princip*, and the General."

"And the Casilani?"

"No one of rank today, Envoy. At least," he added, "not that I am aware of. Whose dog is it?"

"Mine," Colm said. "His name is Peritas."

"An honourable name." The soldier grinned. "No disrespect, Prince, but he'll have to find his place among the other dogs. Expect a torn ear or two while they sort things out."

"I wonder if I will fare any better among the cadets." Colm was smiling—a polite smile, nothing more, but he was making the effort.

I led Colm into the building, Peritas told firmly to stay outside. The saddlebags already sat on the floor of my room; someone had been efficient. "Change," I told him. "Your grey and white. Here's a towel. There's a comb on the sideboard, and wash your face and hands. We need to greet your cousin the *Princip*." I went to my wardrobe, selecting a set of good, but not formal, clothes, in the white-trimmed grey of our house. "I'll go next door to Lynthe's room to change."

Lynthe's indoor boots stood by her bed, and a cloak, still damp to the touch, hung over a chair. So she was here. I smiled to myself as I stripped off my wet clothes and towelled the dampness from my skin and hair. Probably she was at the women's baths, or maybe the junior commons. I'd find her later. I dressed again, combed and tied my hair, and went back to my own room.

Colm was dressed and waiting. "Come," I said, and we walked along the corridor and across the cobbles to the headquarters, Peritas appearing from somewhere to follow us. The door guard straightened: off duty, she was a friend, but she wasn't off duty, and I was wearing grey and white. She swung the door open.

A quick word with the steward, and after a wait of no more than a minute, he came out from Faolyn's workroom to usher us in. My cousin stood as we entered. I knelt, briefly; seeing Colm do the same from the corner of my eye. Raising myself, I went to Faolyn for a quick kiss on the cheek. "Gwenna. How are your parents?"

"They'll be here before long," I said. "Life must continue." He nodded.

"And this must be Colm. I haven't seen you since you were four or five. Welcome." He strode forward to embrace my brother. "Now, sit, please. Wine? Food? When did you leave the *Ti'ach*?" He called for his aide, giving quick instructions, and a few minutes later we had wine, and a dish of olives, and fresh bread to go with them. "You will dine with us tonight?"

"Tomorrow, surely," a voice said from behind us. I hadn't heard Talyn come in. "They'll be tired, and needing the baths and rest this evening." I stood for her hug; I loved my father's cousin, and there was true warmth in her embrace. Nor did she stand on ceremony; before I could work out who had precedence—my brother the heir after me, or the *Princip's* mother—she'd gone to Colm.

He took the offered hand. "General."

"Talyn," she countered. "At least in private. You are family. Which reminds me: what does Cillian want to be called, for the days he is here?" she asked, turning to me.

"Major, I should think." She grinned. "Colm would like to work with the physicians until we sail. Can he just be called by name, please, as I was as a cadet?"

"Of course. None of us are very good at this, are we, even after all these years? Except you, *Princip*," she added, a little wryly.

"One of us should be, or the Casilani will be offended," Faolyn said, "and we cannot afford that. And you will all be models of Ésparian royalty in Casil, of course." A sardonic note to his voice, but he meant it.

"Indisputably," I answered.

"I have given Lynthe very strict instructions," Talyn said. Faolyn rolled his eyes.

"Orders, I hope."

"Orders," Talyn confirmed. We talked a while longer, drinking wine, until Faolyn stood.

"I go to the baths about now, most days," he said. "Colm, would you like to come, this one time? After today, if you wish to be just another cadet, you will use the ones by the wall of the fort, but you are welcome to join me today. Afterwards I will have you introduced to the physicians, and a place found for you in the cadet quarters."

"That is very kind of you, *Princip*," Colm said. "I would be honoured."

"His bags are in my room," I told Faolyn, as they left. Talyn remained quiet until the door had closed.

"Your brother is a credit to his upbringing. I would not expect less. How is Lena?" she asked, her voice changing.

"Not good," I said, letting myself slump in the chair a little. "None of them are. Colm asked me to bring him here, because he couldn't stand to be at the *Ti'ach* with all his memories of Lianë."

"It is a hard thing, to lose a child," she said. "A different grief."

"Did you?" Lynthe had never mentioned it.

"My second-born, a boy. He was two, and he slipped out a door that should have been latched early one morning and went to the horses. One kicked him in the head."

"Oh, gods, Talyn. I'm sorry." Grief and guilt. She shook her head.

"It was a long time ago. The pain subsides. I'll tell your mother, when she's here." She eyed me. "And perhaps Cillian too? Or is he burying himself in his books, as usual?"

"Not entirely." Fatigue washed through me, suddenly. "I am tired," I said. "I think I need the baths, too."

"Then go. But dinner tomorrow? Siusàn will want to see you, and Colm should meet his little cousin."

"I have a letter for her," I said, remembering. "Ruar gave it to me. I can take it to her later."

"Tomorrow will be soon enough," Talyn said.

Lynthe wasn't at the baths. I'd just missed her, the attendant told me. I washed and soaked, chatting a little with some of the other women there. News of my sister's death had spread, and so I accepted words of condolence as graciously as I could before changing the subject.

When I returned to my room, Colm's bags were gone, and Lynthe was sitting in a chair, wine in hand. She put it down as I came in, rising to kiss me. A kiss that suggested she'd missed me. I broke away. "Hello," I said.

"Welcome back," she said, grinning. "Shall we go to the commons?"

I sat on the bed. "I don't think so. I'm tired, Lynthe. I don't want lots of people telling me how sorry they are, and shouting over dice games, and getting drunk. Tomorrow. After our family dinner," I added, remembering.

She wrinkled her nose. "Family dinner?"

"Colm is with me. He needs to meet everyone."

"You're going to have your little brother at your heels until your parents arrive?"

"He's not little," I said, annoyed. "He's fourteen, and he'll be with the medical cadets until we sail. I doubt I'll see much of him at all."

"Good." She hadn't, I realized, asked me how I was, or offered any words of sympathy. I'd just said I didn't want that. But I did, from Lynthe.

"You could come to eat, at least." She trailed one finger along my arm. "I could be convinced to have an early night."

"I'm not hungry. Faolyn gave us food, earlier." I tried a smile "Go on. I need to sleep more than anything else, I think. After all," I added, shading my voice to placate, "we'll be together for weeks on the ship, and in Casil."

"Together? Probably not in the way I prefer." She bent to kiss me again, lightly. "You sleep. I'll see you tomorrow."

I lay back on the bed, hearing the door close, and then, after her footsteps had receded, silence. Silence that echoed in a hollow deep inside me. An empty place, depleted by the days of being responsible at the *Ti'ach*, of balancing my work and my family's grief, of being the adult for Colm. Tomorrow I had reports to give and would begin whatever work I was assigned for the next few weeks. I couldn't be Lynthe's light-hearted lover tonight.

There are times when we are not just ourselves, I had told Colm earlier.

Tears began to seep. I had many roles in the world; too many. I was a junior envoy with great promise. I was Colm's capable sister, and I was my father's daughter, privy to and inheritor of his dangerous vision of a Western alliance. I was Faolyn's heir, the *Principe* of Ésparias one day far in the future. Soon, I might be asked to marry the Emperor of the East, a different alliance but one perhaps beneficial to the land I would someday lead. So many demands.

The trickling tears became sobs. I rolled over to bury my face in the pillow. You're just tired, I told myself. Go to sleep. Things will look better in the morning.

Chapter 8

~FATHER~

"CILLIAN?" LENA STOOD IN THE OPEN DOOR of my library, sweaty and dishevelled. She had, I surmised, been out on the training field with Druisius. "Sorley said you were here. Can I come in?"

"You don't need to ask, *käresta*." She knew I was alone.

She took the chair across from me, glancing at the books lining one wall. "If you buy any more, you'll need more shelves."

I had already asked Roel to build them while we were away. I told her so. She smiled, a little distantly. "Will I even see you in Casil?" she asked. "Between Eudekia and the libraries?"

"I will be one of many minor princes escorting daughters." I put down my pen to stretch my cramped fingers. "The Empress will not have time for me." Not much time, I hoped silently. That she would request my presence at least once was certain. The last nineteen years would only have honed her considerable diplomatic skills. I doubted I could best—or even equal her—now.

"The less time she has for you, the more you have for the libraries." Lena sounded resigned, but not upset. "I'll have to be Gwenna's chaperone most of the time."

"We must both play roles we dislike," I said. "For a few weeks."

"I know." She glanced down at the paper in front of me. "What are you writing?"

"A letter to Iorlath, asking her to send Colm's belongings home. And a warning that he will likely not come back to her *Ti'ach*. I believe he will choose to remain at Wall's End when we return."

She nodded. "Probably. He'll learn a different sort of medicine there."

She sounded detached, almost uninterested. Unmoored, I thought: no longer a mother of a small child, her other children grown, without even the routines of the *Ti'ach* to anchor her. Nor would she—or any of us—have either familiarity or definition to cushion our days for some long time, until we knew whether Gwenna would marry Alekos. I too felt this dislocation, this sense of a foundation shifting.

"I came," Lena said, "to ask to borrow books for the voyage."

"What would you like?"

"Which of Cotta's do you have?"

"The *Commentaries*. They were Perras's."

"I remember us talking about them as we crossed the Durrains." Twenty years past, around our evening campfires. Discussions of the Casilani general's writings on history and tactics, so I could maintain distance between me and the young soldier who had been my partner in exile. What would you do, and why? I had asked her, a teacher's question.

It hadn't worked. Debating tactics, whether in long-past wars or in *xache*, which we had played with pebbles and a grid inked onto kidskin, had only made me more appreciative of Lena's quick intelligence and surprising insight. But it was not until cold forced us to share a tent and our conversation had turned to more personal things did I allow her to lessen the distance. We'd talked about memories, and our favourite foods, and then she'd asked me the name of my first love.

'I have never been in love,' I'd answered. I had thought it true. Later, when she had taught me what love was, I understood I had not been honest. A fiction I maintained, at least by omission, although we—all three of us—knew the truth.

"What are you thinking about?"

"Travelling," I said. "Leaving a life behind."

"Would you? If you could now?"

I glanced around my library, toward the hidden bed behind the screen, the rows of books, the cat watching us with half-closed eyes from the windowsill. Then I looked at the woman who was both my greatest love and my greatest blessing. "Travel, yes. Leave this behind forever? Not by choice."

"When does a refuge become a prison?" Lena murmured. She stood. "Where are the *Commentaries*?" I directed her to them. "Talyn told me to read them," she added, as she turned to go.

⌘⌘⌘⌘⌘

We sat around the long table in the hall, the scent of cut hay drifting in from the fields. Mhairi had gone to take harvest cake to the workers, Apulo with her. "I should go too," Sorley said, without conviction, and without moving.

"Roel knows his work," Druisius said. "Do not insult him by supervising."

"Maybe you're right." Sorley yawned. Neither he nor I had slept until the early hours. But I had learned to live with little sleep; not so Sorley. He yawned again.

Lena returned from the kitchen, carrying a mug, in time to see the second yawn. "You need to stop playing *xache* so late," she said.

"Practice for Cillian, when Eudekia summons him," Sorley said, almost with a grin. "Although I suppose her husband might object to night games."

Druisius snorted. "Of all sorts. But he is not in Casil."

We could, now, maintain this semblance of normalcy for a little while. Then something said or unsaid would remind one of us, and the mood would change. Even last night, what Sorley and I had sought had been largely the solace of forgetting for a short time. I would, in truth, not be loath to leave the *Ti'ach* for the rest of the year, to be where no memories of Lianë confronted me at every turn.

"Where is he?" Lena asked.

"Who? Hathus?" Druisius said. "Gone to quell the unrest in the east, I am told." By whom? I wondered, not for the first time. Druisius would not tell me who his informants were. Letters arrived, or he went to Wall's End and returned with rumours and whispers, usually accurate. "The country, Qipërta, is a province of Casil, but it borders the Boranoi lands too. Maybe he is wearing both crowns, yes? The consort of the Empress, and the prince of the Boranoi. Threats from both, to make little Qipërta cower."

"He led the army that took back the western grasslands, didn't he?" Sorley sat up a bit straighter.

"He did," I said. "It was, if you recall, half Eudekia's reason for marrying him, to take back those lands. But by all accounts, he is a strong leader of men, and a skilled tactician."

"I think bored, too, yes?" Druisius said. "Fifty years old, and waiting for his father to die so he can be king. Nothing to do in Casil but advise an Empress who does not need advising, and once the Prince is Emperor, not even that. No sons to prepare for the throne after him. War is a diversion."

Lena had been standing, listening. Now she sat beside me, placing her mug on the table. I recognized the tang of anash. But the moon was a week past full, and her monthly bleeding over. I gave her a questioning look.

"Yes, it's anash. You might as well all know. I won't risk another pregnancy. I know the chances are small, but—" A film of tears glinted in her eyes and was quickly blinked away. "I just can't."

I touched her hand. Had she thought I would argue, had she told me privately? She half smiled, leaning into me. "You said Hathus has no sons?" she asked. "Did he and Eudekia have any children?"

"None," I said.

"One pregnancy, maybe two," Druisius said. "Lost early." I hadn't known that. It was not something an Empress would tell a provincial prince.

"Poor Eudekia," Lena said. "But it makes Prince Alekos's marriage all the more important, doesn't it? Only one alliance to be made. I doubt Ésparias will rank highly in that analysis."

I agreed. And yet . . . *for our children's children.*

Lena closed the shutters of the window before slipping into bed beside me. She turned to me, her hand on my chest. "Do you mind?"

"About the anash? No." She nestled closer. "Neither of us—none of us—want to live through this again."

"Such a common tragedy," she murmured. "How many families have lost a child?"

"Many. But it does not lessen our grief, *käresta*." I felt her nod, and then the cold seep of tears. I stroked her hair. She took a deep, shuddering breath, turning so her back was against me. We had slept this way so many nights, even before we were lovers. My hand dropped to her hip.

Her breathing slowed and steadied into the rhythm of sleep. I lay awake, thinking of a conversation long ago, the night before a battle in which one or both of us might have died. *You have been my refuge, my sanctuary, and you always will be*, she had said then. Had those words been in her mind earlier today?

If I had been Lena's refuge, the *Ti'ach* was mine. The position of *Comiádh* had been offered for as long as I needed it, to keep me and my family safe. I shifted slightly; I would have to turn onto my back soon, before the muscles began to cramp. Lena did not stir.

I had been a boy when Tómas, the *Ti'ach's* young fawkner, had taken me with him up to the high ground at the end of the long meadow to release a *fuádain*. He'd taken off her jesses, and then her hood, and with an upward movement of his arm, let her go. She'd flown; landed, flown again, seemingly confused without the trappings of captivity, until she launched herself again from a branch, flying south. I'd watched her disappear.

"Why?" I'd asked Tómas.

"Keep her too long, she forgets what she is," he'd said. "She'll never hunt freely, or breed, and even if we release her, she'll just return to the mews.

That's not right. Time to let her go when she still knows she's wild, while she'll choose freedom over safety."

Lena had echoed that thought this afternoon. I moved cautiously onto my back, staring up into the dark, hoping she had spoken in the misery of grief, and nothing more.

Chapter 9

~DAUGHTER~

THE MORNING BROUGHT SUNSHINE, and a meeting with Michan, the officer to whom I reported. He'd been one of Casyn's adjutants, alongside my father, when my great-uncle had been *Princip* in the years after the Casilani had arrived; regardless, he treated me no differently than the rest of the young envoys he supervised.

We reviewed the terms of the tariff agreements I'd made with Ruar. He pursed his lips at the rate set for salt fish. "That's very low, Gwenna."

"But within the range I was given."

"It is. But we'll have to give the Varslanders the same rate, which will reduce revenues more than I would have liked."

"Why?" I asked. "Didn't we request more high-value goods from them? Furs and ivory and amber?"

He leant back in his chair. "Yes, but we are getting fewer of those, not more."

"A bad winter?" I suggested, "Hunting and trapping difficult, and if the ice stayed late, amber difficult to find?"

"Possibly. But we've heard nothing about heavy snows or a late spring. Such hard weather would have affected northern Sorham, too, surely?"

"Then they are holding these goods back? Hoping to renegotiate prices, perhaps?"

"Perhaps. Or?"

"Or bypassing us altogether," I said, realizing. By the terms of the treaties signed after the Taiva, the Marai brought goods only as far south as the trading harbour in Linrathe, to be transferred to Casilani ships there. It kept them away from Ésparias, their ships and men held in the north. But the sea wasn't the only way to travel to Casil, just the fastest. "You think they are taking the river route east?"

"I've received no confirmation of this from our agents in Casil, but I believe that route not navigable until only a few weeks ago, so it's not surprising."

"Am I to investigate, while I'm there?"

"That, I think, might be difficult, given why you are going," he said gravely. "Nonetheless, be alert."

"Of course." Inwardly I smiled: it would be something to do that wasn't polite conversation and court presentation. "What is my next assignment, sir?"

"As I cannot send you away from the fort, I thought to use you here. It will be mostly translation, and tallying cargo manifests, and such. Not very interesting, I'm afraid."

I'd spent much of the last year doing similar work—tallying, not translating—in the coastal villages, so I already knew it wasn't, in itself, interesting. At least I'd been listening as well as auditing records, noting what was said about tax rates and prices—and in the weeks spent at Tirvan, I'd got to know my aunt Kira and my cousin Teárdh a little better. I had a good head for numbers, and I'd been trained to be precise, so the work wasn't difficult; as well, I'd enjoyed the travel.

I suspected Michan had another motive: the opportunity to negotiate border tariffs with Linrathe had come rather early in my career, and by assigning me to mundane work, he'd be sending a message to the other young envoys that I was not being singled out for special treatment. He'd taken advantage of my rank for one situation, but it wasn't going to be common practice.

I wrote a copy of my report in Linrathan, to be sent to Ruar—he read Ésparian perfectly well, of course, but it was a courtesy, then checked figures on oil and wine imports for the rest of the morning. By midday I needed fresh air as well as food, so on the way to the junior commons I took a longer route, past the infirmary. Peritas was curled up by a door; he got up, tail wagging, when he saw me. I rubbed his ears, and spoke to him, but he didn't follow me when I continued on.

Lynthe wasn't there, but several of my friends were, and today I didn't mind their quick words of sympathy. "When are your parents arriving?" one of the men asked. He'd had been at the *Ti'ach* with me in our final year of training, a classmate; more, for a few weeks the following summer. We liked each other, but that was all.

"I'm not sure, exactly," I said. "Why?"

"I'm being sent to the mines," he said dolefully. I made a rueful face. Mine audits took careful analysis: it was far too easy for overseers to falsify weights and take the unmeasured ore for themselves. "I leave in two days. I was hoping to be here if your father was going to teach while he's at the fort."

"He didn't mention it. He might, I suppose."

I was just getting up to return to work when Lynthe came in. "Late back from patrol," she said briefly. "Horse shied at a grouse flying up; the cadet went flying too and broke his arm." She grinned. "Something for your brother to work on. Can't you stay?"

I shook my head. "I'm nearly late as it is. I'll see you at dinner."

"Or the baths beforehand?"

"Maybe." I should check on Colm at some point, make sure he knew where to be, and when. But I could do that, and still meet Lynthe at the baths in the late afternoon.

Peritas's presence outside the infirmary told me Colm was still inside. I went in, a little hesitantly: having his sister checking on him would not stand my brother in good stead among the cadets. I wouldn't do it again. A medic pointed to a room when I asked. I stopped in the doorway. Colm was arranging the bones of some small creature into a complete skeleton, watched by one of the doctors.

My presence caught the doctor's eye: Colm was completely absorbed in his task. "Envoy?"

"Sorry to disturb," I told her, "but I need to remind my brother we dine tonight with the *Princip*. He is," I added, "very likely to forget, if there are skulls to be studied, or skeletons to reconstruct."

Colm looked up, smiled—a real smile, I noted—but his eyes dropped back to the bones immediately. "I will ensure he is there," the doctor said. "I am evaluating his knowledge, these first few days, as I understand Colm is to stay with us as a cadet, once you return from Casil?"

"It is the plan," I confirmed.

"The schools north of the Wall are thorough in their grounding," she said. "Very thorough." I simply nodded. Colm had been studying animal skeletons since he was ten. Once, home on leave, I had come across him bent over the carcass of a sheep with Apulo, discussing how muscles and bones worked together.

"Then I will leave you." Outside, I gave Peritas a pat, and made my way to the baths.

We didn't linger; we both had to be at dinner. But there was time, just, for quick, laughing lovemaking before we had to appear in the *Princip's* private quarters. I did have one horrified thought, as we lay on my bed in a tangle of arms and legs. "We're not supposed to be at the villa, are we?"

Lynthe chuckled. "No. The headquarters. But I suppose we'd better get dressed."

I wore my earrings, garnets sent from the Empress when I was just a baby, the setting done by a metalsmith in Linrathe, and put my hair up into a fairly tidy knot. A grey tunic and breeches, and a pair of sandals were all pulled on in a matter of minutes. Lynthe was even quicker, as she disdained jewellery.

On the way to the headquarters we met Colm, so the three of us arrived together. I introduced him to Lynthe. He had met her before when she'd been my bodyguard for a while, but I didn't think he'd remember.

"I couldn't mistake you for anyone but one of our family," Lynthe said to him. "Funny how we all look alike, somehow."

Even with his hazel eyes, Colm was unmistakeably my father's son, the resemblance stronger now his face was gaining the definition of adulthood. Where had Lianë's red-gold hair and blue eyes come from? I smiled, remembering Jordis teasingly telling Sorley he'd be blamed. 'Won't be the first time,' he'd said easily—a response I'd understood only in retrospect, when I'd learned who Bjørn really was.

Talyn was already with Faolyn and Siusàn in their rooms, the table set for the meal. Siusàn's pregnancy was obvious now, and their first-born, three-year-old Constyn, was sitting on his grandmother's lap. He was as dark-haired as she, and for that I was glad, because I hadn't thought about Colm's reaction to a child only a few months younger than Lianë. But he smiled, and greeted everyone appropriately, then went to crouch in front of Talyn and the boy to speak specifically to him. I could tell the action was forced, but at least he was trying.

I took Ruar's letter to his sister. She broke the seal, scanning the words, closing her eyes in pain.

"Bad news?" Faolyn asked softly.

"Not unexpected," she said. "Ruar expects Helvi not to live beyond the end of the summer."

"Then why did he make Daragh come to the *Ti'ach* for the talks?" Colm straightened, coming over to us. "Forgive my interruption," he said. "But it seems to me to take a boy from his mother at such a time is cruel."

"Daragh will be *Teannasach* some day," Siusàn said. "Ruar is showing him that the needs of his country come first, before personal considerations. Did not Ruar himself leave Helvi, who is his wife as much as she is Daragh's mother?"

A faint flush stained Colm's skin. Siusàn had spoken mildly enough, but now she reached out a hand to touch my brother's arm. "You are feeling your own loss. It seems hard to you, cruel, as you said. But learning to be your country's leader has many difficult lessons."

"Then, in all respect, *Princip*," Colm said, "I am glad it is not my fate."

"Then you had best be an excellent physician, and keep your sister well, or it might be, one day," Faolyn said. "But enough of this dismal talk. I too had a letter today, and after dinner, I will tell you what it says."

Now why was he being evasive? Or was he just trying to lighten the mood, an attempt at playfulness meant to build anticipation? A steward brought wine, a nursemaid took the toddler away, and soon after we took our seats for the meal: fish in a coriander crust, with cucumber and lettuce, and afterwards cheesecake. Faolyn had a Casilani—or Casilani trained—cook.

"This is only a simple meal in Casil," he said. "You will be delighted by the food, I should think."

"I've been told it's excellent," I replied. He should know; he'd spent longer there than any of us, most of seven years, although Casyn, as both his grandfather and *Princip*, had insisted he returned home for several summers. Casil was considered too hot in the summer months, and anyone who could escaped it for villas on breezy islands or in the mountains. Faolyn was not the only heir to a province who went home to be seen, and to bring Casil's thinking to their unsophisticated lands. Casyn, my father had told me, had had other motives, ensuring Faolyn did not forget his family and his traditions in the face of Casil's blandishments.

"Was that only Casyn's idea?" I'd asked. He'd smiled, nothing more, but it was at the *Ti'ach* the summer Faolyn was sixteen that he'd been introduced to Ruar's sister Siusàn, the formal betrothal happening before Faolyn returned to Casil. Another strand in the web woven into place.

Honeyed walnuts were brought, with a sweeter wine, and fresh fingerbowls placed before us. "Well?" Talyn asked. "The meal is done. Who was your letter from, Faolyn?"

"The Empress." He picked up a walnut. "You are being greatly honoured, Gwenna, Lynthe. She is sending a ship for you, a 'well-appointed ship', she writes, to ensure you have all possible comforts on the voyage to Casil."

"Does that mean we might actually have a cabin?" Lynthe asked. Like me, she'd travelled up and down from the Eastern Fort to Wall's End on ships. Comfort wasn't something I associated with them.

"Perhaps," I said. "But I doubt it's our ease the Empress has in mind, but rather my father's, since I know he's written to her to tell her he's accompanying us. Wouldn't you agree, Faolyn?"

"You are completely right," he said. "I am to tell Cillian every need of his will be met. Whatever that means. She is remarkably solicitous of him, I must say."

"They are friends, if nearly two decades of letters is proof of anything."

"I would prefer not to go," Colm said suddenly. "Can't I stay here as a medical cadet?"

"We would have no objection," Talyn said, before I could find a response, "but it's your parents' decision, not ours. Do you not want to see Casil, especially with your father?"

"Yes, but . . . " He fiddled with his knife. "Not just now."

"But this will be the only chance there is," I said. "*Athàir* is fifty-three, Colm, and you know travel is difficult for him. He won't make this voyage again."

Could I have said anything worse? The implication in my words, the suggestion of mortality, was not what Colm needed to hear. Talyn shot me a look. My hands had come up to cover my mouth, involuntarily, a reaction to my own stupidity.

"Should he be going, then?" Colm's voice was tight and a little high. "Is this dangerous for him?"

"No," Talyn said firmly. "Cillian will be uncomfortable, perhaps in more pain than usual without the baths, but there is no danger to his life. All Gwenna meant is, inevitably, your father will be less willing to tolerate discomfort. I am completely happy not to be going, and I'm the same age, more or less, as Cillian."

My brother nodded, but I wasn't sure he was convinced. Talyn turned the talk to what the new baby might be called, with Lynthe suggesting some ludicrous combinations of family names, raising, after a few minutes, a smile from Colm.

"Gwenna, you will have to remember these," Siusàn said, "when it is your turn to name a child."

"If she does." Lynthe sounded doubtful. "I'm not planning to."

"But Gwenna hasn't that choice," Siusàn responded. "She is the heir, and she must herself continue the line. It will be her child who is *Princip*, some day."

It would be, wouldn't it? I hadn't given it much thought. Oh, I knew a child of mine would inherit the title, but as I had no expectation of ever truly being *Principe*, except for perhaps a few years in my old age, none of it seemed real at all.

"Maybe I'll displease the Empress," I said lightly, "and she'll make Constyn the heir instead." Did only I see the tiny movement around Faolyn's eyes, the quickly-masked satisfaction at the thought?

Chapter 10

~FATHER~

WE HAD TRAVELLED SLOWLY FROM *TORP* to *torp*, at the pace of a cart pulled by walking horses. Even so, even with the drugs I had allowed— and suspected Apulo had mixed more strongly than usual—I needed both him and Druisius to help me off the cart, and to walk into the halls of our hosts.

Sorley had prepared them, ensuring my needs would be met. A bedroom on the ground floor, so no stairs to be negotiated; a warning that I would want to eat lightly, and perhaps not at the long table in the hall. But after Apulo's massage and manipulations, and more cannabium and willow bark, I had forced myself to join the *Eirën* and *Konë* for a while, to ask and answer questions, to make conversation. An effort expected of both the *Comiádh* of Linrathe and the prince of Ésparias, and a necessary one, were I to maintain their trust in both roles.

Late on the third afternoon we approached the guardpost on the Wall. Guardpost was a misnomer now: it had grown with trade and movement across the border. Now it was a small fort, with its own commander's headquarters, barracks and workshops—and baths. Druisius had ridden ahead, to commandeer those.

In the last dip before the road rose to the natural ridge of land on which the Wall stood, I asked our driver to halt. "Saddle my horse, please."

"Cillian, no," Lena said.

"I must. Why else do I ride every week, *käresta*?" Apulo was already busy at his chest of tinctures and oils. Wordlessly he handed me a cup. I drank it, tasting the bitterness of willow-bark. Lena, her jaw set, turned away to supervise the saddling of my grey gelding. The horse was old, and placid, and used to my poor seat and weak legs.

Sorley helped me mount, the bed of the cart replacing the mounting block I used at the *Ti'ach*. I could tell from his face he wasn't happy with me either. But what people see influences what they think, and for the same reason I had dressed in a grey tunic trimmed in white this morning, I would ride into Ésparias. I was an advisor to the *Princip*, and father to the heir. I would reveal no weakness nor infirmity to the soldiers, lest they doubt my mind as well as my body.

The commander was waiting for me, with half-a-dozen soldiers in polished leather holding shining weapons. He dropped to one knee as we approached. A small part of me—the part that would never let me forget I was the bastard son of a *torpari* girl—wanted to laugh. I kept my face relaxed.

"Captain."

He stood, a little awkwardly. "Prince Cillian." He hesitated. "Major. Welcome."

Gwenna's advice, no doubt. "Major," I said, "is my preference. Thank you, Captain—?"

"Farry," Lena said from beside me. "It is, isn't it?"

A delighted grin spread across his face. "I didn't think you'd remember me."

She swung down off her horse. "We witnessed a terrible event together. I think I remember every face from that day. Cillian, Farry was at the winter camp, and in the tent with me when Elon tried to assassinate Callan."

"You served with my father?"

"I was a very junior officer, sir, seconded to his regiment. As all junior officers were for a time, then," Farry explained. Twenty years and more ago. He'd have survived the Taiva. Why was he commanding a border fort, collecting tariffs and checking manifests? Then I saw his right arm, hanging loosely, the hand shrunken.

I should have known; should have prepared myself to know who the officer here was, and his or her history. I glanced meaningfully at his arm. "The Taiva?"

"Yes, sir."

"Then we share more than knowing Lena," I said, smiling. "My own injuries from that battle mean I need assistance in dismounting, and I do not walk easily. But perhaps my daughter made my requirements known?"

"She did, sir. There is a mounting block waiting, and the baths are ready."

Much later, after what relief the heat of the water and Apulo's ministrations could bring me, and a light meal with Farry, I lay on the bed in the room provided for us. Farry's own room, from its position in the headquarters building, and the quality of its furnishings. He'd been worried about the bed: it wasn't wide. His *quincala* was at Rigg, he told us, one of the grassland villages; he saw her and his children every few weeks. He'd had a second bed brought in. Lena had assured him it was sufficient.

"Should you have more willow-bark?" She'd changed into her sleeping shift, and in the low light, barefooted, she looked barely older than when I had first met her.

"The *fuisce* Sorley left, I think."

She poured me some, adding a trace of water. "I had an interesting conversation with Farry, while you were at the baths."

"Interesting in what way?" I settled back against the pillows. The pain in my back and leg was manageable, and the *fuisce* should ensure I slept for a few hours.

"After Gwenna and Colm rode through, he heard some mutterings among the soldiers." She pulled a chair up close to the bed. "Faolyn's son. There are some who believe he should be the heir, not Gwenna."

"Casyn's direct line, not Callan's?"

She took a mouthful of wine. "There's more to it than that, in my guess. Had we stayed in Ésparias; were you better known to the soldiers, their opinions might be different. While you've taught the young envoys, and a few officer-cadets, over the years, to the men and women who make up most of the army you're a figure in the shadows."

"The banished prince," I said.

"Exactly. Although Faolyn has tried to counter that."

The last time we had made this journey had been nine years past, for Faolyn's succession. We hadn't attended his wedding to Siusàn, Ruar's sister; Lena had been pregnant with Lianë, suffering with nausea more than she had with Gwenna or Colm. I had been concerned for her and had not minded the excuse not to travel. Sorley had gone, taking our presents and apologies.

"Then," I said, "I will have to ride into Wall's End as the welcomed prince, will I not?" In truth, I should ride all the length of the Wall; there would be soldiers moving along the road. The border was not patrolled now, but there was traffic between Wall's End and the cadet school at the White Fort, and to the grassland villages beyond. The idea was daunting. I doubted I had either the stamina or the strength of mind to do it.

"You can't," Lena said flatly.

"I must. It is only physical pain, *käresta*. It passes."

"There is poppy at Wall's End."

"As there was nine years ago. Druise will make sure the senior physician is aware." I swallowed the rest of the *fuisce*, its induced warmth spreading through me. "Leave the flask on the table, if you will.

She did as I asked, before stooping to kiss me. "Try to sleep."

"I will, for a while."

I slept for a few hours, waking to pain. Just enough moonlight lit the room that I could find the flask. In the other bed, Lena did not move. I swallowed several mouthfuls of the distilled spirit, then lay back, focusing on breathing, waiting. I began to recite a *danta* in my mind, concentrating on seeing the words as well as hearing them. Somewhere among dragons and mythical heroes, I slipped back into sleep.

I woke to Apulo bringing me drugs and heated compresses. Lena had gone. She came in as Apulo finished his work, bearing a tray with a small bowl of porridge and tea.

"I spoke with Farry," she said, as I contemplated the tray with little interest. I reached for the cup. "Food too," she directed. "You need your strength today. He will send an escort with us, the six soldiers from yesterday. In full uniform, one bearing the flag, clearly indicating you are the welcomed prince, and not an exile quietly slipping back home."

It was an appropriate compromise, and I told her so. "But," I added, "I will still ride, the last half mile. I should wear both the pendant and my father's ring, too, today. It is not just our children I would honour."

Chapter 11

~DAUGHTER~

A MESSENGER HAD BEEN SENT AHEAD of my parents, to alert Wall's End to expect their party by mid-afternoon. New flags above the arches of the main gate snapped in the breeze: the Eagle of the Eastern Empire flying higher than the White Horse of Ésparias. An honour guard, their buckles and cloak pins and weapons shining, stood at both arches. More men and women in spotless uniforms lined the road inside the fort.

"For our parents?" Colm whispered, standing beside me.

"For our father." My eyes stung with sudden tears. "For a prince of Ésparias, come home."

Slowly they came into view. Colm's intake of breath audible as he saw my father riding. At a walk, but upright, admitting no hint of discomfort. My mother rode on his right; Sorley on his left, with Druise and Apulo just behind. In the summer sunshine, they wore no cloaks, and the silver of the chain and pendant my father wore, a smaller copy of Faolyn's, glinted against his grey tunic. His hair was a badger's mix of silver and black. He looked—magnificent, I decided, a magnificent stranger on a grey horse, not the father I knew.

They passed through the right-hand arch and into the fort. A soldier ran forward with a stool. Druisius dismounted to offer my father an arm—appropriate, for his Captain of the Guard. Behind him my mother and Sorley dismounted. Druise and Apulo had dropped to one knee, Druise beside my father, there if he were needed. My mother also knelt. My father bowed his head.

"*Princip*," he said. "You have my fealty, Faolyn."

"As you have my regard and my love, Prince Cillian," Faolyn said, his voice pitched to carry. I touched my brother's arm, and together, following Talyn's lead, we knelt: Ésparian citizens on the soil of our own land, acknowledging the man who should have been *Princip*. I swallowed, hard, trying to keep from crying. I'd been taught this protocol, but I'd never offered homage to my father. I hadn't known how it would make me feel, this mix of pride and awe and disbelief—and behind it a profound irritation. He must be in enormous pain.

As we had knelt, my mother had risen. Druisius and Apulo had not. Sorley also did not kneel, but then he was Linrathan—although he had bowed to Faolyn, I was sure. He was watching my father, ready to offer a hand or a shoulder. No deference from my mother or from Sorley? My father must have insisted. To the two people he loved above all others, he was not the prince of Ésparias.

But he was to me, or I would not be the heir. His eyes found mine, and he tilted his chin upward, just a little. I stood, hesitantly. Was this what he'd meant? Sorley, beside him, smiled, and then he bowed to me: not the full bow he'd given Faolyn, but still, an acknowledgment—and to my horror, my mother did the same. Why hadn't I been prepared for this?

Because, the analytical part of my mind told me, my father had only decided to do this in the past few days. Not his own entrance: that I had expected. But in the ritual and emotion of the moment, the returning prince was reminding the world it was his daughter, me, who was to wear the silver pendant and ring one day, the leader of her people.

What, then, did my father know?

I took the few steps forward. He held out his hand. I took it, and knelt again, my head bowed for a moment, before I kissed the ring on the hand that held mine. I looked up. "My regard and my love, Prince Cillian." His eyes—the pride in them—told me I'd done what he'd hoped.

A throat was cleared, loudly. I stood, to hear the Governor say, "Prince Cillian, I extend greetings; we are pleased to see you in Ésparias, if only for a short while." Livius was a frequent visitor to the *Ti'ach*; he and my father were friends. He strode forward, and as we moved to enter the fort, Talyn fell in step beside me. She glanced upward at the flag of Ésparias, and back to me, one eyebrow slightly raised.

"The horse," I said, "was chosen years ago, for its smooth walk. And it is grey."

"Nonetheless," she said, almost under her breath. "I doubt my son is pleased. For those who remember, Gwenna, that could have been Callan on his white horse, back from the dead."

"I didn't know he was going to do this."

"I didn't think you did."

Somehow we all made our way to the headquarters, horses being led off to shouted instructions from Druisius, and a yelp from Sorley as he retrieved his *ladhar*.

"Straight to the baths, Cillian," my mother said, sharply. "Forgive any lapse in protocol, *Princip*, but he is in pain, and needs the baths and Apulo's attentions."

"Of course," he said, "They are ready, and closed to all but those he would like with him."

My father looked up; he'd been talking to Colm. Close to him now, I could see the tightness around his eyes and lips. "Thank you. An hour, and I will be refreshed."

My mother made a small sound of disbelief—or frustration, catching Faolyn's attention. "Lena, I am remiss. My deepest condolences, to you both." He was courteous; no one could fault the *Princip* on that front.

"*Mathàir*, would you like the baths too?" I asked. "We could go to the women's, and I am sure they too can be closed for an hour."

"I would," she said. "Will you come, Gwenna? Talyn, Lynthe—forgive me, but could I have this time with my daughter?"

"Whatever you like," Talyn said. "You have your old rooms, and unless you wish differently supper will be brought to you there. I didn't think you'd want anything formal tonight, or even family."

"Thank you," my mother said. "That was thoughtful. Cillian may have other ideas, but I'll try to prevail."

She was thinner than ever, I thought, as we prepared for the hot pool, and she moved slowly. Perhaps only fatigue, but riding at my father's pace shouldn't have tired her. "Are you well?" I asked her, as we settled into the steaming water. "You seem exhausted."

"I'm well enough. Nothing is wrong, except I'm angry with your father. A ridiculous display." She rolled her shoulders. "All is well with you? Is Colm adjusting?"

"He seems to be. He looked happy enough the one time I went to see him in the infirmary. He was assembling animal bones, with one of the doctors watching." I changed the subject. "I'm told a ship is being sent for us. One with all possible comforts. For *Athàir*, of course."

"Of course," she said. "Eudekia still favours him, after all these years. You do realize, Gwenna, that because she does, you are almost certainly her first choice to marry Alekos? If she could not have the man, her son shall have his daughter."

"Doesn't Alekos have a say? Don't I?"

"Alekos is making a political marriage: he will do what is best for his Empire. But Eudekia has wanted you since you were a baby, to be brought up there as Faolyn was, and if we had let that happen I think she would have betrothed you to Alekos as a child. Cillian has defied her wishes several times, and she has allowed it, but you must never forget that she *is* allowing it: had she chosen to have you sent to Casil, there would have been little we could have done, except go with you."

"And if I say no?"

Her eyes were closed. "I don't know," she said. "Nor does your father." She opened her eyes. "But, Gwenna, if no is your answer, then say it. Marriage is not easy, and when politics and intrigue are part of it, which they would be, married to the Emperor of the East, it is all the much harder. Without a true connection, without complete trust, it would be unthinkable."

"But I have to marry, don't I?" I said. "I am the heir, and there must be an heir after me."

"Then have a child, or two," my mother said. "This is Ésparias, and you need not marry, Gwenna, nor pair with a man for any length of time except by choice."

"You did."

She sighed. "It was necessary. To make the *Ti'ach* possible."

"A political marriage was asked of Faolyn and Ruar," I said, very quietly. "The wishes of the Empress are not the only consideration."

"Pieces in a game," she said. "First the game was Callan's, and we thought, your father and I, that we were free of it, but of course we weren't. And now there are two games: Eudekia's and Cillian's, and you are a piece in both, as much as I swore you would not be."

"But I have known that since I was fourteen."

She sat straighter in the water. "I suppose you have. We owe Sorley a lot for that summer, don't we?" She tilted her head. "May I ask you something? Something personal?"

"Of course you can."

"You and Lynthe are lovers, am I right?"

"We are," I said.

"Is she . . . " She hesitated. "Just women, Gwenna?"

"No," I said. "There's been a man or two, as well. I'd have no problem with Alekos in my bed, if that's what you're asking."

She smiled, just a little. "Assuming he's presentable, of course." Her eyes took on a distant look. "When I was eighteen, I made a decision based on little more than intuition, and perhaps a wish for excitement, not from education and upbringing. You have an advantage I didn't, and I will have to trust to what we've instilled in you, all of us, in guiding your choice."

"Do you regret that decision?" I stepped from the pool, holding out a hand to her.

Water dripped onto the tiles of the floor. Around us, painted on the walls, the gods listened. "I regret things resulting from it: your father's injuries, for one. But very little, for myself." She picked up the towel that lay folded on a bench. "We've had seventeen years of peace at the *Ti'ach*, and I've rejoiced in each one of them. But I think they're done."

We gathered as a family in the rooms where I had spent the first months of my life. I had no recollection of them, of course, although I did vaguely remember them from when we had been here for Faolyn's accession. Apulo would sleep in what had been the nursery, to be close if my father needed him. Looking at how drawn *Athàir* was, I decided that had been a wise decision.

"Give me the wine," my father said, as Sorley lifted the jug to pour, once we were all present.

"Gods, Cillian, I can do it for once," Sorley protested.

"It is mine to do."

Sorley's jaw tightened. "At least stay seated." He took the jug to my father. I brought over the cups, green glass from Casil. The first to my mother, as always, from Sorley's hand; then mine. Sorley's last, and because I knew now to look for it, I saw the brief touch of my father's fingers on his as the cup was passed.

When we all had wine, we waited for my father's words, almost always something from Catilius. Not tonight, though. "There is no such thing as good or bad fortune for the individual; we live in common." I recognized the quote: the Casilani philosopher Annaeus. "We are here at Wall's End for a brief time, before we return to Casil, where our lives together began. A strange retrogression, in a way. Shall we drink to our lives in common?"

How contained they were, the four of them, I thought, as I lifted my cup. I was part of this life in common, and Colm, and yet somehow we weren't.

The bonds among them remained, even as my brother and I moved into our own lives. The thought reassured me.

"Even Gwenna," my father said, with a slight smile, "can lay claim to Casil as her beginning." His gaze was on my mother. She blinked, and the briefest of answering smiles took some of the sadness from her eyes for a moment.

"If I have no claim to Casil at all," Colm said, "then why should I go?"

"There is more to the world than Linrathe and Ésparias, Colm," my father replied, "and I would like you to know it."

"The libraries," Druise said. "You must see the libraries, Cub. The medical texts, and the ones on plants and animals. More books than you can imagine."

"But I can go later, when I'm older."

"But maybe not with us," Druise replied. "You can go back again if you want. There is always a ship."

"We do not have to decide now," my father said, weariness evident in his voice. "Present us your arguments logically, *mo mhac,* and we will listen."

"We will," my mother said. "But now we should eat. Your father needs an early night."

I had time to go to the junior commons after I bade my parents good night, but I didn't want to. I'd worked so hard not to be the princess here, to have my classmates and friends ignore who I was, and they'd all seen me in a different light today. But on the way back to my room a friend hailed me. He was with two or three others. "Coming for a drink?"

I hesitated—but if I didn't, what would that imply? "One," I said. "I have pages of numbers to add up tomorrow. I'll need a clear head."

"Your father must have been a handsome man in his prime," one of his companions said. "If I may say such things about a prince." I didn't know the man well, but enough to know his appreciative comments were reserved for men.

"Why not? I've heard you say as much about the *Princip*." I grinned to tell him I didn't mind. "And from what my mother says, he was." And that, to my surprise, was all. At the junior commons I drank a little more wine, and threw the dice a few times, but I really did need a clear head for the next day. Someone—probably the classmate who had heard my thoughts about being a princess in the weeks we'd been lovers—had warned the others not to bring it up. I'd been among friends tonight, though.

I woke early, and alone. Lynthe had begun late duty yesterday, so I wouldn't likely see her for several days. She'd be in a terrible temper this morning, anyhow: a storm had come in from over the sea in the early hours. I'd roused, briefly, to rain and thunder. The night patrols would have been drenched.

The quality of light when I opened the shutters told me it was only a little past dawn. I washed and dressed. Outside, water drops sparkled on spider webs strung along eaves, and a blackbird sang its morning benison to the newly-washed world from atop a building. The clouds were gone.

The door to my parents' rooms wasn't locked, and as I had guessed my father was up, sitting under the open window, reading. "Gwenna," he said softly. "You are awake early. Apulo has gone to the kitchens for tea. You will join me?"

"Gladly." I bent to kiss his cheek. "Is *Mathàir* still sleeping?"

"She is."

I sat on the floor beside him, so I could keep my voice low. He ran a hand over my hair. "Yesterday," I began. "How did you know?"

"Know what, *mo nihéan*?"

"You made it very clear I am the heir. That was your intent, wasn't it?"

"It was. The captain at the border post—Farry—mentioned to me there were mutterings, among a few of the men, that Ésparias had always had an emperor. A foreign Empress was bad enough, but a leader of their own—our own—should be a man."

Then he didn't suspect Faolyn. "Druisius had told me much the same. He has his informants, as you know. As I had planned to make," he smiled, wryly, "an entrance worthy of my father—in his honour, you understand—but also to ensure that my fealty to Faolyn was clear, I thought to add a reminder that both I and Faolyn understood your role."

"I believe the reminder was most obvious," I said, matching his expression. "But, *Athàir*, I think Faolyn may agree with the muttering." I told him what I had seen the night Colm and I had dined with the *Princip*. He listened, leaning forward, intent.

"Perhaps not surprising, but concerning, nonetheless." Apulo came in then, carrying a tray.

"Good morning, Gwenna." He put the tray down, and poured my father tea, and then me. I took the warm cup from him, murmuring my thanks. "I had better remember to call you 'my lady'," he said, filling his own cup.

"In public. Not here." I wanted to finish this conversation, but I couldn't with Apulo present. But after eighteen years with us, Apulo understood the mood in a room.

"You have things to talk about. What will tempt you to eat this morning, Cillian? Don't argue with me: you barely touched your supper. There is fresh bread; if I brought that, with butter and honey?"

"Just butter."

"Are you staying to eat, Gwenna?"

"Breakfast?" I wrinkled my nose. "I suppose," I said, when he'd left, "it stops *Mathàir* from having to harass you."

He laughed, which had been my intent. "Not always." A hand went through his hair, the sure sign he was thinking. "Had I been born a girl, I doubt Callan would have been as eager to acknowledge me. Or would have done so with less . . . expectation? Sons mattered—matter—to men in Ésparias, as they do in Linrathe and Sorham, and even Eudekia is abdicating in favour of hers."

I'd never heard him speak of this. "Would you have preferred me to have been a boy?"

"Not in the slightest. Girl or boy, you were a blessing, one I had never expected to have."

We both turned at the creak of a door. My mother came into the sitting room, a robe wrapped around her, her hair tousled.

"You look barely awake," I said. She went to my father, bending to kiss him.

"Hello, my love," she murmured. "Good morning, Gwenna. Is that tea?" I poured her a cup. She sank into a chair, yawning. "Did you sleep at all?" she asked my father.

"For a few hours. Apulo is fetching breakfast. I have had willowbark, and after we eat I will have my massage, and exercises, and cannabium if I need it. I promise, *käresta*."

Breakfast arrived, Apulo followed by a kitchen cadet carrying a second tray. From inside his tunic, he produced a letter. "For you, Lena. It came just now."

My mother frowned. "For me? From whom?" She took the paper, turning it over. Breaking the seal, she read the contents. "An invitation from the Governor's wife. It is her birthday today, and she wishes me to visit her. She writes, 'I shall expect you.'"

"Not quite an invitation, then," I said.

"Not quite," she agreed. "I'll have to go. Come with me, Gwenna? Or can you?"

"I think Michan will let me go, given the circumstances. Does it say when she expects you?"

"No, but I would think mid-afternoon. I'll send a note back."

"I'd best go and start adding up, if I'm to take a few hours off this afternoon," I said. "Thank you for the tea, Apulo."

Michan made no objection, and in the early afternoon I returned to my room to wash the ink off my hands and change. At the southern gate, I found my mother waiting with our horses.

The day had clouded over, but it didn't feel like rain. We took the clifftop track, my mother drawn always to the sea. The track passed the houses and workshops and marketplace which had grown outward from Berge toward the fort. Where it forked to descend the cliff to Berge's harbour, we stayed on the clifftop; the villas—one the *Princip*'s, one the Governor's—occupied lands south of Berge. Faolyn's was closer to Berge, but far enough from the village for privacy, and another twenty minutes ride beyond was the Governor's.

As we approached, my mother, who was leading, signalled me to stop. I reined my gelding in from his trot. "What is it?"

"Look how badly the cliff is eroded here." She sounded angry. I gazed down at the fissures, closer to the track than I remembered.

"From last night's storm? I'm sure it wasn't like this the last time I rode this way."

"The cliffs at Tirvan could crumble under the weight of a person, let alone a horse, when they began to collapse like this," she said. "We need to leave the track, and it should be blocked to prevent anyone else from riding over this section."

I glanced over at the *Princip's* villa, a short distance away to our left. "If we tell Faolyn's people, they'll see to it."

The detour to find Faolyn's steward made us a little late, but if the governor's wife was put out, she didn't show it. She embraced my mother, murmuring words of condolence, before kissing my cheek. She'd come with Livius, once or twice, to the *Ti'ach*; there had once been some talk of their children attending, but it had come to nothing. We were served pastries and a sweet pale wine, before Severa, always direct, told us why she had invited my mother to visit.

"I am so glad you brought Gwenna," she said. "For this will concern her too. It has been many years since you were in Casil, Lena, and fashions have changed. You will not want to be thought rustics, now will you? You must have new clothes."

"We sail very soon," my mother said. "Will not our formal clothes do, at least until we get to Casil? We can have things made there."

"Oh, certainly, and you must. But you need garments for the first few days, and what if the Empress requests your presence, as well she might? Gwenna—" she turned to me, "must look her best. This is what we will do."

There was, she told us, a dressmaker of skill in the extended village, a woman who had followed her soldier husband here. We would visit tomorrow, so measurements could be taken, and Severa herself would accompany us, with examples of her newest clothes to be used as patterns. "She has fine fabrics," she assured us, "silks and the best linens."

"My cousin Lynthe will need clothes too," I said, trying to keep my voice expressionless, imagining Lynthe's reaction.

"Then bring her along."

She chatted on about Casil, about new temples and extensions to the palace, and the games we would no doubt be taken to see. After another half hour a servant came to remove plates and the flask of wine, and Severa stood. Our visit was done.

"Tomorrow," she told us, "I will send someone to show you the way, just after midday. Thank you for honouring my birthday with your presence."

We said our polite farewells. When we were some distance from the villa I asked, "Was that just Severa being helpful?"

"I'm not sure," my mother admitted. "Although she is right about the clothes, so, yes, probably. The dignitaries of Casil will judge us—you, particularly—on what we wear."

"Then maybe I should wear nothing but grey, or undyed linen."

"Perhaps you should," she said, slowly, as if she was thinking as she spoke. "Grey and white, beautifully cut and sewn, of course. It would send a message. You are not another client ruler's daughter out to catch

Alekos's eye. You are heir to Ésparias by his mother's decree. Marriage, if you choose it, must be as advantageous to you as it is to him."

I liked the idea. I liked it very much. "Severa will not be pleased."

"Do we care?" she said, with some asperity. "This is all so ridiculous, really. Callan's father was a soldier, nothing more. Emperor was an elected position, with officers of demonstrated skill in strategy and leadership competing for it, not something to be inherited."

"I know." This wasn't the first time she'd told me this. "But the treaty and the Empress changed that. And so here I am, whether I want to be the heir or not."

Heavy logs blocked the path near the crumbling cliff; Faolyn's steward had done his job. At the fort, I left my horse with a cadet and went in search of Lynthe. She was eating an early supper in the commons. I gave her a quick summary of what Severa had told us, and the plans for tomorrow.

"Must I?" she said, as I'd known she would.

"Yes." I didn't tell her what my mother and I had decided.

She rolled her eyes. "I suppose I'd better find out what my dear brother will let me spend. I'm not using my pay for this."

A point I—for all my accounting work—hadn't even considered. How was this all to be paid for? My mother hadn't seemed concerned. I'd never really thought about money, either growing up at the *Ti'ach* or after my years as a cadet. I had room and board, both at the fort and on the road, and sufficient pay for wine and dice and my clothes. Ésparias provided me with my horse and my weapons.

My parents had salaries: my mother as an officer, my father as the *Comiádh*. The school itself was supported by its *torp*, and by the fees paid by landholding parents; *torpari* children admitted for their intelligence or skill were taught for free. Other than my father's books—more seemed to arrive on every ship from Casil—my parents would have few expenses. Except—I would barely give shape, words, to the idea—except for the unnamed men and women who spread my father's ideas of a Western alliance so carefully, so subtly, in Varsland and Linrathe, Sorham and Ésparias. Were they paid?

I thought not. Because if they did it for money, then someone, suspecting sedition, could offer more. I would have to ask, though. I needed to know, for the day when the mind directing them was mine.

I decided to return to my desk for a few hours, so the work I hadn't done this afternoon was completed. Michan would appreciate it, and I would feel less indulged, allowed license the others weren't, because of who I was. I could eat with my parents, to escape my friends' insistence that I stay with them.

At my parents' rooms, I found Sorley, but no one else. "Your father is at the baths," he said, "with Apulo."

"And you're not?"

"I was. But Cillian has never liked me to see his treatments, so here I am." I poured a little wine, watering it well, and sat down.

"Where's Druise?"

"I don't know. Looking at weapons, or drinking with his friends." He sounded unconcerned. Druise returned to Wall's End several times a year. Partly, I knew—as did Sorley, I was sure—for information, and to make his reports. If there was more to it, I had no need to know. "But I expected Lena to be here."

"We've been back for over half an hour," I told him. "I left her at the stables. Maybe she met someone she knows, or went to see Colm."

"Likely." He stretched. "It's strange, being here. Eighteen years ago, I was advising Casyn, and teaching, and riding back and forth to Dun Ceànnar. And constructing my *ladhar*, and studying for my exams. Now I have nothing to do at all."

"You can write songs," I said, which led me to my next thought. "Who is taking your place on the *scáeli'en* council? You must have a deputy."

"Amlodd. He did before, when I took Ruar to Casil."

"Are you looking forward to going back?"

"I'm looking forward to being there with Druise. I've never met his family; I walked through the district, fourteen years ago, but I didn't try to find them. He has a brother and at least one sister still in the city, and a host of nieces and nephews and their children."

"I'd like to meet them too," I said. "Would he take me along, and introduce me as Kitten, do you think?"

"He'd love to," Sorley said, seriously, although I'd been half jesting. "But I doubt you can, Gwenna. The heir to Ésparias in the *subura* markets of Casil? You'd be a target for kidnappers, as your mother was. We'd have to take at least four guards."

"Kidnappers?"

"She's never told you?" He shook his head, smiling. "Typical Lena. She and Druise were out—I don't remember why now—and she was dressed, I suppose, richly enough to make the men think someone would ransom her. But they picked the wrong woman, because she put her secca into the ribs of one of them, while Druise and a couple of patrolling guards took care of the others. Casil's streets aren't exactly safe, away from the palace."

"Did she kill him?" That would explain why I didn't know. She hated talking about the men she'd killed, even Fritjof.

"No. They were sentenced to the quarries. Cillian," he said thoughtfully, "always believed it was Quintus's doing. Decanius's uncle."

From my work, I knew who Decanius was. Every so often I came across a paper with his signature from the years he'd been Procurator. Michan had nothing good to say about the man. "Was Quintus as nasty as his nephew?"

"No. Far more gracious, and far more devious." Sorley grinned. "I think your father learned a thing or two from him. It is possible Quintus was behind the attempt to kidnap your mother. Druise didn't think so then, but his opinion's changed, over the years." Given Decanius had had Druise tried for desertion, that didn't surprise me.

Druisius had his informants in Casil: members of his family, old friends—and lovers, I guessed—among the palace guard. Possibly others, more highly placed. "Even I do not know," my father had told me. "Druisius will not say." Some of these, I thought, my mind circling back to my earlier musings, must be paid. How?

⌘⌘⌘⌘⌘

"Gwenna, no," Severa said, frowning. "You cannot wear just grey. You will look like you have taken vows to some god or goddess. All the other girls will be in the finest silks, with many jewels."

"Nonetheless," I said, "it is my decision." The governor's wife exhaled, loudly. She turned to my mother. "My lady Lena, are you allowing this?"

"I agree with Gwenna," my mother said. Making it sound as if it had been my idea, I noted. Her flat tone stopped Severa's argument. She sighed again, turning to Lynthe.

"And you?" She assessed her, seeing the same dark hair as mine, but eyes as blue as milkwort flowers. "Blue for you, Lieutenant, I would say."

"But simply made, Lady Severa. I am not comfortable except in uniform."

"But you are the *Princip's* sister, and must look the part." Severa turned to the seamstress, waiting patiently. "Take their measurements, and I will choose cloth."

She knew what she was about, I admitted, watching her find greens and russets for my mother, colours which enhanced her eyes and the reddish sheen her brown hair had in certain lights. For Lynthe she chose the blues she had alluded to. Then, "Bring me everything you have that might be considered grey."

There wasn't much. But one was a silk which shimmered as it was unrolled, hints of blue among the silver, and one was a fine wool, nearly white. Severa nodded. "These two for your formal clothes. And perhaps the Lieutenant's best can be trimmed with the silk too, as a reminder of her position." She pointed to another bolt, another fine wool but of a deeper grey. "And this, for your other tunics, with panels of the silk inset at the collar and hem. Will that suit you, my lady Gwenna?"

"It will," I said, in my best diplomat's tones. "Lady Severa, I appreciate your assistance, both for myself and for Lynthe and my mother. We will not disgrace the *Princip* in Casil now."

Severa smiled graciously. "A week," she said, turning to the seamstress. To us, she added, "Now, shoes."

"The poor seamstress," Lynthe said, as we rode back to the fort, "will be working every hour of the day to finish the sewing."

"At least it's summer, and the days are long," my mother said. "She will have assistants, no doubt."

"Severa was most disappointed when you said we had jewels," I commented.

"But she knew she'd lost the argument when you said the Empress had sent them," Lynthe added. "Do I really have to have my ears pierced?"

"If you are to wear earrings, you'll need to," my mother said. "One of the medics will do it, with a heated needle. I was much your age when mine were done, so I could wear the earrings Eudekia sent. The sapphires would suit you."

"But they are yours."

"Cillian's," my mother said, "in truth, but he gave the smaller stones to Gwenna."

I had planned to give the sapphires to Lianë, at the appropriate time, for her blue eyes. The memory hurt, more than I expected. Did I want Lynthe to wear them? But before I could speak, my mother continued. "I did have one thought, but it wasn't one I wanted Severa to hear, although it will get back to her in time. I think we should have a silver pendant made, like your father's, Gwenna."

Once the symbol of the Emperor, and now of the *Princip* of Ésparias. "Is it ... can I wear that now, *Mathàir*?"

"You are adult, and the heir," she said. "It is your right. The fort's metalworker, I think, not the one in the village."

I glanced over at my lover. Her expression was not one I could decipher: not envy, not surprise, but something else. She was looking at me as if I were a stranger, as if I were someone she thought she had known, but had been mistaken.

Chapter 12

~FATHER~

"WE ARE TO DINE WITH FAOLYN and his family tonight," Lena said at breakfast, several days later, her eyes still on the just-delivered note. "They will come here, to save you travelling to the villa, Cillian."

"Do you want me to tell Colm?" Gwenna asked. She often joined us for the morning meal, drinking tea as we ate.

"I will," Lena said. "I'm going out for a ride, as the day is fine, so I'll do it on my way."

"Do you want company?" Sorley asked, finishing his tea.

"Not really, if you don't mind."

"Of course not. What are you doing today, Cillian?"

I looked up from the letter that had arrived for me from Casil. "Teaching, this afternoon," I replied. "A lecture to the junior officers, on our treaty with Casil. Do you want to attend? You could speak to the relinquishment of Sorham, and Linrathe's acceptance of the terms better than I. You are Linrathe's signatory, after all."

"I could. Yes, all right, I will. But shouldn't Lena be there too, to speak to ending the Partition agreement?"

"I was thinking to address only military matters today; the considerations of defence."

"I could do that, you know," Lena said, "but not today. Talyn wants to see me later, I assume to assign me some duties until we sail."

"About time, yes?" Druisius said. "You need to be working, Lena."

"I know." She stood up. "I may not be back for the midday meal. Make sure Cillian remembers to eat, Sorley, will you?" She bent to kiss me.

"I will walk out with you." Druisius followed her from the room. He had taken up training duties almost immediately, never liking to be idle.

"More tea?" Sorley poured me another cup, and one for himself. He did not offer Gwenna any, I noted. As did she.

"I'll leave you to discuss how to teach the treaty," she said, almost immediately. "Although ... "

"Although?" I asked.

She shook her head. "Nothing,"

"Gwenna?"

"It just seems strange, hearing you talk of military considerations. I don't think of you—either of you—as soldiers. *Mathàir* and Druisius, yes."

"We were all soldiers," I said. "The times demanded it. What I will speak of today was Turlo's doing, not mine. But I was there to hear his arguments, as was Sorley."

"But once you understood Turlo's view, you too argued for it," Sorley said.

"And Ruar accepted the need. But Gundarstorp is yours again, my lord Sorley, and if the gods are kind, it always will be."

"We need another tie to Varsland," Sorley said, very quietly.

"Perhaps Faolyn's second child will be a girl," I suggested. Bryngyl's son was only two or three.

"And perhaps," Gwenna said, "the trade treaty with Varsland could be examined, and better terms negotiated? Marriages are not the only way to make strong alliances."

She had a point, one that would have effects sooner than a betrothal made in fifteen years or more. "How well do you know the treaty?"

"Fairly well, but I can't be sure of the fine details. I'll read it again, if you think it would be useful."

"It might be. A good thought, Gwenna."

Gwenna and Lynthe were late for dinner: Lynthe's unfamiliarity with her new earrings the explanation offered. "Now you are here," Talyn said, handing them wine, "we have a toast to make. To Ésparias's newest major. Your health, Lena."

Lena's expression reflected her mixed feelings, but Gwenna ignored it, giving her a hug. "Congratulations, *Mathàir*."

"A necessary promotion," she said, "so I am of sufficient rank to represent Ésparias's military at the investiture, not for my skill with troops or tactics."

"For more than that," Talyn said, calmly.

"It is deserved, *käresta*," I said.

"For eighteen years of guarding the Emperor's son?"

"For eighteen years of not using your secca on him, more likely," Sorley said. "That degree of forbearance should earn you a promotion." A ripple of laughter lightened the mood, as he had meant it to.

The meal passed pleasantly enough. Siusàn had not brought their son, nor was there any discussion of her pregnancy. Talk was of the lecture I had given, and speculation on the ship that would be sent for us. Toward the end of the meal, Colm spoke. "May I ask a favour of you, *Princip*? As my cousin?"

"You may, Colm, of course. What is it I can do for you?"

"I wonder if you would keep my dog for me, if I go to Casil? Then he would be here when I return." He turned to Faolyn's wife. "If you agree, of course. Constyn likes him, I think."

"Indeed he does. We met Colm and his dog the other day, when we were out for a walk," she told her husband. "The dog is gentle, and did not mind Constyn trying to climb on him. I would be happy to have him as a companion for our boy while you are gone, Colm."

"Of course," Faolyn said. "But you said, 'if you go to Casil'? Why ever would you not?"

Colm flushed a little. "I am reluctant to leave my studies. Perhaps Casil should wait until I know more and could benefit from its libraries and its physicians."

"What do your parents think?"

"We have not yet discussed it fully." Faolyn would recognize my tone, from his days as a student at the *Ti'ach*. Perhaps it was inappropriate to the *Princip* of Ésparias, but this was a family meal, and I wanted no encouragement of Colm's reluctance to travel.

"I see," was all he said. "I won't interfere." Silence, for a moment, not entirely comfortable.

"Major?" Lynthe was the first to break it.

"Are you speaking to me, or to Lena?" I asked, infusing amusement into my voice.

"To you, sir. I—"

"He's teasing you, Lynthe," Lena said. "It would be simpler if you called us by name, wouldn't it? Or at least me," she added, seeing the doubt on Lynthe's face. "You can't call us both Major for the next three months or more."

"Both of us," I said firmly. "A long sea voyage, Lynthe, is a time like no other. The world around you changes constantly, but you yourself are passive. It is a time for reflection and relaxation, not a time for formality."

"I'll try, sir," she said. "I don't know if I can."

Druisius chuckled. "Wait until he's been seasick for several days. Hard to call him 'sir' after that, yes?"

Sorley groaned. "Don't remind me. Can we not talk about this at table?"

"I was seasick too," Faolyn said. "But shall we be gracious to the lord Sorley, and change the subject?"

We talked instead of Casil; of its buildings and streets, and the changes Lena and I could expect. "You must go to the Bassanian Baths," Faolyn said. "I believe you did not, before? Huge baths, wonderfully decorated, and with libraries?"

"Baths with libraries?" Gwenna said. "*Athàir* will never leave them."

"You almost do not need to," Faolyn said, "There are places to eat and drink, as well. Men gather there, for debate and discussion; women, too."

Books and talk, in the gracious, beautiful buildings of Casil, the light reflecting off the marble; the heat of the streets and the cool of the courtyards. I wanted to see it one last time, to show my children—and to counter its seduction. "Then we must," I said, meaning it.

Not too long afterward, Talyn rose. Lynthe had already excused herself. "Faolyn, forgive me, but I have an early meeting."

"And I am tired," Siusàn said, "so perhaps you will excuse me too?"

"I'll walk with you," Lena offered.

"I won't be long, *käresta*," I told her.

Around us, servants cleared plates. Colm hid a yawn. "May I be excused? My day begins early, too."

Here was the opportunity I had wanted. "If you would accompany us, Gwenna, I will walk with Colm to his room. The night is fine, and I would like to talk to you both for a few minutes."

Faolyn had a last question: which of two philosophers should he read next? Sorley and Druisius waited with Colm. I said good night to the *Princip* and made my way out into the corridor.

"You will walk back with Cillian?" Druisius said to Gwenna. "Or should I send Apulo?"

"Do not disturb him," I said. "I will be all right."

"Colm," I began, once we were alone in the corridor, "I would like you to consider what I have to say. No answer is expected tonight." We began to walk. Torches lit the walls and the floor. "It would please me if you would come to Casil with us. I will not compel you, but I would like to be there with you, to show you all we spoke of tonight, and perhaps to introduce you to some of the men I correspond with—Bruccius, for one, from whom my letter came today. I am not young, *mo mhac*, and I doubt we will have this chance again."

My cane tapped the flagstones. Gwenna moved a little closer to my side. Colm said nothing, his head bent slightly.

"It's also possible I won't be coming home," Gwenna said. "I'd like you to be there, too, Colm."

"You're not really going to marry Alekos?" He sounded shocked.

"It is a possibility," I said. "Another consideration." We rounded a corner into the corridor that led outside. A torch had gone out; the hall was darker than it should be, but beyond it the next light burned brightly in its wall sconce. I took one step forward.

Chapter 13

~DAUGHTER~

I YELPED A WARNING. TOO LATE. My father's cane skidded. He fell, his shoulder hitting the wall, his head snapping back against the stone. He cried out. "Go!" I shouted to Colm. "Get a doctor!"

I knelt beside my father, Colm's running feet echoing. My father was gasping, his face contorted. "What do I do?" He didn't answer. "*Athàir*?"

"Do nothing," he said, the words strangled. "Wait. Then Druisius, and Apulo."

I took his hand. Shouldn't there have been a guard on the door? I called; no response. I heard my father's rapid breathing. Fear roiled in my stomach, sour and biting. Where were Colm and the doctor?

The door at the end of the corridor opened, and then Colm and a young man were kneeling too. "Go for Druise," I told Colm. The doctor had opened his bag, a small vial now in his hands.

"This first." He held the vial to my father's lips. "To ease the pain. Then I will examine you."

"No!" Colm's hand shot out, knocking the vial away.

"What? Boy, what have you done?"

"It was poppy," Colm said. "He can't have it. Ever."

"Was it?" I said sharply.

"Yes, of course."

"My son is right," my father said, barely above a whisper.

How had Colm known? A question for later. "Get Druise and Apulo," I told him. He scrambled to his feet. "Go on. I'll be here."

The doctor touched my father's head, frowning at the blood which stained his fingers. He was probing his back and leg when Colm returned with Druise and Apulo, and, of course, Sorley.

"Nothing is broken," the physician reported. "The head bleeds, but it is a scrape. The shoulder is bruised. His back and leg are in spasm, A stretcher will be needed, and he should be brought to the infirmary."

Druise had taken the extinguished torch from its holder, lighting it from the one further along the corridor. He bent to examine the floor. "Oil." He touched a finger to the floor, and then to his tongue. "Lamp oil."

"An inattentive cadet," the physician murmured. Apulo had taken his place beside my father, his strong fingers making their own examination.

"Oh." He drew the word out. "Cillian, this is bad."

"I am aware," my father whispered. There were tears on his cheeks. Sorley made a choking sound.

"Sorley." Druise, his voice firm. "Go ensure a stretcher is brought."

"Colm, take my place." He did as I asked. "Druise, a word."

I took him a few steps away. "The torch was out, as you saw. There was no guard on the door."

"The oil was fresh." He chewed his lip, and then he swore, savagely, and turned back to the small group around my father. "Not the infirmary," he said, in his command voice. "His rooms."

The doctor protested, but Druise wasn't to be gainsaid. "I am Prince Cillian's guard. My orders come from the general. Argue with her in the morning." I'd never, in all my life, heard Druise call my father by his Ésparian title. A reminder to the physician, of course.

The stretcher party arrived. "Sorley, go warn Lena," Druise ordered. Sorley hesitated, his eyes on my father, but when Druise growled his name again, he left. "He cannot bear seeing Cillian in pain," Druise said quietly to me. "Your father will scream when we move him. Be prepared. And say nothing to your mother of your suspicions."

My mother met us at the door to their rooms. One glance told me she was angry. "How did you let this happen?" she snapped at me.

"I wasn't quick enough," I said. "I saw the oil, but—"

"Lena," Druise said. "The hall was dark. A torch had gone out. Do not take your fear out on Gwenna."

Her eyes followed the stretcher. There was blood near my father's head. They carried my father to the bedroom, to move him to the bed. He would scream again. Colm had gone with the doctor. Sorley hovered, his face pale.

"Fetch your *ladhar*," Druise said to Sorley. "Go. Music will help, later." Then he walked purposely to the sideboard, poured not wine, but *fuisce*. He gave it to my mother. "Drink it."

A long moan came from the bedroom, and then a sharper cry. "Oh, gods," my mother whispered. I went to her, trying to hold her. She didn't let me.

"He is in pain," Druise said, "but both the doctor and Apulo say nothing is damaged." That wasn't quite what had been said, but I wasn't going to contradict Druise. Colm came out of the bedroom, with the men who had carried the stretcher.

"We need hot compresses. I am going to the kitchens." He'd left the bedroom door open. I glanced in to see my father face down on the bed. Apulo straddled him, kneeling, his hands working on my father's lower back.

Druise and Apulo stayed with my father. The doctor, after salving the bruised shoulder and preparing a cannabium mixture, came to talk to my mother. "The man Apulo knows his job, and the cadet is a competent assistant," he told her. "I have told them to keep a watch on the Prince; do not let him sleep more than an hour, because of the head injury. I will come in the morning,""

"Is it dangerous?" my mother asked, her voice sharp. She'd been dozing in a chair, but had roused herself for the doctor.

"I do not think so. But sometimes when someone has had a blow to the head, they fall asleep and do not wake. It is a precaution, my lady, nothing more."

"Major," she corrected, wearily. "Do not concern yourself," she added, at his apology. He was young. Likely why he had night duty, I thought. "Perhaps you could ask your senior physician to visit, in the morning?"

"Of course, Major."

"Would you like wine, before you go?" She smiled, a movement of her lips. "It is very good wine, and a way to say thank you, if you would."

He accepted the wine, and we made some stilted conversation while he drank it. I had a watered cup to keep him company.

"The poor man was terrified," my mother said, once he was gone. With cause, I thought, had Colm not stopped him from giving the poppy.

From behind the bedroom door, the notes of Sorley's *ladhar* drifted out, muted. My mother listened. "At least there is something I can do now," she said. "I'll sit with Cillian, and wake him when needed, although he will tell me to leave when Apulo begins his work again." She picked up the blanket, folding it neatly. A mindless, automatic action. "I'm sorry I accused you of negligence, earlier."

"Don't worry." My mother's anger was always swift, coming and going.

"You can go back to your own room. There's really no reason for you to stay."

"I suppose I should." I did have work to do in the morning, only a few hours away now. "All right. But I'll come back for breakfast."

Purposely, I took the same route I had with my father and Colm earlier. As I left the building, the door guard stood aside in surprise. "Envoy," she said. "You're up late. Tell me, isn't this your brother's dog? It's been curled up here for hours."

Peritas came to me, tail waving. I rubbed his head. "It is." I told her what had happened, making it sound less severe than it had been. "You weren't here when I shouted for someone to go to the medics. Had something taken you away?"

"A brawl, or so I was told," she said. "But when I reached the spot no one was there. Warned of my approach, I suppose."

"That's odd. Who told you about it originally?"

"I don't know. Someone called to me. Is your father all right?"

"He will be. A day or two of rest and massage." Perhaps. I looked down at the dog. "You didn't see this," I told the guard. "Come," I said to Peritas, and went back into the building, the dog padding at my heels. I opened the door to my parents' rooms and watched him slip inside.

Stars glittered as I returned to my room. I yawned, deeply, thinking about what the guard had said. I'd tell Druise what I'd learned. But who would want my father injured? And why?

And where had the dog been, if not outside, waiting for Colm?

Only my brother was awake when I let myself into my parents' rooms the next morning. He sat up as I came in. He'd been stretched out on the floor, the dog beside him.

"How is he?" I asked softly.

"Sleeping, I think," he said through a yawn. "Apulo gave him more cannabium, and valerian a couple of hours ago."

"*Mathàir?*"

"With him. Apulo's sleeping too, and Druise made Sorley go with him back to their room." He yawned again and rubbed his eyes. "Sorley was upset. Almost more than *Mathàir*. She was reassuring him, at one point."

"They've been friends a long time." To forestall any possible questions, I added, "Tea's coming. I stopped at the kitchens on the way. Colm? How did you know about the poppy?"

"I worked it out," he said. "At the *Ti'ach na Iorlath*, we learned about poppy, both how it's used for pain, and its other effects. I thought, if it's so good for pain, we should have it for *Athàir*, and we didn't. Apulo had shown me all the drugs he uses. Then last time I was home, I asked Druise."

"A good thing you did."

He glanced at the closed bedroom door. "There is poppy at our *Ti'ach*," he said, very quietly. "Druise has some, in case any of the *torpari*, or anyone else needs it. It's in a locked box in their rooms. He told me where, and where the key is. But no one else knows."

Practical Druisius. "Colm? When Sorley told me about the poppy—it was that summer I went north with them—it made me feel, oh, I don't know—not ashamed, but like I didn't know *Athàir*. I couldn't picture him in the thrall of a drug."

"It wasn't his fault," my brother said. "Gnaius made him take it for so long. Druise said it happens to many soldiers who are badly injured, and Iorlath taught us the same. Most don't overcome it. *Athàir* may not have a strong body, but he has a very strong will."

"Well, we knew that." I'd hoped to make him laugh, or at least smile, but he only looked thoughtful.

"I'd better take Peritas out." He got up. "Did you let him in last night?"

"He was curled up at the door waiting for you. Was he there when you went for the doctor?"

"No. But he wouldn't have been: that wasn't the door I came in."

"Then why was he there later?"

"Because I did go out it, and back in, and he'd know that. So he came to where I was last." A simple enough explanation. He went to the door.

"Colm? If the guard gives you trouble over the dog, tell them it was my doing."

The tea arrived while he was gone. I heard no sounds from my parents' bedroom, or from Apulo's. I sipped the hot infusion of mint, wondering if I should stay or go. I'd almost decided to leave when I heard the bedroom door open. My mother, looking as if she hadn't slept at all, came to sit across from me.

I gave her tea. "He's sleeping," she said. "I told Apulo to double the drugs. He'll be angry about that, but it won't be the first time." She wrapped her hands around the mug. "Gwenna, if we didn't come to Casil, who would you like to accompany you?"

"Not come?"

"I don't know we can, or should. The last time your father's back was hurt again this badly, you were still a baby, less than a year old. We were here at Wall's End, and so was Gnaius, and it still took weeks before he could travel."

"I see." I thought for a minute. "Sorley and Druise?"

"They can go, of course. If Sorley will leave Cillian."

"Druise, at least, then."

She almost smiled. "Druise isn't going to let his Kitten go to Casil without him, is he? I was wondering about Talyn."

"She's Faolyn's chief advisor, isn't she? And the general overseeing the north. Could she leave on such short notice?"

"Probably not. But who else is there? There has to be someone of sufficient rank to represent Ésparias at the investiture, as well as to be your escort."

"Michan? Or one of the Eastern Fort officers. Finn."

"Possibly. But protocol says you need an older woman, too."

"To ensure my virtue, and Lynthe's?"

"Something like that, yes."

"Would Severa go?" I regretted the words as soon as I had spoken them.

Her eyes widened. "Perhaps she would. I was surprised she and Livius weren't attending, but he has never shown the slightest interest in returning to Casil. In most provinces, the Governor usually stays no more than five years, and he's been here eighteen."

"She could see her daughter, and the latest fashions." Inwardly, I winced at the idea of three months or more in Severa's company. Why had I suggested it? I had wanted to see Casil through my father's eyes, the libraries and the buildings, its monuments to great leaders. I wanted to learn more of its alliances and enemies. Without him—and with Severa—

little of that would happen. It would be silks and shoes, jewels and gossip, instead.

I would be in Casil without my father's subtle, analytical mind to guide me. I raised my cup to my lips, hoping to hide any expression. Think it through, I told myself. What can happen in Casil if my father is not there?

⌘⌘⌘⌘⌘

I swore, not silently. I'd added the numbers up twice and got a different total each time. I'd just started on the column of figures again when Michan returned from wherever he'd been. "Your ship has been sighted," he told me. "It's expected to arrive by the middle of the afternoon."

"It's more when they'll expect to leave again." I abandoned the numbers. Michan knew what had happened to my father: all the officers did, and I supposed the soldiers and cadets too. They must, as those responsible for filling lamps should have been questioned by now.

"There will be some flexibility," he said. "Would you prefer not to work today, Gwenna?"

"I'm just short of sleep, so I need to check my sums more carefully. I'll do every calculation three times, or five, or whatever it takes."

By late morning I needed fresh air and some exercise; more importantly, I wanted to find Druise. Would he be out on the training ground, or with my parents? I'd try outside first.

He wasn't teaching. Likely he'd stayed with my father, to help Apulo move him. *Athàir*, I thought, would hate for any of the medics here to see him incapacitated. But Druise had had his own suspicions last night, or he wouldn't have insisted my father not be taken to the infirmary. I glanced over at that building, to see my brother's dog sitting outside the door.

As I approached, Colm came out, carrying a box. He'd been sent for drugs, I surmised, a guess he confirmed. "How's *Athàir*?" I asked.

"Maybe a bit better. The senior physician examined him, but he said the same as everyone else: nothing's broken, and he needs rest and heat and massage. He's a little concerned about him hitting his head, but not much. When *Athàir* can walk, Druise and Apulo and I will take him to the baths."

"Where is Druise? I wanted to talk to him."

"I don't know. He said he had people he needed to see."

"Tell *Athàir* I'll come to see him soon. I need to talk to Druise." I watched Colm walk away for a moment. The petulant boy of a few days ago had gone; I preferred the focused, intent young medic who had taken his place.

The steward at the senior commons shook his head. "Haven't seen Captain Druisius." Then where? I turned to the barracks.

I shouldn't really enter this part of the fort: I wasn't a soldier. But I had friends who were, and the rules weren't stringently enforced. Not all soldiers ate at their commons, some preferring the open air, especially in summer. I asked the first man I saw sitting outside his door. He gestured with his chin at my question, still chewing.

Druise sat on a camp stool, throwing dice with two other men. I watched for a moment. Each man bent low as he shook the dice, muttering prayers or incantations—or were they? Over the noises of the fort, and the rattle of the dice, I couldn't hear. But Druise could.

"Captain?" I said quietly. The men looked up, and Druise stood.

"I am needed?"

"No. I didn't mean to concern you." How to say this without alerting the soldiers? "A question about Casil I thought you could answer."

"I will come." He grinned at the two men, as if all they had been doing was dicing, and dug in his belt pouch for some coins. "My losses." We were well away from the barracks before he spoke again. "What is the question, Kitten?"

I looked around. No one was in hearing distance. "Who benefits if I am in Casil without my parents? *Mathàir* is talking about sending me without them. She says my father cannot travel now. Could that have been the plan?"

Druise rubbed his unshaven chin. "Maybe."

"You know the guard was called away from the door?"

"For a brawl, yes? But there was no brawl. It was quiet last night, my friends say."

My stomach rumbled, loudly. Druise grinned. "No breakfast?"

"I don't like food in the morning, as well you know. I'll eat soon."

"Come to the senior commons with me. I have a reason," he added, at my frown. I acceded—the food would be better, anyhow—and followed him. As we walked, he said, "Watch who comes to offer sympathy, or ask questions. Act worried for your father, and see who is most solicitous. Or is not."

"You're very good at this," I murmured. He gave his characteristic shrug.

"Many years, even before I served your father."

In the senior commons, much quieter than the one reserved for junior officers, we were given a table against one wall. Several heads—Michan's among them—swivelled at our entrance. At my entrance; Druise was no stranger here, even if he did visit only a few times a year. The tables were placed apart, allowing for private conversation, groups of two or three at most of them.

I accepted wine, watering it well: I still had work to do. The food would be a few minutes, the steward told us. Almost immediately an officer came over to me. "How is your father?" she asked. She was the first of several, with the news being shared among tables, too. I expressed my worry, nodded at reassurances, and accepted messages of concern for my mother. Druise watched and listened.

Once the food arrived we were left to ourselves, and Druise just shook his head when I gave him a quizzical look. I ate with hunger and appreciation: we didn't get chicken like this from the junior kitchens, slowly cooked with spices and wine, the bread still warm. But when we had finished, and fingerbowls and napkins brought, another officer—a Casilani, and young to be a captain—approached us.

"I hear your ship arrives today," he said, after the usual question and expression of concern.

"So I am told," I said.

"Will your father's accident delay you?"

"He is not badly hurt; just bruises and muscles that cramp, yes? I keep telling Gwenna this," Druise said. "Massage and the baths will take care of it."

"That's a relief." No reflection of his words in the officer's eyes, or in his voice, studiedly neutral. "Give your father my best." I kept my face impassive as we rose to leave.

We were nearly at the door when the steward stopped us. "Major Michan would like a word."

"With me?" I asked.

"The captain, if you would, please."

I waited at the door. Was Michan displeased Druise had brought me as his guest? But why would he be? Michan himself had brought me before, as he had other junior envoys. We needed to understand the dynamics of the room: who sat with whom, who spoke quietly, who asked for tables against the wall. It was part of our training. I watched the conversation, seeing no tension in either man. Druise nodded, shrugged. Michan clapped him on the back.

"What did he want?" I asked, as soon as we were outside.

"If I would play one evening. I do, whenever I am here." He grinned. "They believe I am a captain only because of who I guard, yes? A necessary rank. But they like my music. And if they think of me that way, they do not suspect me when I dice with the men, or ask to have things explained."

Or bring a worried young woman for a quiet meal, when everyone knew how much he doted on her. "What have we learned?" I asked.

"Nothing yet. There may be letters for me on the ship. We might know more, if there are."

Chapter 14

~FATHER~

I HAD INSISTED ON RISING, REGARDLESS of the dizziness that assailed me. Druisius and Apulo helped me to a chair in the sitting room. With my leg propped on a stool and cushions supporting me, the pain was no greater than it would have been had I stayed in bed: a dull throb, punctuated by stabs if I moved.

I knew what Lena would say, had likely already said to everyone but me. I had to address it today, before plans were put into motion. My arguments were prepared, rehearsed in my wakeful periods. But I waited: I wanted Gwenna to hear them.

She arrived late in the afternoon, coming to kiss my cheek. "I am so sorry, *Athàir*," she murmured. "I wish—"

"It was not your fault. I am glad you are here; there are things we must speak about."

"*Mathàir* told me," she said. "I will need to go to Casil without you."

"No!" Surprise flitted across her face from the sharpness with which I'd spoken. I had been more vehement than I had meant. "I will not let you go to Casil without me, Gwenna. The Empress is—" I thought better of shaking my head to emphasise my words. "She was a match—more than a match—for me at thirty-four. Artful and clever, to say the least. You are not yet her equal, *mo nihéan*, not at eighteen."

"How can you travel?" Lena spoke from across the room. "Cillian, you are dreaming."

"Am I?" I bade myself to stay calm. "Eighteen years ago, Lena, you demanded a promise from me: that I would never let Gwenna be a piece in Eudekia's games. If I have any chance of keeping that promise, then I must go to Casil."

"Gwenna is an adult," she said. "At eighteen, I led a cohort of women and girls. I made decisions that helped save this land. I asked for that promise when she was a baby."

"Does she not still need our guidance?"

"If you go to Casil—Cillian, think of the strain on you. Do you want to shorten the time you have to be her guide?"

"*Athàir*," Gwenna said, "I will have Druise, and maybe Sorley, and a high-ranking officer with me."

"Do not let your mother's fears be yours," I said. "I am in pain, and movement will be difficult for some time. But there are six weeks on the ship for Apulo to remedy that."

Sorley had been sitting quietly, his *ladhar* on his lap. "I will go with Gwenna, Cillian, if you want."

"We are all going."

"Cillian," Lena said, "this can wait until you have recovered."

"It cannot," I said. "I have a responsibility."

"What about your vow to me?" she snapped. "If you disregard my wishes and do something that—that frightens me, how is that shelter?"

"We have lost one child." Anger I could not mask rose, worsening the ache in my head. "I will not lose another to Eudekia's snares. And there is more to why I need to go to Casil than just Gwenna's future, Lena. Do I need to remind you that under Casilani law, children of a marriage are the father's to control?"

"You would claim control of our daughter?"

"Don't be ridiculous," I said wearily. "You know I have not and would not. But Gwenna is not just another princess, and if she wishes to marry Alekos, that is only one of many complex considerations."

"Ones only you can solve?"

"Tell me who else," I said. "Who else, Lena, can come close to matching wits with Eudekia, or who can devise a marriage contract that cannot be broken? Faolyn? Michan? You?" Biting pain was running down my leg and up my spine.

"Not me. I am not competent. You have made that clear."

"Neither may I be. But I am going to Casil, Lena, with or without you."

I could hear the others' breathing. No one spoke. I closed my eyes against frustration and pain, waiting for someone to say the obvious: if I could not present this argument in a calm and reasoned manner, my claim to be the only person capable of negotiating with the Empress was as ridiculous as I had just accused Lena of being.

"Is that why someone would try to prevent you from going to Casil?" Gwenna asked. "The marriage contract?"

"Try to prevent him?" Lena said. "Are you saying the spilled oil wasn't an accident?"

Of course it wasn't, I thought. The extinguished torch alone should have been warning enough. I let Gwenna explain.

"The guard was missing, too," she said. "Druise's informants among the soldiers say there was no brawl, even though the guard was called to one. That's why Druise had *Athàir* brought back here and not to the infirmary."

Lena swore. "You have learned nothing else, Druise?"

"No. Not yet. I must be careful in my questions. I have paid for information, men I trust." The door swung open, interrupting anything more he might have said. Colm and an older man stood in the opening, a delighted grin on my son's face.

"Look who I found!" he said.

"Gnaius?" Lena rose. "What—why are you here?"

He strode forward to embrace her. "The Empress sent me, to ensure Cillian's health on the voyage. My arrival is opportune, it appears."

I regarded him from my chair. He had changed little, from what I could see: in truth, my vision was blurry, his form moving in and out of focus. "Gnaius. Welcome, my friend. I am very pleased to see you."

"Your son has told me of your fall, and given me a summary of the treatments," the physician said. "Shall I examine you?"

"I will be glad to assist," Apulo offered from behind him.

"Apulo!" Gnaius turned. "I have heard great things of you. Cillian has kept me informed. Come and show me what you have been doing to alleviate his pain."

Druisius and Sorley helped me stand. Supported by them, I limped through to the bedroom and onto the bed. Colm hovered.

"Can I stay to see Gnaius at work?" he asked.

"You may," I told him. There would be no question of him not coming to Casil now, I thought. I settled onto my stomach, closing my eyes against the spinning sensation movement had caused. If Eudekia had sent Gnaius, then my fears she planned to have me arrested the moment I stepped foot into the city were likely unwarranted—unless she wanted me at my best for a show trial, a public spectacle in which she or her surrogates bested me in every argument.

"If there is any danger in travel," I heard Lena say fiercely, "he cannot go. You must tell him so, Gnaius."

Chapter 15

~DAUGHTER~

SORLEY PICKED UP HIS *LADHAR*. Soft music filled the room, muffling other sounds, and precluding conversation. Perhaps half an hour passed before Gnaius returned to the sitting room, everyone but Apulo with him. He accepted wine and settled himself in a chair. "So," he said. "There is no new damage. Inflammation, yes, and spasms in the muscles of the back and leg."

"The head injury?" my mother asked.

"Not, I think, severe. The brain is shaken by such a strike, but he speaks coherently, and his eyes behave normally when shown light. I have told him to expect headaches for some days, and perhaps dizziness." My mother's shoulders dropped. The physician took a sip of his wine.

"I am very pleased at how small the wastage in the affected leg is. Apulo has done well with the exercises, and he tells me Cillian himself has insisted on walking and even riding." He smiled. "Other activities remain unimpeded? Your youngest is—what, three now?"

No one had told him. But he could not help seeing the pain on my mother's face. Sorley explained, in a few rapid words, and Gnaius, truly upset, I thought, took her hands. "Lena, I am so sorry," he murmured. "Tell me."

"As Sorley said. A sudden fever. Her neck hurt, and then her back. We gave her anash, and bathed her in cool water, but none of it helped. Less than a day."

"She screamed and screamed," Sorley said. Colm moaned. I hadn't known this, either. "When she fell unconscious . . . it was a blessing."

Gnaius nodded, his lips pursed. "You did all the right things; I could have done no more. I know this fever. It is almost always fatal." He studied my mother for a minute. "And so you worry more than is reasonable for Cillian, do you not? Even though you know if he is up in a chair so quickly, nothing can be seriously wrong."

"But you told us . . . " She stopped. "Twenty years, you said. Maybe twenty-five, if he lived a quiet life."

What? Did my mother's words mean what I thought? I glanced at Sorley, but his eyes were on my mother and Gnaius.

"That was my belief," the physician said. "Men whose bodies have been grievously injured; this is what my profession believes, and what we have seen, many times. But I expected to find a frail man, old beyond his years. When he wrote to say there was another child—"

"You wondered who the father really was?" My mother laughed a little. "She had golden hair, and blue eyes, and probably half of Linrathe thought she was Sorley's. But I assure you she was Cillian's."

Gnaius smiled. "So we must disregard my words from so long ago. Once again, Cillian has put my reputation as a diagnostician in doubt. The voyage to Casil will put him in no danger, Lena."

"You could not have saved Lianë?" Colm, in a rush of words.

"Almost certainly not," Gnaius replied. "Rarely, a child with this fever lives, but it is nothing the physician has done. And often they are— damaged, shall I say? In the mind." His eyes rested on my brother. "It is a truth of our profession, Colm. We are not gods. Some diseases, some injuries—we can do nothing but alleviate pain."

"But —"

"We will talk of this more," Gnaius said firmly, "but not now. I have not seen your family for eleven years, and we have much to catch up on."

I went to the kitchens and ordered food. My father got up again for the meal, although he ate little. I listened to the conversation: Gnaius clearly had been a friend, not just my father's physician. But when the meal was done, I excused myself, and took Colm with me. "They don't need us there," I told him.

"I am coming to Casil," Colm said, as we crossed the yard.

"Six weeks with Gnaius is an opportunity you can't pass up?"

"Yes," he said, "But—Gwenna, what did *Mathàir* mean, about twenty years?"

"I don't know."

"Yes you do."

"I don't," I repeated, more sharply than I meant, "but if I had to guess? Gnaius said it's how long *Athàir* would live after his injuries. Twenty-five years at the most."

"But that's only another seven or eight years."

"He said he was wrong," I pointed out. "Now he's seen *Athàir*."

Colm's frown eased. "He did, didn't he?" He put a hand on Peritas's head; the dog, as usual, had appeared at his side as soon as we had left the building.

"Colm!" A group of cadets were leaving the infirmary. "We're going to look at the Casilani ship. Want to come?"

He glanced at me. "Go," I said. He—and the dog—ran to join them. Relieved, I made my way to the junior commons. I wanted company, and wine. My mother's question to Gnaius had shaken me more than I wanted to admit.

Lynthe was with a group of our friends: she had a couple of hours yet until her late duty. She leant over to me. "How's your father? I heard this morning, but I couldn't find you."

"He'll be all right," I said. "You don't know anything about a fight, a bit before midnight?"

"Nothing I heard about. In the fort?"

"Supposedly." The steward had brought me wine. I added a little water and drank.

She shook her head. "No. It was quiet at the docks, too. Why?" I told her about the missing door guard. "Some cadet playing games," she said. "A bet, probably. But now everyone's talking about the ship."

It was, Lynthe told me, both very new and very large. "There are several cabins, private ones, I mean, at the stern, not just a women's and a men's." That was the usual arrangement, on ships sailing between the Eastern Fort and Wall's End, and sometimes both farther north and farther east. Or there was the deck, which had been my preference, the few times I'd sailed.

"Well, surely no one expected my parents to sleep in shared cabins," I said.

"No—but if there are no other women, then maybe you and I will have one to ourselves, too."

"Maybe," I said, grinning, to a raucous comment or two from the others. Six weeks together? We'd rarely had so much time, between her assignments and mine. And that was just the voyage.

I started back to our quarters with Lynthe: it was time for her to begin supervising the guards at the docks. She wanted her cloak: even in summer, night watch could be cold. Her hand found mine, surprising me: she was rarely affectionate outside our rooms, although our relationship was known to all our friends. But not officially to our superiors, as we weren't declared *consori*, partners.

"That joke the lord Sorley made at dinner last night," she said suddenly. "Is your mother really your father's bodyguard? I thought Druisius was."

"He's captain of the guard at the *Ti'ach*, but she's his guard at night. No one stands outside their door, not like at your brother's villa. Her secca is within her hand's reach, always. It makes sense, doesn't it?" I gave her a nudge with my elbow. "It worked for us." Lynthe had been my bodyguard when we'd first become lovers, a year or so past, an assignment that had ended with her promotion to lieutenant. As the *Princip's* sister, she too should have been guarded, but given her skill with weapons, it had been deemed redundant.

"And where did your guard sleep at the *Ti'ach*? Or shouldn't I ask?"

"In a room across the hall from mine. Or maybe with Ruar's man: he's more to her taste," I said. "And she is not to mine, except as a guard." She laughed, and stopping, pulled me to her for a kiss. Another surprise.

"Wish I didn't have late duty," she murmured.

"But you do."

"For another week. The baths tomorrow, after you finish work? Or do you have to see your parents?"

"I don't," I said. "*Athàir* will be fine. I'll meet you there, the usual time."

⌘⌘⌘⌘⌘

The next week passed in work and fittings for the new clothes and shoes, and too much wine and hilarity in the junior commons. My friends, usually so good at ignoring who—or what—I was, reminded me of my royal status more and more as our departure grew closer. Lynthe got less of it, in part because she had to leave earlier in the evenings. But my father's dramatic arrival, with its clear reminder of my position as the heir, had done its work too well.

I visited my parents every morning before work, and once or twice for dinner. The lines of pain on my father's face diminished, and my mother relaxed a little. I found time to talk to Druisius, but he just shrugged when I asked what he'd learned. "Nothing," he said. "Nothing new in the letters, and nothing from my friends."

"The Casilani officer? The one who came to talk to me in the senior commons?"

"He is new. I am still investigating. It takes time, yes?"

I supposed it did; Druise could not be too obvious in his questions. But I had avenues he did not. A last fitting for my best tunics was scheduled for the next morning, and Severa had said she would attend.

The Governor's wife kept her promise, overseeing with a precise and practiced eye. The tunics—of varying length depending on whether they were meant for day or evening—were beautifully made, and the pale silk shimmered.

"Perhaps you were right," Severa said, as I stood on the raised stool to let the seamstress mark the hem. "With your garnet earrings and your hair up, you will stand out. Alekos cannot help but notice you."

"Speaking of noticing," I said, "who is the new Casilani captain? I met him briefly in the senior commons the other day."

She told me his name. "He's very young, isn't he?" I asked. "To be a captain, I mean?"

She rolled her eyes. "Connections to the palace, my dear. His father was a tutor to the Prince, in Casil."

"He's rather nice." He was, truthfully, at least in appearance.

Severa smiled. "But not for you. You must aim higher."

⌘⌘⌘⌘⌘

I relayed what I'd discovered to Druise, who grinned when I told him how I'd learned it. "No names, though," I said ruefully. "I couldn't probe Severa too closely."

"More than I knew," he said. "A place to start."

Chapter 16

~FATHER~

"APULO," I BEGAN, AS HE FINISHED RUBBING unguent into my scars, "may we talk?"

"Of course. About what?" He stoppered the jar.

"The voyage, and Casil. Gnaius has explained the sleeping cabins. Will you mind sharing one with Colm?"

"I was not expecting a cabin." I had thought he might say that. "I am accompanying you as your body servant. It would not be appropriate."

"But I need you close at hand," I countered. "I have a second question, one that may make your answer to the first irrelevant. Are you sure you want to come to Casil?"

He had never told me much about his years enslaved at the baths, nor had I asked. Most of the men who had used him would be dead or infirm now, and those who were not would likely not recognize the cowed boy in this calm and competent man. But the city could hold few good memories for him. I would not—could not, in fact, as he was a free man—compel him to come, and he had said once he would never go back.

"Who would take care of you, if I don't come?" he asked.

"Gnaius will do the massage, and the exercises, or show Druisius how do them again. Lena will help me bathe and dress. We can manage."

"And what would I do, while you are gone?"

"Whatever you like. Take one of the horses and explore Ésparias, or Sorley and I will write you letters of introduction and you can go to another *Ti'ach* and teach. Or simply stay here and relax. You have not had a day without work in eighteen years, *mo charaidh*."

His only reply was to laugh. Pulling a stool out from the wall, he sat down. "It has not felt like work. As to your earlier question, of course I don't mind sharing sleeping quarters with Colm. He may object, though, as I both rise early and retire late."

"Because he is fourteen, and would sleep until midday if allowed? Not with Gnaius to plague with questions, I expect."

"Perhaps not." He hesitated. "Shall I help you dress?"

It was part of his duties, every day except rest days at the *Ti'ach*. Then, he would give me my massage, and cannabium if I needed it, and leave again, knowing Lena would help me dress later, after she had returned to share a leisurely, loving hour with me in the wide bed. Those mornings, he and Mhairi supervised the students at breakfast. But that had been before Lianë had died.

"Please," I said.

"Druisius is waiting to see you. He wishes a private word," he told me, as he knelt to tie my sandals. He helped me up, supporting me while the mild vertigo from standing passed before giving me my cane.

In the sitting room, Druisius stood at the window. He turned as I entered; from the look on his face I knew something troubled him. Apulo went back into the bedroom to tidy it.

"We have been wrong about the spilled oil," Druisius said.

"In what way?" I took my chair, careful to grasp its arms.

"No one could know you would be there, yes? So it was not you who was the target."

How could we have all missed such an obvious conclusion? My own impaired thinking, Lena's worry spilling over to our daughter. Only Druisius had been thinking about it, asking questions, deducing the truth.

"Gwenna," I said.

"Her route to the barracks. Colm should have gone another way; the door his dog waited at."

"She is young," I said. "Falling would not likely have hurt her badly."

"Maybe a banged knee or head. Enough to unsettle her, so when she steps outside, she is not paying proper attention. The guard has been called away. An easy attack."

Plausible. Perhaps more than plausible. "What have you heard?"

He chewed at his lip. "Nothing much. Mutterings, mostly from Ésparian men who do not want a woman as their leader."

I rubbed my forehead, a headache threatening. Had I heightened the unrest when I'd arrived at Wall's End, my reminder that Gwenna was the heir a misjudgement? It would appear so.

"How much danger do you think she is in?"

"Daytime, in the fort, not much," he said. "Outside the fort, or at night, more. Her guard needs to know, and her friend Lynthe."

"And Talyn," I said. "But leave her to me, Druisius. You will deal with the rest?"

"Who tells Gwenna? And Lena?"

"You, if you will. Your judgement will be respected, whereas I—"

His teeth flashed as he grinned. "Respected? You just want me to be shouted at, not you."

I sent Apulo with a note to my cousin, and a few hours later went to see her. Papers littered Talyn's table; in peace, her work would be more administrative than strategic. "Cillian." She greeted me with pleasure. Grey streaked her dark hair now too. She wasn't much younger than me—half a dozen years, perhaps. "You're feeling better?"

"I'm improving." I told her why I was there. She leant back, contemplating what I'd said.

"I was worried, after your entrance, but I thought you'd be the target. Thought you were the target. But I see why Druisius came to his conclusion. He's a good man," she added. "Conscientious and intelligent."

"He'll speak to Gwenna's bodyguard, and Lynthe." It was, in truth, outside his authority until we sailed, but I didn't think Talyn would mind. "Will you keep me informed of what is said, or any other concerns you have, while we are in Casil?"

"The ships sail often enough now," she said. "I will. But if Gwenna marries the young Emperor, any unrest will die down. She'll be too distant; they'll forget about her."

"Or it will create a stronger argument for Faolyn's son to inherit."

"Possibly. Should I alert the Governor, do you think?"

I considered. He would likely report it to the Empress, but not with any haste. Not a subject worthy of a special letter.

"He should be aware," I agreed. "Now, will you tell me if Lena's promotion is as unearned as she believes it to be."

Talyn raised an eyebrow. "Does she truly? Of course it isn't. She may not have had the same sort of command as other captains, but her reports on her methods of teaching weaponry at the *Ti'ach*, and how the guard is organized and trained, have been meticulous. She's made some excellent suggestions on improving the teaching of cadets."

"I see," I said. I knew Lena reported to Talyn, but I had never given what she reported much attention. Nor was the training, either of guards or weaponry, only her responsibility. I said as much.

"Druisius bears a great deal of the credit," Talyn concurred, "but Lena is the senior captain. Nor has Druisius been studying the books on strategy and the history of past campaigns which Lena has. I believe he has no interest in promotion past his current rank."

An observation that raised a question, but one for Lena, not Talyn. I murmured agreement.

"Now," Talyn said briskly, "Lynthe? What will you tell her?"

"What proves necessary. I would like to get to know her better before I decide."

"Wise," Talyn said. "There are times I don't know what to make of my daughter. I was surprised when at twelve she chose the military, but she adored her grandfather and wanted to follow in his footsteps."

"Do you think she regrets the choice?" I asked.

Talyn rocked a hand back and forth. "She's a good officer, but she's unsettled. Uncommitted, perhaps, and that makes me wary."

"A complication, considering her relationship with Gwenna." Lena had told me of it, a few days earlier. It was a difficulty, given why we had been summoned to Casil.

Talyn nodded. "Indeed. I argued against her going to Casil, you know, but Faolyn insisted. She and he, well—" She gave me a wry grin. "Brothers and sisters. I'm sure Gwenna and Colm are the same. Faolyn thinks seeing Casil will help Lynthe understand Ésparias's place in the Eastern Empire, and disagree with him less."

"Disagree?" I asked softly.

Talyn looked me in the eye. "She thinks he gives in too much to Livius. Make of that what you will, Cillian, but my advice is to tread carefully."

"You have told her nothing?"

"No. I'll leave it to your judgment. And if she learns things she can't divulge, then she just needs to say you forbade her to speak of it."

"I'll make that clear." I would have to speak to Gwenna about this before we sailed. I started to rise.

"Do you have to go? I haven't seen you in a long time, cousin. Stay and talk." She got up to call for wine. Her aide brought it, then left us again.

"Do you ever consider coming home?" Talyn asked, handing me a watered glass. "As the risk to your life which made my father and the *Teannasach* agree on your appointment as *Comiádh* appears to be past."

"The *Ti'ach* is home," I said.

She gave me a level look. "You are a prince of Ésparias and should be here. Once you return from Casil, why not? There is work here for Lena and Druisius, and students for you to teach." She dropped her voice. "There is nothing you do at the *Ti'ach* you cannot do here."

I smiled, made a non-committal answer. She was almost right: there was work here, for all but one of us. Sorley was *scáeli* to the *Ti'ach na Cillian,* and his appointment was for life, or at least until he felt incapable of continuing. And I would not willingly leave him again.

Chapter 17

~DAUGHTER~

WE BOARDED THE SHIP ON A SUNNY MORNING, gulls wheeling and crying above the docks, the sea calm. Faolyn and Siusàn had come to see us depart, Constyn in his father's arms. Faolyn pointed to the ship. "Someday when you are grown a little more, you too will go to Casil," he said to him.

"Why?"

"To learn, as befits the *Princip's* son. I did, and so you will too."

"But not for some years," Siusàn said. "Not until you are older, like Colm." She had not brought the dog, I was pleased to see. Colm had taken him over to the villa the previous day, returning red-eyed and silent.

Apulo accompanied my father up the gangway, Gnaius a step or two behind on his other side. He seemed to be all right, except for stiffness and headaches. Sorley reappeared at the top of the gangway, waving us up. Talyn gave Lynthe a hug, and then my mother. "Safe voyage," she said. "Lena, treat it as a rest. Don't try to be busy all the time."

"I have my books," my mother said.

Talyn hugged me next, her arms strong. "There is duty, Gwenna, but there is also your heart. Listen to it."

"I will." I wasn't going to think about it, actually; not until we reached Casil. Not while I had all these weeks with Lynthe.

⌘⌘⌘⌘⌘

We passed Tirvan on the second day, the glint of the waterfall as it cascaded down to the sea catching my eye before the cluster of houses and the curve of the harbour.

"Do you want to stop?" The question was directed to my mother, who shook her head. She went to the rail, watching her home village pass. I'd spent a few weeks there, once with my mother when I was eleven, once to discuss tariffs and taxes with the council. My cousin Teárdh had taught me to sail on the first visit, and other things, on the second.

I went to stand beside her. "I'd like to see Kira," she murmured. "But not the other women. Not yet."

"Perhaps on the way back?"

"Perhaps." We stood watching the cliffs and coves pass, not speaking. Lynthe joined us. Another village appeared, nestled in a valley: above it, further south on the clifftop, the bulk of a fort stood against the sky, part of the coastal defences the Governor had had built in his first years here. We'd already passed one.

"I spent a season here," Lynthe said, "as a cadet. We rode patrol as far north as Tirvan. I was frightened of the cliffs at first."

"Not unreasonably," my mother said. "They crumble easily, in places. Where the soil is greyer, do you see?" She pointed to a paler streak on the cliffside. Seabirds glided on stiff wings, landing among the crags and fissures. I listened to my mother and Lynthe talking of the clifftop track and the fort for a while before crossing to the other side of the ship where Colm stood looking out. Nothing but water, greenish-grey except where the white foam of waves broke the monotony.

"Look!" Colm said, pointing. A large grey body, and then another and another, rose out of the water in smooth arcs. "Whales!"

"Yes," one of the Casilani sailors said. "We see them on the way here, too. Different from the ones in the sea near Casil."

"Different how?" I left them discussing the shape and colour of whales. I wasn't interested in whales, or coastal defences, although I should be.

One was the source of traded products, and one was, well, important to a diplomat. Or an heir.

A space had been made on the deck for my father, a chair and table anchored to the boards and shaded by canvas. I sank onto the deck beside him. A book lay on the table, unopened. "Gwenna?"

"I'm restless," I admitted. "I don't know what to do with myself."

"I might have felt the same at eighteen," he said. "Now I appreciate the time to rest. Did you not bring books?"

"A few." I lay back, staring up at the canvas. "The history of Casil you said I should read again. Some others. But we're on this ship for weeks. I can't just read."

"No," he said gravely. "I had thought of that, and there are things you and I—and Lynthe, as Faolyn's sister—should discuss. But for once, *mo nihéan*, I am not ready to teach. I was fighting sleep when you came to me."

"You will worry *Mathàir*, if you sleep in the middle of the day." That my father slept little, often spending part of the night in his library working, was one of those things I'd always known. He smiled, briefly.

"I will, I suppose." He glanced over to where my mother and Lynthe stood. "What are they talking of?"

"Building roads and forts. Supplying them. Soldierly things."

"Good," he said softly. "Help me up, Gwenna; I should walk a little." He dropped his voice. "We must both show ourselves to be interested in our land as we travel. This ship may have been sent for our comfort, but there are people on board who will be reporting back, both to the palace and other factions. Do not think we go unobserved."

⌘⌘⌘⌘⌘

I sat cross-legged on the deck while Lynthe braided my hair. The constant breeze tangled it, and I'd decided it would be easier to keep it braided and tied back. "Tell me," Lynthe said, her voice low, "why do you always call your mother's name, if you approach when her back's turned? Not just you: everyone."

I said silent thanks for her observation: I'd forgotten to tell her. "She was attacked from behind once, a man with a knife. I think at Tirvan, when Leste invaded. Anyhow, she still doesn't like it. So we warn her. I should have told you."

Raised voices stopped anything she might have said. "Say that again." Druise, and clearly angry.

"You deserted Casil," the Casilani sailor said. "Fucking traitor." Druise's huge fist took him in the jaw. The man staggered, fell. Druisius raised a foot. I held my breath. He wouldn't, surely.

"Druise!" We'd all stopped whatever we'd been doing to watch. Sorley's voice was only slightly raised. "Don't."

Druise snarled an obscene reply before deliberately placing his foot on the prone man's chest. I breathed again. "You listen," he said, grimly. "I chose to stay in Ésparias and serve the *Princip*. I fought at the Taiva; I had that choice. The papers are signed."

"Idiot." The ship's captain. The word was directed at the sailor on the deck. "Insult an officer? When Captain Druisius deigns to let you up, go to the oars. Three days of double shift."

"Captain," my mother said, firmly, from under the canvas canopy where she had been writing. She was Druisius's superior officer, now. Druise's mouth twisted. He stepped away. Turning his back on the man, he stalked to the other side of the deck. Sorley followed him.

I couldn't hear what passed between them, but I didn't need to. Druise's clenched fists and the tension in his body told me he was furious with Sorley. I'd never seen him like this. I looked away; I wasn't going to watch.

Lynthe was, though. "If I were Sorley, I'd just leave him alone," she said.

"They've been together almost twenty years," I said. "I think Sorley knows how to handle him."

"Twenty years," Lynthe mused. "I can't imagine spending twenty years with just one person. If they really have."

"What do you mean?"

"They're *consori*, yes. But when Druisius is at the fort alone, he's with other men. Is the same true for Sorley? Does he have other lovers?"

I didn't want to lie to her. But there was no commitment between us. No different than the other things she can't know, I told myself: my father has secrets even from my mother, to keep her safe. "It's not something we talk about."

"So he could?"

"I suppose it's possible," I said, in a disinterested tone.

"He's away on *scáeli'en* business sometimes, isn't he?"

"Lynthe," I said, exasperated, "do you speculate about your mother's liaisons?"

She grinned. "Yes, actually."

"Linrathe isn't as free as Ésparias, not in this way," I said. "And the *Ti'ach* is even more constrained than the *torps*."

Druise swore loudly in Casilan, his fist smashing down on the rail. I couldn't stop myself from looking. Sorley grabbed his lover's upper arm. "Inside. Our cabin. Not here where the crew is listening." Druise pulled away, but he turned from the rail. Neither man looked anywhere but ahead of them as they passed us. I noted, cursing my training even as I did, the flush of Sorley's cheeks, his rapid, shallow breathing, the set of Druise's jaw—and to my horror, the glint of tears on his lashes. I turned my head.

A door slammed. "Gwenna." My father had been in the middle of a *xache* game with Gnaius. "Perhaps some music? Sorley's *ladhar* is just there."

I picked up the instrument, thinking about what to play. Nothing quiet and slow. The music of the dragon *danta* drowned out all but the loudest words from the cabin, which slowly tapered off. But when I was nearly done the long song, a cry—which could have been pain, but wasn't—rose and abruptly stopped, as if silenced by a hand, or a mouth. I didn't look at my parents, or Lynthe, or at anything except the instrument in my hands.

⌘⌘⌘⌘⌘

The sea roughened as we rounded the western tip of Ésparias, the short peninsula on which the first—or last—of the shore forts stood. My father and Sorley declined food, as did Apulo and Colm. I ate lightly, but more as a precaution than from any uncertainty of my stomach. I'd never been seasick in these waters, but why take the chance?

By the time we reached the Eastern Fort in the long light of evening, Sorley was huddled, pale and thoroughly drained, under the rail of the ship; my father, to his voiced surprise, was not unwell. "It is the cannabium," Gnaius told us. "Lord Sorley, you may wish to take a little, for the rough seas continue."

"I remember," Sorley said, barely audible, "and by all the gods, Gnaius, why didn't you say so earlier?"

"You would not have kept it down," the physician said smoothly. "I will prepare some for you before we sail again."

"How long are we here?" Lynthe asked.

"Overnight." The answer had come from Druise. He'd been quiet the last couple of days, talking little and mostly to my equally subdued mother. "I am going ashore. Who else?"

Lynthe and I, I thought; we'd find friends here among the junior officers. But should I take Colm, show him around?

"And I, with your leave, Cillian," Gnaius said. "Colm, you might like to come with me. I wish to see the infirmary here, and consult with my colleagues."

We boarded the ship again in the early morning. Only my mother was awake, leaning against the rail, mug of tea in her hand. "You're up early."

"Watch change," I said, yawning. "Our neighbours were less than quiet."

"On purpose," Lynthe added. "We'd beat them at dice in the commons. It was revenge." This, at least, elicited a brief smile from my mother, one that didn't touch her eyes. I wondered if she'd ever truly smile again. I didn't want her to forget Lianë, but I didn't want her to be sad all the time, either.

Lynthe went to get us both tea. I stayed at the rail, watching the men and women working around us. Gulls cried, and sea-pies and smaller birds fed along the breakwater. On a separate jetty, a large ship, almost as big as the one we sailed on, lay at anchor.

"Isn't that the Ésparian flagship?" I asked, pointing. "*Erne*?"

"It might be," my mother said. "Would I know?"

As I turned to take my tea from Lynthe, I saw a man—an officer from his dress and bearing—approaching from the fort. He saw us at the rail of our ship and changed his trajectory. "Lena?" he called, from a distance away.

She'd been looking in the other direction. His call made her turn. "Dern? Come aboard, if I'm allowed to invite you."

Dern. Commander of the Ésparian fleet. I'd attended a few lectures he'd given, as would have Lynthe. I knew he knew my mother; he'd stopped me to ask after her, once.

He strode up the ramp. "It's been years," he said, embracing her.

"Since Faolyn's accession."

"Gwenna." He smiled at me, the skin around his blue eyes crinkling. An attractive man, dark hair barely touched with grey, skin tanned by the sun and wind. "And Lynthe. Lieutenant," he amended, as she saluted him. "Although we do not need to be formal just now." He glanced around him. "Cillian?"

"He's in our cabin, being massaged and exercised by his aide. A morning routine," my mother said.

"Please give him my greetings. I'd like to stay, but," he grinned, "now

I've been cheated of a voyage to Casil by the Empress's decision to send a ship for you, I'm returning north. The *Princip* wishes my advice, and he doesn't want to travel south."

"You were to take us?"

"I was, yes."

"Then I probably owe my promotion to the fact you are not," my mother said drily. "I am going as the military representative to Alekos's investiture, not just as the wife of Ésparias's senior prince."

"I hadn't heard. Congratulations, Major. I am less than upset that you have saved me that role." He grinned again. "And now I must go. Safe voyage to you all."

"I always liked him," my mother murmured, watching him walking to his own ship.

"I might have more than liked him." I nudged Lynthe to tell her I was joking.

"I turned him down."

"What?" I said. "Really? Why?"

"Loyalty to Maya. Misplaced loyalty, but it was how I felt that summer." She looked at the tea in her mug, frowned, and emptied it overboard. "I'll let you explain to Lynthe. I want more tea."

"So?" Lythne asked, when she'd gone. She knew the history of Leste's attempted invasion, and the tactics use to repel it; it was only Maya she didn't know about.

"Maya was *Mathàir's* partner, when she was my age," I told her. "Tirvan chose as a village to learn to fight; Maya voted against it and was banished. She and other women who'd been banished from all over began the village over by the Durrains."

"The one where they keep entirely to the old ways, even sending the boy children away at seven?"

"That one."

"Sounds like your mother was well rid of her," Lynthe said. "Those poor boys. Although the school at Casilla's not a bad place to be brought up, I suppose."

"Better now *Athàir*'s had some influence, and it's run like a *Ti'ach,* with women as well as men teaching them."

A breeze ruffled Lynthe's hair. She pushed it back, out of her eyes; it needed cutting. "Why isn't your father *Princip*?"

"You know why." It was part of our education.

"I know what we're taught. But that's never the whole story." She turned to face me. "I think my grandfather was appropriate, while your father recovered from his injuries. But Faolyn just panders to the Casilani."

I'd never heard her criticize her brother before. "Not entirely," I said.

Her hand moved impatiently. "When my mother or another advisor tells him he should make an objection, maybe. But without them? He'd just go along with anything the Governor proposes."

The harbour wasn't the place for this conversation. Voices could carry over the water, even when pitched low.

"My father chose to influence in other ways." I picked my words carefully. "Through expanding the *Ti'acha* into Ésparias, for one, so we know our history, and Casil's."

"But they're still not teaching music," Sorley said, from behind us. "Ésparias will never be civilized, regardless of what your father thinks, until music is a required subject."

"There's more to life than music."

"But there is less to it, if there is none," he retorted, without rancour.

I laughed. "Where's Druise?"

"Sleeping." Something in me relaxed. He had come back to the ship, then. "And I will lay a bet he'll be seasick today, even though he never is."

"I'll take you up on that," Lynthe said immediately. Soldiers. They bet on anything. Diplomats were taught that outcomes could never be predicted, and wagers were a fool's game. "Wait. When do we sail?"

"The tide's high just before midday. But you accepted, Lynthe. I'm not letting you out of it."

I left the two of them arguing and went to our cabin to change. My tunic smelled of spilled beer, a mug overturned by a too-enthusiastic dice throw. Lynthe's words disturbed me. She'd occasionally been vocal enough about orders she didn't like, but to criticize her brother? *He panders to the Casilani.* I needed to think about what it implied.

In the dim light of the room, my bed looked inviting. I hadn't had much sleep. Perhaps I'd rest for a few minutes. I could hear, faintly, Apulo singing as he massaged my father, punctuated by the occasional snore from Sorley and Druise's cabin. Familiar, safe sounds. Out on the deck, Sorley was teasing Lynthe, and my mother—she'd be all right, in time. We'd all be all right. The ship rocked gently. I closed my eyes, and let sleep take me.

Lynthe won her bet—too much to drink or not, Druise wasn't seasick in the rough waters beyond the scattered islands dividing the Lantanan Sea from the Nivéan. I lost mine, if a bet it had been. A wish; perhaps a foolish prayer. The four adults who were my bulwark and my touchstone were not all right; not at all.

⌘⌘⌘⌘⌘

I had started to read to father in the mornings; the sea light was hard on his eyes. On the second day, Colm came over. "What are you reading?" I showed him the book.

"Oh," he said, wrinkling his nose, "politics."

"What would interest you?" our father asked.

"Books about medicine. Or making things." Colm pointed to the gulls hanging in the sky. "Birds fly. Why can't someone make wings so people can?"

"You know the tale of Vikar, whose father built wings of wax and feathers."

"That's a story," Colm said, a little impatiently. "About setting our ambitions neither too high nor too low. I mean really fly."

"No one has yet managed it," my father said, "but a machine was built which flew; by a Heræcrian mathematician. Powered by steam, and shaped, reputedly, like a bird."

"I have seen this pigeon of Archyte." Gnaius joined us. "Or at least one built from its description. It did not fly properly, but the man who built it thought he could make it do so, in time."

"Perhaps it was too heavy," Colm suggested. "Did you know, *Athàir*, that birds' bones are hollow? Maybe," he said thoughtfully, "that's why people can't fly. We're too heavy."

"You may be right," Gnaius said.

"Maybe very little children could, though," Colm mused. "Like Lianë." His face crumpled, and then he gained control. "*Athàir*? Could you teach me more of Catilius's philosophy? Gnaius says it is fitting for a physician."

"In the evenings," my father replied, "if you like."

⌘⌘⌘⌘⌘

While our days were mostly spent in learning, and sometimes music, my nights and early mornings were for a different sort of education. The physical relationship between myself and Lynthe, which had been casual: pleasurable, but nothing more, was changing. With no reason to rise early, we often, after waking, spent a leisurely time learning more about each other's bodies and responses, needs and desires. With that came a deepening of the attachment between us, at least for me. Was this love? I wasn't sure. Was it for me to declare? I might be the heir, but Lynthe was older, and more experienced. I would wait, I decided.

This morning, Lynthe wasn't in a cuddling mood. She lay with her hands behind her head, her attention not on me. "Your mother surprises me."

"How?" They'd been together a lot, she and my mother and occasionally Druise, talking of military matters: past battles and tactics, mostly. Sometimes my mother borrowed the *xache* pieces, to illustrate a point.

"I thought . . . " Her voice trailed off. "You can't tell her this."

"I won't."

"I didn't think she'd have anything to teach me. I know she's a senior officer now, but that was mostly for show, wasn't it? It's not like she's commanded troops or planned defences recently."

"Not recently," I agreed. Not, in the world's eyes, since before I was born, except at the *Ti'ach*. Even that had been mostly Druise's responsibility, although she'd had a voice in it. But in a strategic, long-term defence of her land, and Sorley's, and maybe even Varsland—there she had had a role, and still did, but not one I could reveal to Lynthe. "Just at the *Ti'ach*, really."

"And the guards aren't even real soldiers," Lynthe said. "But she knows so much, and she has ways of thinking about tactics which are—unusual. My mother told her to read some books, you know, the ones senior officers must know. One is by a general who conquered most of the lands we're passing by, hundreds of years ago. Before even your father's favourite philosopher lived. She's read what he says about certain battles to us, and she says he's exaggerated the numbers of the enemy, to make his exploits look all the greater."

"Why does she think that?"

"She said she's been in those lands, and they're too dry to support so many people. Who else among our senior officers has that experience? Maybe, too, she's benefited from not having to attend all the lectures and discussions the officers generally are required to. She's developed her ideas independently."

"Not entirely independently." I could say this much. "She'll have talked about it with my father, and Sorley and Druise, no doubt."

"Druise doesn't know this book," she said, "although he's heard of the general. He became an Emperor, and then was murdered by his own people."

"Cotta?" I asked. I hadn't made the connection.

"Yes. How did you know?"

"We studied why he failed; why his supporters turned against him." Let her think 'we' meant my cohort of diplomatic students, not my father and myself. And perhaps he had discussed Cotta's downfall with others: I didn't know.

"And?"

"He took too much power, leaving the people with none. It is in part why your brother and our military commanders still have roles in the governing of Ésparias. A lesson learned." One my father had made clear he knew to Livius, and to Eudekia, too, in his letters to her. Couched in questions and observations, opinions given and sought. Nothing more than an exchange among scholars—unless one was skilled in the nuances of diplomacy. He had kept copies of them all, a record and a rebuttal, if needed.

"I'm getting up," Lynthe announced, swinging her legs off the bed. "We're coming to a big town soon, the captain said. I hope we can get off. I'm tired of the ship."

"With guards, maybe." I watched as she washed and dressed—the cabin wasn't big enough for us both to move around in at once. There was so much I couldn't say to her. It didn't seem right—and yet the adults I'd grown up with accepted the same secrecy. I had, too—so why was I baulking now?

Chapter 18

~FATHER~

I HANDED SORLEY THE UNGUENT MEANT to make our growing beards less irritating. Apulo had been preparing to shave me, the second day out, when Gnaius had stopped him. "Wait," the physician had said. "I should tell you beards are the fashion now in Casil." He stroked his own neatly trimmed one. "It perhaps would not be amiss to appear knowledgeable of such things."

"I forgot how much red there is in your beard," Sorley said, taking the jar. "I haven't seen you with one since we found you in exile."

Lena was leaning on the rail, watching the land pass, as she did now whenever she was not talking to Lynthe. I'd asked her to get to know our daughter's partner better, to form a judgement of her trustworthiness. At night in our cabin she would share her thoughts on this, but otherwise she was uncommunicative, accepting my brief kiss goodnight, and my hand on her arm or back, but nothing more. She didn't cry now.

A voyage was a time for reflection and relaxation, I had told Lynthe. Lena was not relaxing. A dark unease clouded the back of my mind, bleaker every day.

"I wish he still had that beard," she said, turning from the rail, "if it meant we were free of Casil and politics."

Sorley winced, glancing at me with a gesture of apology. "*Käresta*," I said. She turned away. My jaw tightened, involuntarily, and a spasm gripped my leg. I forced myself to breathe rhythmically. *Examine this.* Perras's voice, from so long ago. I barely needed to: I knew what troubled me. "Accept the things fate brings you," I murmured.

Lena heard me. "Fuck Catilius," she snapped, "and you too, Cillian. I don't need philosophy."

"That wasn't helpful," Sorley said, before I could speak. He went to her, but she shrugged him off, stalking to the bow to join Druisius. Sorley turned, his eyes narrowed. He shook his head before he walked to the other side of the ship, to stare down into the grey-green water.

I rubbed my eyes, pressing my fingers hard to stop the stinging. When I looked up again, I saw Gwenna and Lynthe watching.

"Gwenna?" She came, leaving Lynthe behind, to crouch beside me.

"*Athàir?*" Her voice was tight with worry.

"My solace is not your mother's," I said, glancing at the book on the table in front of me, "as Sorley reminded me. She needs space and solitude, and in insisting we accompany you to Casil, I robbed her of any chance of it."

"What can we do?"

"Nothing, except be patient." This was unlikely to be true now, but Gwenna did not need to know that yet.

"And Sorley?"

Her protectiveness almost made me smile. "I am familiar with his anger, too." I reached out to touch her hair. "I am going to our cabin to rest my eyes. Will you ask your mother, in a few minutes, if she will join me?"

I lay on the bed to think. The simple stools, which were all the seating in the cabin, provided no support for my back. I had borne the brunt of Lena's anger before, but never so prolonged as this, or as cold. She believed Lianë had been the price for my life. How could she ever be reconciled to that cost? Or, therefore, to me?

Whatever private arrangement we came to, we—the four of us—must not show ourselves divided to the captain and crew. I would have this same conversation with Sorley later, but I had to address it with Lena first.

First. As she was for me, had been from soon after we had met. Behind my carefully marshalled, logical arguments was a shadow I did not want to confront. *Free of Casil and politics.* Free of me, as well? Vows could be broken. I had shown her that.

The door opened. I raised myself on one elbow. But the figure in the space was a man's.

"We should talk, yes?" Druisius said. "*Idióta.*"

"I know. The words were for myself."

"Then think them, do not say them. Lena is furious."

"With cause."

His teeth flashed, almost his familiar grin. "With me. I told her she could not act this way, a major of Ésparias. Not in front of Casilani sailors, and a lieutenant of her own army. She was not happy. Sorley is talking to her now."

"He too is angry with me."

"Only for Lena. Not really." He stood beside the bed, looking down. "Fix this, Cillian."

"I don't know how." I had no need to pretend with him. There were no secrets between us, not personal ones. The single exception was by mutual consent.

He folded his arms. "Ask her. Stop thinking you know what is best."

I hadn't asked, afraid of what she would tell me. *You do tend toward making decisions without proper consultation.* She'd said that to me when we had debated our unborn children's future. The decision we had made that night had led directly to this voyage, and what awaited our daughter in Casil.

"It is not that simple," I said.

"Maybe not." He turned to go. "But usually it is. You think too much."

I thought quite a bit more while I waited for Lena. She came in, pulling shut the door Druisius had left open. Even in the dim light of the cabin, I could see the streaks the sun had left in her hair, and the browned skin. She looked as she had on our long walk across the plain, alone together in all that empty world. She sat on a stool, not on the bed.

"Lena," I said. "Please tell me. Do you wish to leave me?"

A long, indrawn breath. "I don't know. Yes, sometimes."

"Marriages can be ended, in both Linrathan law and Casilani."

"All marriages end. Death ends them. If—" Her voice caught. She took another breath. "If I left you, Cillian, it would be to learn to live without you."

I had weighed every possibility, I had thought. I had been wrong. "*Käresta*," I said, "you will have years enough for that. Can it not wait?"

"No," she said. "It can't. I—if you had died when you fell, as you could have, what would I do? I would not be lady of the *Ti'ach*; I am not Dagney, to hold that role for my own skills, nor am I Linrathan. I am an officer of the Ésparian army, but I don't deserve the rank I have; this promotion is a political sham. I have no child who needs me now. I cannot—" She stopped, shaking her head in mute frustration.

One fear was draining from me. "What would you do, if you left?" I held out a hand. "The stool is uncomfortable. You could join me."

She came to the bed, but to sit cross-legged at the end. "I could learn to fish again," she said.

"Do you want to?"

"No. Not really. I was a reluctant soldier, once, and glad to leave Wall's End, but I could be of use there."

"And the work would not end with my death," I said. "A life you chose, not what fate gave you."

"I made you a promise."

"We have been apart before. Officers have leave, and Wall's End is close enough, for a good rider." She was too far away for me to touch her. "When we made our vows, *käresta*, we truly had only each other. But I do not wake alone, even if you are away: I wake to a house where I am loved and cared for. And perhaps you have outgrown shelter."

"Perhaps I have. I can't decide yet, Cillian. Not until after Casil, and whatever happens there." She unfolded herself. "I'm too old to sit like that for long."

I expected her to get up. But instead she stretched out beside me. When I put my arm around her, she turned to rest her head on my shoulder, as she always had. *To learn to live without me.* If my fears for Casil were correct, it could be earlier than she thought.

But that was always true, and so I would not tell her what might await me. It was a possibility, an interpretation, nothing more. I kissed her hair. "Whatever happens in Casil; whatever you decide," I said, "I love you."

"Good gods," she said, "is that twice this year you have forced yourself to say the words?"

"I believe so," I answered, matching her tone.

She looked up at me, laughter mixed with the sadness in her eyes. She kissed me, once, and again, deeper, raising herself to straddle me, her hands moving on my chest. Desire pulsed, rose.

We made love gently, telling each other what there were no words to express. As it had always been, between us. Afterwards, she fell asleep. My hand lay lightly on her ribs, rising and falling with her slow breaths. I had not spoken the truth, of course. Even when she had been gone for only a week or two, to Han or Tirvan, I woke every morning to a hollow absence.

I had never—how could I?—expected the twists and turns my life had taken. I had never expected a woman's love, or children. When, under a cobalt sky, Lena had told me she loved me, I had never expected her to stay. I was too difficult, too complicated. I'd offered her freedom, more than once. She'd always refused. Not this time. I must make it simple for her.

Chapter 19

~DAUGHTER~

"HOW COULD HE SAY THAT?" I DEMANDED of Sorley, keeping my voice low. I'd seen Colm's shoulders tense when my mother had sworn at my father. Gnaius was talking to him, and I didn't want to disturb them.

Sorley exhaled, loudly. "I love your father, Gwenna, but sometimes his idea of duty comes before the needs of the people around him."

"And sometimes it doesn't," I said, pointedly. He had the grace to nod.

"Perhaps the only time in his life," he said. "I told Druise once that almost everything Cillian has done since then sprang from that moment."

"What moment?" Lynthe asked.

"You haven't told her?" Surprise flitted over Sorley's face.

"It's not really mine to tell, is it? But I will, now. Many years ago," I began, turning to Lynthe, "when Sorley was sixteen, my father prevented him from being revealed as—as a lover of men. Something forbidden in Sorham, and shameful. Sorley would have been disowned. My father broke an oath he had made to do so. An important oath, made to Linrathe."

"But that's not very different than what he did later, when he and your mother were exiled," Lynthe said. "He foreswore Linrathe to become Ésparian, so he could accompany your mother into exile and keep her safe."

"Is that what's taught?" Sorley asked.

"What's said," Lynthe answered.

"How stories change," Sorley murmured. "There is a grain of truth there, Lynthe, but if anyone was keeping someone safe, it was Lena protecting Cillian. I should sing the *danta* for you, I suppose."

We had not been eating as a family, instead taking our bowls of food to wherever there was space to sit on the deck. Someone usually kept my father company, but it was as likely Apulo or Gnaius—or me—as my mother or Sorley.

But tonight, when my parents emerged from their cabin, they stayed together, my mother sitting on the deck beside my father to eat. When we had finished the food, Sorley reached for his *ladhar*. "I discovered today Lynthe doesn't know my *danta*," he announced quietly. "I'm going to sing it for her. Druise, do you want to play?"

Druise shrugged. "If you like."

As Sorley began the first verses, all conversation on the deck ceased. He was singing in Linrathan, of course, which meant the ship's officers and off-duty men couldn't understand him, but the tune itself was enough to gain their attention. Colm came over to sit beside me, hugging his knees. I was sure he was taller than he'd been even at Wall's End. I glanced at my parents. My mother leant against my father, just slightly, but the familiar sight gave me hope. Just a disagreement, my mother's temper short from the confinement of the ship.

The *danta* was long, but it changed tempo and mood frequently, enough to keep someone's attention, even if they didn't understand the words. The ending Sorley sang this time wasn't one I knew: it was more thoughtful, sadder, speaking of the price of both war and peace.

"Gods," Lynthe whispered to me, as the last notes faded into the air, "that's so different than what we were taught. Which one's right?"

"Both," I said, shifting my position. "What we learned in class were the facts of the treaty, and the battles."

"And your parents' bravery."

"That too. But Sorley was there for most of it, and he's a poet and a musician. The song is about how it felt."

⌘⌘⌘⌘⌘

We came to a river mouth, a channel cut deep through the cliffs and spilling over boulders to meet the sea. Our ship was well out from the coast, avoiding rocks, and we were huddled under the canvas shelters, trying to keep dry. Low clouds drizzled a steady, warm rain. Not a day for books. Sorley and Druise played music, casually, chatting softly as they did. I'd been watching my father beat Gnaius at *xache*, and Colm was studying a gull's wing. One of the sailors had brought the bird down with a boathook the day before, and Colm and Gnaius had dissected it. I had been thankful when all but the wings and head had gone overboard when they were done.

The cliffs rose even higher. As we passed a headland the shape of a Casilani fort—looking exactly like the ones built recently along Ésparias's coast—became visible. The clouds hung lower here, and the tallest watchtowers were almost lost in the coastal fog. The rain had stopped.

"They were building that fifteen years back, when I took Ruar to Casil," Sorley observed. "It didn't take long to re-establish their control of these lands."

"Casil had men and weapons to spare, once the Empress's marriage to the Boranoi heir had ensured peace between them," my father said. He was standing now, his hand on the rail covering my mother's. She stood close to him, not quite touching, her hood pushed back. Colm had joined them. Huge white birds with equally huge beaks floated on the water, but he wasn't, for once, looking at them.

The sweep of the oars brought us around the headland, where the land fell away to marsh and flat field. The clouds hung on the heights, but here the sun had broken through, lighting a town and its busy waterfront, with jetties and warehouses, the jingle of rigging and the shouts of men loading and unloading—and a Marai ship at anchor.

So Michan had been right: Varsland was taking the longer river route to trade directly with Casilani merchants. But with the fort up on the headland, and Casilani ships at the wharves, this must be an open secret. What did that mean?

We stayed out of the way of the crew as the boat glided into the harbour to be brought up against a stone jetty and tied, prow and stern. "Sylana has grown a little," my mother said, at my side. "When I was last here, there were open fields on the western side of the harbour, and perhaps two or three jetties for the boats. I wonder if Mihae is still headman?"

"No," Druise said. "He is dead. His son has the title, but this is Casil's town now."

I wanted to be off the ship, to feel firm ground beneath my feet again, even as I puzzled over the presence of the Marai ship. My father's eyes were also turned to it, as were Sorley's.

"By Rögnir!" Cupping his mouth with his hands, using all the power of his trained voice to be heard over the clamour of the harbour, he shouted, "Nyle? Nyle!"

On the deck of the Marai ship, a man turned, shading his eyes as he looked our way. Another man—clearly pale-haired, tall and bearded—joined him. The first man pointed. Sorley went to the stern, waving. "Nyle!" he shouted again, "It's Sorley!" A memory rose: Gundarstorp, four years past, a homecoming.

"Who is Nyle?" Lynthe asked.

"Sorley's half-brother," I said slowly. "I've never met him." *Where's Nyle?* Sorley had asked, as his brother's family had crowded around us. *Gone trading,* had been the answer. *East, down the Ubë.* But with the Marai?

"Sorley!" The shout was faint, but clear. Nyle swung over the side of his low river vessel, jumping easily onto the jetty, followed by the second man. As they ran toward our ship, Sorley gave a low laugh.

"I'm almost certain that's Bjørn with him," he said, turning to my father, a question on his face. I, and perhaps only I, other than my father, knew the reason.

"Your son?" my mother asked. Only me, then.

"I might be wrong," Sorley said. "I haven't seen him for a long time."

"I will finally meet him?" Druise had never seemed perturbed by the idea his partner had a son. He knew Sorham's attitudes toward men who loved men; Sorley, just out of boyhood, would have done his best to hide his nature.

The gangplank for our ship was out. Nyle strode up it, Bjørn just behind him, to wrap his arms around his brother. Taller than Sorley, and a lither build, but I could see the resemblance. Bjørn—who, were the fiction maintained, would be Nyle's nephew—shared only the light hair and eyes.

Bjørn grinned at the embracing brothers and extended his hand to my father. "Bjørn Sorlison. You are Cillian of Ésparias?"

"I am," my father said. "I know who you are, Bjørn. I am pleased to meet you, finally."

Sorley turned, one arm still around his brother. Bjørn's lips twitched. "Father," he said. "It has been some years."

I glanced at Nyle, seeing nothing but a pleased smile. He was either very good at dissimulation, I decided, or he had no idea who Bjørn really was. Was that possible? Of course it was, if Nyle had spent the last four or five years as a trader away from Sorham and Varsland. After all, neither my mother nor Druise knew. Bjørn was a common enough name among the Marai.

Sorley embraced Bjørn, as a father should. Further introductions were made, my mother and Druise and Lynthe by their military ranks, and Colm and I only as 'son' and 'daughter'. I grinned inwardly at Nyle's appreciative assessment of Lynthe. Unlike me, she had no interest in men. He was attractive enough, I decided, but not nearly as much as Bjørn. His presence disturbed me.

But not because he had broad shoulders and eyes more grey than blue, or a quick smile. That a Marai trading ship was here was concerning enough. That the King of Varsland's brother was on it rang a warning in my mind as loud as watchtower bells.

Chapter 20

~FATHER~

"I KNEW NYLE WAS A TRADER," SORLEY SAID, as we gathered on the jetty, "but not that it was a joint venture with Varsland." He sounded worried.

We had been invited to leave the ship. An escort had arrived from the fort where we would be given beds for a night or two. They'd brought a litter for me, with four men to carry it, and horses for everyone else.

"This is your doing?" Lena asked Gnaius. The physician inclined his head.

"It is a long and steep road to the fort," he said. "I did not know if Cillian could ride, so I arranged this on the outward voyage."

"It was thoughtful of you," I said. "Thank you, Gnaius."

"In Casil, of course, you must all use litters," he went on. "A family of your rank would never walk."

"Except me," Druise said, without rancour, "and Apulo."

"You as well," Sorley said, "if I name you *quincalum*, surely?"

"I am your *consor*, not *quincalum*," Druise said. "And I do not like litters. I want to see and hear, yes? Not be shut behind curtains." The idea of travelling in a moving box did not appeal to me, either, but I had—and would have—no choice.

"But why are the Marai here?" Lena said, returning to the subject of Nyle and Bjørn. "Aren't they breaking the peace treaty with Casil?"

"Perhaps not," Gwenna answered, while I was ordering my thoughts. "I read the treaty again, just before we came. If they are arriving unladen, to use coin to buy goods at Sylana, or even Casil, they are not violating the terms of the treaty. The intent, yes, but not the terms." Her analysis was correct, I thought, as Apulo helped me into the litter. It would be simple: amber and ivory sold to the traders of Sorham, who were permitted the river route to Casil, and then that coin brought east to buy things which were too dear at the Linrathan trading port. Or things not available, forbidden to be traded to Varsland.

At the fort we were greeted and shown our rooms and the baths: there was no question of us dining with Sylana's Procurator and the fort's commander until we'd bathed. Some time later, clean and oiled and massaged, we were ready for the meal. Apulo had shaken out a grey tunic for me. Lena had dressed in uniform, her new major's insignia bright against the fabric. A clear message to the men here, and perhaps to me.

We gathered in the dining room, Apulo quietly finding a place in a corner among the servers. I was less steady than I would have wished, and not, I believed, just from weeks aboard a ship. Even now my head ached a little. I would be glad of Apulo's arm later.

The wine was good, and the food fresh, a welcome change from the ship's fare. We spoke of the upcoming investiture of Alekos, the unrest in the east, and the young women who had been summoned to Casil from all points of the Empire to be considered as brides for the Prince. Both the Procurator's wife and the commander's were present, and so perhaps there was less talk of politics than their might have been. I could see, to my private amusement, that they were unsure of what to make of Lena and Lynthe. Both had worn uniform, and neither were more than politely interested when the talk turned to clothes and ornaments.

I was proud of Gwenna. Dressed in a grey tunic with white trim, her hair up to show the garnet earrings, she engaged both the men and their wives in easy conversation. When the pastries and fruit and a sweet golden wine had been brought, she turned to the Procurator. "I was surprised to see a Marai ship at harbour. Do they come frequently?"

"One or two last season, and now this one." He did not volunteer anything more.

"It is not an easy journey," Sorley said. "Did you know, Procurator, that three of us here have made that voyage? I from the northlands, and Prince Cillian and the major from the grasslands." He smiled, not his usual grin, but a polite, *toscaire's* smile. "They had the easy part, not having to carry the ship and our supplies between the two rivers in the north."

"A village has sprung up there," the Procurator answered, "with strong men who make their living in part by assisting with that. The trading ships from Sorham are often heavily laden, and glad to give a little coin to speed the transfer."

"The Sorham ships?" I asked. "Not the Marai ones?"

"No," the Procurator said. "You have not been to Casil in some years, I understand, Prince Cillian? You will be amazed by the harbour, then: there are more jetties, and many ships now from the east and south. The treaty with the Boranoi you helped craft has benefited the city greatly."

"The Empress has told me the same. A small service, which has had wider implications than I expected." The headache that had been threatening all evening began to pound. A little too much wine, I thought, although I had been careful to water it. "A wonderful dinner, and a gracious welcome, Procurator, but I will excuse myself now. No," I said to Gnaius, who had risen. "Apulo will provide all the assistance I need." I took Apulo's arm, and the cane he handed me.

By Gwenna's chair, I stopped. "Come to me when you can," I said softly.

Somewhat more than an hour later Gwenna joined us. I was sitting, leg up on a footstool, listening to soft music from Sorley's *ladhar*.

"Are you all right?" she asked, immediately.

"A headache, nothing more," I said. "They have plagued me since Wall's End. Gnaius says they will pass, in time. But I trust my memory less than I once did, and there were things said tonight I wanted to record, so, a convenient excuse to leave."

She sat across from me. "What things?"

"Who else is sending young women to the investiture, for one. Tell me what you heard, Gwenna."

"Their own representative, of course. The headman's daughter." She listed others. "The one which surprised me was Halachia. They are not a province."

"No. They are looking for an alliance. What are your thoughts on Qipërta?"

"Are they not the source of the unrest?"

"Unrest may be a mild word. I believe it to be closer to war. Druise may tell us more. He is drinking with the fort's commander."

"Of course he is," she said, with a quick smile. "Surely it is a war they would prefer to avoid, if a marriage can solve the issues? Peace, in return for their candidate."

"They may well offer a considerable dowry, to find a diplomatic way out of the situation," I said.

"As Varsland did, when they offered Sorham as Helvi's dowry," Sorley said. A shadow crossed his face. "Poor Helvi. She is dead by now, I expect."

"Poor Ruar," Gwenna murmured. "And the boys."

"And speaking of Varsland," Sorley said, "you noted, of course, the Procurator changing the subject when you asked about the ship."

"I did," I agreed. "You've made arrangements to meet your brother and Bjørn tomorrow?"

"I have." Sorley grinned. "Although they want me to bring Gwenna and Lynthe."

"I think we should go," Gwenna said. "They might be looser of lip, if they're trying to impress us."

"Nyle, maybe." Sorley said.

"Why not Bjørn?" Lena asked. She'd been listening, sipping a cup of tea.

"He's older," Sorley said.

"Is that all?" She put down the cup. "For seventeen years I've watched you when you speak of Bjørn, Sorley. Is he really your son?" A direct question. Sorley's oath as a *scáeli* meant he could give only two possible answers; which would he choose?

"Who else would he be?" The third option: a question for the question.

"Bryngyl had a brother," she said. "He disappeared. When the earls made Bryngyl king, no mention was made of him, but there were rumours."

"There are always rumours," I said.

"You forget something," Lena answered, and I heard the sarcasm that preceded anger for her. "A talent I have. One you should have cause to remember, Cillian. We travelled for weeks with Irmgard. Bjørn looks very much like her, and whomever you dallied with as a young man, Sorley, I doubt it was a princess of Varsland." Ice in her voice, now. "Nothing to say?"

"*Käresta*, you know there are things we cannot share; secrets which must be kept."

"I know. I know, and I agreed to it, but this is personal." She turned to Sorley. "Does Druise know?"

"No."

"But you will tell him now." Not a question.

"I suppose I must."

"And you, Gwenna?" She didn't wait for an answer. "Did you tell her, Cillian?"

"Yes." I held up a hand to stop her from speaking. She glared at me, but stayed silent. "Lena, Gwenna has known everything for the last year and more. A contingency. Had I hit my head harder when I fell, I could have died, or been left as Dagney was after the apoplexy. Would you have our years of work mean nothing?"

She took a deep breath, her lips thinning. "I don't know what I think. I don't care that I don't know what messages Sorley takes and brings, or Druise, or what subtle teaching is done at all the *Ti'acha*. I don't care that

I don't know who you suggest should be appointed to what position, or what inducements will make this earl or that look more favourably on Ésparias. Or even what you write to Eudekia to make her think you are loyal and appreciative." No tears in her eyes; no quaver in her voice. Just cold precision. "But this is different. This is about us, our family." She stood up. "I'm going for a walk. I will stay within the walls of the fort, so you needn't worry."

I didn't try to stop her. No one spoke for a moment.

"Shall I go after her?" Gwenna asked.

"No," Sorley replied. "She needs time alone. Let her be."

He convinced Gwenna to go to bed, promising to stay with me until Lena returned. The window, open to the night air, carried both a light breeze and the occasional voice into the room. Sorley sat across from me. "We should have told her."

"Perhaps we should have," I said. "I did not foresee this meeting."

"How could you have?"

"Regardless, I can do little right in her eyes just now. It is not just Bjørn she is upset about."

"I can see that," he murmured. "I worry for you both. Is there anything I can do?"

"I doubt it."

He stood, and without asking went to the table where the flask of *fuisce* stood beside the wine. He poured a little into one of the small glasses and handed it to me. "I wonder if we brought enough." He poured himself wine before sitting again.

I sipped the *fuisce*, warm on my tongue and in my throat. "I expect her to leave me. Either in Casil or once we return home."

Sorley coughed, spluttering wine. "No!"

"We have spoken of it."

"And you are not trying to stop her?"

"How long can you keep a *fuádain* jessed and mewed?" I asked. "Never all her life. She is always allowed her freedom; it is the implicit bargain."

"Between a man and a captured bird, yes," he said angrily. "But Lena is a woman. A woman who loves you, Cillian. How can she do this?"

"The love is not in question." She had told me that, wordlessly, an afternoon not very long ago. "But think, Sorley. Imagine yourself, if you can, as simply a minor *scáeli*, a teacher and nothing more. Take away your work as the head of the *scáeli'en* council, and the time you spend advising Ruar. Would you not be restless after all these years?"

I took another sip of the *fuisce*. "I was thirty-six when we came to the *Ti'ach*. I had been travelling, in one way or another, for eighteen years then. I was ill, and exhausted, and I wanted peace, and that is what I found at the *Ti'ach*. Lena wanted that too, for me and for herself, then. Now she wants something more. Love requires I put no barriers in her way, just as she has put none in mine for all our years together."

Sorley smiled, wryly, acknowledging the layered truth in what I had said. "The night you came, the two of you, to tell me how you saw the future, what needed to be done—do you remember? Lena stayed behind to talk to me."

"I remember."

"It was to tell me she was frightened of what the future held, but that she was willing to face it." A memory flickered in his eyes. "I suppose it's all we can do. But by all the gods, Cillian, I hope she changes her mind."

"It is not yet certain. But Annaeus, in his writings, says she is doing the right thing, preparing herself for the future she must someday face."

He scowled. Sorley found little comfort in the philosophers, I knew. I finished the *fuisce*. Weariness seeped through me. "I should go to bed."

"I'll find Apulo." He stood, bending to kiss me gently. "Unless you will let me help?"

I let myself, for a moment, take comfort from his touch, from his hand on the back of my neck. "*Somhairle*," I said. "*Meas, mo duíne gràhadh. But it is best not.*"

Chapter 21

~DAUGHTER~

I MADE MY WAY BACK TO THE ROOM I shared with Lynthe, dawdling a little to give me time to gather my thoughts. "What's wrong?" Lynthe asked, as soon as she saw me. "Is your father ill?"

"No. Just a headache." I flopped down on my bed. "Nothing I can tell you. I'm sorry."

She moved to sit beside me. "Roll over and I'll rub your shoulders." I did as she asked.

When her strong fingers were working, I said, my voice muffled by the pillow, "Doesn't it bother you that I can't talk to you about some things?"

"Bother me? No. You're a diplomat, and Faolyn's heir. I'm curious, sometimes, but there are all sorts of things I can't know in the army, things above my rank."

"But . . . " This was a good a time as any to say this. "I can't tell you what it's about, but my mother has just learned something my father and Sorley have kept from her for a long time, but which I knew. And she's furious, and I understand why. She feels like her trust in them—and maybe me, too—has been betrayed. I don't want that to happen to us."

Lynthe's fingers stopped. "But she told me the other day it's part of being married to someone who has a public role."

I rolled over. "That's true about political things, like . . . oh, I don't know, like what is offered to Varsland to keep them happy with the trade policies. Or who should be governing Leste. But this is more personal. I wish I could tell you."

"Personal how? She's just discovered they've been secret lovers for years?"

My training meant I stayed calm. "Why would you say that?"

She chuckled. "Sorley's not hard to read, now I've been around him all these weeks. And your father doesn't call anyone else 'my beloved man'."

Mentally, I swore. "It would be dangerous to spread that idea," I said. "Dangerous for Sorley, I mean, in Linrathe, and for my father as *Comiádh*."

"So it's true?"

"Lynthe, you have to promise me to say nothing." I sat up, pushing my hair back from my face. The muscles around her eyes tightened. I put a hand on her cheek. "Please."

I watched her eyes. "On my oath to Ésparias, Gwenna. I promise I won't."

"It's true." I told her the story. She listened without interruption.

"So," she said when I was done. "They're more Ésparian than I thought. But if they've been lovers most of your life, that's not what your mother's upset about. What's changed?"

"It's not that, not directly." I searched for words to explain. "But the three of them, they're so close. Say you had two really good friends, people you loved, and you thought they valued you just as much. Then you find out they've both known a secret for years and years, and they've never told you, but they have told someone else. How would you feel?"

"Angry," Lynthe said. "That's what's happened here?"

"More or less."

"Is the secret about your father, or Sorley?"

"Sorley."

"I'll wager that's worse," she said, surprising me. "Your father is more than he appears on the surface. Maybe you were excluded from the talk at the cadet school, but he was always a subject of speculation."

"I wasn't," I said. "I heard a lot of it."

"Well, I know much it was ridiculous rumour, but there's a grain of truth in some of what's said, isn't there?" She didn't wait for me to answer. "So Lena knows your father is—what he is. But Sorley's different."

"He's still a diplomat of sorts," I said. "He advises Ruar."

"Yes, but," she shrugged, "it's Linrathe. Smaller concerns. Your father has the ear of the Empress, and his influence spreads all the way to Casil. Sorley's more human. It's like Siusàn—she loves Faolyn, but sometimes she and I sit and talk about how irritating he is. He's my brother, and I do love him, but when he's being the *Princip*, he can be annoying. I'm guessing that's how it's been with your mother and Sorley. They share their frustrations about your father."

I hadn't expected her to understand. "I think it's that exactly," I said. Except for my mother's reaction to discovering I was privy to all my father's plans. I couldn't share that with Lynthe.

"I really like your mother," Lynthe said. "There's a lot of wisdom, as well as common sense, in her. She'll sort this out, but I'm not surprised she's angry." She yawned. "I wouldn't mind her as my commanding officer, permanently, I mean."

"Not likely," I said, "as she'll be back at the *Ti'ach* once we're home."

"Seems a waste of her promotion," Lynthe said, yawning again. "Are we going to do anything in this bed other than sleep? Because if we are, shall we stop talking?"

I woke before Lynthe in the morning. I lay still, thinking about the previous night: what I'd witnessed, and what Lynthe had said. She'd never admitted to loving anyone before. I could hope, just a little.

Servants brought hot water and told me where and when breakfast could be found. Washed and dressed, we found the room. Sorley was there, looking subdued, and Druise, who just looked worse for last night's wine, I thought. No one spoke over tea and what little food was eaten—other than by Lynthe, who always had a good appetite.

"Do we have to stay in the fort today" I asked finally. "We're not sailing until tomorrow, right?"

"I don't see why you have to stay here," Sorley said, "but Druise and I will have to go with you, or your mother. Sylana's customs require it."

"I doubt my mother wants to chaperone us," I said. Why pretend? "You said yourself she needs time alone. But if you don't want to, I'm sure the fort's commander will find us guards."

"No," Druise said. "My job."

"Mine, once, too," Lynthe said, smiling softly. "I'll have my secca on my belt."

"As will I," I replied. "Have I ever told you the last time I used it was protecting these two?"

"Not fair," Sorley almost grinned. "We were all fighting. Let's go, then." We stood. "A word first, Gwenna?" As the servants cleared the plates and cups, he asked, "What does Lynthe know?"

"Not very much. I'm not sure I can tell her any of the secrets, not yet."

"Some you never can."

"You don't mind, that *Athàir* doesn't tell you everything?" I asked.

"He has told me the purpose. That is trust, Gwenna, and it is what matters most, because whether I love him or not, I could have betrayed him. I could still. I never will, of course," he added, at my widened eyes, "any more than your mother would, as angry and hurt and lost as she is just now." He sighed, wearily. "So Lynthe doesn't know who Bjørn is?"

"No. But—" I looked him in the eye. "She guessed about you and *Athàir*." He swore, mildly.

"She's sworn to secrecy, Sorley, on her oath to Ésparias." I grinned. "But all she said was we were more Ésparian than she thought. Did you tell Druise about Bjørn?"

"Yes."

"And?"

He chuckled. "In language fit for your ears, what he said was he'd always doubted it, and he wished he'd made a bet he was right. And that was all. But Lynthe shouldn't know, until we know why Bjørn's travelling incognito."

From the corridor outside, Lynthe called my name. I frowned at her tone, and with a glance at Sorley, opened the door. My father stood there, Apulo at his side.

"Have you seen Lena?" my father asked.

"Not since she left last night." Confusion flickered over Sorley's face. "Why?"

"She slept—elsewhere. Apulo has determined from the servants that she told them I was mildly unwell, and she wished not to disturb me. But she is not in that room, or here, and—"

"She left you no note? No message?"

"None."

"Is that so unusual?" Lynthe asked.

"Yes," I said shortly. "I'll explain later."

"Her bed was slept in, I am told." Apulo had one hand on my father's back, steadying him. "Cillian, you should sit. Lena cannot be far."

My father began to shake his head, then closed his eyes, swaying a little. Sorley was at his other side in a second. "Another dizzy spell?" Apulo asked. "Come. There is a chair not far. Gnaius says not to worry," he added, addressing the rest of us. "This happens after a blow to the head,"

"This is true," Druise said. "I have seen it among soldiers. Shall we go look for Lena?"

"We should start at the training field," Sorley said, glancing from my father to his partner.

"You think?"

"She's angry. She's used sword practice to work that out before."

"She might also have gone riding," I said. "We'll go to the stables."

Outside, I told Lynthe of my mother's vow: that my father would never wake alone. "Clearly she can't always be there: she travels, sometimes, but if she can, she is. Otherwise, she says she's there in spirit, if not in body. This behaviour's completely unlike her."

The stable cadet hadn't seen her. We circled round to the training fields.

As soon as we were free of the buildings, relief coursed through me. My mother was talking to Druise, a sword in her hand. Sorley stood some distance away.

"I will come when I am done here." Her voice carried in the clear morning air. "The sooner you leave me to it, Captain, the sooner I will finish the routines." A Casilani soldier squatted at the far end of the field, waiting.

"Major." My mother went back to the field without a glance to us.

"You heard her," Druise said. "Go tell Cillian she is safe, Sorley. I want to watch this."

"So do I," Lynthe said. I didn't; watching my mother work out anger with a sword didn't appeal, and, I thought, my presence might inflame her more. I walked with Sorley back to the headquarters. He was quiet, and so was I. Whatever equilibrium I thought my mother had reached, it hadn't lasted. What it would mean for the weeks ahead, I didn't know.

I had thought the bond between my parents indestructible, and now I wasn't sure. I wanted both to fix what was wrong, and run away from it. I wanted to feel safe again, but my world kept changing.

Apulo had just brought more tea when my mother walked in, sweat streaking the dust on her face and limbs. "Apulo, will you leave us, please?" she asked. My father's face was still, showing almost nothing. She poured herself tea and drank it, standing.

"Shelter," she said, addressing my father. "You vowed to shelter me, and it was here in Sylana I heard you tell Turlo that. But you have gone too far, and so I neglected my own vow this morning." She looked over to where Sorley and I sat. "I am going to say some things, and then I would like you both to leave. I understand Cillian's desire to protect me; to protect us all. Sorley, I know you were only following the agreement we all made. But as Cillian has said himself, what if his fall had been fatal, or brought on an apoplexy? Gwenna may know all the pieces of your game, but is it fair to leave an eighteen-year-old, no matter how you have prepared her, with that burden?"

"Perhaps not," my father said quietly.

"Perhaps?" She made a derisive sound. "It is time we all knew your full plans. If a charge of treason comes, we will all be complicit, regardless. Although I could claim I know nothing of the last few years' schemes, occupied as I was with a very young child. Since Bryngyl chose to marry an earl's daughter, making my trips to Han unnecessary, what have you shared with me, truly?"

"Those trips were about a marriage alliance, then?" Sorley asked.

"Did Cillian tell you that?"

"No. Cillian has kept his word. It was Gwenna who suggested it, four years ago."

A flicker of surprise on her face. "Well done, Gwenna." Her voice was still cold. "So now you know." She took a deep breath. My father was leaning back in his chair, watching her.

She turned back to us. "It is time you left, both of you. Gwenna, I have asked to inspect the coastal defences shortly, and Lynthe will come with me. If you want to see the town, it will have to be without her."

I wasn't going to argue. "Come," Sorley whispered to me. In the corridor he visibly sagged. "I've never seen her like this. Angry, many times, and occasionally coldly furious. But to forgo her vow to him, and their morning ritual—"

"It's like a treaty," I said. "And she thinks he broke its intent."

"No," he said. "Rather he overstepped its intent; instead of sheltering her, he's constrained her. When I gave him the *li'ítho,* he said he would accept them if Lena did not see them as jesses. She hates to be caged, your mother, and perhaps that's how she's been feeling, these last few years."

"Lianë."

"In part. But you heard what she said about the trips to Han; they had a secret purpose, but they were also time alone for her, and time in the grasslands, with all their space." The door guard let us out into the sunshine. Already the heat was intense. "No children, none of the duties of the *Ti'ach*, no Cillian. Just sky and grass and horses, and the company of other women for a week or two." He glanced at me. "Whatever it is you need for that wholeness, Gwenna, don't deny yourself. Nothing good comes of it."

Whatever I needed? I had no idea.

Sorley's question had unsettled me, and I said little as we walked down the hill from the fort. The gate guards had wanted to call a litter, but I'd refused. What, in my life, took me out of work and study? Not the nights spent drinking and gaming; those relaxed me, but I knew that wasn't what Sorley meant.

Soon enough we were on the flat ground below the fort and crossing the arched stone bridge over the river. "The Casilani built this," Sorley said. On its far side, occupying a paved square, a market teemed with people.

"Can we look?" I asked.

"Stay by me," Druise said. "Have you a purse, or coin?"

"No."

"Good. Nothing to be stolen. Sorley?"

"Yes. But inside my belt."

Druise grunted approval, and we entered the rows of awned stalls. Everything from fruit to silk tunics was for sale. "This isn't all made here, surely?" I asked.

"Sylana is a trading hub now. Some of this comes from far beyond Casil, and I'd guess there are things here which originated in Varsland, or Sorham." Sorley stopped to look at a *xache* set, exquisitely carved. "That will be walrus ivory from Varsland, like your father's."

The stall holder began to praise its beauty, in good Casilan. Sorley shook his head, smiling, and then reached out to pick up something else. He turned to me. In his hand was a small blue cat, crouched, its tail wrapped around its front paws. "Cillian's cat."

It did look remarkably like Pangur, who kept my father company in his library at the *Ti'ach* most nights. Sorley bargained with the seller, good-naturedly. Once it was paid for, Druise slid it into his belt pouch. No one was going to try to rob Druise, armed with both knife and short sword.

"Don't tell me I paid too much," Sorley said, as we moved away.

"Would I know? But probably." Druise grinned. "I will do the bargaining in Casil."

As we moved through the crowd, I noticed eyes turning our way. "Why are people looking at me?"

"Not you," Druise said, after a glance. "They have not seen many men with hair like Sorley's."

"So not many traders from the north yet?" I asked.

"Nyle's been coming for four years now," Sorley said. "I'd guess they see two or three ships a year, no more. Perhaps it's just I don't look like a trader." He glanced at the sun. "We should go to the harbour soon."

"Look here first," Druise said. We crossed to the stall he'd indicated. Bowls and cups in deep blues and greens, some touched with silver or gold, stood in shallow boxes. Fleeces draped the shelves between them, and the floor of the stall.

"Oh." Sorley pointed. Druise nodded.

"Or that one." He indicated a bowl on a higher shelf.

The vendor's eyes had narrowed, seeing Druise in his uniform. He gave Sorley an assessing look, noting, I was sure, the quality of his tunic and belt. His eyes dropped to Sorley's hands, his clean, even fingernails, the lack of any calluses except those of a musician. "My lord? You are interested?"

"I might be. You can pack for sea travel?"

They discussed shipment, and then price, for some long minutes, Druise adamant in the bargaining. I turned away to look at the market. Further down the aisle I saw silk scarves; I'd suggest we go there next. The stall-holder was a woman, her face wrinkled and brown. I glanced at the next stall: another woman, this one younger. The man who had sold Sorley the cat had been grey-haired, as was the glass dealer. I took a step away. Without turning, Druise put a hand on my arm.

Boys younger than my brother loaded carts or carried goods. Women of all ages shopped, and some stalls had girls with grandmothers or aunts. But I saw no man without grey hair, or an infirmity of some kind. Where were the young men? Out fishing, or at the fields and the warehouses?

"Immediately, my lord," the stall holder was saying. The transaction complete, Sorley turned to me.

"The harbour now?"

"Is the market here all day?"

"I would think so."

"Then can we come back later? I'd like to look at those scarves, but we don't have to do it now." We left the square. Partly it had been the heat radiating off the stone surrounding us which had made me reluctant to stay. It would be cooler at the harbour, I hoped.

"Are you really taking those bowls to Casil and then home?" I asked as we walked. Sweat trickled down my back and soaked my armpits.

"No. I had them sent to the fort. I'll ask the commander to send them on the next ship west."

"You bought both? Were they horribly expensive?"

"Not for what they are. And anyhow," he grinned, "I haven't paid for them, not completely. I'm not carrying that much coin. I sent the boxes to the fort under Cillian's name. He'll have to pay the balance."

Sorley's return to his usual equanimity reassured me. My mother's anger was, mostly, mercurial. Maybe her rage of the last day would have passed by the time we returned, the shift I had felt this morning no more than a ship righting itself after the shock of a strong wave.

A breeze caught my hair as we grew closer to the water, cooling me a little. We walked along the stone jetty to where the Marai ship lay moored. Both Nyle and Bjørn were on deck, along with a few other men. The ship, riding easily and high on the ripple of the harbour's waters, wasn't carrying cargo.

"You look hot, princess," Bjørn said to me, after greetings were exchanged. "May I offer you what shade we have, and a drink?"

"Gwenna, please. Both would be welcome."

"There are things we should talk about," Sorley said. "Is there somewhere we could go away from the ship?"

Bjørn scanned the buildings along the harbour wall. "No reputable place will allow the princess in, even escorted. The places that will, I would not take her to. But the harbourmaster has a garden, and perhaps he will allow us to sit in it."

He gave instructions to the men to guard the ship. On the market side of the harbour, we stopped outside a building. Nyle ducked into the dark interior, and after a few minutes of discussion in a language I didn't know, he came out again. "The garden is ours, and his wife will bring us drinks. Come."

The garden was walled and shaded by overhead trellises and vines. Chairs stood around a table, and I took the one in the deepest shade at Nyle's insistence. He sat beside me. "Where is your friend?"

"Lynthe? She is inspecting the Casilani defences with my mother." I smiled, wrinkling my nose. "Soldiers. And my brother is no doubt at the infirmary with Gnaius, my father's physician. Or in the town, talking to the doctors here. But tell me, Nyle, how is your family? They were good to me, the days I spent with them."

He told me of Hairle, married now at twenty, to my relief. Little Lairís was doing well at the *Ti'ach*, her voice a marvel. Bjørn and Sorley chatted, and I tried to listen to that conversation as well. We were brought a jug of water, with the juice of a fruit I didn't recognize mixed into it, and some little pastries. I smiled my thanks to the women as they withdrew.

"Nyle," Sorley said, "what of last year's harvest?"

"A good one, by all I heard. But that is all I know."

"And why should you know more, Nyle?" Bjørn asked. "Neither you nor I are inheriting Gundarstorp; we are sons of the wrong mothers. But I suppose my father wants to talk of sheep and barley. Gwenna, are you rested? Shall we look at the ships? The breeze will be stronger at the end of the garden."

Well done, I thought. I let him help me up. A stone path led to the wall, and a view over the jetties.

"Well?" I said softly in Casilan. "Why are you here, Bjørn of Varsland?" I kept my eyes on the ships, and the men moving between them, sorting out warehousemen and carters from crew.

"I am not here as a prince," he said, his Casilan nearly fluent. He'd been *Ti'ach* educated, after all. "As you must know. To look for trade opportunities, to buy goods."

"Does Nyle know who you are?"

"No. I am his nephew who is older than he. A joke among the men. Two of them are mine, but they say nothing. You are very interested in the harbour, Gwenna of Ésparias. What are you seeing?"

A lack of young men, but I wasn't going to say that to the prince of Varsland. "The ships are different than the ones which come to Ésparias."

"The Western Sea is rougher. These are coastal traders." He pushed his hair, longer than mine, off his neck. "You go to Casil for the young Emperor's crowning, is that right?"

"Yes. No one from Varsland is going?"

He shrugged, smiling. "My brother the king said no. We are not subject to them, unlike your country, or even Linrathe."

"Do you agree with your brother?"

He looked down at me—he was half a head taller than I, and I was a tall woman—a wry expression on his face. "Rarely."

"Perhaps you could send a present? A token of Varsland's regard?"

He studied me. "Perhaps I should. What is Ésparias sending?"

"Fine metalwork," I said, "Buckles and cloak-clasps, delicately worked in gold and enamelled."

"I see. Do you have a suggestion?"

I did, as it happened. "There is a *xache* set at one of the stalls in the market, of walrus ivory, exquisitely made."

A man shouted Bjørn's name from the quayside. He answered in Marái'sta, a quick exchange about someone come to discuss prices. "Nyle," Bjørn called to where Sorley and his brother sat, "you are needed at the ship. You know what we agreed to offer. No more."

"That," he said, as Nyle slipped out the gate to the waiting man, "was fortuitous. Shall we join the lord Sorley, and your guard?"

"Captain Druisius is a trusted confidante of my father's, as well as my guard."

"I see. Does he speak Marái'sta? We should not speak Casilan, so close to the house."

"No. Linrathan, though." We took our places at the table.

"Bjørn, are you endangering Nyle and the others through unsanctioned trade?" Sorley asked, as soon as we were seated.

"No. I am buying silk and spices, nothing prohibited in the agreement made when Varsland withdrew from Ésparias and Linrathe. Who wrote that, by the way? I would have expected your hand in it."

"I was busy with other duties," Sorley said. "The Procurator, with the help of a Linrathan man called Randall, drafted it. Possibly the *Princip* at the time, Casyn, advised on it. But the earls who were regent for Bryngyl ratified it, did they not, later?"

"They did. I am not arguing it is unfair. But it is—incomplete?"

"Leaving you free to trade for luxury goods," I said. "You should be pleased."

"I am," he said, his teeth flashing white. "But here is something curious. There are horses here I like; finer boned than ours. I thought to take a stallion back, to see what foals from a cross with our mares are like. But the prices are very high, and there are few available, even yearlings. Casil wants them all, I am told. I wonder why?"

"Is this new? Casil's demand for the horses?" I asked.

"It appears so. I was told that last year I could have had my pick. But of course this could just be a ploy to empty the purse of this ignorant northman."

"Maybe," Druise said. I recognized his tone; he knew something. Missing young men. A demand for horses. The unrest in the east. *Close to war*, my father had said.

"I think you see this gameboard too," Bjørn said, switching back to Marai'ista. "Does it affect the one we play?"

"I don't know," Sorley said. In Linrathan, he added, "But the fort's commander will not argue if I invite my son to dine with me, and he and the Procurator have done their duty by us. We will not be their guests tonight."

"Thank you," Bjørn said. He grinned again. "I will forgo Sylana's pleasures for one night to dine with my father and the prince of Ésparias. It will be an honour."

I looked away, over the wall to the water. "What is being loaded onto the ships returning to Casil?" I asked.

"Salt. Grain, from the stores. Other foodstuffs. But that is not unusual; Casil has many mouths to feed," Druise said. "It is time to return. Your mother will be done her inspection, and you want to stop in the market again, yes?"

"And I should go back to the ship, to see what price Nyle offered for the silk," Bjørn said. "I will see you tonight, my lady Gwenna."

We were twenty paces from the harbourmaster's house before Druise spoke. "I am not sure I trust him."

"Travelling in disguise as he is," Sorley answered, "it's hard to know what is the act, and what is real. Did he say anything to you, Gwenna?"

"Only that he often disagrees with the King."

"Let's see what Cillian thinks," Sorley said. "They've exchanged letters for some years."

"Why wasn't he educated at our *Ti'ach*? Especially with you posing as his father?"

"For two reasons. One is that his aptitude was for numbers, so the *Ti'ach na Asgaill* was the better fit. But we also thought that if someone came looking for the missing prince of Varsland, our *Ti'ach* would be the first place they looked. We were his mother's friends. Are we going to look at silk scarves?"

"I have no money," I pointed out, accepting the change of subject, "and you spent all yours on the glass."

"Sorley did," Druise said. "I have money. You will pay me back, yes?"

"Of course," I said. "I can't leave you without the means to dice, can I?"

I bought three scarves in the end: one of a brilliant blue for Lynthe; a shimmering green for my mother, and a red one for myself—and I did the bargaining. At the fort, I left the blue and red ones in our room, and, carrying the green one and the coins for Druise, made my way to my parent's room.

The doors that opened onto a shaded porch were open, and I could hear Sorley's voice. I stepped out. Both my parents sat on wicker chairs. My father held the blue cat in his hand. "From a country east of Casil, I was told," Sorley was saying.

"It's charming. Thank you, my lord Sorley." He took Sorley's hand, kissing the back of it.

"I brought you this." I handed my mother her scarf. She smiled, genuinely enough, I thought, running the cloth through her fingers.

"It's lovely, Gwenna. The same green as my court clothes, I think."

"I hope so." I poured myself a drink and sat down. My parents seemed relaxed together, my mother's anger calmed.

"Has the glass arrived?" Sorley pulled another chair closer so he was in the shade.

"Some time ago. I paid the bill," my father said, sounding amused.

"I'll give you the money later. You won't see them until we're home again, but both pieces are exquisite." He began to describe the bowls.

"Where's Lynthe?" I mouthed to my mother.

"I left her at the stables."

Of course. A daughter of the grassland villages, where they did almost nothing but raise and train horses, Lynthe never turned down a chance to discuss bloodlines and breeding.

"Sorley," I said. "The glass is lovely, but have you told my parents you invited Bjørn to dinner?"

"Just Bjørn?" my mother inquired.

"Yes." We were speaking Linrathan, but even so, Sorley dropped his voice. "He is coming as my son, but our conversation will be—otherwise."

My father had been running a finger over the blue cat. He put it on the table beside him. "What did you learn?"

"They are here to buy silk and spices, he says, which he is free to do. He had some interesting observations about horses, or the lack of them."

"And young men." My father arched an eyebrow. "Bjørn didn't say that," I added. "But there are none in the market, and few on the docks."

"Two-thirds of the garrison here was recalled a few weeks ago," my mother said. "When I asked why, I was told it was for the control of crowds during Alekos's investiture and the celebrations. Which I do not believe."

"The situation in Qipërta is worse than is being admitted?" my father asked.

"I couldn't determine that. The commander deflected those questions. Did Druise learn more last night, Sorley?"

"He didn't say. But he's not sure he trusts Bjørn."

"What does he know of him?" The question was from my father. Sorley's brow furrowed.

"Only what he's deduced, over the years: that he was a source of information, and a messenger for us, sometimes. If he's learned more, or thought it, he hasn't told me."

"Nor me," my mother said. "Gwenna, what do you think of Bjørn?" She sounded like she had years before, teaching me how to interpret parts of the *danta*: focused, intent.

"He's bright," I said, "and subtle. And he may not like his brother much."

That caught my father's attention. "What proof have you?"

I told him what Bjørn had said. "I had the feeling he'd like to go to Casil, but Bryngyl has forbidden it."

The three of them exchanged a look. "Not again," my mother said.

"The gods forbid," Sorley said. "But I've heard nothing of this at all. Not a whisper."

"Gwenna," my father said, "tell me how and when Bjørn said this." He listened, a reflective look slowly appearing. "I see," he said. "I want you to consider something, *mo nihéan*. Bjørn may be shaping his story to gain your sympathy and your trust. He is an attractive man, and you are a young woman with knowledge and influence. He was attentive? Asking for advice, perhaps?"

My cheeks burned. "Yes." I hadn't considered this. "I thought he was serious."

"And perhaps he was. But perhaps not."

"I am swayed toward not," my mother said. "Druise's instinct was to protect his Kitten from a tomcat."

"*Mathàir!*" I said in pretend shock, hoping for a smile. But I didn't get one. She was different, somehow. Not angry, but there seemed to be a determination about her, and with it a distancing. Not coldness, but clarity.

She got up. "Come with me, Gwenna?" I followed her from the balcony. She closed the door behind us. "Druise's instincts are good. Don't discount them. He likes Lynthe. So do I."

"You're all soldiers."

"Yes," she said. "We are. And Druise and I see the potential in her, as an officer, and someone who could advise her brother in military matters in years to come, just as you will in a diplomatic role." She did smile then, a little wryly. "It isn't just the theoretical future we concern ourselves with, you know. But now, would you find Lynthe, and bring her to see your father? He wants to speak to her."

"About what?"

"Secrets."

"Which ones?" Had Sorley told him she had guessed their relationship? I thought he probably had. But surely he wouldn't talk to her about that, when he had never with me.

My mother turned her head, looking out at my father. "Whatever he chooses to reveal. His is still the directing mind, Gwenna." She smiled, distantly, and in her eyes were memories. "Long ago, when we were prisoners before our trial, I asked him what all the facts and ideas he was considering looked like in his mind. He said it was like a map, with lines between the ideas, and things he couldn't yet connect off to the side. None of us can see that map but him." She stopped. "Unless you can?"

I could, but only the map he had described to me, drawn for me—in words alone—so precisely, once I'd turned seventeen. I didn't know what happened when you changed part of it. I could surmise; I could weigh likelihoods. Nothing more. "No," I said. "Not fully."

"Then let us hope," she said, "he is with you for a long time yet."

Chapter 22

~FATHER~

"LYNTHE. THANK YOU FOR COMING." I smiled, hoping to put her at her ease. I had had a long talk with Lena earlier, taking advantage of our time alone together. "Are you feeling like a cadet summoned to her officer?"

"A little, sir."

"Please sit. Both of you: there is nothing I am going to say that Gwenna doesn't know." I waited as they pulled chairs close. "I am taking on a role here which is rare for me," I continued, choosing my words carefully. "I am not your officer, Lynthe, nor your teacher. But I am Callan's son, and now the oldest of his line. By the Empress's decree, we—Gwenna, and I, and you—are royal, and royalty confers responsibility." Lena had suggested this approach; Lynthe, she thought, was sensitive to her position as the *Princip's* sister, a position she felt constrained her, but gave her no actual role to fill. Lena had had thoughts on that, too, but they were not for now.

Her eyes flickered at the word 'royal'. "Sir?"

"One of those responsibilities—one of the hardest—is not revealing truths we know. Keeping secrets. Tonight we have a dinner guest." I paused, to find the right tone of authority. "There will be secrets revealed, more than one. I must know before I can permit you to attend that no word of what you might learn tonight will be discussed with anyone except those of us who are here now, excluding Colm and Apulo, until I tell you differently."

"Not Faolyn? Or my mother?"

"Not until I say you are free to discuss it, no."

"But—" Confusion in her eyes. "My mother is my commanding officer."

"She is. And that is so when this exact situation arose, as we knew it would, there would be no conflict. Talyn has said nothing to you?"

"No."

I smiled, broadly, to change the mood. "She did say she was leaving this to me. All you need to say to her—in private, of course—is that I forbade you to speak of it."

"I see." She was relaxing, thankfully. "And if my brother the *Princip* asks?"

"Is that likely?"

Her mouth quirked. "No. He might ask what the latest furnishings in the palace are like."

"He is an ideal *Princip* for a time of peace," I said. "But he cannot know, either."

I saw the indecision on her face, doubt replacing the brief amusement. "Faolyn is a surrogate *Princip* in a way, isn't he?" she said finally. "In your place."

"I declined the title."

"You shouldn't have, if I may say so, sir. Ésparias remained at peace. All your diplomatic skills would have been valuable; my grandfather could have advised you on what military matters there were."

Why would she see it differently? She had been a child when the attempt had been made on my life. "I was a focus of discontent, blamed for my father's death and more. Ésparias needed Casyn's known and steady leadership, not a stranger from Linrathe."

"There have been rumours you favour Linrathe over Ésparias." That, I thought, took courage. Her gaze didn't waver.

"Lynthe," Gwenna said, barely above a breath.

"Is there evidence to support those rumours?" I asked.

"Not that I am aware of," Lynthe said. "Will you tell my mother the secrets from tonight?"

"Perhaps. If I believe she needs to know."

She nodded an acknowledgment. "You are asking for loyalty to you over the oath I have sworn to Ésparias."

"The two are not incompatible," I said. Of all the chances I had taken over the years, this might be the most dangerous. Lynthe was an Ésparian officer. Nor did I know how committed she was to Gwenna. But I needed to trust Lena's judgment, for many reasons.

"But not identical, either. There is more to you than it seems, isn't there?" I didn't answer, and the hint of smile I allowed would have been missed by most.

"If I agree," Lynthe asked, "does this mean Gwenna can share some of what troubles her?"

"It does," I said. Her concern for my daughter reassured me. "Within reason. Gwenna will decide what that means."

"And my mother is aware you might ask this of me?"

"Yes." The questions were a good sign. She was thinking, not accepting—or rejecting—without probing.

"And the major? Lena?"

"Yes."

"Then you have my word, sir." I heard Gwenna take a breath.

"Thank you, Lynthe." I smiled again. "This is a family dinner tonight. You don't need to wear uniform."

"What is it I am to learn?"

"You will find out tonight."

Two tiny lines appeared between her eyes. "You're not telling me?"

"He wants to see how well you can mask surprise," Gwenna said. "Don't you, *Athàir*? It's a skill. You've been warned there will be something. Now you wait to find out what."

Bjørn arrived in the early evening. He carried a long box, which he set against the wall. "I am honoured to be here," he said, smiling.

"Sorley's son will always be welcome," I said. Chairs were offered and taken, and wine served. We spoke of trade and ships, of the river journey and Bjørn's years at the *Ti'ach na Asgaill*, as Apulo and a servant of the fort served the food. Bjørn was easy company, engaging Colm and Lynthe in conversation but equally interested in what Lena had to say. Druisius watched him, and said little.

Tiny tarts finished the meal, rich with egg and honey. When only crumbs remained, Colm stood. "May I be excused, *Athàir*? I have a treatise I would like to read tonight."

Gnaius had not dined with us, but with the fort's physician. With Colm gone, nothing prevented Bjørn's identity from being revealed, at least once the dishes were cleared. Apulo had his part in my network of information, but not at this level.

The last tray of plates had gone, and another flagon of wine put on the table. "Two hours," I said to Apulo. "Sorley or Druisius will find you, if I need you earlier." The door closed.

I straightened in my chair, resting my hands on the table. The mood in the room changed.

"Bjørn of Varsland," I said. "Be welcome."

"Thank you." No deference in Bjørn's voice. "And to you, Lord Sorley, for making this meeting possible." Lord Sorley? The formality was unexpected.

"I may have a favour to ask. A delicate one," he went on. "But there are questions I must ask, before I can decide on my actions. Am I free to speak openly?"

"You are."

Bjørn's gaze swept the room, stopping at Druise. "Bjørn," Sorley said, as the two men regarded each other, "if you for a moment doubt Druisius's loyalty, I'll regret having sent the dog back north, and not you."

A bark of laughter from the man who wasn't his son. "I was pleased when you wrote to tell me she was safely home," he said. "It still surprises me that a sheepdog can make such a journey across all that wild land on its own. But I have no doubts of the captain's loyalty, Sorley. I was only wondering how to couch my question."

"What is it you want to know?" Druise asked.

"You are Casilani, and you were a guard. Do you believe the men of this garrison were sent home to patrol the streets, or to keep order at the port?"

"Maybe the port. But probably not, unless the usual guard were needed elsewhere."

"You have heard the rumours of war in the east?"

"We all have," Lena said. "The Lieutenant," she nodded at Lynthe, "told me this afternoon the remaining troops here are talking of little else."

"And recalling troops suggests a shortage of men?"

"Or a greater threat than expected."

"Would you expect an advance on Casil this autumn?" Bjørn asked me.

"No," Lena interrupted. "Qipërta is offering a marriage alliance, and those negotiations will take time. Were I the Empress, I would choose to investigate the possibility for many weeks, well into winter. Nor is the unrest close to Casil. My guess is the recalled troops will be sent to strengthen the force on that border, to show Qipërta what they are up against: an intimidation, not an engagement."

Bjørn leant back. He sucked on his bottom lip. "An astute analysis. So you think no winter war, Major?"

"No."

"Captain?"

"I agree with the major. I have fought there. The land is high and broken. Winter will be for envoys and threats."

"So. Were I to offer men, the new Emperor might have a use for them in the spring?"

"Is this your idea, or Bryngyl's?" I asked.

"Mine."

"May I ask why?"

Bjørn leant forward, raising the wine flask. I declined. The others, except Lynthe, accepted. He was stalling, but perhaps only to gather his thoughts.

"Men feel constrained," he said finally. "Casil's ships and Casil's forts keep us north. We can sail west, searching for the unknown lands. Or I can take men's restlessness and energy to Casil itself, and expend it there."

"But if the Emperor does not want your men?" Druisius asked. "Then what will you do with them? You have prepared them for blood and battle, and if they do not get it, they will be discontent. Angry."

Bjørn raised his cup to his lips, unhurriedly. I watched his hand as he put it down again: his fingers held it a little too tightly. "We are called the Marai, the sea-farers. But we like rivers too, and north of the river that brings us here there are others leading east. If this new Emperor does not need my men, we will go exploring."

"The songs say those rivers lead only to ice and death," Sorley said.

Bjørn shrugged. "The songs say there is a land of flowers and wine to the west, but my uncle never found it for all his years of trying."

"And because he did not," Gwenna said, "he returned to depose his brother. You too disagree with your brother, don't you? Have you similar plans?"

Someone—Lena?—audibly took a breath. "My Prince of Varsland," I said, "forgive my daughter. She has spoken impulsively."

"But were not her thoughts also yours?" Bjørn said calmly. He stood, holding up a hand to stop anyone else from following his lead. "Let me show you something."

He knelt by the long box he had brought. Undoing the latch, he raised the lid to take out a sword, its hilt worked with animal heads and intricate designs on the blade. Balancing it on his hands, he turned back to us. "This is my present to Alekos. The sword of the second son of our line."

"Fritjof's sword?" Lena's voice was tight with anger.

"Fritjof's sword. I do not want it. He killed my father and made my mother flee Varsland in fear of her life. I thought of giving it to the waters, but instead I am sending it far away from our land, to where it has no meaning but one: an offered sword."

"An offered sword," I said, "has many meanings. Are you offering hirelings, or allegiance, Prince Bjørn?"

"I have no power to offer Casil anything but hirelings."

"Have you even that?" Sorley leant forward.

"I will convince my brother. He has expressed concern about our restless young men."

"Were this unrest in the east to become a war, would Casil recall its men from Ésparias?" Gwenna asked. Her thoughts had followed, or perhaps preceded, mine.

A smile flickered on Bjørn's lips. "And without Casil's troops?"

"Ésparias—and Linrathe—are vulnerable," Lynthe said. "But by offering your men to Casil, recalling those troops might be avoided."

Bjørn inclined his head to her, smiling. "Do you see now where my allegiance lies, my lady Gwenna?"

"I do. I regret my earlier imprudent thought, Prince Bjørn."

She glanced at me. Hoping, I knew, that she had redeemed her mistake. She hadn't, but I would not reveal that now.

"What is the favour you want?" I asked.

"Only that you take the sword, and a letter, to Casil. To the Emperor."

"Simply that? No recommendation on how the Emperor should respond?"

Bjørn spread his hands wide. "I leave that to you, Cillian. You decide if my offer serves our common cause and is worthy of your support." He stood. "I will say good night now. You sail tomorrow? The letter will be delivered to the ship."

Sorley rose. "I'll come with you. Nyle invited me to hear a *danta* one of the men knows, something he hadn't heard before. I said I would, if possible."

Gwenna reached for her wine. She knew she had made a mistake. "I cannot pretend," I said slowly, "that I was expecting his offer. Why have we not heard of unrest in Varsland, I wonder?"

"If it increased over the winter, is it possible the messages simply didn't reach Sorley before we left?" Gwenna suggested. "Michan also told me he'd heard nothing from the north, when we were talking about the decrease in luxury goods being brought to the trading port. He—we—wondered if it had been a bad winter there, heavy snows and a late breakup of the ice."

"It might explain why Bjørn's ship is here so late," Lena said.

Druise stood. "I will go talk to soldiers, see what they have heard."

"Lynthe," Lena said, also standing, "I imagine you have many questions. Come with me, and I'll try to answer them."

"Thank you, *käresta*." The click of the door closing sounded loudly in the still of the room. I met my daughter's eyes.

Chapter 23

~DAUGHTER~

"YOU'VE BEEN CRYING," LYNTHE SAID, almost as soon as I entered our room. "Was your father so harsh?"

Tears rose again. "No. He never is." I sat on the bed.

"Then why are you crying?" She slipped an arm around me. I leant against her, just a little, glad of the comfort.

"I was so stupid. I know better. And not just because I'm an envoy." I sniffed, using the heel of a hand to wipe the tears away. "What did my mother tell you?"

"Enough, I think. That you—all of you—have been planning for what happens if Casil leaves. An alliance among Ésparias and Linrathe and Varsland, through marriages and trade and more, so there isn't a war. But this could be seen as treason, so it is done secretly."

I nodded. "Bjørn has been part of it, but not his brother."

"Nor mine," Lynthe said. "But I understand why. He's too fond of the Casilani. I think it's a good idea, though. I don't really like some of the changes."

She'd never said. But on reflection, why would she? A controversial opinion for the *Princip's* sister to hold, and she'd had no idea of how I felt.

"So do you see? I might—I did—jeopardize all the work my father and Sorley and his brother have done in Varsland, because . . . " I didn't want to say the words again. Especially to Lynthe.

"Because?"

I got up, pacing the room. "Because he unsettles me, and I wanted to do the same to him."

"Unsettles you how?"

"How do you think?" I couldn't look at her.

"Ah. Well, you're not likely to see him again."

Wasn't I? Not soon, if he was bringing men to fight for Casil next year. And he was probably married, with children. Anyhow—

"But I thought I was in love with you," I blurted.

"Oh." I still wasn't looking at her. Silence, for a moment. "Did you tell your father that?"

"Not—directly."

"What does that mean?"

"He asked me if I'd said what I said partly because I was trying to impress you. I answered yes."

The bed creaked a little as she rose. Her arms went around me, and I turned to bury my head in her neck.

"You don't have to try to impress me," she murmured. "You have since the first days I guarded you."

I tightened my throat muscles, trying not to sob. Unsuccessfully. "But you don't love me."

"Did I say that?" She kissed my cheek. "But, Gwenna, even if I do—you have to marry, don't you?"

"No." I pulled back a little so I could look at her. "I don't. *Mathàir* says I should have children, so there is an heir, but I don't need to marry. No one did in Ésparias, until she married *Athàir* so I was legitimate in Linrathe."

The two tiny lines appeared between her eyes again. "So you can behave like any woman of Ésparias?"

"Yes. No. I don't know." I went to the table by the wall, taking off my earrings to give my hands something to do, and my mind time to find some clarity. "My parents have always said I would not be required to make a political marriage. Nor would Colm be, or, had she lived, Lianë."

"But wouldn't it be part of the plans your mother told me about?"

"You'd think so." I undid the clasp holding back my hair. "Ruar's choice of Helvi was entirely political, and Faolyn's to Siusàn was—fortuitous. But I am not expected to do the same."

"Faolyn and Siusàn aren't part of the conspiracy, your mother tells me."

"It's not a conspiracy; it's a contingency."

"Would Casil see the difference?" She sat on the bed again. "That was rhetorical, Gwenna; I know they wouldn't. I understand why my brother can't know. I wouldn't trust him either. I understand why this is all secret. And I am—" she stopped, searching for a word, I thought, "honoured, that your father—your parents—have trusted me."

"Because you are family," I said, "and because you will advise Faolyn some day, probably."

"And for another reason."

I frowned. "What?"

"If you marry Alekos, there has to be someone of our generation in Ésparias who is part of it."

It isn't just the theoretical future we concern ourselves with, my mother had said. Contingencies, for a very real possibility. Had she pointed this out to Lynthe, made the suggestion? Did Lynthe think this was her responsibility, now she knew the plans?

"I might not marry him."

"You'd rather marry the prince of Varsland?" Lynthe said. "Gwenna, I do know you. When have you ever avoided duty for your own pleasure? I think that whatever your mother tells you, if you see a political advantage to Ésparias in marrying Alekos, you will."

I wanted to deny it. I even opened my mouth to say 'no'. "I would help shape policy," I said instead. "And I would know Casil's plans long before they were implemented."

She smiled, but not with her eyes. "At least you like men."

In the morning, Lynthe was quiet as we washed and dressed. "Will you come with me to talk to your parents?" she asked abruptly, as I was tying back my hair.

"What about?" I said, through the pin between my teeth.

"You'll hear. I don't want to say it twice."

I knocked and heard my mother's 'come in'. They were dressed, breakfasting on triangles of bread and a dish of olives.

"Gwenna. Lynthe. What is it?" she asked.

"I would like to talk to you, Major," Lynthe said. "To both of you."

My father put down his tea. "This is something serious."

"Yes. I—" Lynthe swallowed and straightened, like a soldier reporting to her superior. "I wish to arrive in Casil as the major Lena's aide, not as a potential bride."

"May I ask why?"

"Men hold no attraction for me, sir. I would never choose to partner with one, not even to bear a child."

"You knew this before we left," my mother said.

"Yes. But Faolyn insisted I come. I never thought I would be seriously considered. But now—" She shook her head. "I want it to be clear." So she was free to take on a new role in Ésparias, as she had suggested yesterday?

My parents exchanged a look. "Never," my mother said, an undercurrent of anger in her voice, "would I ask that of someone. But I wish you had told us earlier."

"I am sorry, Major," Lynthe said. She'd paled at my mother's tone. I didn't understand the anger, but then, I didn't think I understood my mother at all any more.

"Better now than in Casil," my father said. "I will explain to the Empress, if an explanation is needed."

"You'll need to be in uniform when we arrive, Lieutenant," my mother said. "I am assigning you to be the close guard for Gwenna. Understood?"

"Yes, Major. Thank you."

In our own room, I confronted Lynthe. "Why didn't you say something before?"

"I thought I might not have been allowed to come. And I wanted to." She sat down to untie her shoes.

"Why?"

"Why what?"

"Why did you want to come?"

"To be with you. And to meet the Prince. If I hate Alekos, Gwenna, will you still marry him?"

"I might not even be chosen," I said. "He's going to make a political choice, and Ésparias just isn't that important."

"But if you are?"

"And you hate him?" I sat on the bed. "What are you asking, Lynthe?"

"I thought maybe I'd stay in Casil with you, as your personal guard, or something. If you marry him."

"Oh." I couldn't find words. "You would do that?"

"If you wanted me to." She didn't meet my eyes. This wasn't the brash and confident Lynthe I knew.

"Shall we wait to find out if it matters? Maybe I'll dislike him immediately, and that will be the end of it."

She nodded again. "I just wanted you to know."

I held out my arms. "Come here." But even as I pulled her close, confusion roiled inside. I thought she'd been offering to take on the responsibility I couldn't, if I stayed in Casil. Now she was asking to stay with me. This tacit admission of commitment was what I had wanted, had hoped for. So why did life seem more complicated than ever now?

Part II

> . . . your ambitions, follow them with hesitation and caution.
> C.P Cavafy

Chapter 24

~DAUGHTER~

I LAY ON MY STOMACH ON THE TABLE, the hands of the bath attendant working scented oils into my skin. Beside me, Lynthe was getting the same treatment. I relaxed under the skilled fingers, idly looking at the elaborate decoration of the room in the private palace baths.

We'd arrived two days ago, passing by the Pharos and into the quiet waters of the harbour. Buildings—mostly warehouses, Sorley told me—gleamed in the sunshine, and gulls wheeled and cried above the dozens of ships moored along the docks. The water, within the long arms of the sea walls, was still, but the docks were not. Men loaded and unloaded ships, transferring amphorae and barrels to carts and smaller vessels. Shouts blended with the lowing of oxen and the jangle of rigging in the breeze. "It's grown," my mother said, to no one in particular.

"Even since I was here," Sorley agreed. Colm stood with my father and Gnaius near the bow. Druisius was with them too: coming home for the first time since the year I was born. But he wasn't looking around, or not in the way I thought he would be. His eyes scanned the docks, constantly moving. What was he looking for?

Members of his family, I decided. They were traders; surely someone would be here at the waterfront, supervising a ship being loaded or unloaded. But he didn't seem to find anyone.

A smooth and confident official—he introduced himself, but his name passed me by—waited with three carriages and several carts for our baggage. My father left the ship first, as protocol required. I watched him stand at the top of the ramp for a minute, looking down. He took a breath, and then, with Apulo at his side and Druisius just behind him, descended. The official bowed. They spoke for a moment, before my father turned and beckoned to us.

After appropriate greetings and introductions—I would have to ask the man's name again, I realized, in case he was at some function or another—we divided ourselves among the carriages. Druise, uncharacteristically, insisted on being with my father. He laid a hand on my mother's arm, saying something very quietly. She nodded.

There was difficulty about Apulo: the official expecting him to stay to supervise the baggage and ride into Casil in the open cart. Calmly, my father explained he needed Apulo at his side. The other man gave in with a smile. Sorley joined me and Lynthe in our carriage, leaving the third to Gnaius, Colm and my mother.

As soon as we began to move, I asked, "Why was Druise so adamant about riding with *Athàir?*"

"Protocol," Sorley said. "The prince of Ésparias should have his personal bodyguard with him. Just as you have yours," he nodded at Lynthe, "and your brother his, although I think the official is confused as to who your mother is, exactly." He grinned. "They are not used to female soldiers here, except the horse archers. But I'm sure they've heard stories of Ésparias's women warriors."

"Should we have brought a guard for Colm?"

"Druise says he'll take care of it. Which means," he shrugged, "I'll be sleeping alone, if Druise is going to guard Colm at night."

Lynthe would be with me, and my mother's secca was always close at hand to protect my father. "And in the day?"

"He has connections among the guard still. Someone trustworthy will be assigned."

But last night, at dinner—served to us privately—Gnaius had made a proposal. "Once the formal introductions are made, and I would expect that to happen in the next day or two," he'd said, "perhaps Colm could join me at my home for a few weeks? He is an excellent student, and I would be glad to tutor him while you are here."

"Could I, *Athàir*?" Colm had pleaded. "I can learn so much, if you will allow it, and I won't have this chance again."

"Where is your home, Gnaius?" my father had asked.

"Outside the city. A day's journey south and east, in the countryside at the edge of a town. He will be safe with me, do not worry."

"Guards?" Druise queried.

"I have my own. And there is no need for anyone to know who my new student is."

I hadn't been surprised my parents had agreed, although I had thought my father reluctant. Colm had no interest in the palace and politics, and he was right: the opportunity to learn with a physician of Gnaius's stature was not something to be passed over. He would leave the palace in the morning. Tonight, we had a banquet to attend, where we would be formally presented to the Empress and her son.

The invitation had been delivered the previous evening. But this morning a second request had come: the Empress desired the presence of the prince of Ésparias and his daughter in the mid-afternoon. So I had needed the baths and their attendant services, because I must look my best.

I sat up at the attendant's request, shrugging on the robe she handed me. I moved to a low stool, and for the next twenty minutes she brushed and arranged my hair, pinning it high on my head. Lynthe watched, her own short hair a sleek cap, and laughed.

By the time I was dressed, in a tunic of fine grey wool trimmed with silk, and with the garnets in my ears, my throat was dry. Should I wear the pendant? I held it in my hand, trying to decide. I'd take it to my parents' room and ask.

"What a fuss," Lynthe said. She wouldn't accompany us; bringing a personal guard to the Empress's presence would be an insult of the highest order.

"Isn't it?" I grinned to hide my nervousness.

She got up to kiss me on the lips. "You do look appealing."

"I think that's the idea," I said drily. She gave a wry nod. I hadn't found a time to talk to her more about her conflicting messages about us. In truth, for all my diplomatic training, I couldn't think of a way to broach the subject. But I didn't think it mattered. Lynthe had told me enough. She wanted to be with me, and so I wasn't going to marry Alekos.

My father had been equally pampered and prepared. His hair and beard were trimmed and brushed, and dressed in the colours of our house, his black and silver cane polished, he looked again the prince I hadn't recognized when he'd ridden into Wall's End. He wasn't wearing his pendant, though.

"We're not wearing these?" I held it out.

"I think not. And perhaps simpler earrings, Gwenna? Tonight will be the time for the garnets and your pendant."

I had others; a woman in Berge made intricate ones of silver, and I'd brought several pairs. "I'll get them," Lynthe said. She unhooked the garnets, careful not to snag the wisps of hair which had escaped the pins. "I'll only be a minute."

We went over the protocols: three steps into the room, then kneel, head down, until I was instructed to rise. If she offered her hand, kiss it. Address

187

Eudekia as Empress, Alekos as Prince. Stand until offered a chair. I knew all this, but reviewing it was a reassurance.

Lynthe returned. I slipped the earrings into place just as a knock came on the door. "Our escort," my father said.

My mother had been sitting quietly; she'd been reading when I came in. "Nineteen years ago," she said to my father, coming over to him, "you were as nervous as Gwenna is now." She put a hand on his chest and kissed him.

"You told me an Emperor's blood ran in my veins. It was good advice, and prescient." He touched her shoulder. "I wonder if I will see as much change in Eudekia as she will in me."

"Or will she be just as alluring?" my mother murmured, as she went to open the door.

The guards matched their pace to my father's, along two corridors and through a large room where life-size figures adorned the walls, reading and playing music and dancing. At a pair of doors at its far end, one guard stepped forward and knocked. I felt my father's hand on my back, briefly.

The doors swung open, and we made the requisite three steps in and stopped. I had an impression of a seated woman, not as old as I had expected, before I dropped to my knees, eyes down. Beside me, my father simply stood. She would know he couldn't kneel.

She'd been alone, I realized, as I waited. Silence, except for my own breathing.

"Cillian," she said, her voice—what? Sad? Reflective?

"Eudekia," he replied. Not Empress? But then, she hadn't called him prince. I wanted to look up, but I didn't.

"This is your daughter? Stand, please, Gwenna." I straightened, raising my eyes. Not much older than my mother, I thought, with hair that must once have been as bright as new copper. She wore a green tunic, trimmed in a colour close to that of her hair, and a shawl of the same hues. She looked intelligent, and assured, and somehow sad.

"Do you hate me," she said, "for making you heir to Ésparias?"

I had rehearsed answers to many questions. This had not been one of them.

"It is all I have known, Empress. To hate it would be as pointless as hating that pieces on a *xache* board can move only in proscribed ways."

She laughed. It sounded genuine. "Definitely your daughter, Cillian. But I have been remiss. Please sit."

Her guards moved chairs, and I ensured my father was seated before I took mine. Eudekia was watching him, her expression thoughtful. "The years have not been kind to you."

"On the contrary." He seemed completely comfortable, as if he were picking up a conversation recently interrupted. "No life is without its sorrows, but I have been blessed, too. I have work which I both enjoy and is useful, a family whom I love, and a life that suits me. How many men can say the same?"

A smile played on her lips. "Or women? Is this what you aspire to as well, Gwenna? Your father's choice of how to order his blessings was instructive: work before family and personal pleasure."

"My parents—my family—have shown me the value of such a life," I said. "I am only a junior envoy, but my work is for my country's well-being. As Ésparias's heir, I must put it first."

"As I have," she said. "It is difficult, sometimes, to know what is best for our countries. You are lucky; you have a wise advisor in your father."

"And my mother, Empress."

She inclined her head slightly. "And your mother. How is she? I was forewarned of your family's loss, for which you have my condolences."

"Thank you," my father said. "Lena is well. She is here as the military representative of Ésparias, not—or not only—as my wife."

"The prince and the soldier," she said, smiling. I couldn't help but flick a glance at my father.

"Lena was a soldier long before you made me a prince," he said, "and it was her arrow that ended the war, not my advice on tactics."

"And yet your daughter has chosen to follow your career, and not her mother's. Why is that?"

"Envoys and officers share training until we are sixteen, Empress," I replied. "But as an envoy, I see—or will see, over the years—all aspects of my country; where its revenue comes from, and what pressures taxes put on our villages. I will develop trade agreements and set tariffs. These are, I believe, all things a country's leader must understand."

"Do they not also need to understand war?"

"Yes, Empress. But I believe it is easier to find good military advisors than ones with a thorough understanding of the people and their concerns."

She nodded. "You play *xache*. Can you best your father?"

"I have forced a draw, once or twice. I have never won." And only since his fall. A concern, but not one I would speak of.

Her only response was an arch of one groomed eyebrow. She returned her attention to my father, asking about Colm, and then Sorley. Surreptitiously, I watched them both. They spoke of many things, often without explanation of events. Clearly each knew a lot about the other's life. It disturbed me; I felt—exposed.

He spoke of the schools, their success in bringing the writings and philosophies of Casil and Heræcria to Ésparias, and their introduction further north. As he talked, easily, I began to understand, or to think I did. I schooled my face to reflect interest and said nothing.

"I look forward," the Empress said, after a few more minutes, "of returning to this discussion when my son is present. The idea of sending teachers to the provinces, rather than bringing their sons or daughters here has some merit. Cillian, will you stay a minute? I will have a guard escort Gwenna back to her room."

To my surprise, she rose, gesturing me to walk beside her to the door. "Has it occurred to you to change the rules, so the pieces on a *xache* board may move as you choose?" she murmured in my ear.

My breath caught. "Then it would not be *xache*, but something new," I murmured back. "With whom would I play it?"

"With at least one other who had agreed to the modification. Then it might spread, to two or three, and then more, and become something new."

"Would I dare change the rules of a game as venerable as *xache*?" I asked. "Surely it would be a presumption, Empress." My heart was drumming in my ears.

She smiled. "But perhaps your father would not see it that way?" A movement of her hand dismissed me. The guard opened the door. I stepped out into the corridor.

"Your rooms, my lady?" he asked.

I forced a smile. "My parents' rooms, I think. My mother will be waiting to hear what the Empress wore, and her jewels." He smiled back and escorted me to the appropriate door.

She wasn't in their rooms, but as I didn't really want to talk to her, that was of no concern. I poured a little wine, watered it well, and considered what the Empress had said. We had not been talking about *xache*, I was sure. *Spread to two or three and become something new.* Something new, like a western alliance? Her next words, in that context, had been a threat.

Only one other of us had ever exchanged more than a few words with Eudekia. I went in search of Sorley. But I couldn't find him, or Druise: perhaps they'd gone to the baths, or even out into the city. I stood in the corridor, undecided. Perhaps I should talk to my father when he returned from the Empress. A door opened further down the hall, and a young woman stepped out. She looked at me curiously.

"Hello," she called. "Are you lost?"

"No," I said, "I was looking for a member of our party; this is his room, but he isn't here. But thank you for your concern."

She came toward me. Dark haired, shorter than me, richly dressed, I noted. The older woman with her bore a strong resemblance; I guessed her to be her mother, or aunt. Both had scarves over their hair, and leggings under their tunics.

"I am Dalphe of Sylana," the young woman said, "and I think you are Gwenna of Ésparias, am I right?"

"You are."

"We have been waiting for you to arrive. No formal introductions to the Prince could be made until we—all the candidates for his bride—were here. But now they can," she finished, clearly pleased.

"Tonight," I said, "we were told."

She smiled, her eyes full of pleasure. "Yes, tonight. But why are you alone? Where is your chaperone?" She indicated the older woman. "My mother, Faria."

"My mother," I said, after I had made my greeting, "is also the military envoy for Ésparias, and I believe she is attending to her duties." Surely I was not expected to be chaperoned or guarded every moment of the day?

Dalphe did not hide her surprise. "The military envoy! But she is the wife of a prince."

"But also a senior officer in our army," I said, keeping my voice light. "A soldier since she was eighteen."

"How . . . unusual," Dalphe murmured. "I must go; I am late for an appointment. Perhaps we can talk again tonight?"

"I look forward to it," I said. They turned in the opposite direction. I began to walk back to my room. How often, I wondered, would I have to explain my soldier mother? *When I was eighteen, I made decisions which helped save this land.* The remembered argument reverberated. She had not wanted my father to come to Casil, worried for his health. She had thought me capable to be alone here. Perhaps I wouldn't ask Sorley what he thought of Eudekia's words; perhaps I wouldn't ask anyone. I would navigate these waters myself, I decided, as I opened my door, ignoring the other memory: *You are not the Empress's equal, mo nihéan.*

Four hours later, we gathered again in my parents' room, awaiting our escort to the banquet. Four of us in our finest clothes; three in uniform. Apulo handed a small vial to Druisius.

"In wine, in two hours, if I cannot."

Druise slipped it into a belt pouch. "If Cillian must wait to be presented, sooner than two hours."

"I was assured that would not happen," my father said. Druise grunted.

"If no one has bribed the *senescali*, perhaps."

Lynthe had had some interesting things to tell me, after she'd returned to our room. Druisius had taken her and my mother on a tour of the palace, ostensibly to show them the defences, but also to acquaint them with the passages and staircases that the guards and servants used as shortcuts from one part of the palace to another, and out into the forum and the Arénas. As they'd explored, he'd told them what he'd heard from his contacts among the guards: we were the last of the summoned guests to arrive, and no formal introduction of the potential brides to Alekos had yet been made. Resentment at us simmered among the other retinues.

A rap at the door announced the guard. Apulo opened it. My father turned to us. "You are ready?"

"I suppose," my mother said.

I fell into step beside my father: we would lead. Colm walked on his other side, befitting his rank as heir after me. Then Druise, to support my father if needed, my mother and Lynthe following. Sorley, dressed in the green and grey of Gundarstorp, bringing Linrathe's greetings, was last.

Seemingly endless corridors, and then wide doors were swung open, and ahead of us was a large room, busy with people—almost all of whom turned to look at us. The noise in the room had been considerable; it dipped almost to silence, and then rose again, with a different tone.

One man broke away from a group and strode over to us, outpacing an official who was also approaching. "Cillian of Ésparias?" He bowed. "I am Bruccius. We have corresponded on occasion."

"On the correct translation of certain Heræcrian texts." My father offered his hand. "Your last letter arrived just before we sailed." Behind Bruccius the official cleared his throat.

"There has been a delay," he said. "My sincere apologies to you and your entourage, Prince."

"A chair is needed," Druisius said. Colm, unasked, had moved closer to our father.

"A chair?" the official said. "It is not done, to sit on this occasion."

"Get one," Bruccius ordered. The man hesitated. This little drama was being watched by almost everyone in the room.

"Delays happen, of course," I said clearly. "Affairs of state must take precedence, as you and I know, Father. But did not the Empress say this afternoon you would not be kept waiting? A chair would be the least that could be offered, I should think."

Had I overplayed? The official snapped a few words, and two servants hurried from the room, returning with a chair. Positioning it so it faced the room, they bowed to my father. He murmured thanks and let Druise help him into it.

"Bruccius," he said, "I have been remiss. My daughter, Gwenna, heir to Ésparias; my son, Colm. Bruccius is an advisor to the Empress."

Bruccius bowed to me, and then to Colm. "Welcome to Casil and the palace. I am a *magistere*, yes, but for philosophy and history, nothing more."

"And nothing less," my father said. "Lena, you have heard me speak of Bruccius. The major Lena, Ésparias's military representative, and Gwenna and Colm's mother." Not 'my wife', I noted.

She stepped forward to offer a hand. "Of course. Cillian has read parts of your letters to me." The other introductions were made, but I had stopped listening, although I tried to appear that I was. A servant approached with cups of wine on a tray, giving me a reason to turn. Many eyes were still on us.

I surveyed the room, my face carefully pleasant, looking for Dalphe. My rivals, I thought; or, rather, young women who thought I was their rival. I saw gowns of rich blues and greens, necklaces of matching or contrasting jewels set in gold, elaborately dressed hair. One woman's eyes met mine. She smiled and beckoned.

I smiled back. "I am going to mingle," I murmured to my mother. I made my way through the groups of people, Lynthe behind me. The woman stepped forward, holding out a hand. "You are the princess of Ésparias," she said, in slightly accented Casilan.

"Gwenna," I told her.

"I am Rosale of Halachia. You have just arrived?"

We chatted, the politely interested interchange I had expected. Rosale introduced her mother and uncle, her escorts; I introduced Lynthe.

"Your *Princip's* sister? Then you are also a princess." Rosale did not, quite, hide her surprise.

"I prefer lieutenant," Lynthe said, softening her words with a smile. Rosale rearranged her fine shawl, patterned with green and yellow leaves, accenting the green of her gown. Golden bracelets chimed faintly on her wrist as she did. "Shall I introduce you to the others?"

"I have met Dalphe of Sylana," I told her, "and perhaps I should speak to her first?"

Rosale looked around the room. "She is over there, by the wall. Come."

I wondered, as we wound our way over to Dalphe, what Rosale wanted. *The first person who speaks to you at a meeting has an agenda they are hoping you will support*—or so I had been taught. She was an outsider; her country not a province of the Eastern Empire, but an ally, much as Linrathe was. I sensed no resentment here, but what was it she thought I could help with?

Dalphe greeted me with apparent pleasure, and a flick of her eyes at my gown. Her mother was less restrained. "How simply you are dressed," she murmured.

I inclined my head. "The colours of my house, you understand. A requirement for the heir, by our customs." A response I repeated, in some form, three more times as Rosale took me around to meet the other bridal candidates.

"You look lovelier than any of them," Rosale whispered to me, after the third comment. "Simplicity suits you."

As we approached the final group, standing slightly apart, a drum sounded. The room fell quiet. An official spoke from in front of the double doors which led, I surmised, to the hall where we would be presented.

"The Empress Eudekia and Prince Alekos will receive you now, in this order." He called out the countries represented: Rosale's first; then others I recognized. Where would we be?

More names. How was this order determined? "Qipërta," the official read out. From the knot of people I had not yet been introduced to, I heard a murmur, quickly muted. "Ésparias."

Nothing more. I was to be last.

I touched Rosale's arm in thanks and support before threading my way through the crowd back to my father. "Last?" I whispered.

"Remember," my mother said, equally softly, "everyone in the hall will stand until all the candidates are presented. This may be to lessen the strain on your father."

"Or it may not be," he said. "Last is a signal honour, Gwenna. Eudekia may be making her preference known." To me, as well as to her son?

"Qipërta was upset," I said, before falling silent as the doors swung open and the first announcement made.

We watched and listened. The announcements followed a pattern: the men's names and rank, and the country they represented; the older women of the party, and finally the candidate. But not their military escorts.

"I think, *käresta*," my father murmured, "you should not expect to be presented with Gwenna."

"I didn't," she said bluntly.

From where I stood, I could just see what happened in the hall. The Empress and the Prince sat on a raised platform at the far end, too far away for me to gain a real sense of Alekos, except that he was dark haired and bearded, wearing robes of white trimmed with purple. Each party approached the dais, knelt, and waited. At a command, they rose; a short conversation ensued, and the group moved to the side of the hall and the next was called.

Qipërta was announced, and the last group made their way through the doors. Only the guards and military representatives, and a few others—men like Sorley, I supposed, representing a country who had not sent a potential bride—remained in the antechamber. As the small group made their way along the central aisle to the dais, a short man, richly dressed, joined them, offering his arm to the young woman at the centre.

"Decanius," Druisius growled.

"The reason for the delay, perhaps?" My father sounded unperturbed. "I had best stand now, I think."

He took his place beside me, on my left, to accommodate his cane and to allow me to support him if needed, although it would appear he supported me. Colm, with a deep breath, joined us on my other side. Behind us, Druisius carried the chest containing Ésparias's presents.

"Prince Cillian of Ésparias," the official announced. "The prince Colm, and the princess Gwenna."

We walked slowly forward to the spot where we were to kneel. I kept my head high, my eyes on Eudekia, not her son. At the appointed place, I sank to my knees, my head bowed.

Beside me, Colm also knelt. My father, of course, did not. A low murmur rippled along the sides of the room.

"Please stand," the Empress said.

The silk of my gown slid along my body as I straightened, falling again into the simple lines the dressmaker had promised. Only then did I turn my eyes to Alekos.

Eyes as dark as my own, deep set; thick hair swept back from his forehead; the neat beard framing a wide mouth. Muscled shoulders beneath the finely woven tunic. This was the man the Empress expected me to marry. Under my scrutiny, he smiled. Then he stood, stepped down off the dais, and bowed to me.

"Gwenna of Ésparias," he said. "Heir to your country, as I am heir to my Empire. Welcome."

Nothing had prepared me for this. I inclined my head, smiling. "Thank you, Prince Alekos." The gasps and gabble in the room had been quickly silenced.

"You are newly arrived," he said. "Was your voyage difficult?"

"We were lucky with the weather, and the ship sent for us was exceptionally comfortable." Easy, meaningless conversation; I'd been adept at this at fourteen.

"And this is your first time in Casil?"

"Yes. It is magnificent, what I have seen."

"You must see all its glories, while you are here. Perhaps you would accompany me to the games one day? And you too, Prince Colm," he added, acknowledging my brother with a smile.

"I would be honoured, Prince Alekos," my brother said. "Except I am travelling outside of Casil tomorrow, to spend time learning from the physician Gnaius."

I tensed—imperceptibly, I hoped. Alekos's invitation should not have been declined, and Colm should have known that. But Alekos just smiled again. "A scholar, then, like your father? You could not learn from a better man than Gnaius. But you will return for my investiture, and there will be games then."

"Of course, Prince Alekos," Colm said.

"You will come?" Alekos said to me.

"If you wish me to, I would be honoured." There was no other possible response.

"I will let you know which day." He turned to my father. "Prince Cillian. Welcome, and forgive me. I have presumed to ask your daughter for her company, without gaining your permission first."

"No permission is needed, Prince Alekos," my father said. "My daughter is an adult, and her choices are her own."

"I am sure she has been taught to make those wisely," the Empress said, "if not always by example." My mouth went dry. That sounded like a very public warning—and yet no one could hear, except those of us close to the dais.

My father—who had shown no reaction at all—gestured to Druisius, who came forward, the chest resting on his large hands. "Ésparias offers the best pieces from our metalworkers in honour of your investiture as Emperor, Prince Alekos." Colm opened the box to reveal the brooches and buckles, the colours and gold gleaming.

"How beautiful." Alekos picked up one piece for closer examination. "But we have kept you standing too long, Prince Cillian. Shall we take our places? We will meet the military representatives and the ambassadors after the meal."

The chest was handed to an official. Druise returned to the back of the hall, while we were shown where to sit; near the dais where Eudekia and Alekos would eat. My mother and Sorley were at the far end of the room; I couldn't see Lynthe. As we reached our seats, our dinner companions arrived: to my hidden dismay, it was the party from Qipërta.

"Cillian of Ésparias," the oldest man in the group said. "I am Timor of Qipërta, brother to its king." He bowed.

My father inclined his head. "You will forgive me for not bowing."

The man waved a hand. "If you are excused by the Empress and the

Prince, then of course. An old friendship, I understand?"

"Is one friends with an Empress?" my father said, smiling. "She has been gracious toward Ésparias, and we correspond occasionally."

"Does that graciousness extend to the head tax rate?" Timor asked.

"Uncle!" the young woman protested.

"Forgive me. I am thoughtless. May I introduce the princess Sahira." She stepped forward, extending a hand. Shorter than me, with hair the colour of chestnuts, she wore a gown which shimmered between green and blue. My father took her hand to kiss it. "Princess." She smiled.

"My daughter, Gwenna," my father said. I smiled at Timor and gave him my hand, then turned to Sahira.

"Sahira," I said. "How very nice to meet you. What lovely earrings you are wearing." They were a stone unknown to me, close in colour to her gown but nearly transparent.

"They come from the east," she said, "but I am surprised you do not know them. They are reputed to protect against dangers at sea, and you had a long voyage, I understand." Before I could answer, she added, one eyebrow slightly arched. "Your little garnets are pretty."

I wrinkled my nose, shading my voice toward a confiding tone, "I must wear them, Sahira; they were a gift from the Empress when I was just a baby."

Her eyes widened, but she made no reply. Other introductions were made: Colm, the other man, the women from Qipërta. We had been standing for some time, I realized. I glanced at my father, seeing the almost-hidden strain on his face.

I wasn't going to sort out protocol and precedence here. "*Athàir*," I said, "you should not be on your feet." Servants hovered, waiting to place platters of food. Boys with jugs filled wine glasses as we sat. Timor spoke again.

"You have no female companions, Princess Gwenna?"

"My mother is a major in the Ésparian army," I said, for at least the fourth time today, "and its military representative to Prince Alekos's investiture. She is seated nearer the doors, with the envoy from Linrathe, our northern neighbour."

"How unusual," Sahira murmured. "I thought only the uncivilized people of the plains had women warriors."

"You are forgetting the horse archers of Casil," I said.

"Oh, them," she said. "But they are not natural women, are they? Even if it were allowed, no man would marry one."

"It could be said I did," my father said mildly.

Sahira's cheeks held a faint flush as the talk moved to inconsequential things: the minting of new coins with Alekos's face, not his mother's; the flurry of repairs and new construction to mark the occasion. "And the games," Timor said, "every week until the ceremony, and every day for three days before it."

Sahira became animated again then. "We will go, won't we, uncle?"

"Of course," he said. "We all must, to see the spectacle, and be seen ourselves."

"Prince Alekos asked me to attend with him," Colm said, "but I am leaving tomorrow, so I had to say no."

"But you will attend the week of the investiture," my father said, forestalling anything else Colm might say. "A generous offer from Prince Alekos; a kindness to a young man from far away."

"The Prince is a generous man," a voice said from behind us. I turned in my chair. Decanius stood there, wine cup in hand. "No, do not rise, Cillian. I know it is a hardship for you."

Cillian. As if they were old friends, and at the same time an insult.

"*Magistere* Decanius." I stood, holding out my hand. "I am Gwenna of

Ésparias. Your name is known to me from the work you did reorganizing and developing the mines and salterns." Work which had left the women of Ésparias angered at the expropriation of their property and livelihood. "I work as an assistant to the major Michan," I added, "and sometimes meet with the current Procurator."

"Welcome to Casil, Princess Gwenna." Decanius took my hand, almost bowing as he raised it to his lips. He was shorter than I. "Although your title seems at odds with how you tell us you spend your days."

"Not at all, *Magistere*. What better way for me to learn both the resources and the needs of the land I will someday lead?" The same question as Eudekia. Did that mean anything? I withdrew my hand. "No doubt you have ensured Prince Alekos is well informed in the same subjects."

"Informed, yes, but to do the actual work? It would not be appropriate."

"And yet it was once," my father said. "The heirs to Emperors, like their fathers before them, worked in civil or military positions, learning the machinery, if you will, of government. Much as my own father did for the years before he became Emperor. I have long thought the model has merit, and I find it entirely appropriate for my daughter."

"Your father was the Emperor?" Timor said. "Then why are you not *Princip*, if that is not a presumption?"

"Not at all." I recognized my father's insincere smile. "For this exact reason, Prince Timor. I had not the training and experience in governance I believed to be a requirement, especially for a country newly adapting to the oversight of an Empire. I was educated as an historian and a diplomat, not a leader. My father's brother was far better suited, and his grandson properly prepared to be his successor."

"But the Empress," I added, "made me the heir after my cousin Faolyn, so my father has ensured I too am properly educated, and experienced, to take on the role when it is my turn."

"Prince Cillian's birth and acknowledgment by his father the Emperor was . . . irregular," Decanius said.

"Not by Ésparian law," I said, stretching the truth, "and regardless, *Magistere*, the Empress has confirmed it, or I would not be Ésparias's heir, would I?"

His already thin lips tightened. "As you say, Princess."

Chapter 25

~FATHER~

PAIN COILED, TWISTING ALONG MY LEG, threatening to spring into full attack. Tension stiffened my body with every step as I waited for its claws. "You need the baths," Apulo murmured beside me.

"I am too weary," I said. "Just massage."

"And cannabium." I didn't argue. When our place in the presentation order had been announced, last after Qipërta, fear had crawled down my spine. How better to give an unequivocal message that rebellion of any kind would not be tolerated than to arrest the treasonous prince of distant Ésparias in full view of all the gathered provinces? The tension had dissipated, but not entirely: not after her less than subtle warning.

In our room Apulo gave me the tincture, then helped me undress. I lay on the bed, feeling his hands begin their work, the first pressure increasing the pain. I concentrated on breathing steadily, and the fire in my muscles began first to flicker and then to subside.

By the time Lena returned, I was dressed in a loose robe and sitting in a chair. Apulo was tidying up, singing as he did. She unpinned her insignia of rank, dropped it on a table, and came to kiss me, resting her forehead against mine for a moment before she straightened.

"Are you all right?"

"I am."

She dropped into the chair across from me. "That was exhausting."

"I doubt there will be another event so large, until the actual investiture."

"Wine, Lena?" Apulo asked softly.

She shook her head. "Thank you, but no. Not until the others return."

"Go to bed if you want," I told him. He was welcome to stay, and he knew it.

"I will wait." He settled down on a stool.

We talked of the evening, random observations, until Sorley came in. He looked tired. "Gods," he said, tossing the short cloak which was part of his formal dress onto a chest, "it was hot in there." He came to kiss me on the forehead. "You're all right?"

"Yes. Where are Druisius and the children?"

"Colm went to his room an hour ago. Gwenna and Lynthe are still talking to other guests, and Druise is quietly watching them. Watching the room, no doubt."

"No doubt."

Apulo turned to us. "Will Druisius be long?"

"Probably not," Sorley said. "Colm left just after Alekos withdrew, so I'm surprised others are still lingering. But there's a lot of manoeuvring going on among the prospective brides, either trying to align themselves with Gwenna or ignore her. She's handling herself well."

"Did you want to talk to Druise, Apulo?" Lena asked.

"I have learned some things," he said, in his quiet voice, "but Druisius should hear them too."

Another twenty minutes had passed before Druisius arrived. "Gwenna and Lynthe have gone to bed," he reported. "Are we having wine? I have had nothing to drink for some hours."

Apulo got up again, to fetch the wine and cups, setting then on the low table beside me. We followed our ritual: first Lena's from Sorley's hand; his the last, from mine. I raised my cup. What was appropriate for tonight? "What fate brings to us," I said. They all knew the unspoken words which completed the quote.

"I think I prefer the saying from Karst," Lena said, unexpectedly. "Choice is better than chance. I should remind Gwenna of it."

Was there a message here for me? Catilius's words continued with *love whom fate brings to you.* It had been fate, or chance, which had brought Lena and me together.

These were not thoughts for now. Apulo had things to tell us.

"Apulo? Your information?"

He cradled his wine cup in his hands. "The palace servants and slaves see me as one of them. So they gossip in front of me. They said the Empress and her son were late to the banquet because her advisor Decanius insisted he had to meet with them. The cook was furious: the grilled kidneys had been timed to the minute, and they would be ruined.

"But the cook was not the only one angry: whatever Decanius delayed the Empress and the Prince for, they did not find it compelling. One slave overheard the Empress chastising him. They do not like Decanius," he added, "and so are spiteful, and happy if he is in the wrong. And that is all. I will leave you now."

"Thank you, Apulo," I said. Decanius. I knew from Eudekia's letters he was part of her council, advising on—and controlling—financial matters. He had replaced Quintus, his uncle. If the delay of the banquet had been purposeful, then it may well have been done with my inconvenience in mind.

"But why?" Lena asked. "Decanius did not suffer from being recalled from Ésparias; he has risen to a senior position. Why would he still want to hurt Cillian?"

"Perhaps for no reason except that I bested him," I said.

"Qipërta," Druisius said. "Where the rebellion is, yes? They have sent a princess for Alekos. Decanius was the sub-Procurator there, before he was sent to Ésparias."

If I had known that I had forgotten. I had given Decanius little thought this last decade or more; neither he nor his uncle Quintus had liked me, but I understood Eudekia's need to balance factions in her appointments to her council.

"If he can broker a peace through a marriage, especially a peace that could be argued to be favourable to both Casil and Qipërta," I said, "he will be seen as a hero. A statesman worthy of advancement."

"Meanwhile filling his purse through payments of gratitude from Qipërta," Sorley said.

I nodded. "Likely."

"And therefore Gwenna is a threat to his plans," Lena said.

"All the other candidates are," Sorley argued.

"None of the other candidates has Cillian negotiating the marriage," Lena said. "You bested Decanius once before, as you said, and you were ill and barely thinking clearly. He will be who settles what is given and received in the terms, am I right?"

"He is the *fiscarius* for the palace, yes," Druisius said. "He controls the money, among other roles."

"Why," Sorley asked angrily, "are we talking as if it is inevitable that Gwenna will marry Alekos?"

"We're not," Lena said. "It is her choice. But she is intrigued by him: I could see that tonight, even if none of you did. I saw it, and Lynthe did."

"The same as with Bjørn," Druisius said. "She is young, and aware of who she is, and she is meeting powerful young men for the first time. Her equals, yes? No one in Ésparias is that."

Nineteen years earlier, I had experienced the same seduction; the attraction of a mind trained to the precision of governance and with the confidence of power. Even as I had rejoiced in the wonder of loving Lena, so new then, so unexpected, I had felt that pull. As I had still this afternoon. Both today and all those years before, I knew I was not alone in the feeling. What could we have been together, the two of us?

A question never to be answered. But Eudekia hoped to see that unwritten drama played out by her son and my daughter. Was Druisius right? Would she grant me my life for a marriage made?

"Cillian? Is there real danger here?" I glanced up to see Sorley frowning, concern in his eyes. Had he somehow discerned the threat? But his next words removed that fear. "Decanius had Druise arrested once, and if he hears he's asking questions—"

"Do not worry," Druisius said firmly. "The officer commanding the guard in the palace? His father was my family's neighbour."

"But he does not command the soldiers in the candidates' escorts," Lena said. "Lynthe and I—or you, Druise—are not subject to him. If Decanius was behind the attack on Cillian at Wall's End, his reach is wide."

Druise chewed his lip. "Maybe, yes. But we are here only to protect our own people."

"Would that stop someone Decanius has paid from pushing Cillian in a corridor, or worse?" I could hear the tension in her voice. "This means Lynthe and you and I are on duty all the time. Sorley, I'm sorry, but I want Druise with Colm tonight. And can you arrange for door guards as well?"

"Yes," Druise said, getting up. "Then I will go sleep in Colm's room." He gave Sorley a wry smile and a touch on the arm. "Later, *amané*."

Lena too got up. "I'd better brief Lynthe. I doubt they'll be asleep yet."

"They're young," Sorley said, "and they've had an exciting night. Knock and wait, Lena."

She almost said something sharp—I recognized the expression—before her face changed and she chuckled. "You're right, of course. I will." She picked up her major's insignia again, pinning it on as she left the room.

Sorley poured himself more wine, raising an eyebrow and the flask to me. "No," I told him.

"Are they right?"

"Possibly," I said, not hiding the weariness. Gwenna had likely been the target in Ésparias, not me; nonetheless, extra guards were prudent. "That is enough for Lena's demands to be reasonable."

He studied me for a moment. "How was Eudekia this afternoon? How are you, after seeing her again?"

"She is still Eudekia." He had never told me all he had said to her, or she to him, and I would never ask. But I thought he understood.

"You would have been well suited, in another life," he said softly, confirming it.

"A life with Eudekia, rather than a life with Lena and you?" I asked. "Not by choice." In my deepest self, I knew I spoke the truth. The other was only a conjecture, an intellectual question to be considered in my sleepless hours.

"What was that all about, when Lena joined you after dinner?"

Called forward to be presented, the leather and metal of the dress uniform of Ésparias gleaming, Lena had knelt to the Empress and her son, but as a duty, not in deference. Eudekia's eyes on her had shown nothing; Alekos's, frank interest. Then she had come to join Gwenna and me, still with the Qipértani, Prince Timor and his companions rising as she approached.

Apulo had helped me stand. I had taken her hand, raising it to my lips. "*Käresta*." The tone would be understood, if not the word. I had turned to the others. "May I present the major Lena, military representative of Ésparias, mother of the princess Gwenna and the prince Colm, and my wife."

"You saw, then," I said, smiling. "The princess Sahira had been dismissive of women soldiers, earlier."

"So you were making a point."

"More than one, I hope. Not just that Lena's role was valued within Ésparias, but that our expectation was the wife of a prince—or an Emperor—was more than someone to grace his arm."

He nodded. Weariness crumpled his face; like me, Sorley hadn't had to play the diplomat's role for some long time, except briefly, and the strain of tonight showed. "*Somhairle*," I murmured, holding out a hand.

He came to kneel beside me, resting his head on my shoulder. I put my arms around him, the familiar scent of his skin comforting. A faint stirring of desire surprised me; I was far too tired, even if we had the privacy.

Which we did not, and would not, until we returned home to the space that was ours alone.

I kissed his hair, feeling his fingers tighten on my shoulders. He pulled away to look at me, the blue of his eyes almost swallowed by the dark centres. He swore, nearly under his breath.

"How long are we here?" he asked. "And then six weeks back on the ship?"

"Not very long, for us," I said, which was true: making love was a grace note in our lives, a few times in any year.

"I suppose not," Sorley said, standing. "But at this moment, I wish we were home."

I smiled. "A wish I might share, *mo duíne gràhadh*. But we must be patient."

Chapter 26

~DAUGHTER~

I LAY STILL, WONDERING WHAT THE TIME WAS; the room was light, but not bright. I would have to get up soon. I needed the latrine, and water to counter the headache throbbing behind my eyes. The air felt heavy: the beds stood in an alcove at one end of the room, enclosed by walls on three sides. Was Lynthe up? I rolled over to look at the second bed: empty. "You're awake," she said from across the room. I sat up, gingerly.

"Mmm," I said. I pushed back the covers and stood, padding across to the latrine in a second recessed space. Bladder relieved, I washed my face and hands and pulled a robe on over my sleeping shift.

Lynthe rose from where she had been sitting, coming to put her arms around me. Sensibly, she kissed my cheek. My mouth tasted foul to me; I guessed hers was little better, although she had drunk no more wine after my mother's visit last night.

"Don't underestimate the potential danger," my mother had said, when I'd protested. "I'm not saying you can't sleep, Lynthe; just have your secca within reach, and your short sword close. And lock the doors. Druisius is arranging for guards, but perhaps not for tonight."

"Who is guarding Colm?" Lynthe had asked.

"Druisius, tonight."

"Then there is no one with Sorley?"

"Sorley," my mother had said, "can take care of himself, and he is unlikely to be a target."

She'd left us then, and an hour or so later I'd finally fallen asleep, wine and the sensations and release of lovemaking enough to calm the images and conversations crowding my mind. The last one I remembered before sleep took me was the Prince, rising to greet me as an equal.

A knock at the door brought me back to the present. Lynthe went to unlock and open it, to Apulo, bearing a tray with tea. "You wonderful man," I said, the scent of ginger and other spices rising from the pot. He placed it on the table.

"Good morning. Would you like breakfast, Lynthe?"

"I would," she said. "But you shouldn't be waiting on me, Apulo."

He smiled. "I don't mind. He glanced back at the door, but Lynthe had closed it firmly. "The more I act the servant, the less I am seen as a stranger."

"And the more will be said in front of you," I added, pouring myself tea.

"Exactly. Gwenna, the other bridal candidates usually walk in the atrium at this hour, for exercise before the sun is overhead. Should you join them?"

I laughed. "Apulo, sometimes you are as diplomatic as my father. That wasn't really a suggestion, was it?"

"You'll be talked about, if you aren't there. The Prince singling you out as he did last night has made you a person of interest."

"Gossip, you mean," I sipped the tea, considering the idea without much joy. "You're right. I'll go."

"With a chaperone," he said.

"I don't have a chaperone. Except Lynthe. Or my mother, and I can't see her wanting to stroll around the atrium for an hour." I turned to Lynthe. "We should have brought Severa."

"Maybe we should have," she said. "Some older woman, anyhow. We're missing a source of information without someone who can talk to the chaperones."

"I can," Apulo said unexpectedly. "There are two other eunuchs among the bridal parties. We are always considered appropriate chaperones for young women, of course."

"But . . . " I stared at him. "Apulo, do you want to do that?"

"Anyone with eyes to see knows what I am," he said. "It is a position not without honour, to be a eunuch in a prince's court."

"We don't have a court!"

He grinned. "We know that. The others don't. I can tell stories of the *Ti'ach* which will make it sound like a court, one where learning and song are valued."

"Were you always this duplicitous? Or has my father taught you more than *xache*?"

He picked up the tray. "He didn't teach me *xache*, only to play it with forethought and care. I will bring food. You should be ready soon, Gwenna."

I cleaned my teeth and washed and dressed in a light tunic that fell to halfway between my knees and ankles. Lynthe did my hair, and I chose a pair of the silver earrings as my only jewellery. Apulo waited in the corridor.

We walked along the passage and down the stairs into the atrium. I paused under the arch leading out into the open space, surveying. Several groups of young women already walked sedately around the central fountain; older women, and, yes, one man, sat on benches at its edge. Guards stood near the pillars, watchful. For what? Lynthe moved away to take up a similar stance.

A woman waved, beckoning. "Gwenna!" Rosale was walking with Dalphe. Like Ésparias, Sylana was only recently under Casilani control; Rosale's land was a client kingdom, not a province. We were the outsiders, no doubt lacking, in the eyes of the other women, the years of belonging to Casil, and all the sophistication and status that was meant to bring.

I had been an outsider before, the royal heir brought up inexplicably in Linrathe. Cadet school had taught me to handle it.

"Good morning," I said. "Am I the only one with a headache?"

Rosale laughed. "No. I am used to more water in my wine." She wore a tunic of similar design to mine, but a rich blue trimmed in green. Dalphe's tunic was a lighter blue, and over her head she had draped a scarf in a similar shade.

"I bought scarves in the market at Sylana," I told her. "So beautiful."

"The fabric comes from beyond Casil, but our seamstresses are very skilled." We chatted about Sylana and its market as we made a circuit of the atrium. I glanced at the other groups every so often, making note of who walked with whom.

"Speaking of seamstresses," I said, "I need more clothes made. Is there someone here you would recommend?"

"Yes," Rosale said, "if you think what I am wearing is of the quality you would like. It was made here. I can give you the name of the seamstress."

"It's lovely. Yes, give me her name, and I'll visit her."

"Oh, no," Dalphe said. "She will come to you. We do not go to the shops. The streets are not safe."

"Not safe?"

"The crowds," she said. "You go to the shops in your own country?"

"Yes."

"The same in Sylana. But not here, Gwenna."

I murmured an insincere thanks for the advice. My gut tightened at the idea of being restricted to this atrium, the corridor, only going out in a litter. How did anyone live that way?

The sun was higher now, and the enclosed space we walked in warmer. No breeze could reach us here. "It will be time for the midday meal soon," Rosale said. "I . . . " She hesitated. "I would like to ask you to join me."

"I would be glad to," I said, "another day. Today I must eat with my family; my brother is travelling on, with the physician Gnaius, to be his student for a few weeks. I must say goodbye to him."

"How odd," Dalphe said, "for a prince to be a physician."

"He must do something with his life. He cannot spend it in idleness."

"Do not most princes? Those who are not rulers, I mean."

"Do they not usually hold some role at court, or in the army?" Rosale suggested. "This is not possible, for your brother?"

"He has no interest in military matters," I said, "or in the history and politics which are my father's occupation. Medicine is what interests him, and surely it is valuable work?"

"Your father's court must be very different," Dalphe said.

"Learning is what matters to him, the writings from Casil and Heræcria, and music." Apulo's words, almost.

"And yet your mother is an officer?"

"She is also skilled in the interpretation of the *danta*, our story-songs," I said, "and has written an account of what has happened in Ésparias in the last decades. She can be an officer and a scholar." Had I sounded sharp?

"Rosale!" Her chaperone beckoned to her. Rosale sighed.

"It is time to go in. I will see you tomorrow, Gwenna?"

"No doubt," I replied, smiling. "And you, Dalphe."

"What did you learn?" I asked Apulo, in the privacy of the room.

He didn't sit, although both Lynthe and I had. "The candidates have a routine of meals together, and a hierarchy has developed."

"Led by Sahira, I suppose?" I asked.

"Yes. I suggest you send her an invitation immediately, for wine and sweetmeats, tomorrow."

Lynthe wrinkled her nose. "Will she come?"

"Almost certainly. Curiosity, if nothing else. And perhaps ..." He paused.

"Perhaps?"

"Perhaps not in your rooms. Invite her to the Bassanian Baths, Gwenna. It is where Casilani go, to see and be seen."

A memory stirred. "These are the baths with the library? Can I go alone? Can women, I mean?"

"You could, with a chaperone and guard. But I think your father would not object to accompanying you, and if he cannot go, then Sorley will."

"If my father comes," I said, wondering how to word my question discreetly, "then you must. Do you know these baths?"

"I do not." So they were not the site of his enslavement. I considered the idea. If nothing else, it would get me out of the walls of the palace, even if it meant travelling in a litter.

"I'll ask *Athàir*," I said, "after we say goodbye to Colm today."

Colm, at the meal, was as animated as I had seen him since Lianë's death; leaving his family to live with Gnaius for several weeks clearly pleased him. Well, I thought, I was equally happy to go travelling with Sorley and Druise when I was fourteen, although the lessons I had learned that summer were very different from what was planned for Colm.

When we had finished eating, Colm gave us all hugs. "I will miss you, Cub," Druise said. Gnaius stood by, patiently waiting. For the first time I could remember, Sorley kissed my brother's lips, the Linrathan custom between men when a long absence began or ended.

As did my father, who followed it immediately with his customary kiss on Colm's forehead. They had spent an hour together in the morning, my mother had told me. He did not let Colm go, but rested his hands on his shoulders, looking down at him. "Do not argue over what a good man is," he said softly. "Be one."

"I will," Colm said. Our father smiled, gave him one more kiss on his hair, and let him go.

"He will be much happier with Gnaius," I said to my mother, who was still looking at the closed door.

"I know." She almost visibly shook herself back into the moment. "This palace is no place for him."

Or me, I thought. "Can we talk?" I asked. We took chairs again, and I told them of my morning's occupation, and Apulo's suggestion.

"Colm and I saw you in the atrium," my father said. "The requirement for both a chaperone and a guard strike me as excessive."

"I said as much to another guard," Lynthe told him, "and he said it was the expectation."

"Why, though?" my mother asked. "Just elaborate court protocol, excess for its own sake, or is there real danger?"

"Not of the sort you are thinking, Major," Lynthe said. "The guards are for show, and the chaperones to ensure no impropriety between the guards and the candidates,"

"Gods," my mother said, rolling her eyes, "the restrictions some countries place on their daughters."

"An old story, is it not, between those who must be guarded, and those who do the guarding?" A hint of mischief coloured Lynthe's voice.

"For you, perhaps," my mother said drily. "I was Cillian's lover first, and his guard only later."

"Guard, yes," my father said. "But guide, from the beginning. I would have died without you in the Durrains, Lena."

"As I would have without you," she said, matter-of-factly. She seemed calmer, centred. "But about this idea of Gwenna inviting Sahira to the baths. Apulo, why there?"

"The others do not know what to make of her. This is what I heard from the chaperones. She does not dress properly, they say, and her mother is a soldier and her guard a woman, the practices of barbarians. What sort of bride would she be? Even Rosale, who is not even from a province, behaves more like a Casilani woman. And yet Gwenna has had a private audience with the Empress, and the Prince stood to bow to her. If the invitation is to the baths, it will show the others that Gwenna does understand Casilani ways, but is choosing which to follow, and which to not."

"Putting her in a position of power," my mother said. "Druise, do you agree?"

He grinned. "I thought you all barbarians at first, too. Apulo is right. Gwenna is not like these others; she is the heir, and the Prince has acknowledged that, yes? If she just follows the others' lead, the Qipërtani will shun her and Decanius will have the upper hand."

"What if he does?" I asked. "If he convinces Alekos to marry Sahira, he'll be happy, and we can go home." But what would that mean for my father?

"Then there will be a division between the Prince and the Empress, at the very least," my father said. "You are almost certainly her preferred candidate to be Alekos's bride, Gwenna. There is a question of how a rift between mother and son benefits Decanius, and what it might mean for the Empire as a whole, were Decanius to be in a position of influence, even confidence, to the young Emperor."

"As he will be, if Alekos marries Sahira," I said. "What do I do, *Athàir*?"

"At the very least, it cannot hurt Ésparias if you and the woman chosen to be the consort of the Emperor of the East are friends," my father said. "Such a simple thing could tip the balance regarding how we are treated by Casil in the future."

"I should invite her, then? Who is accompanying me?"

Everyone, it turned out. The baths themselves were set aside for women until two hours after midday, but the spaces where food and wine were served and musicians played were used by all at any time. The libraries, which were truly why my father wanted to go, were open from morning to night.

My mother and Lynthe and I would go to the baths, we decided; the men would join us at the hour indicated on the invitation to Sahira and her party. We would travel by litter, of course, with hired guards.

Then I wrote the invitation and sealed it, giving it to Apulo to deliver. "One last thing," my father said, as Apulo turned to go. "If you are to be Gwenna's chaperone, you need clothes in the colours of our court." Amusement in the last words; I'd heard Apulo explaining his deception as

I wrote the note. "I leave it to you to choose what is right. The merchants are to send to me for payment."

"Just a sash, in grey, and perhaps a cap," Apulo said. "Thank you, Cillian."

"When you have delivered the invitation to the princess Sahira, will you help me change?" my father asked. "The Prince has requested my presence this afternoon."

"I will help you," my mother said. "Apulo should do his shopping, to be ready for tomorrow." My mother had written her own note while I had devised mine. I thought it might be to Sahira's chaperones, but now she handed it to Apulo as well. "While you are out in the city, will you deliver this? And wait for an answer, if possible?"

I wanted to know to whom she had written, but my father's news caught my attention. "Alekos?"

"There is a sword to give him." And a letter, I knew. "Lena, are you free to come with me?"

"Free? Of course I'm free. What else would I be doing? But why?"

"Practically," my father said, "I need someone to carry the box. But Druisius could do that. We will be discussing military matters, I hope. I want you to hear what is said, and perhaps your thoughts, Major."

The look she gave him was considered, an assessment. "Is that your only motive?"

He smiled, his eyes soft. "What other might I have, *käresta*?"

"At least two I can think of," she said. "But if we are both to become our formal selves, then we had best make a start."

Chapter 27

~FATHER~

DRUISIUS INSISTED ON ACCOMPANYING US, to carry the sword in its long box: not something Lena should be seen doing, he said. I capitulated; his sense of the palace protocols was likely better than mine. We had not been such honoured guests last time.

We were not kept waiting long. Alekos himself opened the door to us. "Prince Cillian. Major. Please, come in."

"I will take that now, Captain," Lena said. He handed her the box, and she brought it into the private room. Alekos indicated a table. He was alone, no secretary or visible guard. Free of the burden, Lena dropped to one knee.

"Stand, Major," the Prince said easily. "We do not need to be formal. But I am curious: what is it you have brought me?"

"A present for your investiture," I said. "From the prince of Varsland, Bjørn. A personal gesture, you understand, not an official one."

"I see." He freed the elaborate catch on the box and opened the lid. For a minute he simply looked at the sword, before reaching in to lift it out. "Exquisite workmanship."

"The metalworkers of Varsland are skilled," I said.

His dark eyes met mine. "This is not a new sword."

"No. It is the sword of the second sons of the kings of Varsland."

"And why has Bjørn given it to me? No," he said, as I began to speak, "forgive me. Sit, first. My mother would scold me as if I were ten still, were she to know I had kept you standing."

I took the chair indicated. "May I say I have shared that experience, and it is not one I would wish to repeat?"

He laughed, genuinely. "Have you? Will you tell me?"

"Perhaps one day," I said. "But about the sword, Prince Alekos. How much of the western lands' history do you know?"

"Enough, I think." He thought a moment. "The current king is the son of Åsmund, who was the husband of Irmgard who fled to Casil for safety when I was just an infant. You were both with her."

"Åsmund's younger brother, Fritjof, had him killed and took the throne. The sword was Fritjof's, once. Fritjof was killed at the battle of the Taiva." I stopped, glanced at Lena. "By the major's arrow, I should add." Alekos inclined his head to Lena.

"The sword was taken, and kept, and eventually passed to Åsmund's second son, Bjørn." I had to choose my words carefully now. "He wanted no memory of his uncle's deeds, but the sword, as you have noted, is a thing of beauty and worth. In this land, in your hands, that is all it is, a sword without memory or meaning."

He rested a loose fist against his lips. His eyes were intelligent: I would have expected no less in Eudekia's son. "Without memory, yes," he said. "Without meaning, I doubt. You have brought a sword and your military envoy. That is not a coincidence, is it?"

"We were in Sylana not very long ago," Lena said. "The fort was at a quarter-strength, and the young men missing from the market and docks. Sent to patrol the streets of Casil, we were told, but a city guard is not made up of untrained men." I watched Alekos, seeing no flicker of surprise in his eyes. "There is unrest in Qipërta," Lena went on. "Perhaps it is greater than what you might like to be widely known?"

"And if it were?" I saw him find the answer. "Prince Bjørn is offering me both a blade, and blades. For a price, of course. How did he know there could be a need?"

"We met him in Sylana," I said. "There to trade, legitimately. But he too noticed the missing men, and also the scarcity and price of horses: he had wanted a young stallion. Simple observation, Prince Alekos, coupled with rumours of unrest, and a mind trained to analysis."

He flicked his hand, as if annoyed. "We are both princes. Can we forgo the formality, please? Are you acting as Bjørn's envoy, then, Cillian?"

"I am not," I said evenly. "I am only delivering a gift. Look in the box again, Alekos. There is a letter."

He read it, no visible expression on his face. He will play *xache* well, I thought.

"Next year," he said.

"Is the threat that imminent?" Lena asked. "It is not a land for winter war, I am told."

"You are well-informed, Major."

"By coincidence. Druisius, Cillian's bodyguard, fought there many years ago as a young soldier."

"So you are not aware of the details of the conflict?"

"No. But troops have been sent to strengthen the border, I believe."

"That is not a secret. My mother's husband commands them; it is why he is not in Casil."

"What is the conflict over?" I asked. He shrugged.

"Taxes. Qipërta believes their relationship to my step-father should give them special status, but of course it does not."

"And what is that relationship?"

"You do not know? Their king is married to Hathus's half-sister; the girl they have sent for my consideration is his niece."

Was she? That needed thought. "Such a marriage would give them what they seek and end the unrest," I said, "would it not?"

"Would you expect special treatment for Ésparias, were I to choose your daughter?" He was fast, a quick, precise thinker. In that way, a match for Gwenna.

"Not in the same way as Qipërta."

"Then in what way?"

"If a marriage is something you and my—our—daughter want," I said, "there will be time for that discussion then. My purpose here today was to bring you the sword and the letter."

He stroked his beard, eyes on me. Then he nodded. "That is fair. So tell me. Can I trust Prince Bjørn? Is his offer what it seems?"

"I believe so." I had given this long thought on our last days of the voyage; thought and discussion.

"Neither Prince Bjørn or his brother the king wish conflict with either Linrathe or Ésparias," Lena said, "but they are a people whose young men are restless, raised as they are on songs and stories of raiding and battle. Bjørn's thought is to harness that restlessness, to bring them east to fight for pay, and a chance, as they will see it, for honour and glory."

"Would you hire them, Major, were you in my position?"

"Yes."

"And how would you use them?"

"They are skilled with axe and sword, not archers. All will ride, but few of their horses are trained to war. Qipërta is a rough land, I am told; they will do well in that terrain. I would use them in two ways: firstly as foot soldiers, to advance against mounted troops. Their tactics will be to take the horses down. They would also be well suited to travel in pairs or threesomes among the hills and valleys, killing in stealth." A report made concisely and accurately.

"Even in land they do not know?" Alekos asked.

"They see finding their way in new lands an adventure." She paused for a moment. "The last Marai killed in Linrathe were in lands they did not know, but it did not stop them from ambushing the lord Sorley, who was travelling with our daughter and Druisius. All died, one from Gwenna's thrown knife. She was fourteen."

I might not have chosen to reveal that, but from Alekos's quickly-hidden reaction, I saw Lena's choice had had the effect I thought she had intended.

"I see," he said. "But of course, they have been your enemy, and so you can judge their skills and techniques. I will consider what you have said. Thank you, Major."

"You have men within your own army who fought the Marai at the Taiva," she said. "They may have a different opinion."

He nodded. "I will send a letter back with you, if I may. I must thank the prince for the sword, if nothing else."

"Of course," I said. He stood, as did Lena, and to my surprise Alekos came forward to offer me his arm. I accepted the assistance.

"I may wish to speak to you again," he said.

"At your pleasure," I replied.

Druisius had waited for us, as I supposed he should. But at our room, I stopped. "Go find Sorley," I said to him. "He is likely bored."

Druisius snorted. "He has the new *danta* he heard in Sylana to occupy him. He is fitting the words to music and making them sound better. But if I am not needed, I will go to see my family."

"I am sufficiently guarded," I said. "Unless, Lena, you wish to go out too?"

"Not today. We have things to talk about."

On the table in our room lay a sealed note: Apulo must have left it there. I poured wine while Lena opened it.

"Good," she said, reading.

"To whom had you written?"

"Cassia, Severa's daughter. You know she returned to Casil to marry some years ago. Cassia will meet us at the baths tomorrow morning. Apulo must stay with you, and I have no idea of the protocols. It will do Gwenna no good if we look like the rustics we are."

"My wise Lena." I gave her wine.

"Do you want willow-bark?" she asked. I considered. I had soaked in the private baths early this morning, and been massaged, and taken the morning tincture Apulo had prepared.

"No. It's a good day." I had them, inexplicably, sometimes even two or three in a row. I watered my own wine and touched my glass to Lena's. "You enjoyed yourself with Alekos."

"Mmm," she murmured. "But I was right. You had several motives in asking me to go with you."

"And what were they?" We sat, Lena moving a footstool so I could rest my leg. She looked—engaged, I thought, interested, if not happy, quite.

"You wanted me to hear whatever Alekos chose to reveal about the situation in Qipërta. But you also wanted him to hear my thoughts and ideas, so he took me seriously."

"I also wanted him to see that in military issues, I defer to you," I said. "That Ésparias has different ideas about the wives of princes and what their appropriate roles are."

She regarded me, unblinking. "Is the role of a prince's wife different from the role of a *Comiádh's*, then?"

"It could be."

"But you hate being the prince."

"I would hate losing you more." An unintended echo, but the words took me back to a cold tent on a rain-swept mountainside, and the moment I had first given tentative voice to what I had begun to feel for the woman who was my companion in exile. Did she remember?

If she did, she made no sign. "This is not the time to think about it," she said. "Gwenna must be our concern now. These are not just your games against Eudekia's: there is a third, and the mind directing it is Decanius's."

"The prize being Alekos," I said. "What do you think of him?"

"His mother's son. Intelligent; clearly trained to think rationally. I liked how he offered his arm to you. It spoke of kindness, not just manners."

"It surprised me," I admitted. "Nor did he condescend to you, which I also wanted to know. He would take Gwenna seriously, I believe."

"Nothing told me she should not consider him." Lena put down her wine, rubbing her hands over her cheeks. "But should she? There is Lynthe, and beyond that, I cannot see Gwenna trapped inside these walls."

"Are your needs hers?" I asked gently.

"Are yours? Books and teaching and *xache* would keep you content no matter where you were."

"Once."

"When I was eighteen," she said, "I said no to a man I was strongly attracted to out of principle, because I thought it would be disloyal to Maya. I regretted it, later. My fear is Gwenna will say yes because she thinks marrying Alekos would be the best thing for Ésparias, ignoring what is right for her."

"Our lives change. What is right—or wrong—at eighteen may not be twenty years later."

"I don't think what we truly need ever changes. We might ignore it for a time, but it is always there."

"What does Gwenna need, then?"

She shook her head. "I don't know. I hope she does."

I woke in the night, as I always did. I lay still, considering: I could get up, light a lamp, read or write in my chair. But it was not what I wanted. The pain in my back and leg was still muted.

Beside me, Lena's breathing told me she slept, her back toward me. I kissed her neck, tasting a light sweat; the night was warm. I stroked her side, my hand traveling along her hip and thigh. She made a soft sound. I found bare skin beneath her sleeping shift and moved my hand upward.

She rolled over to face me, her mouth finding mine for a long kiss before she sat up to light the lamps hanging over the bed. I could not do even that now, not easily. I watched her, the curve of her back accentuating her breasts as the flame flickered and rose. She pulled off her shift and bent to me.

The world became scent and taste and touch and the encompassing unity I had not known before her, until there was nothing but sensation:

no separation at all between us, hearts and breath and souls merged, fused, one. No words, afterwards; there never were for some time. Lena moved first, her fingers light on my chest. She said my name, so gently.

"You would be asking us to live without this," I said.

"I will have to, some day."

"But why deny us until that day comes?" There was something more I could say, the same plea she had made to me nineteen years earlier, in our room in a house not so very far away from the palace. But I thought she too could hear the words; they hung between us, a memory, a covenant. *Ná mi tréigtha,* she had implored, in words Sorley had taught her to say. *Do not abandon me.*

I would not remind her. If she did not heed the memory, it would be only because her need was greater than mine.

Chapter 28

~DAUGHTER~

THE BATHS WERE ENORMOUS: larger than the palace, standing in grounds where people walked or sat by pools or under trees. We stepped out of the lowered litters Cassia had sent for us, the servant she had also sent catching up, breathless, carrying a bag with the light tunics we would wear in the pools.

I tried not to stare at the sheer size of the building, thankfully distracted by Cassia, who was waiting for us in the shade of the portico. I just remembered her from Faolyn's succession; she had returned to Casil to marry not long after. But she remembered us, or at least my mother, coming forward to greet us with apparent pleasure.

My mother wore one of her green tunics, but Lynthe, as my guard, had kept to uniform. Cassia, introduced, looked puzzled. "But are you not the *Princip's* sister?"

"Yes," Lynthe said. "But I am here only as Gwenna's bodyguard."

"I see." She smiled, as calm and competent as Severa. "You will have to leave your weapons in the changing room, I am afraid. But the woman will guard them."

Cassia led us into the building with clear familiarity. Inside, the building was even more impressive; huge pillars reaching up to a second level; alcoves between them holding statues of athletes, larger than life and with every detail of hair and clothes precisely painted. The tiles of the floor, their pattern echoing the spray of water from the fountains that stood at each intersection of corridors, were cool underfoot as we followed Cassia.

She quietly informed us of the protocols as we walked. They were not so different than the rules for the baths at home—although here the attendants were slaves, which, remembering Apulo's experiences, made me uncomfortable—and the scale and decoration was unlike anything I could have envisioned. As were the number of people: there were hundreds of women, young and old, in the various pools.

We lay on marble tables to be oiled and massaged by skilled hands before slipping into the light shifts to enter the water. My mother's short hair, and Lynthe's, drew attention. I knew enough to understand why: in Casil, the horse archers were the only women with short hair, and they had their own baths. Cassia had noticed, too. She called to an older woman, with two younger ones accompanying her. "Letitia, do come here. These are women you will want to meet."

"Letitia's husband is a high official in the tax office," she whispered to us. "The women with her are her daughter and daughter-in-law, who are also married to men who deal with the administration of the city."

Letitia had a doubtful look on her face; the younger two looked only curious. Cassia held up a hand to stop any questions. "May I?" she said to me. Letitia frowned.

"Princess Gwenna, these women are good friends of mine." She told me their names. "The Princess's companions are her mother, Lena, wife to Prince Cillian of Ésparias, and Lynthe, sister to their *Princip*, Faolyn."

Under other circumstances I might have laughed at how disconcerted the women were, but I maintained my gracious, diplomatic face. The introductions had been made loudly enough to be overheard, and the expressions on faces close enough had changed from disapproving or frankly curious to envy. Status mattered here, and they would know I was a potential bride for Alekos. I might be the future Empress, and they were sharing the baths with me.

Half an hour later we moved to the large swimming pool to cool ourselves, and from there to be dried and oiled and scented, and my hair redone. Our wet tunics given to the servant, we were ready.

"I will show you to where your chairs have been reserved," Cassia said, "and then I will leave you. "Melis," she indicated her servant, "will stay with you. The litters will wait; the men know the Prince Cillian and his entourage arrive shortly, and will align themselves with those litter-bearers, so there is no confusion."

"You will not stay?"

"It would not be appropriate, not today."

I heard the hint. "You will be our guest another day?" I asked. "Here or at the palace?"

"The palace would be an honour," she said.

"Look for an invitation soon," I promised.

Overhead, the ornate ceiling soared, higher than any I had seen and culminating in a dome I just couldn't comprehend. How was it supported? The huge space echoed, even with the dividing pillars, the marble walls reflecting sound. Cassia led us to a group of chairs surrounding a low table, close to a fountain.

Almost as soon as she had said goodbye and we had taken seats, a servant appeared, bearing a tray of wine and small pastries. He placed it on the table, bowed, and backed away.

"I will serve you," Melis said, kneeling. She had just finished giving us wine when I heard my mother's low exclamation. I followed her eyes: Sahira and her chaperone—and a man—walked toward us.

"Decanius," she said, quietly. "Lynthe, go intercept Cillian; tell him Druisius must stay away." Lynthe rose immediately.

"Why?" I asked. "Druise was at the banquet."

"But at the back, except for your presentation. Decanius may not have recognized him. He is the sort of man who does not look at those he considers beneath him." He approached us, just ahead of the women he escorted.

"Decanius," my mother said, her voice neutral. "It has been some years. How are you?"

"Quite well, Major. Quite well. My greetings, Princess Gwenna. You are alone?"

"My father will be joining us shortly," I said. "Princess Sahira, how good to see you. Please sit. Wine?"

Sahira and her chaperone—Debora, I remembered—arranged themselves in chairs. Melis gave them wine and offered the pastries. Decanius did not sit. We made polite queries about their journey here, and comments on the beauty and size of the baths. Sahira did her best to pretend not to be impressed by them, but I caught her covert glances at her surroundings.

"Prince Cillian approaches," Decanius announced. I followed his eyes. My father walked slowly toward us, his black and silver cane tapping the floor. Apulo on one side, a new grey sash around his waist; Sorley on the other. Lynthe walked behind. We were not the only party watching them: my father, I thought again, was a striking man, even here among the glories of Casil.

He greeted the women, smiled at me and my mother, and refused a seat. "I will not disturb you." He turned to Decanius. "*Magistere*, would you be so kind as to show me the libraries?"

"If you would like."

"Lord Sorley?"

"Of course."

"Lieutenant, you are free to stay with the women." My mother's head went up. Without Druisius, my father would be unguarded. Sorley's hand went to his belt, and he turned, as if to speak to her, revealing the knife in its sheath. Only my mother and I—or perhaps too Lynthe—knew it was not his, but Druise's larger knife. They must have switched weapons.

"Who is the lord Sorley?" Sahira asked when the men were out of earshot.

"That depends on the day," my mother replied. "He is the envoy for Linrathe, which is a client kingdom of Casil north of Ésparias; you might have seen at the banquet that he presented gifts to the Empress and the Prince. But he is also a musician, attached to our household."

"A lord who is also a prince's musician? And your son is training to be a physician. What a strange court you have."

"It is what is done in Ésparias. You know I am an officer. My daughter's bodyguard," she indicated Lynthe, "is the *Princip*'s sister."

"Is she?" Sahira turned to look at Lynthe. "A *princess?* Are all high-born women soldiers then? You are not, surely, Gwenna?"

"No. I am a very junior envoy." I smiled. "The most important work I have yet done was to negotiate border tariffs with the lord Sorley's country, a routine matter." Ruar. I remembered the sadness and resolve in his eyes, when he'd given me the formal kiss of farewell outside the *Ti'ach*.

A wave of desire washed through me, to be outside, to feel the breeze and the sun. "Could we walk in the gardens?" I asked. "Sahira, would you like that? I am tired of being inside walls."

She glanced at her chaperone for permission. Words, not in Casilan, were exchanged. Sahira smiled. "I can," she said, "as long as my guard comes with me."

"Lieutenant, I will stay here with Debora," my mother said to Lynthe. "You need not worry for my safety." Out of uniform she might be, but her secca was always somewhere on her body, except at night or in the baths, just as mine was.

Each paired line of columns led to a door to the gardens. As we passed one of the libraries, I looked over to see my father seated with Decanius, in apparently cordial conversation. Servants swung the wide doors open, and we stepped out, still on patterned tiles, under more columns stretching toward a fountain. Small trees grew in a row, shading the path, sparrows chirping from the branches.

Groups—women or men, but not together—walked along the paths or sat on shaded benches. Young children played on the grass, watched over by their mothers, or, more likely, nursemaids.

"Do you have gardens like this in Qipërta?" I asked Sahira.

"At the palace. Not for all to walk in." She looked around. "So many people here."

"So many people in Casil."

"I miss riding," she said. "But women do not ride in the city, I am told. Only officers, and only in parades. At home I rode almost every day. I have a mare, a grey paler than your tunic."

"I would miss it too. My horse is a gelding, a bay."

"When—if I marry the prince, I will ask him to let me ride. If not in the city, at least at his country villa."

We reached the fountain, its spray noticeably cooling the air. "Let's go this way," Sahira said, indicating her left. We were close now to the wall that enclosed the gardens, shrubs, some still in flower, half disguising it.

Ahead of us, a woman screamed, a sharp sound. Then another. Lynthe's hand grasped my upper arm, pulling me to a stop; Sahira's guard stepped in front of her, drawing his sword. The women ahead of us had turned, running our way, glancing back fearfully. "*Rabiosa*," one called.

I saw the dog, foam spilling from its jaws, its gait awkward and stiff. It advanced, making strange sounds, snapping at the air. Sahira's guard stepped forward, his short sword pointed. "No!" Lynthe said, grabbing his arm, pulling him back. "You'd be too close." Sahira whimpered. I stepped off the path, pulling up my tunic, reaching for the secca strapped to my thigh. Perhaps I confused the animal; perhaps it snapped at a fly, but as Lynthe's knife flew, it swung around, biting at nothing. The secca hit its shoulder, drawing blood and a hoarse cry. It staggered toward us a few steps, lips drawn back, trying to bark, before my secca found its neck.

Other guards pounded up, drawn by the screams or the women's shouts. A hand touched my arm. "You are all right?" Druisius asked. "No saliva touched you? No spray from its mouth?"

"I'm fine," I told him.

"Stay here." He and Lynthe approached the dog, Druise's sword out. But its eyes held the glaze of death, and the ribs were still. Avoiding its jaws, Druise bent and pulled the secca out, wiping it first on the grass and then on a cloth from his belt pouch. Lynthe retrieved her knife. She said something to Druisius, who nodded, his face grim.

I heard a gasp, someone trying not to cry. I turned to see Sahira; she had moved a pace or two away to a bench. Tears glittered, and she hugged herself. I went to her.

"We could have been bitten," she said. "It's a horrible death. Horrible."

I sat beside her. "But we weren't. No one was, and the dog is dead."

"You killed it. But you're not a soldier."

"That doesn't mean I can't defend myself," I said gently. It was beyond her experience, and she was shaken, upset. Lynthe came to crouch beside us, her hand touching my shoulder for a moment.

"What happens to—" she indicated the body.

"It will be burned," Druisius said, coming over to us. "I will wash the seccas, Gwenna. Then you should go in, and perhaps the princess Sahira should have some wine, yes?"

"Yes," she agreed. "Wine would be welcome."

We waited while Druisius cleaned the knives. But he gave mine to Lynthe, not me. I understood: putting it back its sheath would mean exposing my leg almost to the hip, surely not something a princess, or any woman, should be doing in a public garden. Not that I'd given it a thought earlier.

I bent to Sahira. "Are you all right? Can we go in now?"

She smiled, a little unsteadily. "Who is the guard who cleaned your knife?"

"Druisius? He's my father's bodyguard."

"He called you by name."

I tried not to sound exasperated. "He's known me since I was a few minutes old." I didn't think I'd tell her he'd changed my diapers. A second too late, I remembered: Decanius shouldn't know Druise was here. I thought, rapidly. Nothing. I couldn't find any reason to ask Sahira not to mention him, not that sounded plausible.

We returned to the building, Sahira's fear changing to excitement; she had a story to tell. As we passed the library, I glanced over again. My father and Decanius were gone.

Chapter 29

~FATHER~

SORLEY DROPPED BACK A FEW PACES as I walked with Decanius toward the libraries. Apulo stayed at my side. "You wish to see the Casilani texts or the Heræcrian?" Decanius asked, politely enough. "They are housed separately, you know."

"I wish to speak to you privately," I said, in Heræcrian, "so the library that is emptiest would be the better choice."

"What have we to say to each other, Cillian of Ésparias?" He had gained some civility in the years since he had been Procurator of Ésparias, a refinement necessary in Eudekia's court.

"When we are not likely to be overheard, I will tell you."

He accepted that with a nod. I had, as I intended, indicated that Apulo did not understand Heræcrian, and he should have no reason to doubt it. In Decanius's mind, Apulo was a servant, nothing more; little better than the enslaved boy he had once been. He did not see the intelligent, talented man at all.

But with time Apulo had revealed that man to me, first in conversation, and then over *xache*. It had been simple to have him join us when I taught Heræcrian to some of my students. Now, when I thought my memory still in doubt, I was glad for my sake he had wanted to learn.

We found an alcove with chairs. Apulo supported me as I sat, then went to crouch against a pillar within hearing distance. Sorley sat further away, where he could watch both us and the larger space. He didn't speak Heræcrian, but Decanius might be unlikely to believe that.

"Well?" Decanius said. "We are here at your request. What is it I can do for you?"

I regarded him for a moment. He'd thickened, his tunic curving over a stomach which told of a love for food and wine, and his head had only a thin strip of hair left. A neatly trimmed beard covered his chin.

"Not at my request," I said, "but the Empress's. She is aware of our past differences, but she wishes us to put them aside." The note had come to me in the morning, an order carefully worded as a suggestion.

"To what end?" He folded his hands together, raising the tented fingers to his lips.

"Peace in Qipërta."

His brows raised. "The Empress is asking you to intervene?"

"I assisted your uncle Quintus with the Boranoi treaty. As then, the Empress believes a mind unfamiliar with the conflict's history might find a way to reconcile the two sides, where someone closer to it may not."

"You think there will be an overlooked detail you can use to force an agreement, Prince Cillian?" Said mildly enough, but his shoulders had risen just a little.

"Just now, I have no opinions, *Magistere*. I am acting on my Empress's wishes, not my own."

I waited. Across from us, Sorley sat, legs outstretched, looking bored, half asleep.

"You are very loyal to the Empress."

"Should I not be?"

"Her days of power are nearly done. Is it not the Prince Alekos's wishes which should prevail?"

"Are they not aligned?"

He didn't answer. Somewhere in the last eighteen years he had discovered the power of silence. But I had learnt it long before him.

"You are prepared to support the princess Sahira's marriage to the Prince over your own daughter's?" he asked abruptly.

"We are here at the Empress's command," I said. "But my daughter will marry Alekos only if that is what he and she both want. I will neither encourage nor discourage it."

"You will let an eighteen-year-old girl decide her own future?"

"As much as possible. She carries a burden of responsibility to Ésparias not of her choosing. It is only fair she makes her own choices where she can."

"I see you do not fully grasp Casilani law," he said. A smile accompanied the words, one which was nothing more than a movement of his lips. "You are her father. She is under your control."

"I am well aware of that. But the law does not define how my control is expressed. A fawkner owns his falcon, but he may choose to let it free, may he not?"

"An indulgent father. But I suppose it is not my concern, if you are prepared to see Sahira as the better candidate."

"I did not say that."

"It is the way to peace with Qipërta."

"It is one way. You seem very sure Prince Alekos can be persuaded. Is he so pliable?"

He shrugged. "His mother was. My uncle persuaded her that marrying Prince Hathus was the better choice for Casil, when her heart was set on the son of a man who called himself Emperor of a land we had forgotten. Alekos can be made to understand his responsibility."

He was trying to rile me. But his barely-veiled insult was of no importance, and I alone—I and Eudekia—knew the truth. I let myself hear that conversation again, nineteen years past. 'Tell me,' she had said, after Sorley had gathered all his courage to confront her, 'your soldier. Do you love her as truly as your friend believes?'

'Yes,' I had replied.

She'd been silent, for a moment. 'It took great courage for him to challenge me.'

'I know.' I'd taken a breath. 'You intrigue me, Eudekia. You test me; and there is an attraction I cannot deny. But my love is given elsewhere.'

She'd smiled, a little sadly. 'Quintus tells me I should marry the Boranoi heir; they have men and arms to spare, and known lands. I will let him think he persuaded me. But he did not. The lord Sorley and you have. Go and thank your friend, and beg your soldier's forgiveness on your knees.'

"Decanius," I said, my smile as insincere as his, "it is a poor *xache* player who has only one plan for his game. If Alekos proves less agreeable than you hope, what then?"

"Young men," he said, "like war. It would enhance his first year as Emperor, to put down a rebellion."

"Is that the choice? Marriage or war?"

He spread his hands. "That is what I see."

"Then perhaps," I said, allowing a thread of disdain to colour my voice, "that is why the Empress asked for my help. Are you going to obstruct her wishes, *Magistere*, or can we explore possibilities beyond the choices you see?"

A thumb tapped on the arm of his chair. Even as the dowager Empress, Eudekia would hold considerable influence, if not power. Angering her—seriously angering her, as defying her request would—was a dangerous chance to take. One that might have repercussions for us both.

"It cannot hurt to consider other paths to peace," he said. "I will have my secretary find some times we can meet, and you will be informed. If that is all, Prince Cillian, I will leave you to the books; I am a busy man."

"I understand. Thank you, *Magistere*."

He heaved himself out of his chair, and without a word to Sorley walked away, not toward where Debora sat with Lena, but in another direction. I sagged, pain tearing at my back.

Sorley took the chair Decanius had vacated. "You unnerved him," he said in Linrathan.

"What did you see?"

"He jiggled his foot a lot. But it was his voice. I don't know the language, but it doesn't matter. When he's afraid, his voice is tight, just as it was at Wall's End all those years ago. At the end, he was afraid."

"Of what, I wonder?" The conversation had tired me more than I had expected. "Apulo?" He rose. "Is wine possible?"

"Not here. It is not allowed in the libraries. But just over there."

"Go arrange it," Sorley said. "I'll help Cillian up." He held out an arm. We followed Apulo to another group of seats away from the library. "What did Decanius say?"

"Either Alekos marries the princess from the land in question, or there will be war. But I must write down what was said while I remember." I sat again. "Apulo has paper and ink in his satchel."

"While you remember? When have you ever forgotten anything?"

"Since my head hit the flagstones at Wall's End," I said bluntly. "Gnaius says it will pass. But it is why I needed Apulo to also hear what was said."

Apulo brought the wine, and without asking dug into his satchel to add willow-bark to mine. I didn't object. At my request he produced my writing materials, and for the next minutes I wrote, as precisely as I could, a record of my conversation with Decanius. Neither Sorley nor Apulo broke my concentration. When I was done, I gave the record to Apulo. "Read it, but not here. I left space for you to add anything I forgot, or which you heard differently."

"At the palace," he said. "Are you ready to go back?"

"Prince Cillian?" a voice asked. I turned slightly to see Bruccius approaching. "I had not thought to see you here. No, do not rise." He offered his hand in greeting first to me, then to Sorley. "Have you been reading Heræcrian texts?"

"Not this time," I said. "My daughter is entertaining the princess Sahira here, and I came to see the building. It is magnificent. Will you sit and have wine?"

Bruccius pulled a chair over, waving Apulo away. "Are you also a student of the philosophers, Lord Sorley?"

Sorley smiled his self-deprecating smile. "I am only a musician, *Magistere.*"

"Bruccius, please. Ah, thank you," he said to Apulo, who had brought him wine. "I doubt that, for two reasons. One is that you are also your country's envoy. Nor can I see the prince having a close friend who is 'only a musician'."

"There is another reason," Sorley said.

"And that is?"

"I can reliably lose to him at *xache*." He pitched his voice to sound both regretful and resigned. Purposely, of course; playing the courtier who knows he is overshadowed by his prince.

Bruccius laughed, a deep, amused sound. "Perhaps we can find time to discover how well matched we are at the game, Prince Cillian?"

"I would enjoy that," I said, meaning it. A new opponent at *xache* was always to be welcomed, and I thought from his letters and his precise and nuanced translations that Bruccius would play the game well.

The murmur of other conversations had risen and fallen around us as we talked, like the ebb and swell of waves, surging occasionally. But now the sound became louder, urgent. Bruccius cocked his head.

"A rabid dog," he said, listening. "In the grounds. They are not uncommon, at this time of year. This one has been killed."

"By a girl who threw a knife," I added, hearing the shocked words.

"Yes," Bruccius said. "Who?"

"My daughter." I did not need to hear her name to be sure of it.

"The princess?" A flick of surprise on his face.

"Last time," I said, "it was a man. He was trying to kill her, to be fair."

"I see," Bruccius said. "Her mother's influence, I expect?" He had regained his composure.

"Entirely. Sorley, would you find her, please?" My head had begun to throb. I had hoped to discuss what Decanius had said with Sorley, to order my thoughts, but that chance had been lost. It would be hours now before we could find another.

"The Empress favours her," Bruccius said quietly, when Sorley had gone.

"It is not the Empress who is marrying. Will Prince Alekos be directed in this matter? I would," I added, at his questioning look, "prefer, if it comes to it, to think Gwenna was his choice, not his mother's."

"I taught him our history. It is peopled with Emperors—and Empresses—who married for the greater good of the Empire. He did not argue against it. And of course, he has his own mother's choice of second husbands as an example." He sipped his wine. "If I may say so, your marriage is an exception among princes, if it was indeed for love."

"It was, and is," I said, "regardless of what you may have heard."

"I did not fully trust the source," he murmured. "Nor do I now. And here," he added, "is the princess Gwenna, and her mother." He stood. "I will leave you, but I look forward to *xache* when we both have time."

Chapter 30

~DAUGHTER~

"YOUR FATHER WOULD LIKE TO SEE YOU," Sorley said in my ear. He'd tried waiting for Sahira to stop talking, which was like waiting for a fountain to stop its spill of water.

I put my hand on her arm. "Princess, you must excuse me. My father the prince wishes to assure himself of my safety."

"I'll come with you," my mother said. A few steps away, she turned to Lynthe. "Get them more wine, Lieutenant, please. Then join us."

Sorley went with Lynthe. My mother looked at me. "What did you do, Gwenna?" Sahira's tale had been garbled.

I told her, succinctly. "You couldn't let the guards take care of it?" she asked.

"Lynthe's first secca only angered it. Should I have let it attack?"

"No," she admitted. "I would have done the same."

I grinned at her. "I know. It will be a nine-days wonder, if that, *Mathàir*."

"Perhaps. This is not Ésparias."

We reached my father. He looked tired, as he had since we had begun this journey. Tired and in pain. I would not reveal what I had let slip to Sahira, not now. He smiled; no anger in his eyes at all. "*Mo nihéan treún.*"

"I wasn't brave. I just did what needed to be done."

"That is all any of us can do. Still, it will be seen as brave, and perhaps barbaric. Are you ready to return to the palace?"

"I should say goodbye to Sahira and Debora first. And Decanius? Is he still here?"

"Not in the public rooms." He reached for his stick, Apulo immediately at his side. "Go and say your farewells. Lena, will you stay a minute?"

I'd been dismissed. Why? But I went back to where Sahira was still talking, Lynthe beside me.

"Are you leaving now? Will you walk with me tomorrow morning?" Sahira asked in a rush of words. "We will have such a story to tell the others."

"Of course," I promised. If my intent in inviting Sahira to the baths had been to lessen the rivalry she felt toward me, I'd succeeded.

Outside Druise waited, Melis crouching in the shade nearby. "Is Cillian coming?" he asked.

"Soon."

"Do not leave until we can all go together. You should not be alone on the streets. I did not hire the litter bearers."

"You didn't object this morning," I said.

"Your mother was with you. And that was this morning." He wouldn't say anything else. I found a sheltered bench. In the afternoon sun, heat radiated off the building and the pavement. Lynthe stood beside me.

"Does he think I can't protect you?" she muttered. "Just because I didn't kill it?"

"Don't take it personally. It's just Druise. I'm his Kitten." I smiled up at her. "If Faolyn died tomorrow and I became *Principe*, I'd still be his Kitten."

"The gods forbid," Lynthe said with a grin. "He'd probably insist on sleeping outside your door, and I don't think I'd like that."

"Neither would Sorley."

We didn't wait long. When my father had made his way into his litter, we stepped into ours, and were hoisted up to be carried through the crowded streets. I went over the events at the baths in my mind while we made the short journey. As we disembarked at the palace, I beckoned to Sorley. "Can we talk?"

We walked a distance away. "I made a mistake," I said. "When the dog appeared, there was a lot of screaming. Soldiers came running, and one of them was Druise. Afterwards Sahira asked me who he was."

"You told her his name."

"Without thinking. I'm sorry."

His lips thinned for a moment. "It's done. I never believed we could keep his presence here from Decanius. Does Druise know?"

"No."

"I'll tell him, and your parents, in a little while. After Cillian's had a chance to rest."

"Sorley? Is *Athàir* all right?"

His jaw tightened. "I hope so. But I wish Gnaius hadn't left."

Fear clenched at my throat. "But surely he wouldn't have, if *Athàir* needed him?"

"I keep telling myself that." He touched my arm. "But he wouldn't have, truly. I just worry."

So do I, I thought. "What were *Athàir* and Decanius talking about today?"

He hesitated. "That is not mine to tell, Gwenna." The *scáeli's* formal answer, when he could not speak a truth he knew. There was no point in pressing him.

I sat on the shaded balcony of my room, writing in my journal: notes on what Sahira had said, mostly, but also my private impressions of the baths. *So many stone buildings*, Ruar had said. Not a mention of the decorations, the colours, and the sheer magnificence of the soaring dome of the baths or the arches of the palace. Perhaps they hadn't pleased Ruar's eye; perhaps he measured beauty by the forests and moors of Linrathe and the grey stone of Dun Ceànnar.

The thought surprised me. But here, even the gardens, as lovely as they were, had been ordered by minds and hands. Would I grow tired of geometry in time? I put my pen down, staring into the atrium with its fountain. I wondered how my mother was coping with the confinement: she needed space and solitude, my father had said, and she certainly wasn't getting either here at the palace. But at least she seemed—what?

Happier? No. Accepting, perhaps, of this hiatus in her life, and perhaps too of Lianë's death.

Lynthe came out to the balcony. She had shed the leather of her uniform, wearing only the light undertunic, although her secca was at her waist. She ran a hand over my neck and shoulders.

"You shouldn't," I said, wrinkling my nose as I smiled to lessen the rejection. "We can be seen here."

She grimaced. "What's happened? You've been different since we got here."

I'd tried not to let my concerns affect us; my suspicions were only—suspicions. But the Empress's subtle threats reverberated in my mind constantly.

"This isn't Ésparias," I countered. "There are protocols to be maintained."

"Are you seriously considering marrying Alekos?" I hesitated, but that was enough. "You are, aren't you?"

We were speaking Ésparian, but even so . . . "Let's go in." I pulled the doors closed. "It's a possibility," I said, as gently as I could.

"Why, Gwenna?"

My father's life, but I couldn't say that. "Politics."

"So it would be a diplomatic assignment, but a permanent one, and if you take it, you're expected to share his bed and bear his children?"

Wasn't that exactly how I'd been thinking of it? "Yes."

"Do you find him attractive?"

"Enough." Not like Bjørn, whose physical beauty had engendered an immediate reaction.

"So you wouldn't mind sharing his bed?"

"You'd prefer I hated it?" I asked. "Forced myself to participate? Lynthe, you know I've made love with men."

"Yes," she said, her voice tight. "I do. But never instead of me." She walked to the sideboard. "Do you want some wine?" I nodded. She poured two glasses, handing me mine. She didn't sit. "What we talked about before? Can I stay?"

"As my bodyguard?"

"Yes. Or more."

"You want us to stay lovers? Even if I marry Alekos?"

"Couldn't we?" she said. "I know you have to have children. I don't care. That's how we all used to live in Ésparias, before Casil came."

"I don't know if it's possible."

"But if it is, would you want me to?"

I took her hand. "Sit down. We need to think about this practically."

"No," she said. "Tell me first. Do you want me to stay?"

I did. Oh, gods, how I did. I wouldn't be alone in this crowded city of stone and statues. "Yes."

She grinned, her fierce, almost wicked grin, and pulled me to her, nothing gentle in her kiss. My hands found the buckle to her belt, fumbling to free her of it.

"Wait," she murmured, letting me go. I stood, breathing hard, as she checked both sets of doors were locked. Then she pulled her tunic over her head and reached for me again, and I stopped thinking about whether I should have said yes, or about anything at all.

⌘⌘⌘⌘⌘

Several days passed. I walked in the atrium and drank tea or wine with various bridal candidates, and I told the story of killing the dog a dozen times. Bored beyond tolerance, I invented a private game: how much could I get the other women to tell me about their countries, about their attitudes to Casil, about the threatening war? I listened, and made noises of agreement or surprise, and later I wrote it all down, along with my assessments of the other women.

Early one morning, my mother joined us on the balcony, where we were eating flatbread and cheese and olives. "I thought I'd visit the horse archers today. Lynthe, would you like to come?"

"I'd love to," she said.

"I can't," I told them, before the offer was made. "The seamstress will be here in late morning. And I can't put her off if my new tunic is to be ready for the games." Alekos, as he'd promised, had sent me a formal invitation to accompany him to the next games, in two days' time. There was a style of tunic to be worn, I was told, modelled on the one worn by a statue of the divine huntress: nothing else would do.

"Do I actually get to be unguarded for a day?" I asked.

"Druise has made arrangements," my mother said. I rolled my eyes.

Druise's arrangements, though, were to guard me himself. "Hello, Kitten," he said, with his habitual grin. I had just decided to read until the seamstress arrived. I put the book down, matching his grin.

"Druise! Who's with my father, then?"

"Sorley."

He sat down. I hadn't seen much of him, except at dinner, the only meal we ate together.

"So. What do you think of Casil?"

"How would I know? All I've seen is the palace and the baths."

He grinned again at my tone. "The day after tomorrow you will see the Arénas Ingenírus, yes?"

"Yes. I wish I could have gone with my mother today, though. Somewhere I didn't have to be the princess." I didn't have to pretend with Druise.

One sandaled foot tapped against the other. "What are you doing after the seamstress is done?"

"Nothing, except the usual atrium stroll, and then wine later with one of the candidates."

"You could make an excuse?"

248

"I could. Druise, what are you thinking?"

"Your father meets with the Empress this afternoon. He does not need a guard; it would be an insult. So I am taking Sorley to meet my family. You could come, yes?"

"Could I? How?" To be out of these walls and distracted from the fears that haunted me would be a relief.

"Wear what you wore on the ship. I will take you out through the tunnels the guards and servants use."

Excitement bubbled. "Oh, Druise, thank you." A thought struck me. "Sorley won't say no?"

"I think not. I will talk to him first."

A knock sounded on the door. Druise got up to open it, ushering in the seamstress. "I will go sit on the balcony," he said.

I endured the arranging and pinning of fabric, raising and lowering my arms as requested. The garment—it wasn't really a tunic, but a gown of sorts, the fabric crossed over my breasts and falling in multiple layers to my knees—took time to ensure it would drape and move properly. I would look like the goddess herself, the seamstress told me.

Did I want to? This was the goddess my mother thought had taken Lianë. She would be glad of her uniform: I thought she would have refused this gown, no matter the protocols.

Finally the woman was done, the finished work promised for the next day. I dressed again, in one of the plain tunics I'd worn on the ship, and braided my hair, pulling it back with a plain clasp. Then I went out to the balcony. "Will this do?"

"Yes. Can you cover your head?"

"I have the scarf I bought in Sylana."

"It will do. You only need to look ordinary." He glanced up at the sun. "I will go see if your father has any instructions for me. Then I will fetch Sorley. We will eat with my family, yes?"

I didn't have to wait long. Sorley gave me a quick grin, that of a fellow conspirator, as Druise opened a small door at a corner of two passages and led us down a set of narrow stone steps into an arched tunnel, and from there to another door that opened into the grounds of the palace. We passed a couple of servants, but no one else.

After a quick, low conversation between Druise and a guard at a narrow gate in the wall, it was opened for us. We stepped out into a wide street, edged with drains and cobbled, and thronged with people. I pulled the scarf up over my head. The sun was hot, and while my skin had darkened during our voyage, the days indoors meant I was likely to redden and burn again. Sorley took my arm. "Stay right beside me," he said. "I'm going to feel your mother's secca if she ever finds out about this."

He too was dressed in a light tunic, but the quality of the belt he wore and the worked hilt of his knife spoke of status. Dodging donkey carts and litters, we followed Druise across the street and into a narrower one, lined with what looked to me like expensive houses. We crossed another street, and turned a corner, and the lanes grew less wide, if not less crowded. Sorley kept a hand on my upper arm. I didn't like it, but other men were guiding women that way. The houses here were narrower and taller, shops on the lower levels opening onto the streets, selling food and pots and cloth and a dozen other things.

I slipped on a piece of squashed fruit, nearly going down onto the cobbles, but Sorley caught me, eliciting a ribald comment from a man approaching us. "She's his daughter," Druise growled, adding an insult that should have made me blush.

"Watch your mouth," Sorley snapped, perhaps a moment too late. Smells mingled and clashed in the thick air, some good, some not. I swallowed with some difficulty—but was the tightness in my throat from the smell? Even with Sorley and Druisius, I was, I realized, apprehensive.

We squeezed by a cart full of cabbage being unloaded and into a larger space; not quite a square, and still lined with shops, but wider, the brick cleaner, the cobbles swept. Nor did the shopfronts have tables crammed with wares, but neat rows of pots and bags. I recognized it from Casilla: these were traders' shopfronts, dealers in oil and grain and fish, not storekeepers for the populace.

"Come," Druise said, beckoning. He lengthened his stride. "Marius!" he called, and near the end of the row of shops a man turned.

"Druisius?" Marius said something to the man he'd been conversing with and strode forward to envelop Druise in a hug that I thought might injure him. He was taller than Druise, with arms that had lugged amphorae and sacks of grain since boyhood, and a grin exactly like his brother's. "I was not expecting to see you again so soon."

Sorley and I stood a little distance away, waiting, until the men stepped apart. Druise motioned to us. "Marius," he said. "This is Sorley. *Amané*, this is my brother."

No pretence, then, in what Sorley was to Druise. With a smile, Marius offered his hand. His hair, like Druise's, was greying at the temples. Did I know who was older?

"You are a fine musician, I am told, Sorley." Marius looked down at the hand he was shaking, and then a little more closely at Sorley. He'd be skilled in assessing men, I thought.

"You are not a soldier," he said.

"I did not say he was," Druise interjected. "I said we taught swordplay together, yes?"

"You are an important man in your own country." Not challenging, but stating a fact. Sorley glanced at Druise, smiling wryly.

"I see close observation is a family trait," he said lightly. A woman had emerged from the shop to stand a few paces behind Marius. Her hair was as black as Apulo's, her skin darker than his but lighter than Druise or Marius. Her eyes were on me.

"He may be important," she said, "but perhaps this woman is too?"

Marius's gaze shifted. He was a trader, experienced, impassive. They were diplomats of a sort. Nonetheless, I saw the slight rise of his brow as he looked at me. So did his brother.

"Marius. Vita. This is Piása." Linrathan for kitten.

"That is what we are to call you?" Marius asked.

"Please," I said. Vita—who I guessed was Marius's wife—hadn't spoken again. But suddenly she appeared to remember what she should do for guests.

"Have you eaten, Druisius?"

"No. And we are hungry."

"Come, then." She ushered us into the shop, and through a door and up a flight of steps to a room above. An unexpectedly lovely room, with walls painted with figures and designs, and unusual furniture of a dark wood.

"Please sit. I will not be a moment." She disappeared, calling names as she did; daughters or servants, I guessed. I didn't sit, though. I went to take a closer look at a bowl sitting on a shelf: I'd never seen anything like it. It was bronze, that much I could see, but elaborately decorated with rows of loops in the same metal.

"From my family's land," Druise said, coming to stand beside me.

"Which is where?" He was Casilani, wasn't he?

"Across the Nivéan Sea. South and west. My father's father was a trader on the coast, but my father said their home was further south. Where this bowl was made."

"When did your family come to Casil, then?"

"I was small. Five, they said, but I think I was seven. Marius was three."

"Why would they say you were younger?"

"No fee to pay for children under six, yes? So they lied, to save the coin. More money for the business, shipping oil and grain."

"Which your brother does still." If Druise was the oldest, then why did his brother run the business? This wasn't the time to ask, especially as I heard returning footsteps.

Vita, followed by a servant, carried trays of food into the room, followed by Marius with wine. "This is not good enough for you," she said to me. The tray held barley bread, and small fried fish, olives and a soft cheese, and pastries dripping honey.

"*Matrone*," I said, "at home I am a very junior official of our government. This," I indicated the food, "is more than good enough, and better than what I often eat. And it looks delicious."

She looked doubtful, but Druise grinned. "Kitten tells the truth. I have better food than she, at the fort."

"But not," his brother said, "better wine than this, I will wager." He poured a cup, then hesitated. "Who should taste?"

"Sorley," Druise and I said in unison. Marius handed Sorley the wine. He took a sip, and his face, always expressive, brightened.

"This is excellent. Don't waste it on your brother."

After the laughter subsided, we ate the food. The wine was very good; even I knew that. The men talked of trade: I listened, filing information away. If I was to be Alekos's wife, I needed to understand this, and more.

"Is the unrest in Qipërta affecting your business?" Sorley asked.

"We ship more grain and oil east," Marius said, "to feed the troops. But that is all."

"What is said on the quayside there?" Druise's voice was casual.

Marius shrugged. "I do not go myself. But the captains say life goes on as normal. The fighting is somewhere distant, not at the port."

"Do you sell directly to the Casilani army, or to a Qipërtani agent?" I asked.

"The shipments for the troops are paid for here. The sacks and amphorae are stamped, to show they are not for sale in Qipërta. They go from the boats to a warehouse, and from there to wherever the army is." He grinned, looking so much like his brother. "I do not know how strong the Qipërtani are, but our men should be their equals, at least. They are very well fed."

"Does the army pay the usual price?"

"No. Somewhat less. But it a steady market."

"But just now, with so many people in the city for the investiture, isn't the demand for food, and its price, rising?"

He smiled. "You know of what you speak, I see, my lady Piása. Yes, it is. But we planned for this: it has been known for some time that the Empress would give up her title when her son turned twenty-one. So for the last two years I have contracted for more grain and oil and wine, and leased more warehouses."

Sorley asked a question about the warehouses, letting me think about what I'd just heard. Food, already purchased a year or two earlier at a standard rate, sold at an inflated price caused by the greater demand in Casil.

I glanced around the room again. The frescoes and furnishings, the bronze bowls and some unusual glassware spoke of wealth. Druise's brother was a shrewd businessman, clearly. I caught Vita's eye. She'd been quiet while the men talked, offering food, keeping wine cups filled. "This is a beautiful room," I said to her.

She dipped her head. "Thank you, my lady."

"Piása, please." I stood, going to examine a glass jug standing on a sideboard, its blue and green hues reminiscent of the bowl Sorley had bought in Sylana. She followed me over. "From my homeland," she said shyly.

"Where is that?"

"East. At the end of the Nivéan Sea."

"And I am from beyond its western end," I said. "Do all peoples meet in Casil?"

"I think so."

The sound of feet on the steps made us both turn. A woman, not young, came in through the door. She stopped, staring at Druisius, and the expression that crossed her face was not one I could read. It almost looked like hatred.

But it was gone in a moment. "Druisius?" she said. He was standing, smiling.

"Bernikë. You are well?"

"Well enough. I did not know you were here." An implication, there.

"I brought friends to meet Marius and Vita. Sorley, Piása, my sister Bernikë." He hadn't offered an embrace, or even a hand in greeting.

"Have you eaten, Bernikë?" Vita asked. "Sit and have food."

"At least wine," Marius said, a shade too heartily. "Vita, fetch more, please."

"I'll come and help," I said. She demurred, but I insisted, and she gave in. At the bottom of the steps I put a hand on her arm. "I do not need to know the reason, but is there animosity between Druise and his sister?"

She looked away, then back. "Yes. Since they were young. Druisius—"

"Don't tell me. But she cannot know who I am, in that case. Earlier today Druise said I was Sorley's daughter. That is what they will tell her, I think."

"I will say nothing. Come into the kitchen; perhaps you could carry more food? I will get wine." She smiled. "Druise? Is that what you call him?"

Chapter 31

~FATHER~

"YOU DO NOT NEED TO WAIT FOR ME," I told Apulo, as we entered the antechamber to the Empress's rooms. "Have you even eaten, between chaperoning Gwenna and escorting me here?"

"Gwenna did not walk in the atrium today," he told me. "Druisius told me she had a bad headache and was resting."

"Too much wine last night?" I had had my share of headaches at her age. Apulo grinned.

The interior doors swung open. Eudekia sat at her worktable, papers in front of her. We had spent many hours there, negotiating the terms that had brought Casilani troops west to help defeat the Marai. Today's would be a different negotiation.

I inclined my head. "Empress." We were not old friends, not today.

"Prince Cillian. Please sit." To the door guard, she said, "Leave us." He stepped outside, pulling the doors closed.

"You are well?"

"Yes, Empress. Thank you for your concern." Well enough. The dizzy spells had subsided, and with them the blurring vision. She had no need to know they had ever happened.

"With the other candidates, we have had my *fiscarius* present, as there are dowries to be considered. But that is not the case with Gwenna. We do not ask a dowry for a woman who will be *Principe* herself."

"The *Princip* Faolyn is a young man, and healthy," I said. "But lives always hang on a thread. My daughter could be *Principe* in thirty years, or three. Were it three, Empress, I might doubt the Prince—the Emperor as he will be—will wish to be separated from his wife. And yet a *Principe* should reside in the country she leads."

"For part of the year," Eudekia said. She had been prepared for this question. "Half, perhaps, with a trusted council for the months she is away. Three years from now, perhaps that would be you, and the *Princip* Casyn's daughter?"

"Talyn," I said. "The general Talyn, she is now."

"You were prepared to be regents, if needed, for the current *Princip* in his youth. I can think of no better governing council than a general and a diplomat." She watched me, looking for a reaction. I did not show her one.

"I too could be dead. A plan for an alternate council would be required."

She smiled. "You are more than capable of devising that plan, Cillian. Do not distract us with minor points."

"It is not a minor point if the plan requires the approval of Casil."

"A formality. We would expect your reasoning as to why the people proposed were suitable, but I do not expect you would suggest someone who planned to depose our Governor and reclaim Ésparias as an independent country." It was said lightly, with a smile, but there was no amusement in her eyes. My back twinged, the muscles tightening involuntarily.

"There are far more who believe one of Faolyn's sons should follow him as *Princip* than think Ésparias was better off alone," I said. "The sentiment exists, of course, but it is a fancy among a few, a nostalgia for something that most never knew."

"What of the other fancy?" I had diverted her.

"That the succession should be direct to Faolyn's heirs? Ésparias has never had a woman leading them. You, Empress, are a figurehead to them, unreal, and soon you will give up your title and your power to your son. The sentiment will grow, I fear, especially if Gwenna is an Empress-Consort in Casil."

"What of your son?"

"Colm?" I said, genuinely surprised—although I should not have been. "He is less suited to leadership than I."

"You are not unsuited to lead a country not at war," she said, but mildly.

"We could debate that for some hours, and it is not why I am here. Colm is observant and intelligent, but his mind is drawn to the puzzles of disease and healing, not politics."

"And yet he is the heir after Gwenna."

"Empress, I will not force either of my children into a role they do not want." I stopped myself from running a hand through my hair. "My daughter has accepted the position you placed her in; beyond that, her choices are her own. She has wisely chosen to be educated as a diplomat. Her assignments have primarily been concerned with the production of goods, and trade and taxation, a solid foundation for someone who will lead a country at peace. She has, Lena tells me, also accepted the responsibility of giving heirs to Ésparias, children who will succeed her, to keep the leadership in my father's direct line, as you wish."

"Your line. Do you truly think I wished the leadership of Ésparias to be in Callan's line? I did not know him. I know you."

You think you do, I thought, but you see what I have let you see. "My line, then. Here, Empress, is where I see a problem."

"Explain."

"May I ask something first?"

She made an impatient gesture. "If you wish."

"When you married Prince Hathus, how did you ensure Alekos remained the heir?"

"It was detailed in our marriage contract. Any children I bore to Hathus were to inherit in his line, in the Boranoi lands—" She stopped. "I see."

"By Casilani law, any children of Alekos and Gwenna would be Alekos's to control, and dually heirs to the Eastern Empire and Ésparias. And while

Ésparias may accept a Casilani governor, and its laws and taxes, they will not, Empress, accept a *Princip* whose first allegiance is to Casil."

She leant back almost imperceptibly, her hand still on the arms of the chair.

"You are saying this marriage is impossible?"

"I am not. Not if the marriage contract follows Ésparian tradition."

Eudekia blinked. "Explain."

"Girls stayed with their mothers; boys, after the age of seven, went to their fathers."

"You would find that acceptable?"

"I would. My daughter might not." It was time to remind her. "A marriage must be Gwenna's choice, and one made freely. I will neither counsel nor coerce."

"Alekos is intrigued. You have seen that, surely."

"Intrigue is not love."

"Love." She waved a hand. "I have lived harmoniously with Hathus without it, and Casil has prospered. Is it needed?"

"It has been for me," I said.

"And no doubt you and your soldier have brought your daughter up to believe it necessary." Her voice had grown colder. "What will you tell her?"

"Gwenna, or Lena?"

"Gwenna."

"What we spoke of, and the proposal I made. Is that acceptable?"

"To discover her thoughts, yes. Do not present it as an accepted compromise."

"How could I? You have not consulted your son."

She acknowledged the point with the barest nod. Silence lay between us for some moments. Then she took a deep breath, her face softening. "Cillian."

"Eudekia."

"Will you play *xache* with me?"

I smiled. "Was that not what we were doing? Of course."

She stood. "I will fetch the game, and call for wine."

But as we neared the end of the game, which I was coming perilously close to losing, a functionary came to whisper in her ear. "I must go," she said to me. She stood, and I did too, a little awkwardly; my leg had stiffened. She glanced down at the board. "Perhaps we can finish this later."

"Whenever you like."

"I doubt that," she said. "Your soldier would not like it if I called you to play late at night." But she was smiling, and there was no animosity in her words this time.

"You misjudge," I said. "My soldier would not mind."

"No?"

"I do not sleep well. If you wish a partner in *xache* or conversation, even in the night, Empress, I will attend you if summoned. But other games are not possible."

She smiled, ruefully. "What a man you are, Cillian of Ésparias. Now, before I go, tell me. Decanius. Have you spoken with him?"

She must know we had. "Yes. He will let me know when we can meet."

"He has been told to cooperate," she said. "I want no war." She gestured to the door. "Knock. The guard will open it." She began to walk toward her private exit.

"Empress?"

She stopped, turned. "Yes?"

"You do not want war. Does your son share your views?"

"He is a young man. Young men see glory, and not the cost." Much what Decanius had said. Eudekia, I thought, wanted peace found before Alekos succeeded to the throne of Emperors.

Apulo was waiting for me. "I went for a meal," he told me, "but you were not in your rooms when I checked. So I came here."

"Thank you." In truth I wished he hadn't; even the brief walk to our rooms would have been a few minutes of solitude. "Is Lena back?"

"No."

Then I would have some time alone to think. The proposal I had made to Eudekia had been spontaneous, a thought that should not have been spoken. Not without consultation with Gwenna. Or Lena. I deserved the ire that would result.

Even before that, the suggestion was faulty. It presumed multiple children, and the birth of both boys and girls. But that was not guaranteed. Casyn had fathered only girls; Ruar had only boy children. I should have required—had planned to require—that all children resulting from the marriage were Gwenna's, for her to decide who was to inherit Ésparias, and who the Eastern Empire. In consultation with Alekos, but hers would be the binding decision. Why had I deviated from my plan?

In our rooms, I accepted watered wine but no drugs—I needed a clear head—and then I sent Apulo away. I sat on the balcony in the late afternoon heat to examine my motives.

The answer, when it came, was simple: my original plan was untenable. Eudekia would no more agree to have the choice of the next ruler of the Eastern Empire resting in Gwenna's hands than I would of the reverse. Had I insisted, it would have ended any possibility of the marriage.

But I hadn't insisted. Why? I did not know what my daughter wanted. If Alekos was her choice, compromises would have to be made. I was laying the foundation for those compromises, nothing more. The conclusion fit the facts. I did not, in the depths of my heart, think it was true.

I was still on the balcony when Lena returned. She sank into another chair with a sigh. "I'm tired," she said. "It's so hot here, and the streets—I don't remember the crowds."

"People have come for the games, and the ceremony," I reminded her. "How was Junia?"

"She commands the horse archers now, all of them. But she made time for us, the entire day. Lynthe did some training."

"Not you?"

"Only a few passes at the pavo, for fun, really." She drank some wine. "I have some things to tell you, but not now. I need to consider them a little more." Apprehension tightened my throat. "Things Junia told me."

The constriction loosened. "Were they told in confidence?"

"Not exactly. I can't tell Gwenna, though."

"Why not?"

"Because the gossip says she'll marry Alekos, and this was not something Junia wanted to get back to him." She put the wine down and stretched, rolling her shoulders. "I'm glad Lynthe didn't hear that."

"How serious is it, between her and Gwenna?"

"I haven't spoken to Gwenna. But Lynthe is in love."

"Eudekia accused me—us—today of bringing Gwenna up to believe love was necessary in a marriage."

Lena made a wry face. "Gwenna certainly didn't think so when she was younger. Remember Sorley telling us she was prepared to marry Bryngyl? Regardless of what she feels for Lynthe, I think she well may put what she sees as her duty to Ésparias first, just as Eudekia did what was best for Casil."

"Eudekia," I said gently, "did not love me."

"She would have." Said matter-of-factly. I smiled.

"She did suggest today I join her for *xache* late at night."

Lena grinned. "What did you say?"

"That I would be pleased to play *xache*, or talk, but that other games were not possible." She laughed. How, I thought, could there be such harmony between us, and yet not?

"*Käresta*." The shift in my tone made her look up. "I did something ill-advised today. You will be angry with me, with cause."

"What?"

I told her, watching her face change.

"You had no right." Ice in her voice: not her quickly flaring, quickly gone anger, but the deeper, colder resentment I had engendered only once or twice before.

"I did say it was ill-advised. But it is a proposal only, a suggestion, and one which would need Gwenna's agreement."

"Ill-advised? How could you even consider it? Or did losing Lianë not affect you at all?" Her voice was growing lower, colder. "Have our children, and theirs, just become game pieces, Cillian? Another vow you will break?"

"You know that is not true," I said.

Lena got to her feet, looking down at me with an expression I had never seen before. But I recognized it: contempt. "What has happened to you, Cillian, that you would suggest sending a small child away? Have you forgotten what it did to you?"

She did not wait for an answer. I heard the outer door close. I didn't try to follow her; I could not have. Fatigue had abruptly suffused me, and with it the melancholy that was never far away. I had been thoughtless once again, seeing a challenge, a puzzle, pieces on a gameboard, not the lives of my daughter and the children she might bear.

I don't know how long I sat there, half fighting the despair, half welcoming it: wanting above all to forget my stupidity, to find a welcome oblivion. When footsteps approached along the balcony, I didn't open my eyes.

"Look at me," Druisius said.

"Leave me be."

His big hand took hold of my chin. "Look at me, you fucking idiot."

Distantly, I felt surprise. In all our years together, even in the worst weeks of freeing myself from the grip of the poppy, he'd never spoken to me like this. I opened my eyes. "I value my life," he said grimly. "Otherwise I would hit you."

He picked up the two wine glasses, emptying the dregs onto the floor. From his belt pouch he took Sorley's flask, pouring *fuisce* into each glass.

"Drink that and listen to me."

I swallowed the *fuisce*, feeling its burn. Druise sat. "I met my sister today."

It took my sluggish mind a moment. "The one—"

"Yes. I saw her eyes. Thirty years, more, and she has not forgiven me. Mothers and children, yes?"

I rubbed my eyes, trying to think. "I suggested nothing more than the tradition Lena was raised with."

He snorted, a derisive sound. "And babies are exposed here every day. Bernikë still hates me." He threw back the *fuisce*. "Cillian. I did not tell you this, before. When my father forced me to take the baby away, I put her in a place where I thought she would be found. Temple servants take girl babies. Better than death, yes?"

"But?"

"The river rose. Rains in the mountains. The flood took her."

"You are sure?"

"I asked. I am sure."

"How old was Bernikë?"

"Fifteen, just."

"Lena is forty, and well-versed in history and politics."

"You think that matters? She has lost one child."

We both had, and Gwenna was an adult. But Druisius had more to say. "I told my sister where I would put her baby. I promised her she would be safe. That was my mistake. All these years you have sworn Kitten's choices are her own, as much as they can be. Now you are finding ways to make this marriage possible. As if you intend it to happen, yes? This is not what told me you would do."

Weeks before, in the mews at the *Ti'ach*, Druisius had suggested the Empress would forgive my treason, if I agreed to the marriage. I had said I would not, unless Gwenna truly wanted to marry Alekos. But what I had proposed to Eudekia today forced a question: was the compromise I sought for my daughter's happiness, or to save my life?

Apulo came, did my exercises and massage. He left, returned with food. I refused it. Druisius didn't. He stayed on the balcony, feet up on the table, as night fell.

I tried to think, with little success. I picked up Catilius, stared at words that meant nothing. Voices drifted in from the balcony. A few minutes later Druisius came in. "Lena will stay with Sorley tonight."

I nodded. He'd take care of her. "What about you?"

He stood with his arms folded. "There is a carpet. Apulo will bring cushions."

"You cannot sleep on the floor."

"I have, many times. I am your bodyguard, yes? Without Lena, I must not leave you."

"I will be all right, Druisius."

"You think? Easy for you to tell the door guard you are in pain and send him for poppy, if I am not here."

I smiled, almost. "You have told him not to go. And warned the doctor." Unnecessarily. The oblivion I sought was that of sleep, not the dreams of poppy. But for all the trust between us, I doubted Druisius would believe that tonight.

"Yes." He unfolded his arms. "I am too old to go through that again. So are you. Do you want music, or *xache*?"

"Thank you, *mo charaidh*, but no. I must think."

He indicated the balcony with a tilt of his head. "I like the night. The chairs there are comfortable." From his belt pouch he took the *fuisce* flask, holding it out to me. "Sorley filled it again. But he warns there is not much left."

Chapter 32

~DAUGHTER~

WE SLEPT LATE THE NEXT MORNING, and got up even later. Midmorning, nearly at the time for exercise in the atrium, I walked along the balcony to my parents' room. No one was there. On a table beside the chair my father used lay a book, not one I'd seen before. The binding and the paper appeared new. I picked it up and went back outside to wait. I'd just started to read when I heard the corridor door open, then shut.

"I just need to get my clothes," my mother said. "I won't be long." Clothes? I put the book down, listening.

"Wait," Sorley said, with some force. "Listen to me, Lena, please. You cannot leave him." He was nearly shouting. Sorley never shouted.

"You did," my mother retorted.

"For a winter, and you know why." The meaning of Sorley's first words sunk in. My mother was considering leaving my father? My hand came up to cover my mouth. "Lena, you can't. It would destroy him."

"And if staying is destroying me?" Bleak misery in her voice.

"How is it? I know you're unhappy. We all know."

A long silence. Was she not speaking, or could I not hear? I sunk lower in my chair, hoping they would not look out and see me.

"He's betrayed me. I am leaving for the same reasons you did."

Sorley swore. At my mother. I tried to breathe quietly. "Do you remember how angry you were at me for that? When I arrived at the *Ti'ach*, you ordered me gone, and when Cillian overrode you, you would barely speak to me for weeks."

"Maybe I should have seen then that he would disregard my wishes when it suited him."

"Lena, be reasonable!" I heard a long exhale, and when Sorley spoke again his voice was controlled. "Have you even asked him why?"

"No. Does it matter why?"

"Yes!" The momentary calm had disappeared. "If I had not run away that winter, if I had stayed to listen why, I would have reached the same conclusions and saved us all a lot of pain."

My mother's retort was rapid and sharp. "Would you have? Without time and distance?"

Silence again, and pacing footsteps. "Where will you go?"

"I will say Cillian is sleeping badly, in pain, and I need not to disturb him when he can sleep. There will be a room somewhere."

"You're not leaving the palace, then?"

"No. Junia would give me a bed, if I asked, but I am Ésparias's military representative. I should stay here."

"I know now why you were so angry with me that spring," Sorley said, his words clipped and curt. "Get what you need. I'll wait."

This time his steps did bring him outside. For a moment, he didn't seem to see me. I said nothing. Then his eyes focused, and he looked down at me. I made a questioning face. He shook his head. "Later," he mouthed, and made a shooing gesture with his hand. I slipped off the chair and as softly as I could escaped along the balcony.

⌘⌘⌘⌘⌘

"You are not well?" Sahira said to me as we walked in the atrium. "Yesterday you were not here at all, and now you are very quiet. That time?"

I smiled wanly and nodded: it wasn't, but as 'that time' didn't bother me, she'd never know. It was as good an excuse as any, and it let me turn down offers to eat together. I left the atrium as soon as I possible could.

"I need to see my father," I told Lynthe. "Apulo, is he in his room?"

"Yes." He looked troubled.

"What's wrong?" Lynthe asked.

"My parents are fighting again," I said. "My father's done something my mother doesn't like. I don't know what. I'm not sure I care what, but she's really angry. And . . . "

"And what?"

"I heard something yesterday I need to tell them."

"Something political?"

"Maybe."

"Can I know?"

"Not yet. To the senior officer first, you know that."

I went, alone, to find my father. Deep lines scored his face, and his hair was unkempt. He gave me half a smile. "*Athàir*," I said, rehearsed words, "I know *Mathàir* is angry with you. But I have learned something I think you both need to hear."

He just nodded. "Your mother told me yesterday she too had things to tell me. We did not have the opportunity. Will you take a note to her? She should be with Sorley."

I fetched what he needed and watched as he wrote the brief request. I could read upside down easily—we had been made to practice as cadets—but I looked away after the first word: 'Major'. Out on the balcony, I could see Druise, apparently half-asleep in a chair.

My father folded the paper, handing it to me. "*Mo nihéan*. The disagreement between me and your mother will find a resolution. We have our differences just now, but your welfare remains the prime concern of each of us. Do not think otherwise." He indicated the note. "I have asked her to come in the afternoon, at our usual time for tea. Sorley too. Bring Lynthe." His tone told me not to ask questions.

In the corridor, I stopped. He hadn't sealed the note. I only wanted to know one thing, I told myself, opening it. He'd signed it simply 'C'.

Tears stung my eyes. I thought they'd worked out whatever was wrong between them. *Your welfare remains the prime concern of each of us.* An implication there, I thought. An implication I didn't like at all.

Sorley was alone. "I don't know," was all he said when I asked where my mother was.

"I have a note from my father for her." I explained what he wanted.

"We'll be there." I didn't think Sorley was in the mood to talk, but I wanted answers.

"She wouldn't really leave him, would she?"

His lips thinned. "I don't know that either, Gwenna. She says she will, and your father—" He made a helpless gesture. "He seems to expect her to."

"But *why*?" Even to myself I sounded like a bewildered child. "What did she mean he'd betrayed her?"

"She thinks he's broken a promise to her. A vow."

"Not with the Empress?"

Sorley gave a dry laugh. "Not in the way you're thinking. But yes, Eudekia's involved. More than that is not mine to tell."

"You're angry with *Mathàir*. I heard you swear at her."

"I'm angry with both of them," he said flatly. "So is Druise." He closed his eyes briefly. "Gwenna, both of us love them. This is hard to watch." His voice softened. "As it is for you, I know."

He held out his arms, and I stepped into them. But I wasn't a child any longer. There was no reassurance in the embrace, just two people sharing their fear.

In the hall I hesitated. I didn't want to go back to my room. At the far end, where the corridor turned, I could see light from an arch opening to the outside of the palace. I went to see where it led.

Which was out onto a flat roof, a wide, sunny space that overlooked the temples and obelisks of the forum. A low wall made the edge safe without obscuring the view. My hands flat on its top, I stood looking at the buildings and the people walking among them. A breeze caught at my hair. It felt a little like being in one of the watchtowers of Wall's End, where I had been illicitly a few times.

I saw a city of stone and brick and tile, of brightly painted statues and triumphal columns and arches. Above me, in the hazy blue sky, crows and kites circled, and the breeze, coming from the river, carried a faint scent of decay. No wonder Ruar had disliked Casil, after the moors and streams and the clear air of Linrathe. Maybe that was what was wrong with my mother; the city oppressed her.

But no. Sorley had said she thought my father had betrayed a vow, one, I was sure, that concerned me. What, though? He had told me repeatedly my choices were my own. He'd told Alekos the same. *Eudekia's involved.* In a way Sorley couldn't tell me.

Then one or the other of my parents was going to. If I was the cause— or part of it—of the strife between them, I should know.

"My lady Gwenna," a voice said from behind me. I turned. Decanius approached me, blinking in the sunshine. "I did not expect to find you here, alone and unguarded."

"*Magistere.* I was enjoying the view," I said, motioning with a hand.

"Of course." He came to stand beside me, closer than I liked. "I have not congratulated you on your feat at the baths. You are very skilled with a knife, it appears."

"Very. My mother made sure of that."

"A useful skill in your untamed lands."

"And in this city. The dangers may be different, but they are still real."

He conceded the point with a smile. "You have killed a man, I understand."

Who had told him that? "Yes," I said shortly. "He was trying to kill me."

His eyes travelled down my body. "Kill?"

"I was an obstacle to his purpose, as were the lord Sorley and Captain Druisius, who were with me. There were three of them, and three of us. A fair and even fight. They all died." I pitched my voice to frost. "And then I ended my horse's pain with the same knife. She had been mortally wounded by a thrown axe. When death is necessary, I have no compunctions, *Magistere*."

"Perhaps a useful trait in a woman who will lead her country one day," he said, "or be a wife and mother to Emperors. You are the Prince's guest at the games tomorrow, are you not?" He had not outwardly reacted to my tone.

"I am, yes."

"May I tell you what you would see, were you standing here tomorrow? A procession such as you have never imagined, coming through the forum between the temples, and then down this street beside the palace, and into the Arénas." A sweep of his hand outlined the route. "Soldiers on horseback, dancers, athletes—the strongest and lithest—and musicians. All to honour the Prince Alekos with their prowess. The people come out to see them on their way to the Arénas, those who cannot afford even the places to stand inside, but also some who can."

I tried to picture it, interested despite my wariness. "How many dancers and athletes?"

"Scores. You will see from the imperial seats tomorrow." He kept talking, telling me of the wonders I would experience. I moved so the low wall was at my back, creating a little distance between us. He didn't close the gap.

He spoke, I thought, from a real pride in the city and its customs, taking pleasure in instructing me in its ways. I asked a few more questions and he answered without condescension, beyond saying, "I expect our sport and spectacles are not among the Prince Cillian's interests."

He had just started to tell me about the training regimes for the athletes when a voice made us both turn to the door. "You will excuse my interruption," Druise said. "Princess, your parents await you."

"Druisius," Decanius said. His stance changed; legs spread, chest pushed out, challenging. "I did not expect to see you here."

"Druisius is our captain of the guard," I said.

"You are responsible for the security of the Princess?"

"*Magistere*," Druise said, almost respectfully. "Of both the Princess and her father, yes."

"Then why was she alone?"

"Alone," Druise said, "does not mean unguarded, *Magistere*. Shall we go, Princess?"

Druise shot me a grim look as we made our way to my parents' room. "You should not have been alone."

"What danger was there?"

"That man. He did not try to touch you?"

"No. He was pleasant." Why was I lying to Druise? I didn't know, and I didn't have time to work it out. Perhaps I just wasn't in the mood for a lecture. And Decanius had been pleasant, after I had subtly warned him.

My mother wore her uniform, her insignia of rank pinned to her shoulder. She and Lynthe stood near the open door to the balcony. "Close that," Sorley said. "What we have to say here cannot be overheard." Lynthe did his bidding. The hall guard had already been dismissed. "Tell us what you learned from Junia, Lena."

"Tomorrow, the horse archers ride in a display in the Arénas, part of the games. Junia requested new equipment a few weeks ago, for them to look their best. The request was declined." Her voice was neutral, measured, an officer giving a report. "Junia assumed it was a mistake, so she went to enquire. She was told it was not an error; there was no spare equipment. Everything had been sent east to the troops at Qipërta. Even training weaponry."

"Why was Junia surprised?" my father asked. "Many men have been sent to Qipërta, some of them new recruits. They would need equipment, both for training and for battle."

"I thought the same. But the armourer is a veteran, experienced with both men and weapons. He thought too much had been sent; more than what should be needed. No proof, just his intuition."

"Too many weapons and too much food?" I said. "Who is being armed and fed?"

"Too much food?" My father turned to me. "Where did you hear this, Gwenna?"

"Yesterday. From Druise's brother Marius, who is a trader."

"Where did you meet him?" My mother didn't sound pleased.

"At his home. I went with Druise and Sorley." I met her gaze, but her next words weren't addressed to me.

"Without my permission?" she snapped at Druisius.

"Remember I am an envoy, and trade is my specialty. I too have work to do here," I interrupted. "I asked to go. Druise thought it safe, and it was."

"I don't like it," she said.

"He introduced me with a false name. The princess of Ésparias was never there."

"We're here to consider information," Sorley said, "not squabble over Gwenna's safety. I heard what Marius said, but I didn't think about what it might mean."

"There are at least two explanations," my father said, "of which one is benign, and one not."

"You're not the *Comiádh* here," my mother said. "Tell us."

"This is a military matter. What do you see, Major?"

I was sure I knew, but this was not the time to offer my thoughts. She stared at him, her jaw set, for a breath, two. "The benign explanation," she said, in a tight, precise voice, "is that Hathus has recruited more troops than expected, and they need both food and weapons."

"A real possibility, and the likely one," my father said.

"But he could also be arming and feeding the Qipërtani."

"And if he is?" My father's words were soft, not a question to my mother.

"Marriage or war: those were the options, Decanius said. Why is it so important that Sahira marry Alekos?"

I was no longer willing to stay quiet. "Because a child of hers is a child of Hathus's blood," I said, "and would be heir to the Eastern Empire."

Chapter 33

~FATHER~

PRIDE IN MY DAUGHTER LIGHTENED my melancholy for a moment. I nodded, hoping my approval showed on my face.

"Sahira is Hathus's niece," Lena said.

"A Boranoi." As I spoke, Sorley straightened in his chair, understanding dawning. "Her mother is Hathus's half-sister, and, I believe, acknowledged but not a child of marriage. Close enough for Hathus to claim the relationship if it is advantageous to him; distant enough for him to disavow it, if needed."

"So in a generation, the Boranoi rule the Eastern Empire." I saw from Gwenna's face she understood the implications.

"Or less." Druise had been quiet, listening, thinking. "A year, two, before there is an heir. Once there is—" He shrugged. "Casil has had an Empress as regent for her son for two decades. Were Alekos to die, they could again, yes?"

No one spoke. What Druisius had just suggested was treason. Hathus's treason, were he correct. His own, were he wrong.

"This is speculation," Sorley said. "We can't prove any of it."

"I know," Gwenna said, "but it feels right. I see the game board."

"Do you see Decanius's place on it?" I asked.

She stared into nothing, her eyes unfocused. Thinking, I knew. "He was sub-Procurator there," she said. "He knows people. Money and power, I think. Perhaps a place on a regency council?"

"Dear gods," Lena said, pacing.

"I see the same game board," I said. "But knowing how it could work is not the same as being right, Gwenna. We cannot speak of this, or let slip the tiniest hint of suspicion."

"Are we to just let it happen, sir?" Lynthe asked.

That too would be treason. "We need to be surer than we are," Lena replied, before I had framed an answer. "I will be spending more time with the other military envoys, so I have an opportunity both to listen and ask questions if the chance arises. And before," she said, her eyes, fierce and adamant, on me, "you tell me to be careful, remember that Casyn trusted me with a similar task when I was eighteen."

Not one that was equally dangerous, I thought.

"We all listen and ask, yes?" Druisius said. "But not many questions, or it will be noticed."

"Do your best to remember everything, regardless of how trivial it sounds," I added. A soft knock sounded; Apulo put his head around the corridor door.

"Are you ready for me, Cillian?"

"Are we done?" Lena asked.

"I'd like to speak to *Athàir* alone," Gwenna said. "Can I come back later?"

"Come and have supper with him," Apulo suggested. "He might eat more than a mouthful or two, if you are here."

Sorley did not leave, but sat quietly, frowning when Lena left with Lynthe and Gwenna. "I want half an hour with Cillian," he told Apulo.

"Sit with me on the balcony," Druisius said to Apulo. "With wine, yes?"

"All of us need wine," Sorley said. He dealt with it, giving Druisius and Apulo theirs first. Only when they were outside, the doors closed, did he give me mine. I took the cup, my fingers touching only it. He showed no surprise.

"Are you truly just going to let her go?" he asked, dropping heavily into his chair again.

"What else can I do?"

"Apologize? Admit you were wrong?"

"I have." Tiredness dragged at me. I closed my eyes.

"I can imagine. In the way you always do." Sarcasm sharpened his voice. "Cillian, you have more trouble admitting you're wrong than any man I have ever known. It's infuriating."

"Then perhaps you should emulate Lena and leave me alone." I didn't want this conversation; I was afraid of what I might divulge to Sorley.

Sorley swore, violently. Real anger now. "Enough of your self-pity! You're going to lose her because you can't beg her forgiveness?"

"On my knees again, as Eudekia required?"

"Don't jest!" He sighed, a gust of air and sound. "It might get through to Lena."

"Her mind is made up," I murmured.

"No, it's not." I opened my eyes. His, narrowed and assessing, were on me. "You didn't notice?"

"Notice what?"

"For all her anger, and leaving you to wake alone, she is still wearing her *li'itho*."

"Perhaps she has just forgotten it."

"No. When she thinks I'm not watching, her fingers find it, constantly. Leave Catilius behind, Cillian. Don't blindly accept what fate has brought you." He downed his wine. "And don't think I'm not angry with her too. I'll tell Apulo you're ready for him now."

Apulo's hands worked on my back, the familiarity of both the pain and the relief letting me think, as well as I could through the heaviness that permeated both my body and my mind. I did not want to be here, dealing with treachery and politics and my own duplicity. I missed the *Ti'ach*. For seventeen years its routines and structures and the pleasure I found in young minds had, for the most part, kept the guilt and remorse at bay. And beyond and behind that, for all it had been the strange and frightening place I had been sent to as a child of seven, it was home.

Pain shot down my leg as Apulo's fingers dug deeper. I breathed, waiting for it to subside. Would the *Ti'ach* still be home without Lena, if somehow I found a way through the peril I perceived? I was growing old. Age brought loss, of things small and great: the acuity of hearing, the rapidity of thought, an unexpected child. I had thought I had accepted this decline; that both my actions and my injuries had taught me to live with things lost. But I had not expected love to be one of them.

Sorley would still be there; I would not be without love either received or given. But the balance would shift, and there was Druisius to consider. He too loved Sorley, and Sorley him. It would be better if I again chose to be celibate.

Gwenna arrived, alone, just as Apulo brought food. Druisius, who had been playing his *cithar* quietly in one corner of the room while I pretended to read, took his meal out to the balcony.

Neither Gwenna nor I ate much. I had no interest in food when melancholy stalked me, and she was distracted, or worried. She put her plate on the table, reaching for her watered wine "Are you and *Mathàir* fighting about me?"

"Not directly." I ran a hand through my hair. "And yet, yes."

"Then shouldn't I know?" Anger flashed across her face. "You tell me my choices are my own, but don't tell me this?"

"You are," I said, "entirely correct. I have been wrong." Sorley, I thought in a corner of my mind, would be pleased with me. "Listen, then."

I told her why I had insisted I came with her to Casil, because I— speaking for Ésparias—could not allow Alekos to control who was our country's leader, regardless of how nominal that leader's power was. "Faolyn, you—even I—are symbols, Gwenna," I said, "a reminder that Ésparias and her people are more than a province of Casil; that we have a history of our own. Remove that, and what strength have we, when Casil leaves us again? As they will."

"I see that," she said, "but why didn't you tell me? Do you think control is what the Empress wants?"

"How can Ésparias be important enough?" I asked. "We produce nothing unique in the Empire, or in abundance beyond other provinces, do we?"

"No. Then why, *Athàir?*"

"I have to believe it is that she wants something not very different from what Hathus does. He wants a child who bears Boranoi blood on the throne. Eudekia too is taking a long view. Your children and Alekos's would mean her grandchild—and mine—sits on that throne instead."

"So she is not thinking of Ésparias at all?"

"Not in the same way." A distant province she had never seen; why would she?

"This is all because you wouldn't marry her?" Disbelief in Gwenna's voice.

"Had I, our children, were there any, would not have been in line for the throne," I reminded her. She frowned, trying to make sense of Eudekia's motives.

"It's a gift? Your grandchild as the ruler of the Eastern Empire?"

"I think so." Gift, or inducement? History might then remember me as the scholar-prince, not the one executed for treason.

"Then . . . did she love you? Does she still?" Not a question I had expected. Nor, in truth, one I could answer.

"Perhaps. In a way." I heard my own fatigue.

Gwenna did not, or she chose to ignore it. "Is that," she demanded, "why my mother is so angry?"

Chapter 34

~DAUGHTER~

I KNEW MY FATHER WAS TIRED; I could both see and hear it. More than tired; he looked ill. I'd talk to Druise and Apulo in a minute, share my concern, but I wanted answers.

He sighed, running a hand through his greying hair. Grey hair. There was little black left. "No."

"Sorley says she thinks you betrayed her. Broke a vow, and the Empress is involved somehow. He wouldn't tell me more."

"That is the most recent cause."

"Did you break a vow?"

"A matter of interpretation." He picked up his wine. We'd been talking for some time; likely he did need to wet his throat, but I recognized the ploy to buy time. After all, he'd taught it to me.

"I promised your mother that I would not allow you to be a piece in Eudekia's games," he said. "The Empress wanted you to be brought here as a child, as Faolyn was, for education. I suspect even then she planned to shape you to be Alekos's bride, possibly betroth you very young. I refused, more than once, to allow this." His voice, hoarse from exhaustion, dropped away.

"*Mathàir* told me all this," I said, anger subsumed in concern, "You're tired. Tell me the rest another day."

"No. You must hear this." He straightened a little. "Eudekia herself was the daughter of a man high in the government of Casil. He had no sons, and he educated Eudekia far beyond what is usual for girls here. Her marriage to Philatos, Alekos's father, was surprising; a marriage for love, not politics." He emptied his wine glass. I held out my hand; he gave it to me.

I refilled it, adding only a small amount of water, and placed it on the table in front of him.

"When the Boranoi threat arose, her father counselled a military defeat, not a political compromise, and encouraged Philatos to war. When Philatos was killed, Eudekia's father did what is considered honourable here and took his own life. That she managed to not be deposed or killed herself, but convinced the remaining councillors to allow her to rule as regent for Alekos, speaks to her subtlety and intelligence." He cleared his throat before taking the smallest sip of wine.

"Eudekia and I have corresponded regularly over the years. She knows how you have been educated, and she expressed approval at your choice of diplomacy as your work." He stopped to take a breath, two. "In effect, *mo nihéan*, by bringing you up the way I and your mother believed you should be, as heir to Ésparias, we removed the need to have you sent to Casil. You are intelligent and insightful, and you have been trained to think, just as she was. The ideal wife for her son." A faint smile appeared on his lips. "You do see the irony here?"

"You thought you were keeping me safe, and instead you played into her plans," I said. "But you didn't purposely break a promise."

"Not then. Where your mother thinks I did was in my most recent move, if you will, in this game."

He told me what he had proposed, the division of male and female children between Ésparias and Casil. "I made it clear you would have to agree."

How little Eudekia truly knew my father, I thought, if she believed his compliance could be bought through me, through a grandchild who would rule the Empire of the East. He had betrayed his land once. He would not do it again.

My choices, though, were my own. I would not be betraying Ésparias; I would still, someday, assuming I outlived Faolyn, be *Principe*, and a daughter after me. And my father—my family—would be safe.

"Why wouldn't I? It's a reasonable compromise."

My father smiled, tiredly. "It sounds that way. But the actual practice is likely much harder, both on child and parent."

"Faolyn didn't mind," I said, "He'd been expecting to be sent to his father for two years, and was angry it hadn't happened, he told me once."

"Talyn was not perturbed either," he said. "I remember being surprised by that, at the time. My own experience was somewhat different, as your mother reminded me, quite forcibly."

"Thinking about losing a child—in any way—must cause her pain just now," My words sounded awkward in my own ears.

He gave a slight nod. "She is not alone in that."

I slipped off my chair to kneel beside him, putting my arms around him. He felt fragile, somehow. Old. Tears threatened. I blinked them back, his hand stroking my hair. I kissed his cheek. "I'll talk to *Mathàir*."

"No," he said gently. "Do not, please."

"But this concerns me." I sat back on my heels. "She needs to know I don't object to your proposal."

"Then you may tell her that, but you must be the diplomat, Gwenna, relaying a message but not entering into argument, or not into any argument that touches on the dispute between us. That is for your mother and me to resolve, not you. Can you do that?"

Could I? I would have to. "I can. I promise." I leant forward to kiss his cheek again. "And now I am fetching Apulo. Don't argue."

⌘⌘⌘⌘⌘

By midmorning, heat hung in the air of my room. I finished dressing, the new tunic light and cool. I pulled my hair up, looping and fastening it into a neat coil held off my neck. The bowl of the Arénas would be hot, even if the private box I'd be sharing with Alekos and his party was shaded.

I'd had a visit from a functionary the previous evening, briefing me on protocol. My father would be seated with us as my official chaperone, or protector, along with the Empress and one or two senior advisors. The guards would be from the palace: Lynthe and Druisius's services were not required. They were free to watch the games from an appropriate location.

I'd asked about my mother, to be told she'd be with the other military envoys. "In very good seats," he'd added, "so they can watch the displays of troops carefully." The lord Sorley had a place too, he assured me.

The spectacles would begin before we arrived in the imperial box, lesser dancers and boxers to entertain the crowds of common people. I was to join the Empress and the Prince for refreshments prior to walking, via a private corridor, to the box.

Sweat beaded on my neck. No doubt there would be fan-wielding servants at the Arénas, but that wasn't helping here. I stepped out onto the balcony. The air was as still as in the room. Even the pigeons we often heard cooing and scrabbling on the roof were quiet.

"Maybe there's a breeze on the other side," I said to Lynthe. "Let's go out there. The procession might have started, too."

"Should you?" She wasn't dressed in full uniform, but in a light tunic, her lieutenant's insignia pinned to her shoulder and one secca in its sheath on her belt.

"Why not? I have a few minutes."

She shrugged. "I suppose there's no reason."

Cool shade greeted us, to my relief, the walls of our level blocking the sun. I could hear music and shouts from the far end of the forum, and crowds between the buildings, but nothing more.

"I'm surprised there's no one else out here," Lynthe said. So was I. Not the other bridal candidates, but members of their parties with nothing to do, or even palace staff.

"Maybe there's a better place to watch the procession from," I suggested. Probably there was, closer to the front of the palace, where the street widened before turning toward the gate into the Arénas.

I moved closer to the railing. It was warmer here, but a breeze made up for it. But the sun grew hotter, the music no closer, and the breeze was sporadic. After a while I said, "We should go."

We turned to the door. A clatter of wings made me look up, directly into the bright blue sky over the palace. I saw the silhouettes of pigeons exploding off the roof, and a sense of an object falling. Lynthe shoved me. I stumbled forward. Something hit the ground, shattered. Instinctively I closed my eyes. A sudden sharp pain stabbed my cheek.

I leant against the wall, breathing hard. I put my fingers up to my face: blood. "What was that?" I kept my hand pressed to my cheek.

"Roof tile," Lynthe said. She looked upward, then back at me. "Let's get you cleaned up. Then I'll report it."

"You too," I said. She frowned. "Your leg's bleeding."

She glanced down. "I didn't feel it." She bent to touch the flesh nearby. "It's not deep. We were lucky. Back to our room, and I'll go for the physician."

"No!" Didn't she realize? "Lynthe, if this wasn't an accident, we don't want the whole palace to know. Apulo can deal with wounds this small, and we need to tell Druise what happened, and let him investigate."

Apulo dealt with the cuts while Druise questioned us, but we had little to tell. "You heard nothing?"

"No," I said again, as Apulo salved my cheek. He had cleaned the nick and had me hold a cloth against it until the trickle of blood stopped.

I washed my hands in a bowl of water while he tended to Lynthe's leg. "Lieutenant?" Druise persisted.

"Nor I, Captain. The noise of the pigeons' wings would have muffled any sound. I saw no movement except the sliding tile."

Apulo wrapped a bandage around Lynthe's leg; her wound was deeper than I'd thought. "You will let me see them, morning and night."

"I've had worse cuts on the training field," Lynthe said. "But, yes, Apulo, if it makes you happy. What are you going to tell the Prince, Gwenna? He's going to notice."

"Probably an accident, yes?" Druise said. "Boys are sent up sometimes, to clean the dead things the kites leave. One might have loosened a tile. If you report it, someone will be punished."

"Tell them you dropped a wine glass," my father said. He'd been quiet, letting Apulo and Druise deal with what was needed. "It will explain both wounds. Lynthe, go back to your room and drop one onto the tiles, but," he added, with a hint of a smile, "do your best to not be cut again. Gwenna, Apulo, if you are ready, we should go. We are late, but they will forgive that under the circumstances. I will explain."

He rose, without help, I was glad to see, using only his black and silver cane to steady himself. I stood too. "Wait," Apulo said. He looked me up and down. "No blood on the tunic. Very good."

Druise escorted us to the imperial apartments. I glanced at my father once or twice, wondering how he managed to look so regal this morning, when he had been so drawn and exhausted last night. Baths and massage and some concoction of Apulo's, I presumed, but something more than that. His own determination.

The slight displeasure at our late arrival turned to concern once the formal greetings had been made. My father managed to convey, without saying it directly, that nervousness on my part had been the cause of the dropped glass.

"It is of no matter," the Prince said to me, smiling, "since you are not seriously hurt. Although I do hope the cut will not scar, Princess, and mar your loveliness." A servant brought us drinks, a pale, honeyed wine.

"A scar arising from my own clumsiness would be unfortunate." I had other scars from the days of learning to use secca and sword: one on my right thigh, one on the inside of my left arm, where I hadn't been quick enough with my shield to parry my partner's sword thrust. I wasn't going to bring his attention to them.

My reference to clumsiness elicited a comment from him about the dog at the baths, as I had thought it might. To my surprise, Alekos asked only about how I had learned to throw a knife so accurately.

"They are made to be thrown," I told him. "The balance between hilt and blade is such they fly straight, even as they spin. I began with a wooden one when I was eight or nine; it is a skill my mother teaches to all students at the *Ti'ach*, although I was younger than most."

"Your parents were your tutors? No one else?"

"Until I was twelve. History and philosophy and languages from my father; weaponry, primarily, from my mother. The lord Sorley was my music teacher, and Druise—Captain Druisius—also taught weaponry, and music."

"Your guard taught you music?" He sounded puzzled.

"He is talented with the *cithar*, so I can play it too, although I am not very good. And," I said, purposely, "Apulo, my father's aide, teaches us to sing. He is highly trained."

He nodded. "Slaves and eunuchs often teach here. I have had both, among my own tutors."

"You were schooled alone? Not with other boys?"

"Not always. Sometimes princes from other lands joined me, so we could learn to know each other. Your own *Princip* was one, although he was much older than I. But come, let us eat a little."

We moved to the table where food was laid out: breads and sweetmeats, cheese and eggs, fruit. Across the room, my father spoke with the Empress and Bruccius. I caught the name Annaeus. The book I'd picked up on the balcony had been by Annaeus.

How could he talk calmly of dead philosophers when my mother was considering leaving him? I'd spoken to her not long after dawn. What she'd said hadn't reassured me at all.

I tried to calm the rising fear. *Athàir* is doing what he must, I told myself; he is being a diplomat, in more ways than one. An angry opponent needed time to think, to reflect on whatever offer had been made; more negotiation did not further the cause.

"My lady?" a servant murmured. "Is there something you would like that you do not see?"

I'd been blindly staring at the table of food. "No," I said, with a quick smile. I took a few things at random. Alekos hadn't seemed to notice my distraction, or was too polite to mention it. Perhaps he thought me overwhelmed by the array of dishes.

"Bruccius," he said with a nod toward the man, "was one of my tutors. He will remain an advisor to me; his knowledge of our history is unparalleled."

"He and my father—" Another voice interrupted me.

"My deepest apologies, Empress, and to you, Prince Alekos. An unavoidable delay." Decanius. He knelt, his head bowed, holding the pose until Eudekia spoke.

"Your delays are always unavoidable, Decanius. You must learn to navigate obstructions more neatly." Her expression was not quite amused.

"Empress." He rose. "May I say you are looking as lovely as the huntress herself?" Eudekia wore a tunic like mine, but longer, the hem falling below her knees and trimmed in purple. Light sleeves covered her upper arms, whereas mine were bare.

"I believe that compliment belongs to the princess Gwenna," she replied. Decanius turned to me.

"You do indeed honour the goddess of the hunt, Princess." His eyes flicked to the cut on my cheek, and away. "I cannot imagine you have a knife hidden in that gown today."

"Do not presume to speak to the princess in such a way!" Alekos snapped.

"The princess is aware I jest," Decanius said smoothly.

"Am I?" I didn't smile. "The *Magistere* and I have had a previous conversation about knives," I told Alekos. "He was also kind enough to explain the procession of performers and athletes which will enter the Arénas. Does that happen before or after we arrive?"

We ate and talked about the procession and the spectacle. Bruccius, overhearing, called us over. We joined the others, although we remained standing.

"The private passage and the sheltered imperial box were added by Prince Alekos's grandfather," he told me. "He was fond of the chariot races, it is said."

"He was," the Empress said. "My father accompanied him, once or twice, and came home to tell me about it. Shall we now follow in their footsteps, and go to the Arénas?"

Bruccius offered an arm to my father, and at some unheard signal four guards appeared. Two ahead of us, two behind, they escorted us through the palace corridors and into a domed passage, lit by openings in the curved ceiling, the walls and floor painted and tiled with depictions of beasts and chariots and figures racing.

Two carved and inlaid doors were swung open by more guards, and we stepped out onto a wide platform, shaded by a roof supported on pillars but open on three sides. A low rumble of sound from the crowd below became a roar as the Empress stepped forward to acknowledge her people. So many people! Thousands upon thousands filled the stands. I hadn't realized how large the Arénas was; how high the stands rose above the oval below.

Alekos walked forward to join his mother, and the roar grew louder, if that were possible. He was popular, then. I moved beside my father. "I had no idea," I murmured.

"Nor did I, truly, for all Druisius tried to tell me." Far below us, gates at the righthand end of the oval opened, and the procession began to wend its way into the Arénas. Tiny figures, almost lost in the vast space, then a hundred or more horsemen, riding in tight formation. Not just horsemen, but women, too, with bows: the horse archers of Casil.

"Your mother," my father said, "will watch this display with interest."

She should be watching it with you, I thought, but this was not the place to say it. Nor would it have been possible; Eudekia would not have included her in this invitation.

The Empress and the Prince stepped back to take their seats, allowing us to sit too. The riders circled the entire field at a controlled gallop before leaving by the gate they'd come in. "They will return," Alekos said quietly to me. "But first, the dancers."

Chapter 35

~FATHER~

AS PRECISE AND ORDERED AS THE RIDERS, lines of dancers took their places on the inner field, where the hooves of the horses had not churned up the surface. They arranged themselves on either side of the *murum*, the central line of statues and columns. To the faint music of *cithar* and pipes, they began to dance, whole lines moving together like petals of a flower opening to the sun, then closing again. Their numbers, I realized, meant the effect could be seen from the highest seats, their bright costumes enhancing their visibility against the sand.

The flowers curved in on themselves, circled, and became serpents, undulating along the *murum* in opposite directions. I glanced at my daughter: she was leaning slightly forward, a look of delight on her face.

"As lovely as this is," Decanius murmured in my ear, "we have things to talk about. There are rooms off the passage behind us. Shall we withdraw, with the Empress's permission?"

I glanced to my right, where Eudekia sat. Without taking her eyes from the dancers below, she inclined her head. I reached for my cane; immediately Apulo was at my side to help me up. He'd been standing against the wall behind us. I would have to remember to ask him what he thought, the once-enslaved boy now watching the spectacle from the imperial box. If his eyes weren't always on me, that was.

Decanius led us to a small room a few paces down the passage. It held a table and benches: a guards' room, or a place to bring food before serving it to those watching the games. Beside me, Apulo clicked his tongue. "Forgive me, *Magistere*," he said, "but where can I find a chair? Prince Cillian needs support for his back."

"My oversight," Decanius said, pleasantly enough, and sent Apulo off with directions.

"I will stand until he returns," I said, going to the small window to look out. Decanius knew the bench was inadequate to my needs. He had wanted Apulo gone. Why? Was I in danger here?

"I have a question," Decanius said. "One I thought best asked in private."

I turned from the window. "I assumed as much. What is it you want to know?"

"I lived in Ésparias," he said. "Behaviour is different. Morals are different. Is your daughter untouched by a man, Prince Cillian?"

I almost laughed. "Why do you think I would know?"

His brow raised. "You do not?"

"My daughter does not live with me, and for her work travels the length and breadth of Ésparias with a bodyguard, not a chaperone, *Magistere*. As I have said repeatedly, she is an adult, and her choices are her own. Nor," I said, a little more forcefully, "is this something I would discuss with her."

"Would her mother know?"

"Perhaps. But of what relevance is it?" I knew, though.

"An expectation," he said. "It is clear the Prince is drawn to her. I would not want him to be disappointed."

"And if she had the same expectation of him?"

"It is different for men. We both know that."

"Not in Ésparias. I am sure the Prince's education has taught him this."

"I am sure it has. But his upbringing will have shaped feelings more than an abstract piece of knowledge, do you not think?"

"You are suggesting that if Gwenna would not meet the Prince's requirements, she should withdraw from his consideration," I said, controlling my anger with some difficulty. "Firstly, *Magistere*, is not the law only that she has contracted no formal partnership, current or past, and that she is clearly not with child?"

His scalp reddened. "Those have been the expectations in prior generations."

"So that there can be no demands of money or property made."

He conceded the point with a curt nod. "You seem," I went on, keeping my voice calm, "to believe marriage to the princess Sahira is the only route to peace with Qipërta. Were we not charged with finding alternatives?"

"Alternatives would not be needed if there were an impediment to a marriage with your daughter."

"There is not. *Magistere*, you are presuming several things. One is that my daughter wishes to marry Alekos, regardless of what his intent is. Another is that he would choose the princess Sahira at all." I let a thread of anger enter my voice. "The third, I believe, is that I am aging, and in pain, and would prefer an easy agreement to long talks and dispute. But I am prince of Ésparias by the Empress's decree, and loyal to her, and I will do her bidding. Am I to tell her that you will not?"

His lips thinned, then parted. But whatever he had been about to say, he thought better of it. I waited.

"No," he said eventually. "You are not. We will talk. Your eunuch can write? A scribe would be useful."

Apulo returned with another man, each carrying a chair woven of strong fibres, and cushioned. He would be pleased to scribe, he replied to my question. Decanius sent the second man for writing materials and wine.

"I understand the dispute centres on taxes and tariffs?" I began, once we were settled.

"Yes, primarily. Qipërta pays the same rates and fees as other provinces, which is inappropriate."

"Because of a blood tie between the Empress's husband and the king of Qipërta's consort?"

"You are well informed. That is correct. Sahira's mother was a favourite of the Boranoi king; not royal herself, but of high enough birth."

Everything he said agreed with what I had already been told. "An acknowledged daughter?" She must have been, to be a piece in the marriage games.

Decanius rubbed the side of his nose with one finger. "Yes."

I paused. I knew what I would say; I had had enough sleepless hours to think about it. My first proposal was so obvious I could not believe Decanius had not made it himself. His reaction would be instructive.

"Is Qipërta favoured by the Boranoi with regard to taxes and tariffs?"

"Yes. Since the marriage. Over twenty years now." Then the agreement had been made when he was the sub-Procurator.

"When Hathus married the Empress, the same proposal was not made then, to balance the influence of the two empires on Qipërta?" The Boranoi were not an empire but an alliance, but the distinction did not matter just now.

Nor did Decanius correct me. "No. At the time Qipërta was a minor province, insignificant in military terms."

"Not unlike Ésparias," I said drily.

He actually smiled, an apparent genuine reaction. "Not unlike," he agreed. "But without a son who charmed an Empress and thereby gained royal status for himself and his province."

"An unforeseen result of my diplomatic efforts." Stay calm, I told myself.

"Was it?" He shrugged. "Of no matter now. Your treaty that ended the Boranoi conflict nineteen years past was one of balance, of sharing the disputed trade route. You favour compromise, not control."

"I weigh the price of each," I said, "and in this case it is the Empress who does not want the cost of a war. Prince Hathus is in Qipërta. Perhaps she wishes only not to risk losing another husband in battle."

"Perhaps. So tell me, Prince Cillian, what compromises do you propose to avoid a war with Qipërta? If we give in to their demand for reduced taxes only to avoid a fight, then every province will threaten an uprising to gain the same concession." He spoke without belligerence, and his point, I had to admit, was valid.

"What is the state of Casil's coffers?"

Decanius blinked, faint surprise crossing his face. "Adequate, but both the costs of the Prince's investiture and the Qipërtani conflict are significant. Why?"

"Taxes could be reduced everywhere for a year or two, a gesture of goodwill from the new Emperor—and then Qipërta's not raised again."

"That would simply delay conflict, and widen it, as provinces learned of the Qipërtani's special status," he said flatly. "Traders talk. Envoys talk." On the surface, I thought, he is more polished than he was in his years in Ésparias, less hasty in his decisions, but behind the veneer is still a man who favours punishment over conciliation. "It is not that I have not thought of your solutions," he went on. "But I cannot see how they create a lasting peace."

If that is even what he wanted. I could not forget our suspicions. Money and power for this man, and a Boranoi on the throne of Casil in another generation.

"Then," I said, "we need to think differently. You were sub-Procurator in Qipërta, were you not? You must have a good understanding of the land and its people."

"I was. My father was Procurator, and as Qipërta is not a royal province, he also served as its governor. It is not dissimilar to your own land in what it produces, but more of it is mountainous, not suited to crops, and it too has only one city of any size, on the coast." Without asking, he poured and watered two glasses of wine, holding one out to me. A conciliatory gesture?

"What does it trade to the Boranoi?" I asked.

"What Casil allows. Grain and fish, salt, limited amounts of copper and tin."

In legitimate commerce. I had no doubt there would be a thriving market which bypassed official records. But regardless of the treaty I had negotiated with the Boranoi, I had no real expertise in trade. I had simply offered a compromise no one else had.

"May I see the notes?" Decanius asked, holding out a hand to Apulo. He read them over. "Accurate." he commented. "Copy them, so both your master and I have a record. Write more neatly."

The order had been made pleasantly enough, but it was still an order. "Please," I said to Apulo. I had, once or twice in my days as a travelling teacher, been employed by landholders who saw fit to give me orders, enough to know how it felt.

We sat drinking wine while Apulo made his copy. "Qipërta is a beautiful land," Decanius said. "The sea there is blue, not like the cold grey of yours."

"You enjoyed your time there." He was making an effort; I must respond appropriately. "Do you speak its language?"

"Of course," he said. "It is a strange tongue, more like to Heræcrian than Casilan."

"The Empire has sent you far and wide," I said. "With a wife and family, or alone?"

"No wife." After a mouthful of wine he added, "I could have married well, of course, had I chosen to. But I saw a good man destroyed by his obsession with a woman, and vowed not to take the risk. My steward runs my household efficiently, and other satisfactions are not hard to obtain."

It had been the first thing he had asked for on arriving in Ésparias: a woman or a boy, Sorley had told me. He had been disappointed, but here in Casil either was available for a price, and a *Magistere* could afford to pay for the best.

With a slight bow, Apulo handed the notes to Decanius. "A cleaner copy," Apulo said, "as I was not rushing to keep up with your speech. I regret the pen is not sharp."

"I have an hour or two tomorrow," the *Magistere* said to me. "Do we continue?"

"We must. In the afternoon?" I needed time to talk to Gwenna, and perhaps Druisius. He nodded his assent.

Apulo helped me stand. Decanius remained sitting; he'd refilled his wine glass. "Prince Cillian," he said, as I turned to leave. "Earlier you said I thought you elderly. I am but a year or two younger. We are not old men. We have time yet to write our names in history."

The chair had been less than comfortable. My back and leg ached. "I should walk a little," I told Apulo, and we did, down the corridor a short way.

"Will we talk later?" he said, in Linrathan.

"Yes. Perhaps with Druisius, who also knows the country."

He assessed me, frowning. "You need willow-bark."

"Walking will help. I am stiff, more than in pain." We turned and paced slowly back toward the door to the imperial seats. I did need willow-bark, and when I was seated again I would let Apulo give me some. The guards opened the doors, and I stepped out onto the platform.

Below us on the sands two men battled with swords. Muscled, bare except for short leather skirts, they circled and struck, the sheen of sweat on their bodies reflecting light. The crowd roared with each blow, so loudly no one had heard me arrive. All were watching the men.

All but Alekos. He leant toward Gwenna, saying something I could not hear. I watched them for a moment. Gwenna was listening with interest, smiling. Alekos was attractive and intelligent, and he was offering my daughter an empire. Should I be surprised if she accepted, even after all I had told her?

I took my seat beside Eudekia. "A useful meeting?" she whispered.

"A beginning. We meet again tomorrow," I murmured. The noise of the crowd intensified; one man was on his knees. The other raised his sword. The sun flashed off the blade—and my mind, unbidden, went to the field of battle at the Taiva: light flaring off steel, the rush of arrows, no time to turn before pain and darkness engulfed me.

Chapter 36

~DAUGHTER~

ALL THROUGH THE DISPLAY OF HORSEMANSHIP I tried to control my horror at what I'd seen. "They are criminals," Alekos has said to me, sensing my shock, "sentenced to die. Better with honour and glory on the field of games, than hung on a pole to be jeered at and worse. Here the suffering is short."

Put like that . . . I still struggled to understand. Ésparias executed criminals, of course, but cleanly, and not publicly.

"Criminals must be punished, Princess," the Empress said. I turned to her. "Those who are of the common people are rarely offered an honourable death; here they have that chance. It is different for those of higher rank who plot murder. Or sedition, of course." On her far side, my father's face remained impassive.

"As you say, Empress," I managed. The mounted soldiers left the field. Alekos touched my hand, just one finger, lightly.

"Refreshment?"

Perhaps a drink would help. I nodded, and he signalled. Wine was brought, and pastries. I refused the pastries; I couldn't eat.

The wine was lightly honeyed and perfectly watered. I sipped it gratefully. Despite the fans, kept constantly moving by four men, the heat was stifling. What must it be like here in the summer months?

Men armed with spears entered the Arénas, accompanied by two dogs. My stomach tightened. "They fight animals now," Alekos said, "not each other. Just a hunt, Princess. Surely you have hunted, if only with falcons?"

"Not I, personally," I said. "Once our *Ti'ach*—our school—kept hunting birds, but my father says he does not have the heart to keep a falcon captive now."

"He must feel himself a captive of his injuries, or perhaps his role. As you and I are, my lady Gwenna." Alekos had a charming smile, quick and genuine. Not a handsome man, but assured without arrogance. Confident. Well, of course he is, I told myself; he is heir to the greatest Empire in the world. Did that make what I had to do any easier? My gut twisted again, the wine acid in my throat.

A boar ran out on the field, tusks gleaming. A massive animal, in its prime, and dangerous. One of the men shouted. It turned, only to turn again, as the baying dogs lunged and twisted away, avoiding its tusks. The men stepped closer, spears at the ready. The boar charged; the crowd roared. A dog snapped at the boar's legs, but it ignored the threat, intent on the man.

Sweat trickled down my neck. I'd never hunted, but friends had, and they had spoken of it as exciting. A spear thrust penetrated the boar's hindquarters, enraging the animal. It swung to charge the man who had wounded it. He stood his ground, to the delight of the spectators. I held my breath. He leapt aside a moment too late.

I couldn't watch. I looked up at the stands, seeing the people on their feet, screaming, gesticulating. There would have been bets, I realized; some on the men, some on the boar, even on the dogs. Each wound meant money changing hands. What was the price of a death?

"He is up again," Alekos said in my ear. "A graze, nothing more."

To a cacophony of cheers and cries, the terrible dance below us played out to its end. As a spear was raised for the final thrust, I looked at Alekos. His face was impassive, showing neither pleasure nor disgust. Schooled. "Is there more of this?"

"Not today. Each spectacle, as we grow closer to my investiture, will have a fiercer animal, until the men fight the great cats of the plain and forests. But I must acknowledge the men now."

Standing, he walked to the front of the platform. The men on the field dropped to their knees. Alekos spread his arms, encouraging a rising tide of approval from the audience. Then he bowed to the hunters. The roar of sound grew even louder.

The games were done. A pair of men ran out from under the stands to drag the dead boar away, leaving a dark streak on the pale sand. Already people streamed toward the exits, guards holding them back as the best seats emptied first. The Empress stood. Alekos offered me his arm, and with my hand lightly on it, we made our way back down the cool corridor to the palace.

"What did you think?" Lynthe said, sprawled across one of the beds in our room. I sat in a chair, hoping the willow-bark Apulo had given me would ease the pounding in my head. If it didn't, I'd try anash. The Empress's words—*or sedition*—had been a clear threat.

"About what? Which part?"

"All of it. Any of it."

"I don't like killing as entertainment," I said, voicing what I felt. "Not animals, and especially not men."

"The crowd certainly did," Lynthe said.

"Alekos said the closer it gets to the investiture, the fiercer the animal will be. Bulls and bears and big cats. I don't want to watch that."

"He'll ask you again, though." Her voice was almost level. "Gwenna, I have to tell you this. If you do marry him, I'm going back to Ésparias."

Pain stabbed my temples. "I talked to your mother," Lynthe went on. "She insisted I sit with her today. Do you want to know what she said?"

"Should you tell me?" I closed my eyes. The room was too bright.

"She'd planned to stay, if your father had married the Empress. Not, she said, because of you—she didn't know she was pregnant yet, but because she assumed they could be together sometimes."

"And?"

"Sometime later she told Druisius this, and he laughed. Said it couldn't have worked; the Empress would have been told she'd stayed, and your father's movements monitored."

"I see."

"She'd have put him in danger, staying." Even through the increasing nausea, I heard the catch in her voice. "As I would you. So I can't stay."

My stomach roiled and lights flashed at the edge of my vision. I just made it to the latrine.

Lynthe gave me water, and then a little later some *anash* tea. I got these attacks a few times a year; they'd started not long after I'd begun my monthly bleeding. I lay on the bed, cloths over my eyes to block the light. Lynthe went out to the balcony to give me silence

An hour later, the *anash* had done its work. I sat us cautiously, but without consequence. The cup that had held the anash sat on the table. I looked at it, thinking about Alekos, and Lynthe's decision.

I'd gone to see my mother just after dawn, to tell her I saw nothing wrong with my father's suggestion. She'd shaken her head. 'I was a willing piece in the games once, too,' she'd said. 'Never again. Think long and hard, Gwenna, before you decide to pay that price.' Her voice had been as flat as Lynthe's had been an hour ago when she'd told me she was going home.

Choices had consequences: I'd been taught that since earliest childhood, and therefore to not make hasty decisions. 'Although sometimes that is necessary,' my father had said, 'if a life hangs in the balance.' I wasn't making a hasty decision, I told myself.

The heat lingered in the room. I washed and dressed in my lightest tunic; Lynthe had shed her uniform for something cooler too. With my hair braided and pinned off my neck, we made our way to my parents'— my father's—room. Druise had come along the balcony while I was sleeping to ask us to join them. "He didn't make it sound like we had a choice," Lynthe had said.

Just like last time, my mother was seated as far away from my father as she could be. She still wore her uniform. I was suddenly glad Colm had gone with Gnaius; the gods knew how he'd be reacting to their estrangement.

"Is your headache better, Kitten?" Druise asked.

"Just the heat." I smiled at him. "I can't imagine what it's like here in the summer."

"Much like today," my mother said, "as I recall."

"I don't envy those who dined with the Empress tonight," Sorley said. "It's not a night for formal clothes."

"The baths will be busy, yes?" Druise said. "The cold pools, and now the sun has gone down, the gardens. We could go, Sorley, except—" He shrugged.

"Except I must be guarded," my father said. "I am asking too much of you, Druisius. You are home, and you have friends and family to see, and a city to show to Sorley. Is not the palace guard sufficient?"

"Paid men can be paid more," Druise said.

"Take the night off," my mother said abruptly. "I will guard Cillian."

My father inclined his head, his expression grave. "Thank you. Shall we speak of what we saw today, so that we keep Druisius and Sorley here no longer than we need to?"

So formal. The diplomat again. But he would be alone with my mother later.

"Major, your impressions of the mounted displays?"

"Not their best men." She counted facts off on her fingers. "Several collisions among the riders in the manoeuvers, and not the best quality harness. The riders were young, inexperienced."

"Inexperienced horses, too," Lynthe added.

"Which suggests the best mounted cohorts have been sent east." My father ran a hand through his hair. "Druisius?"

"That is what I hear."

"Did you not say the land is high and broken?" my mother asked. "Is that terrain for horsemen?"

"Mostly it is mountains," Druise replied. "But not at the coast, and inland for a distance in the north. Hathus and his men are there, I think."

"It is how we use mounted troops," Lynthe said, "to patrol the coast. As much to be seen as to see."

"Sending the best east suggests the threat is real," my mother stated. "Inexperienced horse soldiers—and horses—are a liability."

"Perhaps," my father said, "it is to maintain the illusion of a real threat. But to leave the city undermanned is a risk, given the crowds here and still arriving. Would the Empress's husband take that chance were it not necessary? I find it unlikely."

"Sorley and I will listen at the baths," Druise said cheerfully. "Recreation and wine might loosen tongues, yes?"

Lightening flashed in the indigo sky, followed by a roll of distant thunder. "A storm will break the heat," Sorley remarked.

"I hope so." My mother stood. "Give me a few minutes to change out of this uniform, Druise, and then you can go. Lynthe, with me, please." She gave no reason.

"Cillian," Sorley said, as soon as they'd gone, "don't ask too much of her tonight."

"Do you think I would?"

"Not purposely, no." He grimaced. "She's hurt, Cillian. Wounded. Not physically, but—" He paused. It wasn't like Sorley to be this hesitant. "I know I wasn't there, not at first, but after the Kurzemë village, you let her heal. You let her choose when to ... approach you. That's what she needs again."

"I remember," my father said.

The Kurzemë village? "What don't I know?" I asked. "What happened to her that winter?"

Sorley looked at me, and back at Cillian, his lips parting in alarm. He swore, almost under his breath. "I assumed she'd told Gwenna."

"We haven't spoken of it in a very long time," my father said. He passed a hand over his eyes. "You must hear this from your mother, Gwenna."

"And I must explain to Lena," Sorley said. "This is my fault. I'll find her."

We waited in silence. Druise had gone out to the balcony, closing the doors. My imagination suggested many things, but listening again to Sorley's words in my mind, I could find only one thing that made sense. I shivered. Please not . . .

I saw the tension in my mother when she came in. She didn't sit. Her arms folded, she faced us, her back to the windows. "I never meant to tell you," she said to me.

"You don't have to," I said. "I think . . . I can guess." I didn't want to hear the words.

She nodded, a sharp movement. "He was the headman's son," she said, without expression. "Arrogant, cruel. He treated all women badly. I had beaten him in an archery contest, and he could not let himself be bested by a woman."

Cold suffused me. I turned to my father. "Where were you?"

"Away. Hunting geese with some of the village men."

Hunting? My father? I couldn't make sense of it. "I told Cillian to go," my mother said. "It was not his fault, Gwenna. I had my secca. But the man overpowered me."

Tears wet my cheeks now. I wanted to hold my mother, and be held, but her stance told me not to approach her. "This is why you told Lynthe she didn't have to be a bridal candidate," I said.

"No one should endure something they are not a willing partner in."

"What happened?" I asked, after a moment. "Afterwards?"

"I left the village that night. Cillian found me a day or two later, and we resumed travelling east."

"And the man? Do you know?" Hatred gripped me. He had to have been punished. Or I would find him and make sure.

"Lena killed him," my father said quietly.

"Or the wolves did," she said. Her face was white, drained of both colour and expression. I'd made her relive something terrible, a violation. I felt sick.

"Gwenna." My father. "Leave us now. Find Lynthe. She may tell her, Lena?"

"Yes. But no one else."

"I wouldn't. Oh, *Mathàir* . . . " I didn't know what to say. "I can't imagine . . . "

"Don't try," she said. "Don't try."

Chapter 37

~FATHER~

"SORLEY HAD NO RIGHT," LENA SAID. She stood, arms still crossed.

"He made an assumption," I said. "One I might have made, too. A mistake."

"So many mistakes." She was trembling. "I didn't want her to know." I pushed myself up, left the cane where it was. She stared at me. I went to her, put my hands on her upper arms, lightly, feeling her flinch.

"*Käresta*, I'm here." Words I'd used the day I'd found her on the plateau east of the Kurzemë village. Would they reach her?

She relaxed a tiny bit. I stroked her hair with one hand.

"No!" She pulled away from me, too suddenly, upsetting my balance. I stumbled. Lena grabbed my arm, steadying me.

"Sit down." She guided me back to my chair. When I was seated, she did not sink to the floor as she once would have, to lean against my good leg. Instead, she took a chair across from me. "I am going away for a few days."

"Where, if I may ask?" A strange calm had descended as she spoke, a sense of inevitability.

"To see the facilities where the young horses are trained, northeast of Casil. Junia has offered to take me, and I have accepted."

"Lynthe would enjoy that too," I said, mildly.

"I know. But I can't take her; Gwenna must have a bodyguard. That's why I asked Lynthe to come with me, earlier." Her voice was returning to her normal tone, or at least that of the major. "I wanted to explain, and also ask what she—or Talyn—might want me to take note of."

"Is anyone else going? Of the military envoys, I mean."

"No. Just me and Junia."

A plain lay northeast of Casil. Grassland, horses, and the company of a woman who had no interest in men. I had never asked Lena what had taken her back to Han year after year, beyond the purchase of horses. We had sworn no vows of bodily fidelity, and the precedent had been set long ago.

"I will have no reason to worry then," I said. "Lena, I am truly sorry for my suggestion to Eudekia. I should not have made it."

She shrugged. "It appears our daughter agrees with you, so I suppose it doesn't matter."

"It matters that you saw it as a betrayal. I did not mean it that way."

"Gwenna told me. How was she with Alekos at the games?"

"Alekos was attentive. Gwenna was . . . interested." I did not want to ask the question, but I must. "Lena, is she a stranger to men?"

Slight surprise, I judged. "No. I determined that before we came."

Should I speak of Decanius's carefully worded threat? Sorley had charged me more than once with not telling Lena enough. "Decanius implied that Alekos would find her unacceptable, were that the case, although it is not the law."

"Truly?" Disgust crossed her face. "But Alekos can have done what he likes, no doubt."

"No doubt. But should Gwenna be told? Or do I ask the Empress if this is an expectation?"

"If you do, then she will know Gwenna does not meet it."

A valid point. "What do you suggest?"

For a moment, I expected a sarcastic response. Instead, Lena said, "I will talk to her before I go. Isn't it simply between her and Alekos?"

"I suppose it is," I said. "My wise Lena." She didn't smile, but neither did she contradict me. Watching her, I thought again of what my life would be without her. A solitary life: austere. I had lived that way once. I had thought most scholars did, that being part of the long tradition of the

Ti'acha was enough. I loved and honoured the *Ti'ach*; I loved and honoured teaching.

But I loved and honoured Lena more. And what was a *Ti'ach*? The building, or what occurred within it?

"What are you thinking?" Lena asked, after a moment.

"About how an arch stands because its stones support one another," I said. "And how it can be disassembled and built again in a new location." Why had I never considered this?

Her brows drew together. "Could you be clearer?"

"Not yet. I have some thinking to do."

"As do I," she said. "Cillian, I—"

Whatever she had been about to say was interrupted by a knock at the door. Frowning, Lena went to answer it.

"The Empress requests the Prince Cillian's presence," the guard sent as a messenger announced. My back twinged as I tensed. She had made a clear statement at the games: her choice of sedition as an example had not been random. Lena turned to me, a wry expression on her face.

"I must change," I said. "I will be there shortly."

"I will wait, sir," the guard said.

"No need," Lena told him. "I will escort the prince."

I put on more formal clothes, with Lena, as dispassionate as Apulo, assisting. She wasn't wearing her uniform, but her secca was on her belt. There were others hidden on her body, I had no doubt.

"I'll wait," Lena said in the anteroom.

"I could be very late. A guard will be assigned."

"Druisius would wait." Her tone told me not to argue. Nor did I dislike the idea, in truth. We could perhaps return to our conversation on our walk back through the quiet halls. If I were allowed.

The guard opened the door. Eudekia, dressed in a loose green tunic, stood at the long table. She smiled, seeing me, and then her eyes moved to

Lena. Her expression didn't change. "Please join me," she said. "Both of you."

"Stop," the guard said to Lena. "Your knife."

"I am the prince's bodyguard. I keep my knife."

"Not in the Empress's presence." He took a step forward.

"Leave it!" Eudekia said. "The major may keep her weapon. She is no danger to me." Then I will be walking back through the corridors, I thought, or neither of us would. Eudekia would know Lena would defend me against any arrest.

The guard withdrew, closing the door. Lena dropped to one knee, briefly. I inclined my head to Eudekia, then turned to the other man in the room. "Bruccius."

"Perhaps you would serve wine, Bruccius?" The Empress indicated chairs. "Your discussion with Decanius, Prince Cillian. I have heard his version. What would you tell me?"

"His first preference is for a marriage alliance. The conflict is over trade and taxes, he tells me, but he countered every suggestion I made with regard to those issues." Bruccius handed me a cup; I smiled my thanks. "Not unreasonably, I would add."

"That agrees with what he reported. What will you discuss when you meet again?"

"The commodities traded, and the methods of trade; where the taxes or tariffs are highest." But I must talk to Gwenna first, I reminded myself. "Perhaps there are adjustments that could be made."

"I do not want a war," Eudekia said.

"The land is mountainous, I understand?" Lena asked. "My captain described it as high and broken."

"There are coastal plains, but mostly it is mountainous, yes," Bruccius replied.

"Dangerous," Lena said. "An army on the plain is subject to raids from the mountains, quick ambushes and retreats into the valleys. A difficult land to subdue and to hold if the resistance is strong." She was calm, unintimidated by making this assessment in front of the Empress.

"Indeed," Bruccius said. "You speak from experience, Major?"

"From the accounts of campaigns I have read, and from the days Linrathe was our enemy, not our ally," she said, "and again when we left Sorham to Varsland, in our last war. I have led ambushes from hidden sites more than once."

Both in a life before I knew her and at the Taiva, Lena had been deadly with both secca and bow. A truth I had allowed to fade over the last decades in the peace of the *Ti'ach*, just as I had stopped reading the histories written by long-dead generals. I had not wanted reminders of my failure at the Taiva.

"My son," Eudekia said bluntly, "wants to take his throne, wed his bride, and sail to Qipërta to lead his army, if necessary. I am doing my best to dissuade him."

"A winter war, under those conditions?" Lena said. "A very poor choice, Empress, if I may speak freely."

"Winter comes later to Qipërta. He believes he can triumph over them before it arrives," Bruccius said.

"They are more likely to fade into the mountains, and arise again in the spring," Lena said. "At the very least it will be no quick victory."

"History bears the major out," I added. Bruccius nodded.

"What troops would he take?" Lena asked. "The mounted soldiers we saw at the games were far from highly trained. The best are already in Qipërta, I assume?"

"They are," Bruccius said.

"So some untried men and a young Emperor will be enough to turn the tide?"

"His presence will give heart to the soldiers," Bruccius said.

"It may," she said, "but what of Casil? Will you rule in his stead again, Empress?"

"He will be Emperor, Major," Eudekia's voice held a touch of ice. "The ruling council is his to appoint. It will be his surrogate in his absence."

"I see," Lena said.

"Your thoughts are noted." Eudekia turned to her advisor. "*Magistere*, please leave us."

Silence, until the door closed. "I expect you to find a solution, Prince Cillian."

"I trust you have told Decanius the same," I said, holding her gaze.

"I have. Thank you for your thoughts and advice today. And my apologies, Major, for an oversight. I did not ask if you enjoyed the games."

"They were a great display of discipline and courage, Empress," Lena said.

"Traits which are valued by us both. Even when they may look, on the surface, like betrayal." The Empress signalled, and the guard opened the door. "Good night, Major. Good night, Cillian."

Lena said nothing until we were back in our room. Apulo waited for me. "What do you need?" he asked.

"Willow-bark, nothing more," I told him. "Then get some sleep."

"What did Eudekia mean?" Lena demanded, when he had gone.

"I don't know." Too many interpretations: a reminder of events nineteen years earlier? A message that she was aware of Hathus's plans? But no: the words had been directed to Lena.

Games of discipline and courage that might look like betrayal. A description of diplomatic negotiations? Or private ones? There were no secrets in a palace. Eudekia, I believed, had been telling Lena to reconsider her anger at me.

Lena would not take advice from the Empress easily, I thought, drinking the tea Apulo had made, and less so were I the subject. I would let her reach her own conclusions. "Perhaps only a reminder that she values Decanius, although he is recalcitrant in these negotiations," I offered, my tone disinterested.

"And that she knows he would argue to be on a ruling council. But it makes no sense. Why is Decanius pushing so hard for a marriage alliance if he wants Alekos out of Casil?"

"What did Ruar do, shortly after he married Helvi?" I asked.

"He went to Varsland," she said slowly. "Of course. Either way, in peace or war, Alekos is gone from the city."

"This is conjecture," I warned. "Perhaps we see a pattern only because of our own years of planning contingencies."

"We? The plans are yours, Cillian. The rest of us are only messengers." But it was said without rancour, a fact stated.

"You see other patterns," I said. "Your analysis of the terrain, and the problems it would bring, for one."

"My education in warfare," she said, "has been more practical than yours."

"To Ésparias's benefit, past and future." She didn't react. "It is late. We should sleep."

"Where did Druise sleep?"

"On the floor. The cushions and blanket are in the chest. But—" Should I speak of this? "*Käresta*, you were made to recall terrible memories earlier. Cannot I be shelter against them, at least tonight?"

"A night to pretend our vows hold?" Tension corded her neck. "You shelter me, and I am there when you wake? No. I will sleep on the floor."

Chapter 38

~DAUGHTER~

I WAS STILL ASLEEP WHEN MY MOTHER knocked; it had been very late before I slept. Horror at my mother's revelation; guilt that I had forced her to speak of it, and then a different shock when Lynthe told me Junia and my mother were leaving the city.

Even after sleep had finally come, I'd woken with a thought that had made me gasp. Lynthe must have been sleeping lightly, because I'd felt her hand on my arm almost immediately. "What is it?"

"When was my mother attacked? Am I even my father's child?"

Lynthe had wrapped an arm around me. "Don't be stupid," she'd said. "You look exactly like him."

Will you indulge an old man, and let me tell you how much you look like your father? Gedwin, the summer I was fourteen, and his was only one of many similar comments I'd heard over the years. I'd relaxed, and, cuddling against Lynthe, slipped slowly back into sleep.

My mother waited while I washed my face and tied back my hair. Lynthe went for tea. "What I have to say is ridiculous," my mother said, her face grim, "but you need to know." She told me what Decanius had asked my father, and what he had implied about Alekos's attitude.

"I am ineligible to marry Alekos because he wouldn't be the first man in my bed?" Anger twisted inside me.

"That is what Decanius suggests. Don't forget he is advocating for Sahira, so he may be exaggerating. Likely he is."

"What do I do? I won't lie."

"Nor should you. But if it becomes," she hesitated, "appropriate, then you tell him. Not only of the men, but women too. There needs to be honesty between you."

I nodded. "I will." I tried to smile. "I suppose," I said, "that was an advantage of Festival. There were no expectations of chastity in the intervening weeks."

She laughed, to my relief. "Certainly not for the women I knew. I never experienced Festival."

I hadn't known that. "Then . . . " Lynthe had not returned. "Was it only Maya, before—?"

"No. Not only Maya, and not only women." She didn't seem to mind my question.

"My aunt Kira . . . " I fumbled for a way to ask what I wanted to know. "And other women in the villages—they have one child only, Marai-fathered. Kira said men were unbearable to them, after."

"To this day," she said, speaking slowly, choosing her words, "I could not . . . not with any man except your father. But he helped me heal, Gwenna. He asked nothing of me, let me choose, but neither did he withdraw from me. I was so afraid he would," she added, her eyes distant. "The memory intruded, sometimes, but the day I believed all could be well between us was the day you were conceived, in a house not very far from here." Her eyes had softened, and then, to my distress, filled with tears.

"I'm sorry," I said, reaching out a hand to her. "I didn't mean to upset you."

She brushed the tears away. "You didn't. Now, Gwenna, Lynthe has told you I am going away for a few days? This is an opportunity I can't turn down. I only wish I could take Lynthe, or that Talyn was here. But I will ask all the questions I can think of, and take notes."

"Enjoy yourself," I said. I didn't like it, but maybe it would help. Space and silence.

"It will be good to be away from the palace," she said.

Lynthe returned then, carrying a tray with tea. My mother refused a cup. At the door, she turned. "I almost forgot. Your father wants to see you, as soon as you're ready."

"Can you get me the trade records?" I asked my father, after he'd explained what he wanted. "We'd be looking for something Casil needs, Qipërta has in abundance, but has high tariffs on it to protect prices of other sources in the Empire. And it needs to be something that, if its trade value drops, does not incite rebellion elsewhere."

"Including," he said, "from the Boranoi, who may be using Qipërta as a key source of some commodities."

"If they have favourable trading agreements, yes," I said. "Removing the tariff on, say, flax, will drive its price higher to the Boranoi, because they will have to compete with the new market in Casil. They then may seek out new sources, perhaps from some of the provinces who have seen the price of their flax drop because now there is more on the market. Do you see?"

"Many ripples from one small pebble." He ran a hand through his hair. "More and more I understand why Decanius thinks a marriage alliance is the only solution."

"But if tariffs are relaxed as part of the marriage alliance," I said, "the effect is the same. The reasons for it don't matter: in either case, Qipërtani trade benefits from a larger market and higher prices than they are currently getting."

He looked mildly startled for a moment "Of course they do," he said slowly. "Then why is Decanius so opposed to an economic solution? There must be another reason for wanting this marriage."

"I would have to think so." I sat back, feeling—what? A sense of something changed. I'd never explained anything to my father before, or understood something he hadn't. "Can you get me the records?"

"I believe so." He smiled at me. "I wish I could take you to the negotiations, but Decanius would not approve."

"Nor would he reveal anything about why he wants the marriage so badly with me there," I said. "But I am happy to study the trade records for you. It will give me something to do."

"May I suggest you do not tell the Prince?"

I laughed. "*Mathàir* says there are things I must tell Alekos, and now you say the opposite."

"They are quite different, *mo nihéan*," he said, with what I thought was mild embarrassment. "One is personal; one is political. I will reveal your role in these negotiations if they are successful, and certainly Alekos should know your contribution. Just not yet."

He was right. "I won't say anything." Rising, I kissed my father's cheek. "Is there anything you need?"

"No. But perhaps we could meet again tomorrow, to discuss today's talks?"

"Of course. In the morning?" Outside on the balcony, Lynthe had seen me stand. She'd been talking to Druise, but now she too stood, waiting.

"After Apulo is done with me. We can share tea."

"Just no food," I said. He smiled, and I smiled back, in anticipation. I would enjoy the analysis of the records, and our talks; I'd missed them. The next time I was with Alekos, I decided, I would engage him in a discussion of history or philosophy. Perhaps I'd better find out if we were compatible, at least in that way.

⌘⌘⌘⌘⌘

My mother was supposed to be gone five days, but on the sixth a note arrived, saying she would be away a little longer. Druise told me; he had some strong words, too, about her absence. "She should be here with you, yes?" I assured him I didn't need her. It was true, mostly.

I shared wine or tea with the potential brides, and once I went to the theatre with Alekos, chaperoned by Cassia, to her delight. The Prince could speak intelligently on philosophy, I learned, and he listened without condescension. On a different evening I dined with him and the Empress, along with Sahira and Dalphe: a test, I knew, of my skills in conversation and my behaviour with women I was expected to see as rivals. I thought I passed; Sahira, who rarely deigned to notice the candidates who were not called princess, did not shine.

Between—and sometimes instead of—these obligations, I read records of trade and tariffs, and reports from the *mensores* and Procurators of Qipërta, and I told my father what I had learned. His meetings with Decanius continued. More lines appeared on his face, and he ate little.

Ten days had passed when a letter from Talyn arrived for my father. "Two things," he said, reading it. "One for us alone, Gwenna. She reports men still argue for Faolyn's son to be his heir, and the numbers may be growing."

"A handful of discontents," I argued.

He nodded, but his eyes were troubled. "What else?" I asked.

"Helvi is dead."

Tears stung. "Oh, how sad for Ruar," I said. "And their sons."

"Will you find Sorley, Gwenna? He should know. But don't tell him. Send him to me, and then—"

"Leave you alone? Of course." I hesitated. "Should I tell Druise, convince him you can be unguarded for half an hour?"

"That would be kind."

⌘⌘⌘⌘⌘

The records had been brought to my father's room, and as it was both larger and had a table, it was easier for me to read them there. My father was with Decanius; Sorley had not long returned from accompanying him to the meeting room. He often sat with us now, after the news of Helvi's death. He brought his *ladhar*—he was still perfecting the new *danta*—and played or wrote quietly as we worked.

I was reading yet another set of old mine tallies, calculating how yield had changed over time, confirming an idea. The creak of the door made me look up.

"*Mathàir!*"

"Lena!" Sorley said at the same moment. "By Rögnir, where have you been all this time?"

Out of doors, I thought, seeing the brown of her skin and the pale streaks from the sun in her hair.

"Learning," she said. "Learning and thinking. Where's Cillian?"

"With Decanius," I said. "He'll be some time; they've barely started today."

"They've made no progress?" She didn't approach either of us.

"Every suggestion *Athàir* makes, Decanius says he'll consider it, but at the next meeting, he argues against it." I put my pen down.

My mother pulled out a chair. "What does the Empress say?"

"She is displeased with them both. *Athàir* argued that he needed time to study the records, which she allowed, but she insisted they meet again today." Should I tell her our belief, that Decanius had other reasons to want the marriage, ones we didn't understand? Something stopped me. "When did you get back?"

"Earlier this morning. I needed the baths first." Out of the corner of my eye I saw Sorley's head turn at that, his eyes narrowing a little.

"A dusty ride?" he said.

"Dusty and long. But worth it. I have many ideas to take back to Talyn. And more, but that must wait for Cillian." She looked around. "Lynthe's not here? Or Druisius? You're not guarded?"

"I have my secca," I said, "Sorley has his sword, and a knife, and both Druise and Lynthe are tired. Druise has slept on the floor here for how many nights now?" I didn't try to hide my irritation. How dare she disappear for days and days, and then return to criticize us?

"Come out to the balcony, Lena," Sorley said. "We can talk there and leave Gwenna to her work." Without another glance at me my mother crossed the room and stepped outside, Sorley following. I felt oddly chastised. I swallowed my annoyance and went back to the records.

I heard the soft murmur of voices from the balcony, but not the words. I turned a page in the records. Copper production had remained constant over the last twenty years; the *mensores* reporting large quantities of ore, easily accessible. The tariffs on it were high: copper was mined across the Eastern Empire, and Casil had chosen to protect other suppliers. What was actually sold to Casil was a tenth of the Qipërtani output: the rest not used within Qipërta was sold to the Boranoi.

In the margins of the new page were written some words in a script I didn't know. I'd come across marginalia many times: sometimes sketches, sometimes comments on the mine manager—usually scurrilous, and obscene—and some, like this one, in a language I couldn't read.

I pushed the page aside to make room for the tea Apulo had just brought. He set it on the table, glancing at the paper I'd moved. He smiled.

"What's funny?"

"This." He pointed to the marginalia.

I frowned. "I thought my father taught you to read? This isn't a script we know."

"Your father taught me to read Casilan, and Ésparian. This is the language of my home. I have known it since I was a small boy."

"What does it say?"

"That a man called Crispus has stolen something valuable from the king. But the writer has described it in colourful terms. Ones I will not repeat."

I grinned. "Not fit for my ears? I wonder who Crispus was. But mine managers stealing ore or ingots is as old as . . . as mines, I think. All we do in Ésparias is try to minimize it." I looked at the script again. "I've seen this hand before, in later records. Let me find them."

A few minutes later I passed two other pages to Apulo. He read the notes, but he didn't laugh. "Gwenna," he said finally, "This is not about copper theft."

"What, then?"

"The hand is the same, but the language different. He is no longer ribald, but using the words of our poets. This one—" he pointed, "says that Crispus's theft is becoming visible, 'like a waxing moon', he writes. And the third one says, 'the full moon has brought the tide which leaves a gaping creature behind, claimed by the king, but the gods know belongs to Crispus.'"

I didn't need him to explain: the imagery was strong. Whoever had written this had taken a risk, twenty years earlier, to tell Casil that a child born to the king of Qipërta was not his at all.

Part III

As one long prepared, and graced with courage,
say goodbye to her . . .
C.P. Cavafy

Chapter 39

~FATHER~

THE GUARD ESCORTED ME BACK ALONG the corridor. I was glad of his presence beside me: I was tired, and the tension of the meeting had sent pain stabbing down my leg. At least Decanius had been a little less obstructive today, admitting that perhaps the tariffs on copper needed a closer look. I would bring figures tomorrow, I had told him.

We reached my room. I thanked the man, and he pushed open the door for me to enter. I wanted wine, and willow-bark, and Apulo's hands relieving the pain.

Lena stood near the balcony doors. I steadied myself with my cane. "Lena," I said, apprehension tightening inside me. I'd seen this look before; she was calm, resolute. She'd made a decision in these last two weeks. "Welcome back."

"*Athàir*," Gwenna said, "I have something I must tell you."

"Not now," I told her.

"It's important."

"It can wait," I said firmly. "Will you leave your mother and me to ourselves, *mo nihéan*? I will hear what you have to tell me soon."

"Come," Sorley said to Gwenna. "I'll bore you with the new *danta*." He touched Lena's shoulder briefly, his face concerned, perhaps a little confused. Without speaking, he stopped at my side to run a hand along my upper arm before he ushered Gwenna from the room.

Lena still hadn't spoken. She went to the sideboard, mixed the wine and willowbark, gave me the glass.

"You look well," I said. "There was space and silence for you?"

"There was." She took a breath. "Hello, my love."

Relief coursed through me, replacing the rigidity in my muscles with weakness. I grasped the walking stick more firmly. "*Käresta*."

"Sit down, before you fall down," she said. She took the wine from me, kept a hand on my arm until I was seated. Then she sat across from me. "Will you listen?"

"Always."

She took a deep breath. "I am not leaving you. But when we are done here, I am going back to Ésparias."

Be calm, I told myself. "What will you do?"

"Whatever Talyn will assign me to. But I can't go back to the *Ti'ach*, Cillian, to be responsible for other people's children. To be around them."

"And if Talyn asks you to teach?"

"I'll ask not to. For a year or two, anyhow."

Talyn would accommodate that request, I thought. I gathered my courage. "What changed?"

Her right hand went to the *li'itho* on her wrist. "I am not angry now, nor . . . " She bit her lip. "Junia is a true follower of the goddess. She convinced me I was wrong; that the huntress would not demand a child as a sacrifice. But . . . " She still played with the marriage bracelet, unconsciously. "Can you accept this? Live in the way this will mean?"

"If your friend Farry can do it, why not I?"

"What?"

"You don't remember? He told us his *quincala* and children were at

Rigg; he saw them occasionally. It is not rare, I should think, among the men and women of the army."

"I suppose it isn't," Lena said. "But not what we are used to."

"When Dagney married us, she asked if our friendship and love and trust would endure all things. I said then they would, and I believe that still."

"All things but death," she said. "I must find a life that will sustain me when you are only a memory, Cillian."

She'd found a fragile peace with herself; I could not disturb it. "You must."

"I thought, now I have been a military envoy, perhaps I could continue in that role. A reason to be in Linrathe more frequently than just my weeks of leave."

"The *Ti'ach* has always been a place to stop between the Wall and Dun Ceànnar," I said. "We would welcome Ésparias's military envoy."

"Mhairi would not even have to find me a bed in the annex," she said softly.

I fought to control the smile that wanted to escape. "Does that mean Druisius no longer needs to sleep on this floor?"

"Yes. But . . . "

"But?"

"I took no anash with me. We must wait three days until it begins to work again."

"We have before." She hadn't left me, not in the ways that mattered. And perhaps we didn't need to be separated at all. I hadn't spoken of the idea that had begun to form weeks earlier; it was not without complications. Or rather, one. Sorley.

We had twenty minutes alone before Druisius came in, the surprise on his face telling me he hadn't known Lena was back. She was sitting on the floor beside me, reading the letter that had come from Colm a few days earlier. Druisius grinned broadly. "Sorley and I can play tonight?"

Lena grinned back. "You can. I'm sorry, Druise, for these past weeks."

He shrugged, of course. "My job. Where is Sorley? I will leave you alone, yes?"

"Sorley is with Gwenna, and, no," I said, running my hand across Lena's hair, feeling her lean into my touch, and the suffusing warmth that brought. "Gwenna had something to tell me, something important, she said. Perhaps you would fetch them?"

Lena finished the letter. "Colm sounds happy."

"He does. Much more than he would have been here in the palace with nothing to do. I would not have had the time to show him the temples and libraries. It was kind of Gnaius to take him."

"He won't want to leave."

"I doubt Gnaius wants an apprentice. You and he can be at Wall's End together," I said lightly.

"And Gwenna, if she doesn't marry Alekos." She looked up at me, her eyes troubled. "Everyone but you." She paused. "How often did Eudekia call for you while I was gone?"

"Twice, for *xache*."

"Is that all she wanted?"

I smiled. "Conversation, too." She had offered more; made it clear by her hand on my arm, her fingers touching mine on the *xache* board. I had declined, gently, and she had laughed.

"About us? You and me?"

"Never," I said truthfully. Eudekia's subtle words suggesting reconciliation might have been addressed to Lena, but it was my composure she had been concerned with, ensuring my thoughts were given to negotiations and not to marital problems. But even the Empress would not trespass so far as to ask. I stroked Lena's hair again. "*Kāresta*, may I ask you not tell anyone else what your plans are? Not yet."

"Because there is too much else happening?"

"That, and because I would like to get used to the idea first, before we deal with other reactions."

"I will be disrupting all our lives, won't I?" she murmured. "I'll wait."

The relief on Sorley's face when he arrived was palpable. Kneeling, he put his arms around us. "Thank the gods," he murmured.

He would be unhappy when Lena told him her plans, and my own—if I could bring them to fruition—would hurt him terribly; more than I wanted to contemplate. That was not for tonight, though. I rested a hand on his familiar back, kissed his hair, murmured thanks. "But now, my lord Sorley," I said, "we have work to do. Where is Gwenna?"

"Gone to fetch Apulo. She said he was needed."

"They are here," Druisius announced. "What is so important, Kitten?"

"I need to show *Athàir*," she said, going to the table to find several records. "Apulo, will you translate again?"

Lena made room for her. Gwenna pointed to the script in the margins. "This all appears to be the same hand; the *mensore*, I think, writing in his own language."

I glanced up at Apulo. "And it says?" He told us.

"Dear gods," Lena said. "How old is Sahira?"

"There is," I said, before anyone could answer, "no reason to believe this refers to Sahira. The Qipértani king may well have had *pallacae*. Women other than his wife, whose children he would recognize," I clarified, at Lena's frown.

"I wonder who Crispus was," Gwenna said. "Someone of status, surely, if he had contact with the king's women?"

"You have not seen his name in the records?"

"No. I have seen Decanius's, and his father—Flavian, his name was— and several others, but not a Crispus."

"It is a common name," Druisius said. "Maybe an officer?"

"Perhaps." I considered what to do. "I could ask Decanius, if I can think of a way to do so naturally."

"The reports mention losses at the mine, the usual amounts diverted, presumably by the manager," Gwenna told me. "You could ask how that was dealt with, mention Crispus's name?"

"Indeed I could," I said. "Well done, Gwenna."

"If that's decided," Sorley said, "shouldn't we toast Lena's return?" He meant from more than her physical journey, I knew. And why not? We were together, a mirror of thousands of evenings at the *Ti'ach*, and our ritual had more than one purpose.

Lena rose, holding out an arm to help me up. Apulo brought the wine, and I poured. I had been reading Tullius earlier; his words were appropriate. "The gods," I said, raising my glass, "have given nothing better to man than friends."

⌘⌘⌘⌘⌘

To my surprise, Lynthe accompanied Apulo and me to the palace's private baths the next morning. "Druisius asked me to," she answered, when I asked why. "I'll stand outside."

Sorley, unexpectedly, was waiting for me at the hot pool. He settled into the water beside me, looking drawn, as if he had not slept. At a nod from me, Apulo withdrew.

"What is wrong, *mo duíne gràhadh*?" I asked Sorley, in Linrathan. The pool water lapped against the tiles. At the far end, the only other two men present conversed quietly.

"Druise," he said. "He says if Gwenna marries Alekos, he's staying. She'll need a loyal guard, and he trusts no one else to recruit and lead them."

That was why Druisius had sent Lynthe to guard me. "Does he mean he is staying long enough to put a guard in place, or—"

"Staying. Permanently." Sorley's voice flat. "I shouldn't be surprised: I always knew his Kitten came first."

What could I counsel? I had not yet made any suggestion to Lena. "You could stay too," I said. "Gather songs, learn the other instruments. Could you not?"

"For a year, by the rules of the *scáeli'en*. But leave you?" He shook his head slowly, staring up at the ornate ceiling of the baths.

"A marriage between Gwenna and Alekos is not certain." But if it were, I would have to tell him my plans. He should stay with Druisius.

"I know," he said bleakly. "But Druise took Lynthe to the markets and taberna yesterday. She thinks Gwenna will agree, if Alekos asks, and she's devastated. She loves Gwenna."

"As you do Druisius." Under the water I touched his hand. He looked over at me.

"And you? Who do you love, Cillian?" A question that told me how anguish wracked him; he had never asked, a tacit understanding between us. He knew, but words mattered. Before I could speak he shook his head, grimacing. "I shouldn't have asked. Forget I did."

"*Somhairle*," I murmured.

"It's all right. I understand." He gave me a wry smile. "And it's not like Lena didn't warn me."

He closed his eyes, leaning back against the rim of the bath, leaving me with my thoughts. My near inability to say three simple words—four, in my own tongue—was a source of amusement to Lena. And perhaps frustration, too.

But if she had warned Sorley, I slowly realized, then my reluctance to say those words to him, believing them reserved for Lena, had been misplaced for all these years. To speak them would not be a betrayal, or a lessening.

The two men at the far end of the pool were engrossed in their conversation, paying us no attention. I raised a hand, resting it on the back of Sorley's neck for a moment. He didn't open his eyes, but his expression relaxed, a hint of a smile touching his lips.

This was neither the time nor the place. But if I must break his heart again, this time I would first tell him that I loved him.

Chapter 40

~DAUGHTER~

THE MESSENGER BROUGHT THE note just as I was finishing my tea, preparing to go back to another morning of reading records.

"What does it say?" Lynthe asked, yawning.

"I have been asked to play *xache* with Alekos this afternoon."

"Again?" She didn't sound happy.

"Lynthe—"

"At least now your mother's back Apulo can be your chaperone," she said.

"You don't want to?"

Lynthe made an impatient gesture. "I don't really enjoy watching the two of you together. What I'd really like is to accompany Sahira or Rosale or Dalphe, to see if he treats them the same way."

"I'm sure you've asked their guards," I murmured.

"I have. But it's not the same as seeing it myself."

Anger flared. "And what do they say?"

"That he's attentive; flattering, the way he is with you."

"He isn't flattering," I said icily, "not any more. But no one looks at guards. I'm sure you could arrange something."

"And leave you alone? Your mother would have my head." She too was growing angry. I didn't need this now; I had work to do.

"Druise will always guard me," I said.

"You're right about that," she snapped. "Ask him what's he's planning, if you marry Alekos."

"What?"

She shook her head. "Ask him. In fact," she added, as a tap came at the balcony door, "you can do it right now. He's here. We've swapped guarding this morning."

Why? I didn't have time to ask. Lynthe let Druise in, and then stalked off along the balcony.

"Druise," I said, "I have work to do."

"It can wait, yes?" he replied. He sat down, looking up at me. "Sit, Kitten. We should talk."

Sighing, I complied. "What is it?"

"I took Lynthe to the market yesterday. And the *taberna*. We talked. She is unhappy."

My shoulders tensed. "I know she is. But what can I do? I'm here for a reason."

He chewed his lip. "But not one you must capitulate to."

Must I not?

"Kitten," Druise said, "listen, please. There are things you must consider. If you marry the Prince, I am staying. There are too many factions here. Too much danger, yes? I trust only myself to recruit and lead your personal guard."

"Druise, you can't! What about Sorley?"

"I have told him."

"You can't leave him, and he can't stay."

"He could. For a year. But he will not; he will not leave Cillian. You see the four of us, Kitten; you think we are solid, like the four walls of a building that stands square. But it is not so. The wall that is Sorley leans more heavily on the wall that is your father, and his wall leans more heavily on your mother's. My wall," he shrugged, "leans on no one, but it has helped hold up the roof for nineteen years. So if I leave, there is still a shelter, yes?"

"A shelter, maybe, but not a house. Not a home." My voice rose with the fear inside me. "And I don't believe you. You don't stand alone. You love Sorley. You love all of us."

"Maybe," he said. "Maybe you too are not being honest about love, yes?"

Heat stung my face. This wasn't the sort of conversation I had with Druise.

"When I swore my oath to Ésparias," Druise said, ignoring my discomfiture, "I made it to the *Princip* and all his heirs, born and unborn. You are the heir. My job is to protect you. That comes first."

"You're my father's bodyguard, not mine."

"There are others in Ésparias who can guard him. Here, I trust no one."

"And if I refuse to allow it?"

"It is not your decision. Your safety is the general Talyn's responsibility. She and I spoke before we sailed."

"But you didn't tell anyone until now?"

He shrugged. "If you did not appear interested in the Prince, what did it matter?"

I had no answer to that. For a moment, I considered confiding my fears to Druise, except I was sure he'd tell my father. But how could I let him leave Sorley? The summer we'd spent travelling, they'd been so comfortable together; affectionate when we were assured of privacy, clearly loving each other.

Love and loyalty, conflicting. I considered the contradiction as Druise sat silent, waiting. His loyalty to me—either as his Kitten or the heir— outweighed his love for Sorley.

How did you decide which one to choose? How did you sort them out, separate them? Was it a greater love, or a greater loyalty, that would take Sorley back to Linrathe, to my father, to the *Ti'ach* and to his work as a *scáeli*? I was prepared to marry Alekos to keep my father safe, but wasn't I also protecting the years of planning and creating alliances? Was I doing it for love, or loyalty?

"This is ridiculous," I said. "There has to be a better solution. But I must work now; the Prince wants my company this afternoon."

"Come, then," Druise said, apparently unperturbed by my reaction. "I will walk with you."

I was tired of escorts and guards, I thought, as we made our way to my parents' room. I couldn't remember the last time I'd been alone. The room was empty. My father would be with Decanius; I'd hoped to speak to him before he went. I could send a note if needed, I decided; sitting, I pulled a stack of records toward me and began to read.

Halfway through the morning my mother returned from wherever she'd been, looking troubled. Notes from Druise's *cithar* drifted in from the balcony; she glanced that way, but pulled out a chair across from me and sat.

"You've been with Sorley," I said, guessing.

"He is understandably upset." She sighed. "But I can't say that part of me wouldn't be relieved, knowing Druise was the head of your personal guard."

"But why can't Sorley stay too? Ruar could appoint him as Linrathe's emissary to Casil."

"Gwenna, you know why."

"Well, he could be here half the year, and half the year in Ésparias."

My mother laughed, dismissively. "You know how seasick he gets. Two six-week voyages a year?"

"Then why don't you all stay?" I hadn't planned to say that, but hearing my own words, I wondered: why not? "I would have not only my personal guard, but my advisors, too: you and *Athàir* and Sorley, and he could still be Linrathe's envoy."

"Too many complications," she said.

"But if there weren't, would you stay?"

"I have no love for cities and walls," she said bluntly. "But walls have gates. The question is what would I do."

"And *Athàir*?"

"He could teach, if he wished. But the libraries here would be enough, I think; that and the company of men like Bruccius. But it isn't possible, Gwenna."

"Because," I said, "there is a question of alliances, and plans, and—how did you put it before? The directing mind."

"Exactly."

"I am supposed to be heir to those plans, be their directing mind someday," I said, my thoughts outrunning my speech. "But if I stay in Casil, then there needs to be someone else anyhow. And not Colm."

"Who, then?" my mother asked.

"Lynthe, didn't you say? And what about Ruar?"

She leant back, crossing her arms, considering. "Perhaps," she said. "Perhaps. Are you going to marry Alekos, Gwenna?"

"I think so. Yes." Was my voice steady?

"For love, or politics?"

I met her eyes. "Politics. I do like him. He's intelligent and thoughtful. We are becoming friends, I think."

She nodded. "One more question. For politics, or power?"

"Not power," I said. "Influence. And perhaps challenge?"

"An Empire to manage, rather than years of trade negotiations and advising Faolyn?"

"Yes. Is that terrible, *Mathàir*?"

She didn't answer. "Does Lynthe know?"

"More or less. Alekos could still choose someone else."

"And if he does, she will still be there? Your second choice?" Her voice was sharp now.

"No!" I protested. "She's not . . . she says she'll wait for me to decide."

"But you have decided. Tell her, and then tell Alekos you want to marry him, and why. Don't let him control this, Gwenna."

Not why; not the true reasons, ever. But maybe . . . "Negotiate my own future," I said.

"No one else, not even your father, should be directing what you do."

I looked down at the papers on the table. "Will you tell *Athàir* my proposal?"

"No. That's up to you." She pushed her chair back to stand. "Marriage to Alekos will mean dealing with the Empress, and the counsellors, including Decanius. You must be able to argue your point to an opposed or doubtful group, not just with your husband. Nothing you have done has truly prepared you for this, Gwenna. Practicing on us will be a start."

⌘⌘⌘⌘⌘

I moved a gamepiece, taking one of Alekos's. He grinned. "And so I do this," he said, capturing one of my higher-level pieces in return.

"Yes, but—" I made the multiple-square move allowed for the figure in my hand, placing his king in immediate and inescapable jeopardy.

He laughed, although there was an undercurrent of disbelief to the sound. "I should have seen that."

"You moved too quickly when I presented a target."

"Perhaps I did," he admitted. "Can you best your father?"

"Occasionally."

"My mother says he is very good. He can defeat her, and that is rare. I would have studied the board longer, were I playing her," he added ruefully.

We were speaking Heræcrian; why, I wasn't sure. He'd greeted me in that tongue, and we'd continued in it. Perhaps he had assumed—rightly—that Lynthe didn't speak it. Apulo had been needed by my father, and Druise insisted on accompanying them to the baths in case my father needed more help. She'd had to act as both my guard and my chaperone, to her disgust.

I wished she weren't in the room, but at least I didn't have to switch languages ostentatiously. I picked up my queen piece and placed it next to his king. "They look well together."

"The set was made so the colours complemented each other," he said.

"And the carvings; they are not exactly the same, but in a style."

"As two people both heirs to leadership are." I wet my lips, forcing the words. "We would be good partners in more than *xache*, Alekos."

Surprise, first, in his dark eyes, and then a pleased smile. "I have thought the same."

"Except I do not bring peace with Qipërta."

An eyebrow shot up. "You are forthright."

"Does that shock you?"

"No." He regarded me thoughtfully. "There is a drama from Heræcria where women bring peace by withholding themselves from the men, forcing them to find another solution. It seems to me that I am being asked to do the opposite, to give myself to a woman to end a conflict."

"You would prefer a war?"

He made a face. "It would be cleaner. A marriage to buy peace could last forty years or more."

"In the lord Sorley's land, their leader made an arranged marriage, and it has worked well. They are happy together." But Helvi was—had been— Ruar's equal, taught for some years at one of the *Ti'acha,* prepared to be his partner in all aspects of his life. He would miss her so much, I thought, seeing again the resignation in his blue eyes as we'd said goodbye. He'd told me to come back from this voyage.

"There is still a chance of a negotiated treaty," I said, bringing my attention back to Alekos. "You know that it is Decanius who turns down every suggestion my father makes?"

"He has told us they will not work, that your father does not understand trade."

"But I do," I said, "and those are my proposals, not my father's. I am confident the newest one will work, if properly considered. Has Decanius explained it to the Empress or yourself?"

He picked up the queen piece, turning it in his fingers. "Your proposals?"

"I am a trade envoy," I said. "It is what I was educated for, and what I do when I am not here in Casil. Surely your mother told you?"

He had the grace to look ashamed. "Perhaps I did not listen closely. I have heard quite a lot about many women, these past weeks."

I couldn't help but laugh. After a moment he did too. "What does a trade envoy do in Ésparias?"

"Study a lot of numbers." I told him what I did at the mines and villages, and why; how I liked the freedom and the responsibility. "I look for discrepancies in records, or, more often, a lack of them, of the mistakes everyone makes. I look for the things that tell me the mine manager is lying, and listen to what he or she doesn't tell me, or tells me too much about."

"Who taught you all this?" He'd put the gamepiece down to lean forward, intent.

"My father taught me how to read records, and people. Then other teachers, and the experienced men and women we are paired with in our last years as students taught me the rest."

"Trade is left to the officials, here," he said. "I was taught strategy, and the campaigns of great generals, back to the man I am named for."

"As has Lynthe been," I said. "But we are at peace, by your Empire's intervention. If I am to be Ésparias's *Principe* one day, should I not understand the production of food and other commodities that my country's economy is based on? Do you know what Ésparias sells to Casil?"

"I do not. Grain?"

"Grain, yes. Also salt, and lead and copper, and fish."

"All things we need."

"Grain and fish and salt to feed your city and your armies, and lead and copper to pipe water from the aqueducts to the fountains and bathhouses and this palace. Casil has a great demand for lead and copper."

"I suppose we do," he said.

"Then why are you forcing outrageous tariffs on Qipërtani copper, with the result they sell most of what they mine to the Boranoi?"

He straightened. "Are we?"

"You are, and have been for many years. I've read the records for the last twenty. What my father proposed to Decanius this morning is that those tariffs—and only those—be lowered, and Casil buy more of its copper from Qipërta. Their increase in revenue will be significant, enough to placate them, I should think."

"What about our other copper suppliers?"

He was quick; good. "They will see a drop in prices, yes, but not an extreme one. Your existing copper imports come from provinces like Ésparias, where we also provide other goods." I hesitated, not wanting to appear too intent on Ésparias's benefit. "As Ésparias builds in the style of Casil, forts and villas, we too need copper. Exporting less would not hurt us."

"Decanius refuses to see this as a bargaining point with Qipërta?"

"I saw my father only briefly after this morning's session, but I understand not."

He tapped a finger on the table, thinking. "Why is he being obstructive?"

"Possibly . . . " I stopped. "May I speak theoretically, without it being construed as an accusation against anyone?"

Both eyebrows raised at that. "You *are* a diplomat. Please do."

"It suggests to me someone benefits from the Boranoi lands having almost exclusive access to the copper from Qipërta."

"Benefits? How?"

"Financially, most likely. If the acquisition of copper is done cheaply, perhaps recompense finds its way to the purses of the people who keep the price low."

His shoulders tightened. Under his neatly trimmed beard, cords in his neck sprang into sharp relief. "You are accusing Decanius of taking bribes?"

"I am accusing no one. I said I spoke theoretically: this is what my training and experience suggests as the most likely reason. There may well be others." But, I thought, find me a mine manager or ship's captain or harbour master—anyone involved in trade—who did not thieve or smuggle or take payments in one form or another. Even Druise's brother, I had no doubt.

"Yes, of course. My tutors did the same, when analysing why generals made decisions in campaigns." He regarded me, his head tipped slightly to one side. "We would be good partners, wouldn't we?"

"I believe so," I replied, my mouth suddenly dry. He reached out to touch the almost-healed cut on my cheek, holding my eyes.

"What an Empire we could create together," he murmured. His finger was gentle on my skin.

"You have an Empire."

"It was greater once. It could be again. Think of your own land, being transformed by our engineers and architects, your people schooled in our philosophers. Yours is not the only province who could benefit from the Eastern Empire's presence."

My own land. I pushed away the thought. "The Princess Rosale would agree."

"That is what I mean. There is much we could do. I am committed to dine tonight with . . . others. But tomorrow? Your parents, and my mother, and the two of us."

"Of course."

"Tell your father I wish to hear his impressions of his talks with Decanius, if you would. And now I must go, my princess Gwenna. You have given me much to consider."

Chapter 41

~FATHER~

"WHAT," LENA ASKED, "DO I WEAR? Am I the major, or am I Gwenna's mother and the wife of the prince tonight?"

Apulo's hands were gentler now, no longer pushing deeply into muscle but smoothing an unguent smelling of lavender into the scars. He had already shaken out a tunic for me: white, the hem and sleeves trimmed in grey silk, reflecting the purple-trimmed garments of Casilani royalty. Gwenna, too, would be in the colours of our house.

"Lena will help me dress," I told Apulo. He helped me up, then smiled and left us to ourselves. I sat on the edge of the bed as she held the tunic for me to slip over my head. When my arms were free, I reached for her.

"Be the major, *käresta*." In her uniform, that she did not wear grey and white would not be noted. "It is who you wish to be, is it not?" Your soldier, Eudekia called her.

Lena rested her forehead against mine for a moment. "It is who I need to be."

"Then be her." I kissed her. She too smelt of lavender from the baths. A memory—and more than a memory—stirred.

She felt the change in my kiss and pulled away, laughing a little. "We haven't time." I watched her dress. In the low light of the bedroom, neither scars from aggression nor the marks of childbearing could be seen. But were they not mostly inside her, in her mind and spirit? My own scars—both sets—were only outward manifestations of inner wounds. We all had them, visible and invisible. Lena's only deepened my love for her.

Voices, in the outer room: Gwenna and Apulo. "Ready?" I asked Lena.

She finished combing her hair. "Ready." She wore a leather vest over a linen tunic, lappets of leather extending from a wide belt almost to her knees. Her insignia of rank on her shoulder caught the faint light. "But you aren't."

"I am not?"

From the chest that held our clothes and belongings she took the pendant I had forgotten, distracted by desire. Sitting beside me, she fastened the chain, letting her fingers trail along my neck.

"Stop." I grasped her hand with mine, laughing. "Or I will not be paying attention to food or speech tonight."

"Or Eudekia?" she said, grinning.

The Empress wore her usual green, her copper hair piled high on her head, revealing her pale neck. My earlier arousal made me more conscious of her, not less, something, I thought wryly, I would not share with Lena.

She gestured for Lena and Gwenna to rise almost as soon as they had knelt. Apulo remained on his knees until she had turned away to catch the eye of a servant.

Wine was offered. "Major," Eudekia said to Lena, "did you find your visit to our training facilities for the warhorses informative?"

On the nights I had joined her for *xache* and wine, Eudekia had not mentioned Lena's absence to me. But she had known, of course.

"I did, Empress," Lena said. "I will take several ideas back to Ésparias for consideration." She spoke briskly, with only the slightest deference. Her uniform gave her confidence, I thought.

"And you are settled, now you have had a chance to escape the walls of Casil for a while?"

"It was a respite, Empress. One that did me good."

Eudekia smiled. "I am pleased to hear it."

"Prince Cillian," Alekos said from beside Gwenna, "your aide is welcome to wait in the adjoining room. Food and drink will be served, and he will be only a moment away if you need him."

"Leave the satchel," Lena murmured as Apulo, at my nod, followed a servant to a door in the far wall. He slipped it off his shoulder: it contained the drugs I might need, and the records to show Eudekia and Alekos later.

My back twinged. I could not sit until the Empress suggested it; even I would not be allowed that privilege, not in company. She looked my way. I tightened my hand on the silver top of my cane, the briefest of motions.

"Please sit," she said. "We will eat now." I smiled my thanks.

Conversation during the meal did not touch on trade or war, but on philosophy and theatre. To my surprise, Lena made several apt comparisons between the *danta* and the dramas of East. "Both frequently deal with moral dilemmas," she said, "or the effects of pride or arrogance."

"Are there also less serious ones?" Alekos asked.

"Many," she assured him.

"I would like to hear some of these songs."

"I imagine Lord Sorley could be prevailed upon," I said. "He is a magnificent musician, and the head of Linrathe's council of *scáeli'en*." I explained their complex, faceted role. "While we stopped at Sylana for water, he heard a tale new to him. During our time here, he has been turning it into verse, and writing music to go with it. I believe it is nearly ready to be heard."

"I would be honoured to be among the first to hear it," Alekos said. "Will you ask him if he will play for me?"

"Of course." I'd have to warn Sorley. Not that he ever minded performing.

"I am pleased the lord Sorley and you have remained friends," Eudekia said. "He loves you greatly."

"Cillian owes Sorley much," Lena replied. "As do I. He is more than a friend, Empress; he is part of our family, and loved greatly by us all."

"Sorley has been another parent to me and my brother," Gwenna said.

"Has he?" Alekos said. "I did not realize you were so close. Should he then be asked to sit with us at the games next week? You will accompany me again, Gwenna? They are the last before my investiture."

"Will there be killing?" she asked. "If so, I'd prefer not. I didn't enjoy watching it."

"There will be," Alekos said. "There must be. The people expect it, and it would not be wise for me to disappoint them. Perhaps you could join me until the fighters take the sands, and again at the end?"

"Perhaps." The servants were clearing dishes, bringing the bowls of dried fruit and honeyed nuts, and a different, sweetened wine. When they withdrew, the real business of the evening would begin.

One more surprise awaited: Bruccius joined us. I greeted him courteously, but with an inner tension. Could I—we—speak freely in his presence? The Empress would expect it, though.

He accepted wine and took a chair. "Now," Eudekia said, "Cillian, tell us what has unfolded in your talks with the *Magistere* Decanius."

"Very little, in truth," I explained the constant objections Decanius raised to each proposal I made on lowering taxes or tariffs. "If indeed this is Qipërta's reason to challenge Casil, perhaps their representatives should be part of these talks. I cannot help but think the *Magistere* has his own reasons for being obstructive."

"Beyond considerations of Casil's economy?" Bruccius asked.

"War is an expensive business," Lena said. "The cost of transporting and feeding so many men and horses; the acquisition of weapons—all these add up. Is the *Magistere* considering that in his calculations?"

"We would be feeding those men and horses anyhow," Alekos said.

"Yes, for your standing army," Lena replied. "But hundreds, thousands, more men have been recruited, and almost every horse ready for the saddle that the grasslands can supply purchased. The cost must have been enormous."

"Why does my step-father need so large an army to quell a small rebellion? I have been asking myself that since we first spoke of this, Prince Cillian."

"It is a difficult land to subdue." Bruccius spoke for the first time. "It took our earlier Emperors many years and many repeated incursions before Qipërta became a province. Hathus will know this. As do you, if you would recall my teaching, Prince Alekos."

"He is being overly cautious, you believe?" Alekos asked his tutor.

"I think rather he is showing the force Casil can muster, suggesting the retribution that could occur were they not to capitulate."

"A forced peace will mean leaving many divisions of men in Qipërta, to ensure our presence is felt," Eudekia said. "That would be reason enough for the increase in men and horses."

"Whereas if I marry the princess of Qipërta," Alekos said, "the peace is settled without bloodshed. Then what are extra men and horses for?"

"When the Empress married Hathus," Bruccius pointed out, "he brought men and horses to Casil's army, to retake the lands north of Sylana. It will soon be time for those soldiers to retire. Recruiting new troops now means they are not green and untrained when the Boranoi soldiers leave the ranks."

They may well be right, I thought. All that had been said was an alternative explanation, reasoned and reasonable.

"None of this explains why Decanius is unwilling to consider an economic solution," my daughter said. "*Magistere*, you may not realize I am educated and trained as an envoy. My specialty is trade."

All eyes turned to Gwenna. Unperturbed—at least outwardly—she went on. "The *Magistere* Decanius was Procurator of Ésparias when I was an infant. Our first Procurator, charged with bringing Casil's order to our land, an immense task. We study what he did, the administration he created, of which I am now part."

She sipped her wine, pausing to heighten expectation as I had taught her. She had praised him; now she would sow doubt.

"It is well known there are unofficial taxes, if you will, imposed by managers of mines and salterns, and by officials of greater rank. A certain percentage of losses. This, within reason, is accepted. While Decanius was Procurator, our salterns provided him with extra income. I expect a similar arrangement existed in his time in Qipërta." She spoke precisely, without hurry or emotion. "And may still."

I glanced at Lena. She was watching our daughter with both trepidation and pride, and listening intently.

"If such an arrangement exists," Gwenna continued, "whether the tariffs are lowered by treaty or marriage, there will be no appreciable loss of income to those who benefit from it." She summarized the way the markets would change, as she had done for me.

"You suggested a reduction in the tariffs on copper, Cillian, did you not?" Eudekia asked.

"It was Gwenna's suggestion, relayed by me," I said, "but yes, copper."

"It would not harm Decanius's interests, and is only to Qipërta's benefit," she said. "Then why is he so opposed?"

We could say no more. The conclusions must come from the Empress and her son. To voice our suspicions was to speak treason.

But, I thought, hearing my own breathing in the silence of the room, if the Prince sitting across from me is the man I hope he is, a man worthy of our daughter, he will speak.

He did not disappoint. "The princess of Qipërta is my step-father's niece," he said. "Is this all so his blood will one day rule the Eastern Empire?"

We were excused—or dismissed—shortly afterwards. I refused a guard: unnecessary with Lena at my side. We did not talk in the corridor, but without asking Gwenna accompanied us to our room.

Inside, Apulo busied himself with my drugs. "Cannabium," I said to him quietly. The calm satisfaction of work done suffused me. I could suspend worry for a while; whatever came next was not up to us. Lena poured wine for herself and Gwenna.

"At your age," she said to our daughter, "I was terrified the first time I spoke to our village council."

"But you too were precise with advice to your Emperor, even the first time you met him," I said, taking the drink from Apulo.

"Did Callan tell you that?"

"He did. One night at the Eastern Fort." I raised my glass. "You were impressive, Gwenna. Well done, *mo nihéan gràhadh*."

We talked for a while of other things. When Alekos himself had come to help me rise, waving Apulo away, he had offered an apology to Lena. "You too of course should be in the imperial box at the next games, Major"

"I would be honoured to join you," she'd replied—what else could she say? Now, recalling it, she grinned.

"I'm not sure Eudekia approved of the invitation."

"I think, perhaps, it was her idea." Lena had dropped to the floor beside me, her hand resting on my thigh. As the drugs relaxed me further, I was becoming acutely aware of her. Gwenna, I thought, go to bed.

Lena was more forthright. "Lynthe will be waiting for you," she said to our daughter.

"I suppose she will," Gwenna said, standing. A smile played on her lips. "Sleep well."

"Am I needed?" Apulo asked softly.

"No." He followed Gwenna out. I ran a hand across Lena's hair and onto the skin of her neck. She still smelled faintly of lavender.

She rose, bending to kiss me, her hands light on my shoulders. Her lips were soft, full, and then firmer, her tongue flicking against mine. I slid my hands under the leather vest, finding the curves of her breasts beneath the tunic. She moaned and pulled away to help me stand.

In the bedroom I lit the lamps as she shed her uniform. Naked, she bent in front of me to remove my sandals. When my feet were bare, she ran her hands up my legs to my hips, her lips following the path of her hands. I gasped her name, sensation and desire flooding through me.

She pulled the tunic over my head. I lay back, as I had on a night so very long ago, under the stars of a cobalt sky, letting her offer and take what she needed to begin another healing.

Later she nestled against me, her head on my chest. I stroked her damp hair, arousal and release still resonating. "Wanted," I murmured. "Valued. Loved. Always, *käresta*."

I felt her smile. "When I woke that morning," she whispered, "I thought about how scarred we both were by life, and how one night could not repair that. Or even many. How life was not that simple."

"But we are given moments when it is," I said. I kissed her hair. "And the memories of those moments to sustain us."

She lay silent. Then, "Lianë was so curious. So many questions."

"So much you," I said, "and yet herself."

"She might have disappointed you," she murmured.

"Disappointed me? How could she?"

"I think—had thought—that at twelve I might have taken her to Tirvan, to apprentice to the boats, or the herds. She was meant for an outdoor life, not books and arguments, I believe."

"I had thought the same," I said.

"Had you?" She looked up at me. The lamps still burned; I could see her eyes, questioning.

"I had. And it would have been no disappointment."

"We never spoke of it," she said after a moment.

"We haven't spoken of many things. Reticence has become a habit again. I shouldn't have let my guarded tongue affect us."

"Or I mine. Things I didn't tell you, because I thought you uninterested, or too busy, or I judged them too unimportant."

"And," I said gently, "because you need a part of your life to be yours alone."

"Yes. Cillian—"

"No." I ran a finger down her cheek. The horse archers of Ésparias lived together, loving each other as part of their worship of the huntress. *Junia convinced me,* Lena had said. "Yours alone."

I woke a few hours later, hearing in the fragment of a dream my own words: *my guarded tongue.* Spoken not by me, but by the Empress. I lay still, trying to hold on to the sense of the dream, the meaning. Eudekia's tongue was always guarded: why was I being reminded of that?

Look for the exception, I told myself. I searched my memory. In our night-time meetings, she had been freer with her speech, as she had always been; nineteen years ago, she had openly told me of the advantages of a marriage between us, and what could happen if I refused. Not something ever mentioned in the formal negotiations. We had spoken now of Gwenna and Alekos, of course; of their complementary skills, the role Gwenna might play here and yet still be a presence in Ésparias; of the problems that might arise. She had mentioned the similarities with her marriage, her consort husband heir to his lands, and the conflicts and compromises that had caused.

There had been a dozen times those conversations had given her an opening to challenge me, tell me either subtly or directly she was aware of my years of planning for a future without Casil. She had not. Each time she had spoken her veiled threats, Gwenna had been present. Their purpose, I could only conclude, was to sway my daughter's decision.

Chapter 42

~DAUGHTER~

"DID HE ASK FOR YOUR HAND?"

Lynthe had been asleep when I'd returned to our room; quite deeply asleep. She hadn't stirred, and I hadn't tried to wake her. What Druise would have said about the fact I'd entered the room without her noticing, I didn't want to think about. But she had no compunction about waking me this morning.

"What?" I said, rolling over.

"Did Alekos ask for your hand?"

"No." I sat up. "Wait a minute." I pulled back the light cover and went to the commode. My bladder relieved, I washed my hands and face before I returned to Lynthe.

"Why are you asking me this?" I took a step toward her, but she moved her head to look out the balcony door. "Lynthe?"

"Wasn't that what was last night was about?"

"No." I hadn't told her much. "No, it wasn't. It was about the negotiations my father has been holding with Decanius, and the records I've been reading."

"So why was your mother there?"

"She was there to give an officer's opinion on some things. If you don't believe me, ask her." I pulled off my shift and began to dress, my jaw tight.

"But he is going to ask, isn't he?"

"Perhaps," I said, straightening my tunic. I had put off this conversation; one I should have had as soon as I had admitted to my mother I would accept Alekos. I'd lied to her when I said Lynthe knew. I took a deep breath.

"I suggested to him we would be a good partnership. He agrees. But there is still the question of Qipërta."

"You didn't tell me first?" She sounded—and was, I realized—completely shocked.

"I thought you understood," I said. The statement sounded weak to my own ears. "Lynthe, we did talk about this." Hadn't we? We'd started to . . . but then I'd been sick. "You said you were going to go home."

"So you'd know I wasn't going to stay, hoping to see you occasionally. I can't do that. But I thought . . . " Her voice trailed off.

"Thought what?"

"That you cared enough about me to tell me first."

"It's not that."

"Then what?"

"I can't . . . " I stopped.

"You can't, or won't? There's something you're not telling me, isn't there? Something you don't trust me with."

"Lynthe, will you listen?" Gods, how to make her understand? Could I tell her?

"No," she said, her face set. "Your father trusted me with secrets that could destroy him—and you. I thought he was doing it so we could be equally responsible, you and me. Together. But regardless, I'm part of it now."

"I'm sorry," I said feebly.

"I'm not. Not about that. I agree with his thinking. It makes sense. I want to be—" She groped for words. "Instrumental, in the plans." Her voice changed, into that of an officer questioning a soldier. "If you marry Alekos, Gwenna, can we trust you?"

I couldn't find words. I just stared at her. "Either your mother or Druisius can guard you today." Lynthe said. "I'm going out. Stay here."

Druise appeared so quickly I realized she couldn't have gone in search of him. I was still braiding and pinning back my hair, which gave me a reason not to look at him as I reached for composure. "I met Lynthe in the corridor," he said. "I gave her leave. Lena can shout at me. Except she will not. I left a note with Apulo. She is still in bed. So is your father."

"Druise." I was glad of the excuse to sound distant, "Don't tell me that." I'd been fairly sure why my mother had suggested I leave last night, but I didn't need confirmation.

He laughed. "You said the same at fourteen. But you are an adult now, yes? Be happy they are reconciled."

Were they, this time? I'd thought the same before. If they truly were, then my plan for them to stay in Casil, at least for a while, had more chance of succeeding.

"They won't want me in their rooms, then," I said. "Druise, can we go to the baths? The Bassanian Baths, I mean, not the palace ones." I could walk in the gardens again, be out of doors, even if the space was still walled and tamed. Think.

He chewed a lip. "If you want. But a litter, yes, for protocol? Not walking."

"If I must."

Druise found a servant, sending her scurrying to make arrangements while I tied my sandals and found my silk scarf from Sylana. Then we walked out into the morning sunshine, and down the long ramp that led to the forum with its temples and monuments. At its base, at the gate in the palace's walls, the litter awaited me.

I stepped into the open box, its seats cushioned and the interior walls painted with nymphs and gods. When I was seated, Druise said something to the four large men, and the litter was hoisted up, slightly swaying, onto their shoulders to begin the slow journey to the baths.

I left the curtains partially open, hoping the sights would distract me from my thoughts. Below me, I could see the heads of people: dark heads and lighter, red hair and pale like Sorley's; straight and curly; covered and bare. City guards with their helmets; eunuchs in their caps; women with scarves against the sun. I could hear snatches of cries from market stalls; the wail of a baby; an irritated mother or nursemaid scolding.

Angry shouts made me lean forward for a better look. A group of boys a bit younger than Colm tore in front of the litter, taunting their pursuers. Market stall holders, I guessed, the boys thieving fruit or baked goods. With the agility of youth the boys scrambled over a wall and disappeared, to profanity from the men chasing them.

We crossed the bridge over the river. Gulls screamed. I saw barges and skiffs, transporting goods and people, and smelled mud and rot. Three kites fed on a dead piglet—or at least I hoped it was a piglet—on the bank.

A sharp breeze ruffled the curtains, clearing the air for a moment. Then we passed through a gate in the huge city wall, and along more streets to the gates of the baths.

Druisius had followed on foot, along with another guard, one I thought I recognized from the palace. One of the men Druise trusted. The litter was lowered. I stepped out.

The second guard stayed with the litter. Druise escorted me into the building. "Are you going to the pools?"

"Not yet," I said. "Maybe tea, and then can we walk in the gardens?"

"Whatever you want. I am just your guard, Princess."

"Don't—" I stopped. He had proprieties to maintain in this public space. I nodded, instead. "Tea, please."

He found me a seat and a serving girl, who brought not just tea but bread and honey. I ate a little. I liked honey, and the bread was fresh, still warm. The tea tasted of fruit.

Sipping the tea, I looked around. Few people were here this early, and no one I recognized. Which was, to be truthful, exactly what I had hoped for. I had made a mistake, a bad mistake, in not telling Lynthe my plans. Before we'd come to Casil, she'd been casual, uncommitted, and I'd been treating her as if that hadn't changed. Because, I admitted, I needed to believe I wasn't going to hurt her by marrying Alekos.

Or by what I was forcing her to do, if I did.

If you marry Alekos, there has to be someone of your generation in Ésparias who is part of it, my mother had told me, weeks before. Someone who knew the plans and the secrets, and the people who were allied, or not. I had reminded my mother of this, not more than a few days past. My choice to remain in Casil meant this would fall to Lynthe. If my whole family stayed, it would be even more vital. *I want to be instrumental in the plans.* Would she accept that meant taking at least nominal responsibility for a girl child, or children, sent back to Ésparias as the heir?

If I was going to ask this of her, she had to know why. I had to trust her with the truth.

I finished my tea. Druise was standing behind me, at what I supposed was the correct distance. Part of me wanted to find Lynthe; a cooler-headed part knew she needed more time away from me. "I'd like to go to the garden now," I told Druise.

I walked the paths for about an hour, rehearsing what I would say to Lynthe, until the increasing heat had me sweating. We went back into the cool of the building. "Can I go to the pools unchaperoned?" I murmured to Druise.

"It is unusual. But not much; there will be no gossip, or only a little."

"What is a little gossip?" I asked drily. He accompanied me to the door that led to the women's rooms.

"I will not be far." He handed me some coins. "For your attendants. Do not leave this corridor without me, when you are done."

I spent another hour bathing and being groomed. Women clipped my toenails and smoothed my feet with salve; they trimmed and washed my hair and massaged me, and I luxuriated in their care. I could, I thought idly, as strong hands rubbed an unguent into my skin, get used to this.

Dried and dressed, the coins distributed, I thanked the woman who had kept my possessions safe and stepped back out into the corridor. Druise was crouched against the wall a few paces away. Seeing me, he straightened.

"I'm sorry I was so long," I said.

He shrugged. "No matter."

"Druise," I said in Linrathan, "why are you always so good tempered? Accepting?"

He grinned. "Life is easier that way."

"Seriously," I said. We began to walk.

"Sorley asked me that once," he said, his voice no longer teasing. "And I am not, always. But we have choices, yes? In how we react, and if we are bothered by something."

"That's what Catilius says, and Serventius, and the other philosophers my father studies."

"So Cillian has told me." We'd reached the open space of the main hall now, with its statues and high, decorative ceiling. "He has offered me the books, but I know what I think. I do not need dead men to tell me the same. Do you want to eat before we leave?"

What Druisius was saying was not so different than what we had been taught as envoys: not to react, but to listen for the intent behind words of anger or defiance. Something, I could remember Michan telling us, causes the anger: fear, usually. Do your best to understand the root of that fear, and you will have the advantage of your opponent. Then choose how you will use that advantage.

"Eat?" I realized Druise was waiting for an answer. "Why not?" As he escorted me across the hall, now considerably busier than earlier, I saw Decanius. He was talking to two women. One, red haired, dressed in green, looked remarkably like the Empress, although I could see she was not. The other—did I know her? Decanius turned his head and looked directly at us. He said something to the women before hurrying away.

Druise muttered something I didn't hear. One of the women approached us. Druise's sister, I realized: Bernikë.

"Druisius."

"Bernikë. I am working." She looked at me.

"So was I. You are not his *quincalum's* daughter, I hear." She folded her arms. "You are a princess."

"Gwenna of Ésparias. I am sorry for the lie, before, but I could not risk being identified."

"Of course not." It was almost a sneer.

"Who told you?" Druise asked, and then he added something in a tongue I didn't know. She answered in the same language, her tone still derisive. Druise nodded, and then went suddenly still.

"What did you call him?" he asked in Casilan.

"Who? The *Magistere?*"

"No. His father. Flavian."

"Old Curly. Bald as an egg on top, the tightest curls around his *mutto*. Which I saw close up whenever he was in the city, not to make you blush, Princess."

"You're not," I said, reflexively. Curly. *Crispus.*

"Why's it matter?" she asked.

The *scraptae* of the baths—because that was what she and the other woman were—would trade in gossip and information, I guessed. Druise was asking too many questions. Bernikë would tell Decanius of our interest.

"I think I saw those same curls once," Druisius said with a grin.

Bernikë shook her head. "Not likely. Always women, for Old Curly."

"A mouth's a mouth, yes?" Druise said. I was going to blush in a moment.

"Maybe it is," Bernikë said. "I'll leave you, before the Princess's reputation is spoiled by being seen with a *scrapta*."

"You are Druisius' sister, and he has been my guard and my friend since I was a few minutes old. I am pleased to meet all his family."

Bernikë's face grew hard. "Has he?" She nearly spat. "What he could not do for one of his own, he does for a stranger?" She said something in the language I didn't recognize before turning on her heel to stalk away, an ankle bracelet jingling.

I looked at Druise. "What have I done?" He was staring after her, his face anguished. "Druise?"

His expression changed. "You could not know. It is not important now. You heard what else she said."

"Crispus."

"Decanius's father." He glanced over at his sister, who had rejoined the green-clad woman. Keeping his voice low, he added, "We need to return to the palace."

I tried not to hurry; drawing attention to myself wasn't sensible. Outside, it took a minute or two before the litter was readied and we could be on our way. The streets, even more crowded regardless of the heat, were difficult to navigate, and inside the box I was jostled more than on the morning's journey.

We crossed the bridge, the smell of rot and mud stronger now, and into the market quarter beyond. I heard Druisius calling for people to clear our way.

A gabble of voices and cries, and suddenly a dozen heads were at the side of the litter. Arms reached up to push. I reached for my secca, strapped to my leg. Shouts from Druisius and the other guard, another rocking of the litter, a cry of pain—and the litter tipped. I grabbed the frame of the opening with one hand, my feet sliding.

An impression of sky, and the sun in my eyes, and then the world levelled again, and the litter was slowly lowered. I got to my feet. "Kitten?"

"I'm all right," I told Druisius. "What happened?"

"A gang of boys. I have sent a guard after them, but he has little chance. They will know these streets too well."

I stepped out, heedless of protocol. Druisius's short sword was still in his hand, as my secca was in mine. One of the litter bearers was on his knees. "Is he hurt?"

"A thrown rock, taken in the calf. He has cramp. It will pass." Druise's eyes were moving constantly. "You should not be out here, Gwenna."

"Was this random? Just rowdy boys?" I pulled the red scarf over my head. A crowd had gathered, and from their excited voices I heard 'princess' and 'palace'.

"Maybe. Maybe not. You are sure you are not hurt?"

"I might have a bruise or two. Nothing serious."

The young guard returned, breathing hard. He shook his head at Druise's question. Druise swore. I was sweating now, out here in the busy street, and the smells of fruit and fish and meat that had spent half a day in the sun were nearly overpowering.

The guard was questioning the crowd. A woman pushed her way up to us. She carried a pitcher and cups. "Wine for the Princess?"

"No," Druisius said. I smiled at her.

"A kind thought," I said. "What is your name?"

She told me. "You have a stall here?"

"A *taberna*, my lady. Just there." She pointed.

"Could I have just a taste of the wine?" She poured with the skill of long practice. Bowing, she handed me the cup. I took the barest sip. It was of the quality served in the soldiers' commons, thin and sour. But it was a taste I knew well, and if it were poisoned, it was with something undetectable to my tongue.

I swallowed, but only saliva. Handing her the cup, I said, "As good a wine as I have drunk elsewhere. You may tell your customers Gwenna of Ésparias told you so."

Her smile of pleasure looked genuine, and I'd seen no flicker of recognition at my name. The litter bearer got to his feet, nodding to Druisius. He called the young guard back. I climbed into the litter, felt it lifted above the street, the slow sway of movement. I sat back on the cushioned seat, pulling the scarf off my hair, willing myself to relax. But I did not sheathe my secca.

Chapter 43

~FATHER~

"I AM ALL RIGHT," GWENNA INSISTED, to Lena's repeated words of concern. "What we learned from Druise's sister is more important."

"I will investigate," Druisius said. "But it will take time. Maybe just boys being stupid; maybe something else."

"What else?" Lena asked. "This is the second attack, Captain. Do you think that is coincidence?"

"The first wasn't an attack," Gwenna said. "Just a loose roof tile."

Lena frowned. "I am not so sure."

"The boys see a litter from the palace," Druisius said. "A woman inside. Maybe they think to frighten the Empress, let her know they want the Prince on the throne, not her."

"Possibly," Lena said, her voice doubtful. "But would the Empress have only two guards?"

"I said stupid boys."

It was possible, I thought; possible, but unlikely.

"You have reported it?" Lena asked. Gwenna sighed with impatience.

"Of course." Druisius said. "Soldiers will go, punish the boys. Then tonight or tomorrow I will visit the *taberna*, yes? The woman will help the princess who praised her wine, if she can."

"You have coin enough?" I asked.

"For wine. Not for bribes."

"Tell Apulo what you need." Gwenna was pacing, impatient to talk. Sorley put a hand on her arm as she passed him.

"Sit down, Gwenna," he said, "and tell us what you learned." He'd been singing the new *danta* to us when Druisius and Gwenna had come in, our daughter flushed and intent.

She stood still. Her lips parted as if to speak, but she stayed silent. Then she shook her head. "I can't."

Druise chuckled. "I will tell them what Bernikë said. Not something easy to say to your parents."

She nodded, turning to look out into the atrium as Druisius, grinning, told us.

"A use-name," Lena said. "I hadn't thought of that."

I saw a good man destroyed by his obsession with a woman. "What do you know of Flavian?" I asked Druisius.

"Not very much. I fought in Qipërta many years past, a small insurrection. Flavian was the governor. He did what was needed with the leaders, and the followers were sent to be soldiers somewhere else. The usual, yes?" He chewed his lip, thinking. "Twenty years ago, when the records mention Crispus, I was a palace guard. Sometimes I did work for Quintus. His sister was married to Flavian."

"Decanius's mother," I said.

"Yes, but long dead. That I knew. But nothing else about Flavian."

"Is he still alive?" Gwenna asked.

"No. Bernikë said today he was dead."

"Would your sister know more?" I asked. "Did she not imply he visited her regularly?"

"She might. But Decanius is her client too. She will tell him we asked about his father."

"Can she be bribed?" Lena asked.

For a minute I thought Druisius had taken offence; the question had been blunt. But his voice when he replied was thoughtful.

"Maybe. Marius will know, or Vita. Do you need me? If not, I will go to ask. I will be gone an hour, maybe more."

"Should I come?" Sorley asked.

"No, *amané*. This is for family, yes?"

"Did anyone overhear your conversation?" I asked Gwenna, when Druisius had departed.

"I don't think so," she said, "but there was another woman with his sister and Decanius, and after Bernikë left us she went back to her. She might have told her what we talked about."

"Would you recognize her?" Lena asked.

"She looked a lot like the Empress, but I think she was a *scrapta* too."

If the woman did look like the Empress, she would command a high price among the licensed prostitutes of the baths, men—and perhaps other women—indulging dreams of desire or power. She should be easy to find, if we needed to.

"Do you recall Decanius's reaction to me, when I scribed for Druisius's trial?" Lena asked. "I was heavily pregnant, and he hated that; didn't want me at the same table."

I didn't remember; not surprising. I had been far from well. "All this is still circumstantial," I reminded them. But the pieces made a pattern. In my mind I saw, not a *xache* board, but the table at the Eastern Fort, a map of what was now Ésparias spread out on it, and the pieces massed and arranged to show a plan of attack.

I had failed then to see treason hidden in those pieces. That failure had cost my father his life, and I lived every day with pain reminding me. I would not make the same mistake twice.

"Sorley." Lena had the rank for this, but I would not risk Eudekia's reaction to her as a messenger. She would trust Sorley. "Will you take a note to the Empress? We must see her, and the Prince, as soon as possible."

"This is dangerous," Lena said, while we waited. She did not sound judgmental, or even frightened; an observation from a soldier, nothing more. Gwenna had curled herself into a chair, saying nothing; perhaps only now allowing herself to consider the attack on her litter.

"It is," I agreed. "Have you any advice?"

"Advice?" She half-smiled. "This is diplomacy, Cillian. I leave it to you."

"Do you think," Gwenna asked suddenly, "that Sahira knows?"

"You've spent more time with her than we have," I said. "Tell us what you think."

"I think not." She uncurled herself to sit upright. "She's mentioned more than once that Hathus is her uncle. At first it was almost . . . defiant." She paused. "No, that's not the right word. As if it gave her status, an advantage over the rest of us. She's stopped doing that, at least with me.

"But she's never mentioned Decanius, not in a way that would suggest she thinks he's her brother. He's been kind to her here in Casil, she said, but that was all."

"Would she, though?" Lena asked.

Gwenna wrinkled her nose. "She has no skill in dissimulation, *Mathàir*."

We all looked up at Sorley's return. "They are coming here," he announced. He handed me a note. I read it, allowing a smile. Of course. Why would the Empress and her son come to us? The court would believe only one reason.

"Gwenna," I said. "Please go change. Your best tunic: you must be the princess. As I must be the prince."

"And I?" Lena asked.

"For this, *käresta*, you are Gwenna's mother, and my wife."

She had always been quick. "Alekos is coming to propose."

"That is what is to be believed. We must play our part."

Gwenna stood, irresolute. "Is it only a ruse?"

"At this moment, yes."

"I once pretended to be your wife, if you recall," Lena said to me. "Ruses can become reality. Gwenna, come. I'll help you dress. How long do we have?"

"An hour. Apulo, will you fetch appropriate wine?"

"And tidy the room," he said. "But do you not need me to help you dress?"

"I can do that," Sorley said.

In the bedroom he helped me pull my tunic off. "Which do you want?" he asked, turning to the chest.

"The white one." I watched him shake it out. He brought it to me, slipping it over my head. He'd done this with the wool shirts I habitually wore in Linrathe a hundred or more times before. The familiarity was reassuring.

I put my arms around him. He tensed. "Cillian," he protested, "this is your bedroom."

"But this isn't the *Ti'ach*, where we have a place that is ours. We have a moment alone. Can we not take advantage of it?"

He smiled, stepping forward to return the embrace. We stood silently, his hands tight on my back, for a long minute. Then I kissed his hair, and his lips, lightly. "You need to change too."

"In a little while. What else would Apulo do for you?"

"Nothing. I can comb my own hair and beard, and he cut my toenails yesterday. But you could give me my pendant; it's in the chest."

"Will Alekos really propose, do you think?" Sorley asked, as he handed me the silver sigil of my rank.

"Possibly. He will certainly let it be believed he has." The silver chain was cold, briefly, on my skin. Sorley found my comb, gave it to me.

"Couldn't that put Gwenna in more danger? Assuming the incident today was no accident?" He sat on the chest, watching me tidy my hair.

"Yes," I admitted. "I'll talk to Druisius about increasing her guard." She wouldn't like it, but it was necessary.

"Lynthe won't be happy," Sorley said quietly. "Druise says she loves Gwenna."

"Lena says Gwenna will marry Alekos," I said. "An alliance of like minds and upbringing. Lynthe must know that." I put the comb down. "It's not what I would have chosen for Gwenna, politics aside. I can only hope she comes to love him, and he her. To live without love, without loving, is unthinkable to me now."

"It wasn't once." When he had offered his love to a cynical, bitter man, and I had hurt him, so much.

"I haven't been that man for a long time." This chance, I thought, would not come again before events overtook us. "Nor am I who I was before this journey."

I saw puzzlement in his blue eyes, and concern. "*Somhairle*," I said, in his own dialect, "you must know I love you."

Disbelief, for a moment, and then growing joy in the smile that curved his lips. "Now?" he said. "Of all the times and places. Cillian . . . " He shook his head, still smiling, but tears glittered. "I did know."

"Knowing and hearing are not the same. I have been wrong, all these years, not to have told you."

"You had your reasons," he said softly.

"Mistaken ones. I will tell you, *mo duíne gràhadh*, but not now. Now you must prepare to present yourself to the Empress and the Prince as Lord Sorley."

"I suppose I must." He got up, coming to where I sat on the bed. "Ready to stand, *kärestan*?" He held out an arm.

When I was on my feet he kissed me, not quite as lightly as before. "You are annoying, still," he said with a grin. I brushed the wetness from his eyelashes with one finger.

"That you have always known." I had hurt him badly twice. I was preparing to do it again. *The third decides*, the proverb ran. A decision that I, in the deepest recesses of my heart, did not want to make at all.

Chapter 44

~DAUGHTER~

"WHERE'S LYNTHE?" I ASKED, when we'd reached my room.

"I sent her to Junia," my mother said. "She was angry, and angry soldiers are careless. They make mistakes. I told her to work it off cleaning stables, or whatever task they gave her." She sounded angry herself. At me? What had Lynthe told her?

"What's wrong?"

"Two guards were not enough for you this morning. What was Druise thinking?" Her mouth twisted. "But that is between him and me. Change your clothes, Gwenna, and I'll do your hair."

I stripped off my tunic and washed the tang of fear from my body. The assault earlier felt unreal, as if it had happened to someone else, and yet thinking about it made my spine tingle and tighten. I pushed the feeling away to dress again in my best clothes, the palest grey tunic with the silvery silk inserts. We'd never had more clothes made here; it hadn't seemed necessary. I slipped the red earrings on, then sat to let my mother arrange my hair.

She combed it, then began braiding. "I didn't know you could do this," I said. My hair had been short until I made the choice of diplomatic service over military and could let it grow.

"I used to do it for Maya," she said, through the hairpins in her teeth.

"How did you feel, leaving her?" I asked impulsively.

"She left me. I was devastated when she chose banishment." She pinned a braid in place. "But she chose a life I could not be part of, and I had to accept it, in the end." A tug as she separated another section of hair. "As Lynthe will have to, and will, in time."

"I do love her," I said, tears pricking.

"Then why are you even considering marrying Alekos?" She finished with my hair and put the comb down, moving to stand in front of me.

"You were considering leaving *Athàir*, "I said, "and you love him, don't you?"

She sat on the bed with a sigh. "Turlo—you remember who he was?—gave me advice once. He told me not to let Cillian's dreams subsume mine, because I was meant to be a leader too." She smiled, wryly. "And then I told Sorley the same thing. But he listened far better than I did."

I saw a chance. If I could persuade her that was my reason to marry Alekos, all the better. "But I am also meant to be a leader, and here I can be. What am I in Ésparias, *Mathàir*, other than a reminder to Faolyn that his son will not succeed him?"

She didn't answer. "Have you thought any more about staying?" I asked.

"A bit. But until you suggest it to your father, and Sorley and Druise, it has little substance. You need to do that soon, Gwenna. Today may be the right time, after Eudekia and Alekos have gone."

The tension inside me coiled again, but this time for what awaited me, not what was past. My mother rose to take my silver pendant from the table where it lay. She fastened it around my neck, her hands resting on my shoulders when she was done.

"Can you love Alekos, in time?" she asked quietly.

I thought of playing *xache* with him; our conversations, his intelligence, the feel of his finger touching my cheek. "I think so."

"Then I will worry less." Her hands tightened on my shoulders for a moment. "We should go back to your father."

Their rooms were extraordinarily tidy, with extra chairs brought from somewhere, and a flagon of wine and glasses waiting on the sideboard. My mother disappeared into their bedroom to change her own clothes. Sorley, in the green-and-grey of Gundarstorp, had been playing quietly. I recognized the tune. *Uncharted paths could be explored . . .* wasn't that what I was doing? I tried not to think about the rest of the words. *Older love is not forgotten.* A ruse today's visit might be, but it presaged what was to come.

I couldn't sit. I went to look out; below us, I heard the splash of the atrium's fountain and the chatter of sparrows. A thought struck. I turned. "Will you explain how we identified Decanius's father to the Empress and Alekos, *Athàir*? I don't think I can."

"You should," Sorley said to my father. "Eudekia will accept it more easily from you."

"She may," he said. "But, Gwenna, feel free to add your own thoughts, or expand on what I say. You may be questioned, too."

My mother emerged, dressed in a russet tunic trimmed in green, the emeralds Eudekia had sent to my father in her ears. She wore no other jewellery but her silver marriage bracelet, and her secca was not visible. "I would like wine," she said, "but I suppose we should not, until the imperial party arrives."

"Are you nervous, *käresta*?"

"Shouldn't I be? What we are suggesting to the Empress is treason, yet again."

"I will tell her what we know," my father said. "The conclusions will be theirs."

Apulo, in a fresh linen tunic, his wide sash neatly tied, had knelt at the sideboard, opening its door. Now he straightened, handing my mother a cup of wine. "Less good than what you will offer the Empress," he said. "Would anyone else like wine? I will take the cups away when the guards knock at the door."

"Please," Sorley said. My father declined, and, after a moment's temptation, so did I. I needed a clear head.

The knock came a few minutes later. Apulo, a tray readied, gathered our cups quickly, taking them into the bedroom. Sorley answered the door.

He stepped aside with a deep bow as the Empress and Alekos entered. My father had pushed himself upright at the knock. As my mother and I knelt, he inclined his head. "You do us great honour, Empress, Prince Alekos."

The door had been firmly shut. "Enough," Eudekia said, with an upward motion of her hand. "You have things to tell us, and protocol can be put aside." She glanced around the room. "Where are the bodyguards?"

"The Lieutenant is training with the horse archers today, Empress," my mother said, "and the captain will return soon. I gave him leave to visit his family."

Eudekia smiled slightly. "I suppose if you are here, there is little need for another guard."

Alekos had remained silent, but his eyes had met mine across the room. He smiled, meaning, I knew, to reassure me. "I think," he said now, "that if Gwenna and her mother both have their knives, Prince Cillian has little to worry about."

"Prince Cillian," the Empress said, "is a man of subtlety and secrets; such men must always worry for their safety." Her eyes flicked to me. I didn't flinch, not visibly.

"Will you sit, Empress?" my father said.

"Of course." She took the best chair without thought. Sorley served the wine, my mother last, as protocol demanded; she bore no title, no rank except her military one, the least among us. I wondered if it bothered her.

"Now," Eudekia said, "what is it we need to know?"

My father laid it out for the Empress and Alekos: the translation of the marginalia; Decanius's answer to his question about a wife; the identification of Crispus as a use-name for Flavian among the *scraptae*. The latter he explained unemotionally, simply saying the name was due to 'the tight curling of body hair, especially noticed where it grows thickest.'

"There was some problem, I remember," the Empress said, when he finished. "Quintus advised recalling Flavian from Qipërta; he pleaded to be allowed to remain. He had projects he wanted to see completed, he said; I do not recall the details. We had originally thought to send him to Ésparias, so we sent his son instead."

"Perhaps one of those projects was an infant he wished to see grow up," my mother said.

"Perhaps it was. But there is no proof here, just conjecture."

"Who would have seen the records, here in the palace?" I asked.

"Some clerk, who would have summarized the information for Quintus, were it important enough," the Empress replied. "May we see the records?"

I took them from the table and knelt beside Eudekia, pointing out the three notes. She scanned them, checking the dates. "They say what you reported, I believe. I have not read this language for some years. Your father's aide is close? I would have him read it to me."

Sorley fetched Apulo. He knelt, head to the floor, until she commanded him to rise. Then he crouched beside her, reading the lines in a clear voice. She nodded. "I see no hidden meaning here."

No hidden meaning? But of course, I thought, marginalia could well hold coded messages, words or even symbols—there were plenty of rats and cats and dragons sketched on the edge of records—meaning something other than the obvious. Or bringing attention to the passage they edged, telling the reader to interpret it in a certain way. Useful, I thought.

"Perhaps Bruccius should see them?" Alekos had been listening attentively. "This is a serious matter."

"Wait," my father said. "Apulo, leave us, please."

"Do you not trust him?" Alekos asked, as the corridor door closed.

"With my life. But this is not for his ears."

Alekos nodded. "If Decanius has his own reasons for promoting Sahira as my bride, beyond that which we attributed to my stepfather, there is potentially great danger here."

"What danger?" my father asked.

Alekos stood. I guessed, like me, he ordered his thoughts better while moving.

"That Hathus wishes me to marry his niece to bring the Boranoi bloodline to the throne of Casil is one thing," he said, his voice measured. "In the fullness of time, were I to marry Sahira, that would happen. Regardless of whom I marry, unless I choose a bride from within the city walls as my father did, my heir will be half-Qipërtani, or Sylanan, or," he glanced at me, "Ésparian." For a minute, he paced in silence.

"But Decanius is a greedy man." He stopped again, as if reluctant to voice his thought. "The gods willing, I will live a long life, and he will be dead before he saw a child of his bloodline on the throne. Unless—"

"Unless the Emperor is dead, and his heir an infant. A regency council would be needed." Eudekia spoke calmly. "Quintus and his allies demanded the same, when your father was killed, Alekos. I stood up to them; I still had my family's friends to support me, and in the end they accepted me as the Empress and regent, with older men to advise me. But Sahira is not strong-minded, nor has she friends at her back."

"Were Decanius able to prove he was Sahira's brother," my father said, "he would potentially have great influence, even power, over a young Empress and her child."

"Power, indeed," the Empress said. "A route to the throne for himself, if he does not baulk at murdering innocents."

No one spoke. Sorley, unbidden, refilled the wine glasses. He stood behind my father's chair, his face grim. The Empress looked up.

"Sit, Lord Sorley," she said, faintly smiling. "There will be no repercussions for Cillian. All he has done is bring certain things to our attention. You will not be required to plead with me for his freedom again. Not over this."

A faint flush stained Sorley's cheeks as he took his chair. Eudekia drank her wine. We waited. She put the glass down.

"We cannot let any hint of our suspicions show," she said. "Nor will I risk forcing my husband's hand, or Decanius's. They must think, therefore, that marriage to Sahira is still a possibility."

Alekos made a sound of protest. "I said 'think'," his mother reiterated. "I know your wishes, as, I believe, does everyone here. A wish shared, is it not?"

My parents' eyes met for a long look. "The decision is Gwenna's," my father said. I swallowed, tried to speak. Nothing came out. I couldn't say the words. I didn't want to.

"Gwenna?" Alekos said gently.

I wet my lips. "We would be good partners." My fingers wanted to curl into fists; I stopped them.

"We must let the palace think we came today with a marriage proposal, one that was rejected." Eudekia spoke briskly. "More negotiations will be needed; further questions of children and inheritance, perhaps, or time spent in Ésparias. I will continue to conduct those negotiations personally with Cillian, and Lena, too, I think."

I was barely listening: had I just agreed to marry Alekos?

"But as the proposal has been refused," the Empress continued, "you should ask Sahira and her party to accompany you to the games this week, Alekos. And if you can imply that the princess of Ésparias was my choice, and you feel you have had a fortunate escape, all the better."

"How can I do that?" Alekos murmured.

"Because you must," my mother almost snapped. "My daughter was attacked this morning; there is more than one way to eliminate her as a bride. If you care for her welfare, Prince Alekos, you will stay away from her."

"Attacked?" Alekos asked, sharply.

"I wasn't hurt," I said. "Just startled." But as I spoke I felt again the tipping of the litter, and the sensation of falling; the faces, the walls . . .

trapped like an animal in the Arénas. My heart pounded. Cold sweat beaded on my neck; I gasped for breath.

Arms around me, strong and gentle. "Gwenna," Sorley said, "it's all right. You're safe. Come and sit."

"No!" I tried to twist away. He kept his hands on my back, but loosely. "I don't want to sit." I was behaving like a child, in front of the Empress. I didn't care. "I need to be outside. Not the balcony. Where I can see."

"Then I will take you."

"No," my mother said. "Stay here, Sorley. I'll go with Gwenna. You will excuse us, Empress, Prince."

"Of course," I heard the Empress murmur. "Alekos, instruct a guard to accompany them, but at a distance." I couldn't look at him.

Outside, I leant on the wall, looking out, not down at the temples and the people below us, but beyond. The hills of the city were crowded with buildings, but at least there was distance, and a sky to be seen, even if it was full of circling carrion birds.

My breathing slowed and steadied. My mother stood close, not speaking, waiting. "I'm sorry," I said. "I don't know what happened."

"A reaction to the attack," she said. "Soldiers often experience this. At the time our bodies and minds concentrate on survival, but later we realize what could have happened, and shock and fear take over. It's happened to me, many times."

That made me feel a little better. If it happened to my strong mother, then I wasn't so childish. "I was trapped in a box, and I couldn't do anything." I shivered.

"Gwenna," my mother said gently, "is there perhaps another reason you are feeling trapped?"

"The city," I said, turning back to the view. "The palace. Walls and more walls."

"And Alekos?"

I stared out, willing myself strength. "No," I said. "Not Alekos." *You will not be required to plead for his freedom again. Not over this.*

"Even if what you say is true," my mother said, "accepting Alekos means accepting the walls of the palace and the city too."

"I'll grow used to them."

"Perhaps. Gwenna, nineteen years ago in this city, I watched your father grow more silent and distant every day, withdrawing from me as he prepared to accept Eudekia and the walls of this palace as the price for the chance of our countries' salvation. You are," she said, her voice softening, "so like him. Perhaps too much like him. I think you are making this choice for reasons other than those you have given me, and I think you are making a mistake."

I fought against the rising tears, and the desire to tell her, to ask what would she do to keep my father safe? But it wasn't just my father, it was her too, and Sorley, and Druisius, and maybe even Ruar and his sons. I swallowed, straightened, faced her. "It isn't a mistake."

She took a deep breath. "Then I will say no more, except this. You owe Lynthe the truth. Maya gave me that, if nothing else."

Chapter 45

~FATHER~

"IS THERE NOTHING DECANIUS DOES NOT have his fingers in?" Sorley asked. The Empress and Alekos had left us just a minute before. Lena and Gwenna had not returned.

"The office of the *fiscarius* means his reach is wide," I said. "But whether the palace guard is loyal to their Empress, or to the man who pays them, is a delicate question."

"The Empress is right to look for alternatives, though." Sorley sat in the chair beside mine, wine in his hand.

"Women seconded from the horse archers to guard the Empress, when she becomes the dowager, will not be questioned, I think." Apulo was mixing drugs; my back was threatening to spasm. "But bringing Bjørn and his men to Casil? It clearly indicates the Prince does not trust the palace guard."

"Alekos's reasoning is almost believable," Sorley argued. I took the cup of willowbark tincture from Apulo, drinking it down in two swallows. I had refused cannabium; I wanted my mind unclouded.

"That the city will remain crowded even after his investiture, if no bride is announced, and so they need more men? The people will accept it, I think. But the guard?"

"He will be their Emperor."

"Emperors have been killed or deposed by the palace guard before," I said. "But Bjørn cannot reach Casil for at least two months. If before then there are problems which the guards, both city and palace, have difficulty containing, perhaps resulting from the rise in the price of food, they will be more amenable to reinforcements."

Sorley grinned. "Gods, you're devious."

Another cramp gripped my back. Apulo, attuned to my needs, noticed immediately.

"You need massage," he said. "Now."

I indicated my acceptance. He helped me up. Sorley followed us into the bedroom. "I'll sing the rest the new *danta* for you," he said.

Half an hour later, Sorley had finished singing about Hrothgar and heroes and monsters, and I could stand without too much pain.

"That is not a *danta* for children," I commented, as Apulo slipped a fresh tunic over my head.

"Not unless nightmares are called for," Sorley agreed. "It's interesting; there are other *danta* about Hrothgar, and others with dragons, but nothing else I know with these monsters of the deep. I wonder what traditions are behind it?"

"When we get home, perhaps you should travel and find out."

"Not until next summer. I'm not journeying into the wilds of Varsland and beyond in winter." He hadn't said no, I noted. Lena was not the only one who needed a life beyond the *Ti'ach*. Maybe it would make my proposal easier for him.

Druisius had returned during my massage; hearing Sorley's *ladhar*, he'd come in to let us know he was back, then retreated to the other room. We found him talking to Lena.

"Where is Gwenna?" I asked.

"With Lynthe. I went with Gwenna to her room, and Lynthe had just returned, so I left them together. I've been telling Druise what transpired with the Empress," Lena said. "Did you talk to your brother, Druise?"

"Yes." He rubbed his chin. "There is something Bernikë wants. I will see her, offer it. Maybe it will be enough." His tone did not invite further questions. Lena didn't push him; she had, it was clear from her next question, her own worries.

"Has Gwenna spoken to you, Druise? About Alekos?"

"The Prince? Words here and there. Why?"

"I want to know why she plans to accept him. I don't believe what she tells me."

"Which is?" I asked.

"That she wants the intellectual challenge, and the political influence. She isn't pretending to be in love with Alekos. But she's turning her back on Lynthe, and Ésparias, and all she is heir to. And that is not Gwenna."

"Leaving the woman she loves, and her country, for something she perceives as a greater good," Sorley said. "Doesn't that sound familiar, Lena?"

"Very," she said, with a sideways glance at me. "I told her only earlier today she was far too much like Cillian. What is driving her to do this? What is she afraid will happen if she doesn't marry the Prince?"

"Maybe nothing," Druisius said. Lena frowned. "Maybe you are looking for political reasons, when that is not why."

"What do you mean?"

"Maybe she is afraid of love."

"Why should she be?" Lena said.

"Because of you and Cillian," Sorley said. "She knows you were planning to leave him, Lena. And that you were not dissuading her," he added, turning to me. Anger was tightening his voice. "So if a love as strong as yours can't survive, doesn't she have good reason to be afraid of it? Simpler to stay here in Casil with Alekos." He gave a sardonic laugh. "A form of running away. I should have seen it before, shouldn't I?"

"Oh, gods." Lena met my eyes, a helpless look on her face.

"*Käresta*," I said. "She is young. And we haven't explained properly to her, or even to Sorley and Druisius." I did not want this conversation now; too much was unresolved. Nor did I truly think this was behind Gwenna's choice, but a question needed to be asked of Eudekia. A difficult question, to be carefully worded.

"Perhaps," Lena said, "this is why she wants us to stay."

"Stay?" Sorley said. "All of us?"

"All of us." Lena crossed her arms. "I wasn't going to say anything, but I think you need to know. She wants Cillian and me to be her advisors."

"But Sorley cannot stay," I said. No more than he could come to Wall's End with us.

"Why can't I? I have little doubt I could convince Ruar to appoint me envoy to Casil."

"You would leave the *Ti'ach*? And the *scáeli'en* council?" Lena's question echoed my own hidden disbelief. I had not expected this response at all.

"If the rest of you are here, yes. There is a lot I could learn about music and verse, and perhaps teach too."

"*Mo duíne gràhadh*," I said, as gently as I could. He hadn't thought this through. "You would be leaving Gundarstorp, too."

"I know," he said. "But perhaps not forever."

"But we can't do this," Lena said.

"Can we not?" It would be a solution; one with repercussions, but not impossible.

"But who would . . . " She stopped, a question on her face. She blinked, once, twice. "You knew we were coming to Casil. Voyages are never without risk. Ruar didn't come to the *Ti'ach* just to negotiate border tariffs, did he?"

From the corner of my eye I saw Druisius grin. "Not entirely," I admitted. "I gave him all the records—the real ones—and the letters, for safekeeping, and we reviewed the plans." I waited, expecting anger.

"Every contingency," she said wryly. "I should have known."

She had guessed only one reason why I had entrusted Ruar with my vision and the records. Perhaps she would never need to know the other, depending on Eudekia's answer to the question I must ask.

Apulo was hovering. "It has been a difficult day," he said. "You need the baths, Cillian, or you will be in much pain tonight."

He was right, and yet . . . What I wanted was solitude: my library, my books, the cat softly purring, not the public space of the palace's baths. I wanted to think about my own weakness in allowing myself to be manipulated by Eudekia. And about what might be possible, if Sorley would leave the *Ti'ach*.

"Come with me?" I said to Druisius. Sorley looked up. I moved my head, a negative gesture. He nodded. He might ask one or the other of us, later.

The baths were busier than in the mornings, but after some pleasantries we found a place away from the other groups of men.

"What is it your sister may accept, in exchange for silence?" I asked Druisius.

"A memorial stone. In a good location, and in my name."

"That is all?"

"Donations to a temple. Every year." He flexed his shoulders. "It will be understood I was responsible, yes?"

"Will that cause you difficulties?"

"Only if I wanted to marry. Not something a girl wants to know about her husband."

"But if we stay, you will have to explain it to Sorley," I said.

He shrugged, as I knew he would. "Then I will."

"The practice is not unknown in Varsland, and on Sorham's northern coast," I told him. "He may be less upset than you think."

"Maybe," he said. "I will tell him if I must. Are you going to tell Lena why else you gave Ruar the papers?"

"If I must." He grinned, then became serious again.

"I have heard nothing," he said. "Nothing about the Empress. Decanius does not like you, and makes that known. But no talk of anything except how the Empress favours you and Gwenna."

"Nonetheless, I believe she has knowledge of our plans, and is using that in another way." I ran a hand through my hair, formulating my words.

Water dripped into my eyes. I brushed it away. "I must find a way to ask her."

Druisius rolled his eyes. "Ask her what? Just tell me, yes?"

"We spoke of it at the *Ti'ach*," I reminded him, "except now I think Gwenna may be directly involved. Has the Empress told her I will be charged with treason unless she marries Alekos?"

We were speaking Linrathan, but the Prince's name caught the ears of another man, perhaps because I had used Gwenna's name too. A mistake.

"I hear that match is in doubt, Prince Cillian?" he called across the pool.

I gave him my best diplomat's smile. "It remains a possibility, but there are aspects that must be negotiated."

"I have good money on your daughter," the man said, "so I hope they are settled satisfactorily." His companion said something to him, and he gave me a nod and turned away.

"See?" Druisius said. "He would not have bet on her if there were rumours about you. But you cannot ask the Empress if she thinks you are a traitor. If you do, you force her to act, yes?"

"I am considering that question. It may be a price I must pay."

"*Idióta.*" He shook his head, his lips twisted in mock disgust. "Ask your daughter instead."

Chapter 46

~DAUGHTER~

"YOU'VE ACCEPTED HIM," LYNTHE SAID, her voice flat.

"I don't know," I said. "Maybe. Not officially. But Casil will think I've refused him, so there can be more negotiations. To give Alekos and the Empress time to plan." I'd explained all this to her once.

"But in the end, you'll marry him." She sat on her bed, abruptly. "I suppose I knew you would, but I kept hoping." Her jaw tightened, her lips pulling inward. She was trying not to cry. Lynthe never cried. Tears sprang to my own eyes.

"Lynthe." *You owe her the truth*, my mother had said. "Can I explain?"

"You don't need to." I crouched in front of her, reaching out to touch her hand.

"Yes, I do," I said. All the truth, I thought. "Lynthe, I love you. Please believe that." She looked up. "Truly."

She jerked her hand back. "Then why?"

I took a breath. Just say it, I told myself. "Because if I do not marry Alekos, my father will be charged with treason. And maybe my mother and Sorley and Druise, too."

"What?" Her brow wrinkled. "How do you know that?"

"Things the Empress has said to me." I rose to sit across from her on the other bed.

"She's told you she'll arrest your father?" I heard the disbelief.

"Not in those words." I fiddled with a hairpin, thinking about how to explain. "She's been subtle. Talking about changing the rules of *xache*, and creating something new only two or three can play. She's said more than once that my father is in danger. She even said that today."

"So you're just guessing this. You don't know for certain."

"I know a hidden message when I hear one. This is what I've been trained for, Lynthe, to hear what isn't said directly. Just like you know to pay attention to birds suddenly flying up, or a crow calling."

"But most of the time there's a simple explanation for those: a *fuádain*, or a wildcat," she argued.

"Nothing the Empress says is simple," I told her. "Even my father says her skills in diplomacy and intrigue are greater than his."

"Does he know what you're doing?"

"No. He would confront her, and I can't let that happen. What choice would she have then but acknowledge what he has been doing, all the secret plans and alliances? That's treason, Lynthe. And the punishment for treason is death."

She said nothing for a minute, her eyes on me. "So," she said finally, "you will marry Alekos on a belief your family is in danger if you don't. You will leave me, and you will risk a war at the gates of Casil—or even in its streets. A war in which many will die, but those lives are just a bribe, a sacrifice, to keep your father safe. Have you weighed the cost, Gwenna?"

Pieces in a game. Acceptable losses, to protect the king and queen. But my father was not the king piece, worthy of protection.

Except to me, and my mother, and Colm and Sorley and Druisius. But every one of the men and women who would die if my marriage to Alekos provoked war with Qipërta had families who felt the same.

One life, or many. Empresses had to make these decisions, I reminded myself. What would Eudekia do about her husband, planning war against Casil?

"What would your mother say?" I asked Lynthe.

"That you have insufficient information to act," she said, without hesitation. "Generals do not deploy soldiers on rumours. They are readied, but scouts are sent to determine what is happening." She half smiled. "Or diplomats."

"But how do we find out? I can't just ask Eudekia." A sudden thought struck. "You're not planning to do what Sorley did, and confront her?"

"No, of course not. I doubt she'd see me, anyhow." She leant forward to take my hands. "Let me think."

"You can't tell my father," I warned.

"I won't." Her fingers tangled in mine. "I'm sorry for what I said before."

"No." I shook my head. "I should have trusted you. I thought—"

"That you could do this on your own," she interrupted. "Just like always. Just like your father, your mother tells me."

The tension inside me shattered like flawed glass. I began to weep, and as Lynthe wrapped her arms around me, to sob. She let me cry, murmuring words of comfort, rubbing my back, until I pulled away. I ran the back of my hand over my nose like a child, blinking away the tears. "I don't want to marry Alekos. I want to go home with you," I said, letting myself admit it, my voice hoarse from crying. "But I don't see how."

"There has to be a solution," Lynthe said. "We'll find it together." I nestled against her, accepting for the moment the comfort of her words and her arms, envisioning a future. I would have what was now Michan's position; she would be a senior officer, maybe a general. There would be a villa overlooking the sea, and a child or two; blue-eyed children, one my heir. In the autumn the hills would be purple with heather, and riding to and from the fort I would hear the peewit's cry, and the inevitable baa-ing of sheep. Home.

Lynthe's hand had still been making circles on my back. Now the strokes lengthened, lightened, tracing my spine, her fingers spreading as they reached its base. I raised my head to meet her kiss, feeling the low tug of desire, my own hands travelling.

I broke the kiss. "Wait," I whispered, reaching up to find the pins that held my hair back. I pulled them out, feeling its weight tumble onto my shoulders. Lynthe plunged her fingers into its waves, laughing deep in her throat. Our lips met again. We fell back onto the bed together, and I stopped thinking about anything except love.

Dawn light woke me. I lay against Lynthe, knowing with calm certainty what I had to do. The idea had come to me fully formed, my sleeping mind shaping the solution.

Lynthe, roused, listened as I explained. "It's a gamble."

"I know. Not a word to anyone, Lynthe. This has to be between me and Alekos. But—" I hesitated.

"But?"

"There is a way to make it certain." I asked a question.

Delight spread across her face. "You are sure?" I nodded. "Then, yes." She looked up at me, touching my lips with one finger. "It's been a while since I saw that smile."

I kissed her fingertip, happiness surging. "I suppose it has. Apulo will be here with tea soon; I'll write a note to Alekos. And we had best get dressed, don't you think?"

"Your father wants to see you," Apulo told me, a little later.

"I may not be free, if the Prince wishes my company." Let Apulo think my note was a reply to an invitation. "I'll send word."

The summons came an hour later. I dressed simply, no pendant of rank, just a tunic and my red scarf across my shoulders; the day was cool, the crispness of autumn in the air. In Alekos's workroom, a brazier glowed. He greeted me warmly, if, I thought, slightly puzzled. "Princess. This is unexpected."

"I know. But there are things I must say to you. Privately." I flicked a glance at his guard. With a movement of his hand, he dismissed them.

"Your bodyguard stays?" he asked.

"For propriety," I said. "And because this concerns her too."

His lips pursed, but he motioned me to a chair. "What is it you have to tell me?"

"Alekos." I saw the flicker of surprise at my use of his name. "This must be between you and me only, at least for now. Will you promise me that?

"A difficult promise, when I do not know what we are talking about."

"Our marriage negotiations must continue until the spring, to allow you time to gather troops and plan a campaign, if necessary."

"Yes," he said, interrupting me. "I was consulting with the *Magistere* Bruccius earlier about exactly this. But we discussed this yesterday. Have you something to add?"

I wished my mouth weren't suddenly dry. "The negotiations can continue, but they must be a ruse. I cannot marry you, Prince Alekos."

His eyes widened a fraction. Arms crossed, he leant back, studying me. "You said we would be good partners. I thought we had an agreement." A thread of anger in his voice. "What has changed?"

"We would be good partners. We are well matched in intellect and education. I like you, Alekos. But I love someone else." I paused, gathering courage. "Lynthe is not just my bodyguard. She is also my *quincala*."

The muscles of his cheeks tightened. "Your *quincala*?" I kept my eyes on him. I would not look away, as if I were ashamed. "Then I am repulsive to you?"

"No," I said. "Men attract me too. You attract me. But I love Lynthe, and I don't want to leave her, even to be Empress of Casil."

He got up, abruptly, pacing the floor. "Why did not you tell me earlier?"

"I thought . . ." I swallowed. "I thought perhaps I could marry you. I was wrong, and I am sorry for that, but, Alekos, think as the Emperor now. I am giving you cause to reject me, whenever the time is right; not a breaking away from your mother's influence, or a failure of negotiation, both of which could cast doubt on your autonomy and power, but a clear, unequivocal reason. The Emperor of Casil cannot marry a woman known to have had a *quincala*."

He rubbed his chin under the neat beard. "Does your father know this?"

"That Lynthe and I are *quincalae*? No. I led him—" I stopped. "No, that's not right. He believed there was no barrier to a marriage between you and me because until earlier today there was not. He does not know I am here, or what I am saying to you. Nor do I intend to tell him."

"Not tell him?" As abruptly as he had risen, Alekos sat again. "Why not?"

I was going to sail dangerously close to the rocks now. "I want no possibility of fault falling on my father—my parents—when this becomes public. Do I understand the customs of Casil correctly when I say that the barrier to our marriage is not that I have had lovers, but that Lynthe and I are formally *quincalae*?"

"You do," he said. "Lovers can be overlooked, male or female, but not a formal partnership, unless death ended it. It was why the Emperor Adricius, whose commander of the palace guard became his *quincalum*, could not marry, but adopted an heir." He was relaxing, I thought, thinking of the political ramifications, and not the personal ones.

But when he spoke again the undertone of anger was still there. "So we keep this secret to protect your parents?"

"What would be said if it were discovered the Empress had continued the negotiations, knowing they were false?" I countered.

He nodded, slowly. "False negotiations happen among countries, as you must know. But in this case, where we are stalling to prepare for war, if it comes to that, accusations would be made."

"And deflected to my father," I said.

"Yes." He fell silent. I had made my move, placing myself in jeopardy. Would Alekos go for the defeat, or concede a draw?

He was almost as good as my father at hiding his conflicting thoughts. The silence stretched out. I waited; not speaking had its power.

"I will tell no one else what you have said to me today," he finally agreed. "But I must think longer on all the implications of your suggestions. If I am not to marry you, then who?"

The question was not for me to answer. "May I withdraw, Prince Alekos?"

"You may," he replied.

I remained calm until we reached our room again. Then I almost fell into a chair. "I hope I can trust him," I said to Lynthe.

She pointed to the table. "There's a note." Apulo must have left it. My father's seal. I broke it open.

"My brother's returned. We're to eat the midday meal together." The thought of seeing Colm again made me surprisingly happy. Among us all, he'd been enjoying himself the most, if his letters had been anything to judge by. And hearing what he'd been doing would be a welcome distraction.

Colm seemed—older. More mature, and not just in physical growth, although he was noticeably taller. He was more thoughtful, more serious, speaking of treatments he had witnessed and sometimes been allowed to assist with.

"Last week I set a broken bone as Gnaius's assistant watched," he told us as we ate. "A simple break, a child's arm. But soon I might be . . . " His voice trailed off.

"Might be?" my father prompted him. "Continue your thought, Colm."

My brother looked at Gnaius, seated a little distance from him. "I have a proposal for you," Gnaius said. "Colm has a propensity I have seen in few students over the years. I believed I was finished with apprentices, but for him, I will make an exception. If, Cillian, Lena, you would allow him to stay in Casil, of course."

Chapter 47

~FATHER~

"STAY?" LENA'S JAW WAS TIGHT. "Colm, you're fourteen."

"Faolyn was nine," Colm said calmly.

"He had people with him," Lena said. "But perhaps if —"

"As could Colm, if we so chose," I said. She frowned at the interruption. "Talyn and Faolyn will not deny him an officer to act as his guardian, or men to protect him."

She understood. "I suppose."

"I could arrange guards for Cub," Druisius offered. He too had seen that I wanted no discussion of us all staying in front of Colm. Before that decision could be made, I needed to talk to my daughter.

"I would be pleased to act as Colm's guardian, if such a thing is permissible," Gnaius said. "But you must discuss this privately. Whether now or in a year or two, the offer remains. I believe that when the records are written, to be remembered as the teacher of Colm of Ésparias will be a great honour."

A reminder to me, I knew, of the responsibility we shared, the unbroken line of learning we had to maintain. We honoured those who had taught us, while expecting one or two students in our lives who would both exceed and succeed us. Gnaius and I had exchanged thoughts on it more than once before he returned to Casil, and in letters after that.

I studied my son. His face showed me both determination and apprehension, but the latter, I thought, was from a fear of being denied this chance. He felt my eyes on him and turned. "*Athàir?*"

He wanted this. He had a life to make, and we—Lena and I—should not stop him. *If I left you,* she had said, *it would be to learn to live without you.*

Our children—the ones who lived—had to do the same.

"We are not saying no," I told him. "There are aspects to be considered." Regardless of how he felt about it, Colm was Gwenna's heir.

"I understand," he said. "When are the games, Gwenna? We are going with Prince Alekos, aren't we?

"Oh," she said. "I'd forgotten." So had I. "They're the day after tomorrow, but I won't be going. But I'm sure he'll welcome you."

"Aren't you going to marry him, then?"

"I don't know yet," his sister said. "But he's already taken me to the games, and it isn't my turn this time."

"You can of course watch the games from the imperial box, if that is what you wish," Gnaius said, "but we could also join the doctors, to watch how they treat the wounds that result from the fights."

"Could we?" Colm brightened. Then his face fell. "But I was invited to watch the games with Prince Alekos, and I cannot say no to him, can I?"

"I am sure a compromise can be reached," Gnaius said.

We spoke of other things, but I was only half-listening. Colm's wish to stay with Gnaius could either be a complication or a simplification, and I had no way to know which until the spring.

Eudekia expected me within the hour, and I had hoped to talk to Gwenna first. Lena, too, would want to discuss Colm's proposal. Too many demands on too little time, but what I might say to the Empress needed responses from them both.

"Cillian?" From the tone of her voice, Lena had tried to get my attention at least once already.

"I am sorry, *käresta*. What is it?"

"Colm wants to go with Gnaius this afternoon, to visit another physician. Do you mind?"

"Not at all," I said, relieved. "Will you both be back for dinner tonight?"

On their way out, Gnaius stopped to murmur a question in my ear. "You may need to think about it."

I did, and I hadn't time now. I told him as much. He nodded, said his good-byes, and took Colm away. Lena eyed me. "We need to talk," she said.

"We do. But—"

"Not now. I know." A trace of sarcasm in the acknowledgment.

"I need a little time with Gwenna," I told her. "Will you allow me that, first?"

"Come, Lena," Sorley said, standing. "We can stretch our legs. It's stopped raining."

Lynthe went with them, at my suggestion. Druisius took himself out to the balcony: I did not mind if he overheard what I had to ask of, and say to, my daughter, but I appreciated his discretion.

"Well?" Gwenna said, once we were alone.

"I am meeting with Eudekia shortly," I said. "The marriage negotiations, ostensibly."

"Ostensibly?"

She was not that obtuse. Why was my daughter stalling? Perhaps the *Comiádh's* tone would reach her. "Gwenna. Do you plan to marry Alekos in the spring?"

"Yes." Was there a thread of resignation in her voice?

"A second question. Do you want to marry him?"

"Yes."

Tread carefully now, I told myself. Gwenna was trained to dissemble.

"If you were a *scáeli,*" I said gently, "could you have given me the same replies?"

Her lips parted, and closed. Her shoulders slumped just a tiny bit, but it told me the answer.

"I think you believe I am in danger," I said. "It has been suggested to you that charges of treason will be brought against me if you do not marry Alekos." Her eyes, wide and watching, glistened suddenly. She started to speak. I held up a hand.

"Eudekia offered me everything you could have as Alekos's Empress: a place of influence, even power, in the centre of the world, and herself as a partner who matched or exceeded me in many of my interests," I said. "Most of our *xache* games ended in a draw, and even nineteen years ago she had studied the work of philosophers of whom I had never heard." I considered my next words; they would be hard to say to my daughter, but she needed all the truth.

"Nor will I pretend that the physical attraction was not there. It was. It still is, and she knows it: it is not something easily hidden between two people, alone late at night over wine."

"You haven't...?" she almost whispered.

"Not then, and not now. I promise you that, *mo nihéan*. But I am guilty of more than one betrayal; you know that. Why would another shock you so much?"

"Because . . . " She took a breath. "Because you love *Mathàir*. And Sorley. And they love you. But you were trying to save their lives, so would it have been wrong?"

"No. It would not have been." I watched confusion cloud her face. "Sometimes sacrifice is called for, Gwenna. Sometimes so is betrayal. But not this time." I held out an arm. She slipped off her chair to sit on the floor beside me like her mother did, leaning against me. "I am nearly an old man, and you are very young. Do not marry the Prince for this reason. Do not give up love to possibly gain me a few more years of life." I stroked her hair. "That is not your responsibility."

She looked up at me, no tears blurring her vision. "But I would know what I had done, if I ignored the threat to you. How would I live with the guilt?"

Not, I hoped, as I had in the years after betraying Linrathe for Sorley, growing bitter and cynical, hating myself and the men that had forced my choice. "I have told you what I think you should do. If there is a sacrifice to be made, let it be mine."

She twisted away from my hand, knelt. Our eyes were level. "No," she said, her voice as sharp and hard as a blade. "I will hear no talk of lives sacrificed. I will decide by weighing what could happen, calculating risk and reward for the greatest good. To take the long view, as the *Principe* I may be one day must. It is what you taught me, is it not?"

Chapter 48

~DAUGHTER~

THE TREMBLING INSIDE ME HADN'T CEASED. Lynthe glanced at me curiously a time or two as we walked the corridors. I needed to move. I had never spoken to my father in such a way; never rejected his ideas so forcefully. *I will hear no talk.*

And yet, in the long, level look he had given me, unspeaking, before my mother's return had interrupted us, hadn't there been pride? Or perhaps respect. Either way, he hadn't been displeased, not entirely.

I turned to go through the door that led out to where I could look over the forum. The rain had ended, but the clouds hung heavily, unmoving despite the cold breeze. Regardless, I stood by the low wall, looking out.

"What happened?" Lynthe said.

"He knows he's been threatened," I said, "and that's why I've agreed to marry Alekos. He told me not to."

"What did you say?" She stood beside me, her arm just brushing mine. Closer than a bodyguard should be, but I didn't care.

"That I would decide based on what I judged was best. I feel . . ." How did I feel? "I feel like Sorley told me once he did, when he knew he'd passed his *scaeli's* examination. Like he was finally an adult, accepted as an equal by the council."

"You are," she said. "You've grown up a lot, these last weeks. *Quincala*," she added. I smiled, briefly. "Your brother has too. He really wants to stay here, doesn't he?"

"It seems like it," I said. "Another reason for my parents to stay."

"And Sorley and Druise."

"I meant them too. They're all my parents, really."

"I suppose they are. Just like all the women of Han were mine; especially after the war began. I barely saw my mother for years."

"And now she's your senior officer."

"Yes," Lynthe said thoughtfully. "As your father is yours, in a way. Gwenna, you've been concentrating on keeping him safe, but what about the reasons he'd be charged with treason? All those years of work can't be lost."

"If he is safe, so are the plans." *If there is a sacrifice to be made, let it be mine.* I frowned.

"What?"

"Something he said . . . there must be someone else who knows everything. Not just the strategy, and the connections that have been made, like Ruar and Helvi, or even Bjørn, but who can be trusted. How he gets his information, and where it's recorded. It can't just be in his head."

"It could be."

"No." I was sure of this. "After his fall, when his mind was foggy, and he couldn't remember certain things—if he'd been keeping everything in his memory, he'd have been worried. Seriously worried, and he wasn't. So it must be written down somewhere too, and somebody knows where those records are."

"Your mother," she suggested, then shook her head. "No, maybe she does, but there has to be someone else."

"Why?"

"Because she's here, and if your father is charged with treason, so might the rest of your family be. He would have planned for that. Someone back home holds the secrets."

"Talyn," I guessed.

She shook her head again. "Don't you remember him telling me there were things I couldn't tell my mother? I was to say he'd told me I couldn't, and she'd understand. So she knows some of it, but not all."

"Then who?" We stared at each other.

"When we get home, Gwenna, we need to see these records. Listen to what your father has to tell us about them. There is always more than what is written down."

We. I was the heir to Ésparias, but no longer was I the only heir to sedition. Lynthe shared the burden now, a choice made willingly, for love. I could barely believe it.

I put my hand on hers, all I could do in this space. "We will, *käresta*," I said. She smiled, raising her smallest finger to caress mine.

A scraping sound made us both turn. Above us on the roof, the pigeons exploded in a flurry of wings, flying out over the forum. Lynthe swore, her eyes moving along the ridge.

"Gwenna!" a voice called. Startled, I jerked my attention to the door.

"Rosale." I said warily, "I haven't seen you for a while." Had there been something else at the peak of the roof—a head, a hand—just before the birds rose?

"You haven't come to the atrium, or the baths," she said. "I've missed you." She approached me, her chaperone staying under the eaves. "Have you been to the temples?" she asked, gesturing to the forum below.

"I haven't."

"They are magnificent," she told me. "Perhaps we could go one day together? But, Gwenna, I need your advice. Will you have tea with me?"

"Now?" My heart was slowing. Likely what had disturbed the pigeons had been nothing more than a kite landing to survey the streets below. Or one of the slave boys, cleaning up the mess the carrion birds left.

"If you have time." Her cheeks were pink, as if she were excited about something.

"I do." Why not? The other bridal candidates were gossiping about me and the failed marriage negotiations, I had no doubt. Rosale had shown herself a friend before, and I should have allies.

The rooms assigned to Rosale and her party were quite far from ours, overlooking the houses northeast of the palace. But they were barely smaller, or less richly furnished, so the implicit message about status could be overlooked.

Her chaperone sent for tea. It arrived with small, sweet pastries, rich with honey and walnuts. I ate one gratefully, conscious of a sagging fatigue.

"I have been asked to be Alekos's guest at the next games," Rosale told me. The reason for her excitement—and a surprise. I had expected he would ask Sahira, to placate Decanius and the Qipërtani.

"You might have my brother with you, too," I said.

"He's back?" We chatted about Colm, and where he'd been, for a few moments, but I could tell she was just being polite. I summoned the appropriate question.

"You have your gown for the games?"

"Oh, yes. For some time now. But, Gwenna, what do I talk to the Prince about? What will entertain him?"

I dipped my sticky fingers into the bowl of water provided for that purpose, wiping them on the accompanying cloth. "Do you want him to remember you?"

"Yes!"

"Then don't try to entertain him," I said. "He will lead the conversation, but listen for ways to bring serious subjects to the forefront. What future you see for your country. The expansion of the Empire; the benefits your land can gain from being part of it. The Prince is interested in these things."

"Aren't these subjects for formal negotiations?"

"If you hope to reach that point, raise them with the Prince yourself." I sipped my tea. "I discussed copper tariffs and trade routes with him. Do you play *xache*?"

"Of course."

"Then suggest a game. And don't lose purposely." I put down the cup.

"Rosale, Alekos has watched his mother rule with diplomacy and skill for his entire life. He has an idea of what an Empress should be. Emulate her."

She nodded, slowly. Then her lips twitched. "Sahira won't be able to." I muffled a laugh. Rosale grinned, and then her brows dropped. "Why are you telling me this? Is there no chance for you now?"

"The talks continue," I said, grimacing a little for show. "My father is meeting with her again now." What else could I say? "I know I'm supposed to be Alekos's first choice, or the Empress's, but there are complications because I'm the heir to Ésparias."

"That's what I'd heard," she said softly.

"I'm telling you because I like the Prince, and I like you. If an agreement can't be reached between my father and the Empress, then why shouldn't you have a chance?" The more uncertain Decanius and the Qipërtani were, the more likely they were to make a mistake. If that was why Alekos had invited Rosale to the games—and I guessed it was—then I would encourage the tactic. Perhaps more would come of it than unnerving the *Magistere* and his collaborators.

I hoped so. Because otherwise, wasn't I making Rosale what my mother had sworn I would never be: a piece in Casil's game?

Chapter 49

~FATHER~

THE FADING LIGHT TOLD ME THE AFTERNOON was well advanced. My back and leg ached, with tension and the hour of the day. It was nearly time for Apulo's treatments, and still Eudekia had not called for me.

The Empress has sent word earlier that she was postponing our meeting, for which I had been initially glad. It had given me time to talk to Lena. She had gone out now, seeking space and quiet to accept the decision we had reached. Decisions; but one, I hoped, was easier than the other.

Druisius closed the balcony door quietly behind him. "I should light the brazier, yes?" He went about it; the room was cool, although I hadn't noticed. When it blazed, he sat down.

"We are staying?"

"Yes. Until the spring, at least."

Lena and I had talked about Colm's request, the benefits to him of an education that would be unparalleled in Ésparias—but also how he would be another child gone from us. All three, in the space of a few months. Staying for the winter would ease that transition, and not just for Lena.

"What of the *Ti'ach*?" she'd asked.

"I will write to Ruar, suggest names for a temporary appointment. Sorley can do the same." She'd nodded, satisfied. "What will you do?"

"Work with Junia. We spoke of the possibility on our travels."

"Will they allow you to?"

"To become fully a member of their cohort, I would have to renounce you," she'd said, seriously. "But as an officer from Casil, I can join them for a time without having to make such a drastic decision." She'd started to smile, saying the last words.

"I'm glad," I'd replied, not trying to stop my answering smile, "that you have reconsidered, *käresta*."

Druisius grinned again. "Good. Should I help Apulo find us a house?"

"I am sure he would appreciate it," I said. I'd known Druisius for nearly twenty years, and his capacity to simply accept a situation and move on still perplexed me. With little education, he was a far better follower of the stoic philosophers than I would ever be.

"I talked to the woman from the *taberna*," he told me. "She was helpful, but I did not learn much." He stopped, cocking his head, clearly listening.

"What?" I mouthed. He shrugged.

"Something on the roof, I thought." He chewed his lip for a moment. "So, the *taberna* woman. There was a man talking to the boys, she said, earlier that day. Just after the litter went by. She had gone to fetch water and saw them. He was not one of the usual city guardsman who patrol there."

"But he was a guard?"

"Not in uniform. But she thought so, from his bearing."

"One from the palace, perhaps?"

"I think so, yes. Maybe I can find out who was not on duty that morning."

"Be careful," I said.

"What else have I been, since I became a soldier? More than thirty years. Do not tell a fish how to swim, Cillian."

I laughed, accepting the rebuke. What would have happened to Druisius, had we never come to Casil? He accepted life as it came, but alongside that was a strong streak of independence, not a characteristic encouraged among soldiers. Unless you wanted someone who could think for themselves, for assignments beyond the usual protection of people and places. He might, I thought, have risen in the ranks of Eudekia's—or Quintus's—spies.

A sharp rap on the corridor door brought my attention back to the immediate. Druisius helped me up before he went to answer it. I smoothed down my tunic, resisting the impulse to run a hand through my hair. My back twinged as I joined the guard sent to escort me to the Empress. No time for more willowbark now. I had to hope the pain would grow no worse.

The two men who attended the Empress did not bode well for my comfort, I thought wryly, taking the seat Eudekia indicated. Decanius and the Qipërtani prince, Timor, sat at the table, their expressions stony. Whatever had been said before my arrival, they were not happy.

I greeted them pleasantly, receiving nods and murmurs in return. A servant placed wine—suitably watered, I noted—in front of me before withdrawing.

"I want a truthful discussion of the status of the negotiations," the Empress announced. "I have spoken to both Prince Cillian and the *Magistere* Decanius privately, and I hear little agreement between them. Now I will hear what you have to say to each other."

She glanced down at the reports in front of her. "Prince Timor. Are you aware of an offer of a considerable reduction in tariffs on copper? Enough to bring significant revenue to Qipërta. Why is this not enough to settle the dispute?"

Watching Timor, I saw the quickly-hidden reaction. He hadn't known. "A reduction in copper tariffs benefits only some, Empress. I seek relief for all my people."

Eudekia raised a groomed eyebrow. "You did not convey that offer to Qipërta's prince, Decanius?"

"I knew it was not sufficient, Empress. Am I right that Prince Cillian negotiates with trade as his only mandate? The answer will not lie there, I am afraid."

"Where will it lie, then?"

"Qipërta wishes treatment equal to what the Boranoi receive from

Casil." Decanius spoke smoothly. I doubted this was the first time he had said this to Eudekia.

"And I have told you before they will not get it," Eudekia said. "The Boranoi prince is my husband."

"Not even were the Qipërtani princess wife to Prince Alekos?" Decanius said. "The precedence has been set, Empress."

"Prince Hathus," Eudekia said coldly, "is heir to the Boranoi crown. He will be king of his lands soon. The princess Sahira has no such claim."

"But the princess Gwenna is heir to Ésparias." Timor spoke heavily. "So do you bargain fairly, Prince Cillian, or do you make offers you know are insufficient, so that your daughter marries the Prince, and Ésparias's head tax is reduced?"

The head tax. He had mentioned it once, at our first meeting. I had forgotten. This was what Timor sought? "I had not considered the head tax at all," I said. Honesty would be best. "It was not part of my instructions from the Empress, nor," I paused, briefly, "nor has it been mentioned by the *Magistere* in our discussion, a matter of record."

Eudekia held out the records to Timor. He read them closely, taking his time, giving me space to think. I was certain he knew nothing of Decanius's real reason for wanting Sahira on the throne, but had been led to believe the tax would be reduced if the marriage occurred.

Timor looked up. "Why did you not speak of the head tax?" he asked Decanius.

"I thought to gain more for Qipërta, to honour its people for my good years there. The head tax would rightly be part of the marriage negotiations, separate from these talks."

Timor grunted. "But it is clear Sahira is not the Prince's choice. You should have changed tactics, *Magistere*."

"There is no marriage agreement confirmed. Is there, Prince Cillian?" Decanius's bald head shone pink, as it had when I had defended Druisius from a charge of desertion, long ago.

"None," I said. "That she is the heir has its complications. I doubt we will reach a conclusion quickly. Do you agree, Empress?"

"I do. But neither will we stop negotiating. Tell me, Decanius, Prince Timor. Were I, for sake of argument—this is not an offer, you understand—were I to reduce the head tax on women in Qipërta by a percentage, would that suffice to end this threat of war?"

"I would think so." Timor's words were made nearly inaudible by Decanius's cry.

"Empress, no!" His scalp gleamed almost as red as the scarf Gwenna had bought in Sylana. He licked his lips, swallowed. "You cannot. I speak as your *fiscarius*. If you do, other countries will demand the same, and we will not have the money needed to bear the costs of the Empire."

A credible argument. I did not believe for one moment that it had caused his outburst.

Nor did the Empress. She dismissed the two men from her presence with a terse, "We will speak again." I reached for my wine glass, drinking a little. My back throbbed steadily in time with my heart.

Eudekia smiled, a smile of satisfaction. "That was informative."

"What will you do?"

"Wait. I have made certain arrangements. The letter or messenger he will send to Hathus will be intercepted. I need tangible proof now, although I am satisfied of Decanius's intent."

"The Qipërtani themselves know nothing," I said.

"So I believe." She picked up her untouched wine. "Alekos came to see me this morning. To ask whom he should marry if it were not your daughter."

"He will court another, to give authority to the story we are spreading?"

Eudekia pursed her lips. Small lines appeared at the corners of her mouth. "I thought that. But on reflection, it is not what he asked. Not to whom he should pay court, but marry."

"Gwenna has said nothing. Perhaps he is simply being wise, making a second choice for contingency."

"As all princes must. Am I right, Cillian?" Her voice was light, almost teasing. Was this it?

"As all wise leaders do," I replied. The tiniest of nods; the briefest flicker of a smile. I breathed again.

"The marriage negotiations must stretch over the winter now," she said after a moment. "To make a decision as to a bride might be all the reason needed for Qipërta—or rather my husband—to bring war to Casil. We cannot risk that." What would she do regarding Hathus? It was not for me to ask.

"You will expect the candidates to stay," I said mildly.

"As you are already planning to do," she said. I raised an eyebrow. "Am I wrong?"

"You are not. Was that a guess, Eudekia? If it were not, I would be curious about your sources."

"Do you think," she said, "I would let a prince of Ésparias leave this city without keeping a watch on him?"

It took me a moment. "Colm?

"I leave little to chance. I trust Gnaius, but your son is heir after Gwenna. He has been quietly watched, and the idea of him remaining here to study reported."

"We had not decided until earlier today."

She laughed. "Cillian. Would you deny your son an education in Casil? The education you wish you had had? But nor would you leave him here, even with Gnaius, so soon after your daughter's death. Lena may be a soldier, but she is a mother, too."

I had not been able to outwit her nineteen years earlier; I had no chance now. It was, I realized, entirely possible that everything I had done since then was at my Empress's pleasure. Everything.

I shifted slightly, pain lancing down my leg. "May I leave your presence?

I would like to spend the evening with my son, if I could." I needed the baths, and Apulo's hands, and time to think.

"You may." She did not call a guard, but rose herself to help me stand. Before I could take my hand from her arm, she covered it with her own. "Alekos does not wish to marry Sahira."

"What have you told him?" She was disconcertingly near, the scent of her perfume spicy in my nostrils.

"That marriage, for an Emperor, is a complex matter. But that I did not think Sahira a fit partner for him."

"You did not think Lena a fit partner for me."

"I was wrong." Our eyes were nearly level. "I am not, about Sahira."

"Likely you are not," I agreed. Her hand moved on my mine, a caress.

"Eudekia," I said, forcing the words. "No."

She smiled, and stepped back, taking her hand away. "You remain incorruptible," she said, regret tracing through her voice.

"With difficulty." Eudekia was the Empress, holding my life in her hands. But she was also a woman whose own life was changing, her power moving to her son, her husband betraying her and all she had thought they had built together. I took her hand again, raising it to my lips. I let them linger a moment longer than protocol allowed. "Had we two lives," I told her, with the roughness of desire, "I would not be saying no."

Chapter 50

~DAUGHTER~

"I WONDER," SORLEY SAID IDLY, finishing a second cup of tea, "if the Empress will recognize the carnelians on my *ladhar*."

"If she does, what of it?" my mother said. "She told Cillian they were his to give to whomever he chose." She glanced toward the bedroom door. "I don't like leaving him today."

"When Gnaius and Colm arrive," I said, "Gnaius will tell you if there is anything to worry about."

"There is not," Apulo emerged from the bedroom. "It is just he missed his full treatments yesterday. Go to the games, Lena. Cillian will be fine."

My mother looked to Sorley, her face irresolute. "I'll be here, and Druise, and Apulo," I said. "The Empress invited you. You need to go."

"I suppose."

"It's easier for me if you do," Sorley said. "You can tell the story in Casilan between verses. I haven't had time to finish the translation." Sorley had been asked to sing his new *danta* for the Empress and Alekos—and I guessed Rosale and her party as well—before the start of the games. He, along with my parents and Colm and Gnaius, were then to be her guests in the imperial box. I hadn't worked out the message here: an indication that, while her son was in the company of another bridal candidate, my family, and I, by extension, were not out of favour?

But my father had barely slept last night, wracked by cramps in his back and leg. Both Apulo and my mother looked tired, the shadows of fatigue darkening the skin around their eyes. Apulo would find moments to rest during the day; I did not envy my mother, who would need to stay alert and polite while with the Empress.

Whatever my mother had been about to say was interrupted by Gnaius and Colm arriving. They'd been out somewhere, seeing other doctors or patients or both: Colm had told us last night what their plans were, but I hadn't been paying much attention.

Gnaius, always alert, said, "Cillian?"

"A bad night," my mother said. "Will you examine him, Gnaius?"

"May I join you?" Colm asked.

"If he says you may," Gnaius told him. "One moment." He disappeared into the bedroom, only to come back to the door to gesture to Colm a minute later.

"We should go," Sorley said to my mother, who shook her head.

"Not until I know what Gnaius says. Go without me."

Why was she so worried? If this had happened when she was away with Junia, or even earlier when she'd been sleeping separately, she would have never known. And it was far from the first time; my father had had these days when his back was bad for as long as I could remember.

"I can't," Sorley said. "I need to know too, now you've worried me." He gave her a one-armed hug, the other still holding his *ladhar*.

A few minutes later, Colm came out. "Gnaius says to tell you *Athàir* will be fine. But he—*Athàir*, I mean—is going to let me examine him too. We will be a while, because I have to be shown how." His smile was a mixture of reassurance and anticipation.

"Well!" Sorley said quietly, after Colm had returned to the bedroom.

"Indeed." My mother's eyes lost their focus for a moment, and then she blinked, and turned to Lynthe.

"Did you familiarize yourself with the lower levels of the Arénas?"

"Yes, Major," Lynthe said. "At first light. They are complex, a warren of rooms and animal pens. I'm glad the physician's guard will be there too."

"Maybe I should guard Cub, yes?" Druise suggested. "I know the Arénas."

"No," my mother said. "If Apulo needs help with Cillian, Lynthe can't do that. I want you here today, Captain. There is a door guard hired?"

"Yes," Druise said. "One I trust."

"*Mathàir* seems too worried," I said to Druise, after she and Sorley had gone. He shrugged.

"She is feeling guilty," he said. "Cillian has been tense and troubled for some time, yes? Now his body is reacting, and she know it is partly her fault. But when these spasms subside, he will be better."

"What was all that between Sorley and my mother, when Colm went to examine *Athàir*?"

"To allow his son to touch him in such a way," Druise said, "it is a departure. A reversal. Colm is not a boy now, but soon a doctor. He is taking care of your father, who once took care of him."

As I had been trying to do, differently. A vague annoyance took hold of me: *Athàir* would let Colm do this, but tell me my concerns were not my responsibility?

My thoughts were interrupted by Colm and Gnaius. Colm looked pensive, and perhaps a little upset: Gnaius was his usual self. "Just spasm," the physician said. "Cannabium and massage, and the baths when he can. It will pass. Come, Colm. The Empress expects us, and you must change first."

⌘⌘⌘⌘⌘

Apulo was singing; his voice travelling clearly through the open bedroom door. Druise began to play along, the notes of the *cithar* enhancing the tune. I listened, wishing I had a *ladhar*. I played well enough—with Sorley and Druise to teach me, how could I not?—and it would be something to do, something to take my mind off my concerns.

What was I going to do all winter in Casil? I didn't want to be idle; I liked working. Then I laughed to myself, imagining my father's reaction: *the libraries of Casil are open to you, and you are wondering what you will do?* I liked learning, too. When *Athàir* was feeling better, I would ask him to plan a course of study for me.

I reached for an olive. Apulo had brought food for midday a little while ago, and I was nibbling now just because it was there. The games would be underway, the fighting men probably now on the sands—which meant Colm and Gnaius and Lynthe would be down at that level. What would it be like? Sweat and blood, I guessed.

I stretched. From the bedroom, Apulo called Druise's name. "Can you help me take Cillian to the latrine?" he said, from the door.

Druise put down his *cithar* and went to do as Apulo asked. He closed the bedroom door; regardless, I went out to the balcony. I leant on the wall, looking down into the atrium. The palace was deserted, everyone at the games.

If I had my journal, I could begin to plan what I wanted to learn this winter. The bedroom door was still shut. My room wasn't far; I could be there and back in a minute or two. If I went along the balcony, no one would ever know I'd gone, and I wouldn't have the intrusion of the guard. Druise would scold me if he found out, but it wouldn't be the first time.

I pushed open the door into my room, closing it so it would not bang in the wind. I went directly to the alcove where the beds stood, and the chest that held my journal. It lay on top of my clothes. As I lowered the lid, the hinges creaking slightly, I heard the corridor door open.

I swore to myself. The guard must have noticed me leave. I looked up. "I'm—"

Decanius stood in front of the closed door. My fingers tightened on the journal. "*Magistere*," I said, "why are you here? Am I wanted?" Had my mother sent for me? Or the Empress?

"Not in the way you think," he said, "not in Casil, not anywhere." He licked his lips. "Except by me."

He took a step or two into the room. *He hates women,* I remembered someone saying. I backed away, instinctively, seeing him smile, sensing danger. I wore only one secca. The other two were in the chest.

"Let me put my journal away," I offered, hoping I sounded calm, "and then we can talk about what has brought you here." Where was the guard? I reached for the lid.

Something smashed at my feet, liquid splashing onto my legs. I stared down at the shards of the lamp on the tiles, oil puddling. I dropped the journal, reaching for my secca.

The second lamp hit my breast, the force spinning me. It shattered on the floor, but oil soaked my tunic. I put out a hand, finding a bedpost, steadying myself. I pulled the secca from the sheath on my thigh and threw.

But as I threw, I slipped, falling hard to one knee, and the knife flew wide, barely grazing Decanius's arm. He laughed, pulling a knife from his own belt.

"So much oil," he said. "There will be a most unfortunate fire. No one will be sure why the princess of Ésparias lit a lamp in the middle of the day, or how she dropped it, setting her tunic on fire. No one in the palace to notice, until it is far too late."

I stayed down, battling fear, trying to think. I could not easily get to the other seccas. I reached for a shard of the lamp, but the clay was thick, the broken edge blunt. Decanius laughed again and took another step closer.

I lunged up, grabbing a pillow from the bed, throwing it at him. He batted it away. My breath came in gasps, the sharp smell of oil making me cough. I clambered over the beds, putting them between us, but still I had nowhere to go. The walls of the alcove trapped me. My only chance would be to outrun him. Why had I closed the balcony door?

Do not let your eyes give you away. My mother's voice, from long ago on the training field. I looked over Decanius's shoulder, at the door behind him, gathering myself to run the other way.

I sprung, racing toward the balcony. He swore, throwing himself toward me, so fast for a man his age, so close. I smelled his sweat, heard his excited breathing. I moaned.

The hall door slammed against the wall, Druise shouting something, knife raised. He ran at Decanius, who turned, his own knife out. Druise stopped.

"Gwenna?" His eyes never left his opponent.

"I'm fine," I gasped, the wall hard against my back. Decanius outweighs him, I thought, but Druise is a soldier. This can be no contest.

Druise took a step closer. Decanius lunged forward; Druise twisted, striking up at the Magistere's belly. Decanius kicked out, unbalancing Druise, slicing down with his own blade.

Druise grunted. Still crouched, he drove his head into Decanius's groin. A knife clattered on the tiles. Decanius collapsed, moaning.

Blood dripped from Druise's arm. He touched it with one finger, the others still wrapped around the hilt of his knife. He gazed at Decanius, doubled up on the floor, still whimpering. Druise half rose, breathing heavily, his lips parted—and lunged forward, to stab his blade deep into the *Magistere's* back.

Decanius convulsed. Blood began to seep, then trickle. Druise gazed at the dying man, eyes hooded, a faint smile on his lips. I stood unmoving, cold, horrified. He looked—pleased, and something else, something that didn't belong here. Thoughts swirled. I saw a downed man on a ship's deck, and Druise's foot raised. Sorley, intervening.

Druisius bent to remove the knife. "No!" I cried, my voice high in my own ears. "Druise, don't."

He looked up. "He wanted to kill you. More, before, too."

"Yes," I said, swallowing hard. "Yes." Think, I told myself.

I stepped forward, knelt. Decanius had tried to have Druise executed, years ago. A matter of record.

"What are you doing?" Druise said sharply.

I reached out to pull the knife free. A crimson lake spread around the body. "He would have raped me, then set me on fire," I said, picking up Decanius's own knife, smearing blood onto its blade. "I killed him in self-defence."

Chapter 51

~FATHER~

"HOW IS SHE?"

Lena sank into a chair, the sag of her body speaking of exhaustion. "Calm. She went to the baths, very early. Lynthe's with her; she needs her more than me now." Silently, Apulo gave her tea. She drank some of it, then smiled at him. "Honey. Thank you, Apulo. I needed that." She finished it, shaking her head at the offer of more.

"And you?" she asked.

"Well enough," I said. The spasms of yesterday had gone, leaving only a residual soreness. Nothing that would distract me from what we must shortly do. "Apulo, please leave that." He was gathering cups, tidying the room. "Sit down. You are as tired as us all."

Tired, and shaken, too. He had just finished settling me in my chair in the sitting room when Druisius's shouts had echoed across the atrium, calling for him. He'd gone running, leaving me in cold fear: not for myself, but for my daughter.

The fear had spiked when he returned, leading Gwenna, white and trembling, her hands and tunic stained with blood. I had tried to rise, couldn't. She collapsed on the floor beside me, burying her face in my lap, sobbing like she had not since childhood. Apulo crouched beside her, rubbing her back. "She is not hurt," he said, "but shocked. Decanius is dead, at her hand. I must go back to help Druisius."

Decanius dead? "Send someone for Lena," I told him.

"Druisius has done so. Guards arrived too at his shouts. He would not let them into the room but sent them to the Empress. Not just Lena must know."

I stroked my daughter's hair and neck. Her sobs were subsiding. "Bring wine," I said, "and then go back to Druisius."

I hadn't let Gwenna speak until Lena had arrived, and not long after her, the Empress herself. Then, haltingly, Gwenna told us what had happened, the stains of oil down her tunic giving mute evidence.

"When he dropped the knife," she said, "I saw my chance. I grabbed it and stabbed him. I just wanted to stop him. He'd hurt Druise. I didn't mean to kill him."

A few minutes later Lena had taken Gwenna into our bedroom, to wash and change. The Empress leant forward to pour herself wine.

"I should have had him arrested," she said. "We had enough to question him, but he is—was—powerful, and I was being cautious. I am so very sorry, Cillian."

I too would have counselled caution, had she asked me. I told her so.

She nodded, slowly. "Any other of the young women would have succumbed to his attack."

"None of the others were a threat to his plans," I reminded her.

Lena had come out then. "There is a bruise forming on Gwenna's breast," she said. "Further evidence of her story, if you need it, Empress."

"I do not, but perhaps Gnaius should see it? He has been sent for." She rose. "Was there not a guard in the corridor?"

"There was meant to be," Lena said. "He had vanished. In Decanius's pay, we assume."

"Have your captain provide his name. He will be dealt with," she said briskly. "I will leave you to comfort your daughter. Will she understand her story is for very few ears? I believe Decanius may have died of a sudden apoplexy, perhaps on the stairs, but I must give that some thought, and take counsel."

Then Gnaius had arrived, and Lynthe, and while they tended to Gwenna I spoke to Sorley, who had gone first to Druisius. Then to Apulo again, and briefly to Bruccius. It was late before our rooms were quiet. Night had fallen, and lamps lit the room. Gwenna, dosed with poppy, slept on our bed, Lynthe with her.

"Druisius," I said, as we picked at food. "Thank you, although that is not enough."

"Do not thank me." I had never seen him look so pale. The wound on his arm had been washed with wine and stitched; a deep cut, Gnaius had said. "It should not have happened. I trusted the wrong man."

"You saved her," Lena said. "That's all that matters. Don't be so hard on yourself, Druise."

He shrugged. "This will all be covered up, yes?"

"Yes." I could speak freely; Gnaius had gone, taking Colm to sleep at his city house so Gwenna and Lynthe could have his room. "Decanius was too powerful. Eudekia must balance that against his corruption."

Druisius chewed his lip. "Bruccius had the body wrapped and taken away, yes? And a dog killed to explain the blood. But guards and servants know, and so others will too."

"Rumours," I said.

"I wonder who will be blamed for the dog?" Lena murmured.

"Not the Qipërtani," I said. "But someone among the bridal candidates will be disgraced, I fear."

We fell silent. Innocents would suffer; the guards' silence could be assumed, or bought, but what of the servants? Freedom from bondage, a purse with enough money to start a market stall? Perhaps. And perhaps the obscure potential bride who would be blamed for the threat to Gwenna would find her country a recipient of the Empress's largesse as well.

"How did Decanius know Gwenna had left these rooms?" Sorley asked suddenly.

"The boy slaves; they are everywhere," Druisius said. "We have heard them on the roof, checking tiles, yes? Easy to pay one to watch Kitten, and report."

"Decanius was close by, then."

"Hiding in the servants' passages." Druisius grimaced. "I did not think it out."

Lynthe emerged from the bedroom. "We should go to our room, but Gwenna's sound asleep. I can't wake her, and I can't carry her."

"I will," Druisius said, beginning to stand.

"You will not," Sorley said. "I'll do it." Druisius snorted.

"She's no heavier than our ewes," Sorley snapped. "By Rögnir, Druise, I'm not incapable, and you'd open your wound again. Stop trying to be indispensable. You could have died today." He stalked off into the bedroom, appearing a minute later with Gwenna, still asleep, in his arms. Lynthe ran ahead to open the door. She, I thought, will not sleep tonight, but remain alert, on guard. Gwenna was safe with her.

Lena had followed Sorley. I regarded Druisius. He was sitting back again, wine cup in hand. Only a few years younger than I, and he'd lost blood today. With Sorley gone, he'd allowed his shoulders and face to droop.

Apulo had left us, gone to tidy the bedroom. "*Mo charaidh*," I said, "Will you tell me now what really happened?"

⌘⌘⌘⌘⌘

The inquest had been set for early afternoon, in the Empress's rooms. The three of them sat at the end of the long table, Eudekia at its head, the two men on either side. We took our chairs, Druisius and Gwenna closest to their questioners. Gwenna did not look at Druise, but sat with eyes downcast.

Bruccius began the inquiry gently, asking first why Gwenna had gone to her room. "What did the Magistere Decanius say to you when he arrived?"

"I asked him if I was wanted. I thought perhaps you, Empress, had summoned me. Why else would he be there?"

"What did he say?"

"That I was most certainly not wanted here in Casil." She looked down at the tabletop, and then up, her eyes meeting Eudekia's. "Except by him."

She told the rest with admirable calm, barely hesitating when she explained his purpose in drenching her and the room with oil. Agitation showed only when she spoke of stabbing Decanius. Tears glistened then. "I didn't mean to kill him," she repeated.

"We know that," the Empress said. "Thank you, Princess. Your bravery may have saved a good man." Beside me, Lena shifted in her chair. I could almost hear her thought: *and rid us of a bad one.*

"Captain Druisius. What did you see when you reached the princess's room?"

"The *Magistere* was chasing her. He had a knife. When I challenged him, he turned on me. I made him drop the knife, but he had cut me. The princess saw I was hurt. She panicked, yes? She wanted to stop him getting up." He made the tiniest of shrug, his face impassive. "Bad luck, where the knife went in."

Apulo was questioned next. Yes, he said, the captain had called for him. The princess was shocked and needed a familiar face. There had been broken lamps and oil on the floor.

"You noticed that, with a dead man and a pool of blood before you?" Bruccius asked.

"I am responsible for keeping Prince Cillian's rooms tidy, here and at home," Apulo said, his head high. "I notice disarray."

Eudekia looked down at papers in front of her. "This is the physician Gnaius's report. He found the princess in some distress, shaking and cold. There was a large bruise on her breast, and one on her knee. No other injuries."

She glanced from Bruccius to her son. "Are there further questions?"

"One," Alekos said. "Princess, you have killed before." Her head jerked at that. Gwenna, I thought, stay calm. "A dog, not many weeks ago, and a man, when you were—fourteen? Is that right?"

"It is," she said, her voice almost steady.

"How did Decanius escape your own knife?"

"I slipped," she said, simply. "As I threw, I slipped on the oil and fell. The knife missed, and I only had one."

"That is why your knee is bruised," the Empress said. "Princess." She paused, her face becoming gentle. "Gwenna. No blame lies on your shoulders."

Her eyes moved to Druisius. He met them without fear. "The captain," she said, "was only fulfilling his orders. His actions are to be commended. You have served both Casil and Ésparias well, Druisius."

His lips pursed slightly. "Empress."

"It is not politic for me to reveal how and why the *Magistere* died." Eudekia's voice was decisive now. "A different story will be told, of a sudden death from a burst heart on the stairs rising from the atrium. Gnaius will attest to this. Your own illness was caused by the shock of finding a dead dog in your room, its throat cut. No doubt meant to be a reminder of the one you killed, a threat that overwhelmed you."

"Empress," Gwenna said. "I understand."

Little more was said. Alekos did not take Gwenna aside for a private conversation, as I had expected he would. The omission puzzled me.

"Prince Cillian?" Bruccius pulled out the chair beside mine. "The Empress asks if you would send the lord Sorley to her. He is aware of the events of yesterday, we know, but he is not a citizen of our Empire. Remaining silent will be through his courtesy, and the Empress would like to convey that request herself."

Would Druisius tell Sorley what had truly happened? Perhaps. He had not, yet; I knew. "I will," I said. "I have no doubt of the lord Sorley's agreement."

"And your son?"

"He believes Decanius died on the stairs." When the guards had come to fetch Gnaius, he had left Colm with the Arénas doctors, telling both him and Lynthe to stay. The orders, he had told them, came from the Empress. What Gwenna had told Lynthe later, I did not know.

"Will that be the end of it?" Gwenna asked, back in our rooms. Lynthe stood behind her, rubbing her shoulders.

"I believe so," I said.

"Better for everyone," Sorley said. He'd gone immediately to see Eudekia, returning quickly. A formality completed.

Gwenna yawned. "Why am I so tired? I slept for hours."

"But drugged sleep," Lena said. "It's never properly restful, it seems to me. Go have a nap."

"Perhaps I will." Lynthe pulled Gwenna to her feet. "I'll see you at supper. Maybe."

"Sleep is what she needs," Lena said, watching them leave.

"Is there more to this than we've been told?" Sorley asked suddenly.

Lena frowned. "What makes you ask that?"

"Because I was there, the last time Gwenna killed a man. And the horse that she loved: I wanted to do it, but she wouldn't let me, said it was her responsibility. So I showed her how. After all that, at fourteen, she wasn't this upset."

"He threatened to rape her, Sorley, and to set her on fire," Lena said. "It's not the same."

"I suppose," he said. I didn't think he was convinced. He would ask Druisius when they were alone, I guessed. As I too had a question for Druisius, one that needed privacy and sufficient time. *You have served Casil well.* Casil, or an Empress?

"I am starting to hate this palace," Lena said, getting up. "I'll be glad when we have our own house."

"We can go to the *taberna*," Sorley said. "Drink bad wine and eat roasted chickpeas. Buy things in the market."

"Play at dice," Druisius said, but it sounded forced. "Make music."

"You can," I said, glad of the distraction. "This prince of Ésparias cannot. It will be the libraries and the baths for me, in a litter."

"We can go to the theatre, surely," Lena said. "Junia was explaining the performances."

"The theatre will be acceptable," I told her. A winter in Casil, with work to be done: a war to plan, while at the same time attempting to avert it. But there would be time—I would make time—for the libraries, and the conversations with Bruccius and other men of learning, and the theatre and other amusements. And, no doubt, evenings of *xache*, played by lamplight with the Empress. All at her pleasure, of course.

A heavy knock, almost a pounding, at the door. We all turned. It swung open, a guard standing aside. A man strode into the room, stopped. I heard Lena's indrawn breath. "Dern?"

He ignored her, turning to me. "Prince Cillian," the commander of the Ésparian fleet said. "Where is your daughter?"

Chapter 52

~DAUGHTER~

I HADN'T TRULY BEEN SLEEPY, ALTHOUGH my body felt heavy, as if I moved through water, each step taking effort. I'd wanted to be away from my parents, from thinking about the lies told, by me, by the Empress, by Druisius.

I'd tried to explain to Lynthe this morning, when I told her what had really happened. "Decanius got what he deserved," she said. "Gods, love, think what he wanted to do to you. Would have done, if the captain hadn't arrived."

I knew that, and yet I couldn't find words for the doubt that circled in my gut. I'd put it aside, told my story—most of it—to the inquest, heard the Empress's decree with remote acceptance. Alekos hadn't spoken to me. I wondered if I should worry about that.

"Lie down," Lynthe said now, "and I'll rub your back." I pulled off my tunic to lay face down on my bed. She straddled me, her hands firm and comforting, working my shoulders. I let myself drift.

Outside, in the corridor, I heard heavy feet, running. My shoulders tightened. Guards? They passed by. "Relax," Lynthe said. "Late for shift change, maybe." She pushed my hair aside to massage my neck.

"We should go back to the baths later," she said. "You can have a proper massage."

"No," I said, "I can't face other people yet. They'll ask questions."

"But about a dead dog, and who would have done such a thing," Lynthe reminded me, "Not about Decanius."

Or Druise, except perhaps to praise his prompt attention when I'd screamed. Had I screamed? I couldn't remember. I thought not, but it would be said I had.

Someone knocked on the door. Lynthe swore, sliding off me. She handed me my tunic. "Put that on. Who would disturb you?"

"Apulo, maybe." I pulled on the tunic. Lynthe went to the door.

"Captain?"

"I must come in," Druise said. Lynthe stood aside. Druise took a step or two into the room. Without thought, I shrunk back, toward the wall.

"Druise?" He was looking at me with—what? Sorrow?

"Kitten," he said, so very gently, "you must come. Put on a good tunic, and your pendant, and come. I will wait in the corridor."

"Why? What's happened?"

"Not for me to say. But you are needed."

Bewildered, I did as he asked, my mind roiling. Had Eudekia reconsidered? Was I to be arrested? Lynthe pinned my hair up, tendrils escaping, but it would do.

Druise shook his head when I tried to question him again. We walked the short distance to my parents' room in silence. He opened the door.

Everyone was on their feet, even my father. A man—Dern—stood with them. Why was he here?

Dern took one step forward and dropped to his knees. He held out his hand, a silver ring on his palm. "*Principe*, I bring you your ring of office. Faolyn is dead."

I stared at his hand, not comprehending. My father took the ring from Dern, reaching for my hand. "It will be far too big," he said gently, "but you must put it on, Gwenna. You are *Principe* of Ésparias now, *mo nihéan*."

He slipped the ring onto my middle finger, then raised my hand to his lips. "I pledge you my fealty and my love, *Principe*." There were tears in his eyes.

Around me, everyone was on their knees. No, I wanted to scream, seeing my mother looking up at me. Druisius. Lynthe. Only Sorley remained standing, and when I met his eyes he bowed his head, and then he too dropped to one knee.

I heard their words, the oaths of fealty: my mother first, her cheeks wet; then Dern, and Druisius, and Lynthe, and finally Apulo. None of it was real. The ring slid on my finger; I clenched my fist to keep it on.

"We must," my mother said briskly, "inform the Empress. Apulo, you will see to what is needed, about packing, and transport to the ship? Can we sail tomorrow?"

"The day after," my father said, "I think. I will go to the Empress. Commander—" He stopped. "Forgive me. Dern, you came straight here, after a long voyage, and we have not offered you wine. Before the world knows; before history changes, while it is just us in this room, shall we drink to the *Principe* of Ésparias?"

The first glass was mine, another confusion. I tried to smile at my father's words. "Accept what fate brings you." Of course he would choose that passage. I drank my wine, the ring clinking against the glass.

My mother took the glass from me. "Give me the ring." She threaded it onto the chain that held my pendant and fastened it again. "We'll get it made smaller at Wall's End. Now, Gwenna, will you please sit, so your father can?"

What? I sat. "*Athàir*," I protested. "You don't have to stand for me."

"I do. For the rank. But not in private, if you grant that."

"Yes," I said. "Let's settle that now. Sit, please, *Athàir*. Everyone."

He didn't move. "I must go to the Empress, and the Commander with me."

"But I don't know what happened," I said. "Shouldn't I know first?"

An accident, Dern explained: Faolyn had been riding home to his villa with his aide, on a wet and windy night. The cliff had collapsed under them. The bodies of both horses and men had been found on the shingle the next morning.

My mother, hearing, swore. "I warned them."

"The general Talyn is acting as regent until you return, *Principe*. The Governor is satisfied with her leadership, temporarily," Dern said, "But we should not linger here."

"Has the unrest grown?" I should have asked that, I thought.

"The death of a leader always raises questions, Major," Dern replied.

"Two days," my father said. "Are you ready, Commander?"

"Should I not come with you to the Empress?" I asked. What was the protocol?

"It is my responsibility," he said. "Not as your father, but as Ésparias's diplomat. Expect her to receive you later." I watched them leave.

"Gwenna." My mother touched my arm. "There are things you must do."

I blinked. "What?"

"Confirm our appointments to you, for one. Our assignments came from Talyn, but Faolyn approved them. As you must, now."

I heard a sound, a strangled sob. Lynthe stood guard at the balcony, as Druisius was at the hall door. Tears coursed down her cheeks. A realization struck me then, as hard as the blow from the lamp Decanius had thrown. *He's my brother, and I love him.* "Oh, *käresta* . . . " I crossed the room to her. "None of us gave a thought to your loss."

"Oh gods," I heard my mother say. "We didn't." I led Lynthe to a chair, crouching beside her as she wept, rubbing her back.

Apulo brought tea—his remedy for most things—so sweet I could smell the honey. Lynthe drank it and wiped her face. "It was just such a shock," she said. "I'm sorry, *Principe*, Major."

"No!" She couldn't—she was my *quincala*. I loved her, and she loved me. This was ridiculous. "You can't call me that."

"I'm on duty."

"Has that ever stopped Druise?" I said. I glanced over at him. He didn't smile.

He'd killed a man he hadn't needed to, with apparent enjoyment. I couldn't think about that just now. I looked away.

Tears wet my eyes too when Colm knelt to offer his fealty a short time later. It wasn't just my life that had changed today: his had too. He was my heir. He always had been, but now the designation felt more portentous. Was he going to be forced into a position he didn't want? Not by me, I promised silently.

That it was on his mind too was obvious as soon as my father returned. Dern was not with him; he was being found a room, and food, and would leave us to ourselves, he had said.

"The Empress will see you tomorrow," my father reported. I could see the lines of pain on his face. "She too believes you need a little time to adjust." He'd barely taken his chair when Colm spoke.

"You're going home," he said. "Does this mean I can't stay with Gnaius?"

"I don't know. Your mother and I must talk. It is less simple now."

"How?" Colm demanded. I gave him a look.

"*Athàir*," I said, "it is not just for you and *Mathàir* to decide. Colm is my heir."

"Gwenna is right," my mother said, although I heard the reluctance. "The education of the heir is a decision of the *Principe*, isn't it? Casyn decreed, and we accepted, that Gwenna needed to leave the *Ti'ach* at twelve, to finish her schooling in Ésparias. The precedent is there."

"I am not decreeing," I said. "But there are arguments for Colm to stay in Casil, aren't there?"

My father took the glass Apulo held out to him. "There are."

"What arguments?" Colm said. My parents exchanged a long look.

"It is only fair he knows," I said. "He can't choose properly without enough information." *Am I wanted?* I had asked Decanius. *Not in Casil, not anywhere,* had been his mocking reply. I hadn't told the inquest the second part.

"Tell him," my father said.

"If you come home," I said to my brother, "I may be in danger. Not everyone in Ésparias thinks I should be *Principe*. They've never had a woman leader."

"They might kill you, so I could take your place?" He sounded unbelieving.

"They might," my father said.

"But I don't want to be *Princip*."

"And so you might be offered abdication, so Faolyn's son can take the title," I said gently.

"Or killed," he said, his eyes widening. "But that could all happen if I'm here, too."

"It could," my father agreed. "But here you are out of sight, and therefore more likely out of mind. If we have reason to believe the threat certain, Gnaius will take you away, further east to other schools of medicine."

When had they planned that? It was nearly the same plan that had been used to keep Bjørn safe as a boy. Would Gnaius give Colm another name, claim him to be someone else's son?

Likely, I thought. My brother had paled.

"May I think about this?" he asked. Then, "What would you choose for me?"

"We will tell you tomorrow," my father said, "after we hear your thoughts. The decision is your sister's. The *Principe's.*"

"I will fetch food," Apulo said, a little later. "You all need to eat. Something simple?"

"Please," my mother said. I supposed I was hungry; maybe that's what this hollowness in my stomach was.

"Apulo." My father stopped him. "There are guards on the door. Introduce yourself as our steward."

"Guards?" Druisius growled. "You did not tell me?"

"I am telling you now," my father said patiently. "Two on the balcony, two in the corridor. The Empress insisted. You may—you should—make yourself known to them, as our captain."

"I had no say?"

"Eudekia's doing, not mine, *mo charaidh*," my father said. "None of us had a say."

"Their presence will raise questions," my mother pointed out.

"It will. Which is why, Apulo, you are to whisper the news in the kitchens: you are too proud to serve a *Principe* to keep it to yourself."

"Certainly," Apulo said. "It is almost true."

Was there nothing my father did not think of? But he was right, of course. Before whispers of my arrest, or my betrothal—both reasons I might suddenly have palace guards assigned—spread, the truth too should be one of the rumours.

"I am going to talk to the guard," Druisius said, getting up. "Lena?"

"Yes. You too, Lynthe. They need to understand we are also bodyguards."

There was suddenly space in the room. Sorley and Colm were playing *xache* quietly in a corner. My father held out his arms. "Come."

I slipped off my chair onto the floor beside him, the familiar feel of his hand stroking my hair so comforting.

"I am so sorry, *mo nihéan gràhadh*," he murmured. "I did not wish this for you."

I needed him; I couldn't be *Principe* without his calm counsel, his wisdom. He'd been prepared to stay in Casil for me. Could I ask?

I could compel, I realized. My mind recoiled at the thought. Perhaps I could, but I wouldn't. "*Athàir*? Will you stay with me at Wall's End? For a while, until I am used to being *Principe*?"

"If you wish," he said. "For a while."

Thinking of Wall's End reminded me. "Someone at home knows the plans, don't they? In case none of us came home?"

He smiled, smoothing my hair. "Have you not worked it out? Who was the last person I saw, before we left the *Ti'ach*?"

The stars had wheeled toward morning before I slept. Alone with me, Lynthe had wept for her brother again, and I for what fate had brought me. Acceptance did not come easily. And, I admitted, lying in the dark, aware of the guards I could not see, trying to imagine what waited for me in Ésparias, I was frightened. I was going home to be the *Principe*. That alone was cause for fear. But I was also returning to a country where some wanted me dead.

Chapter 53

~FATHER~

I MADE MY WAY OUT ONTO THE BALCONY. One of the guards outside Gwenna's room turned, saw me, nodded. Overhead, stars glittered.

I leant on my cane, looking up at the unchanging stars. They had hung over this city since its founding; watched it rise from a village, the buildings and walls of brick appearing, and then the temples and columns and the palace of marble and splendour. They would watch over it still when its grandeur had crumbled to dust.

Soft footsteps approached. Sorley. He stood beside me. "What are you thinking?" he asked.

"Of impermanence." His hand touched mine. I allowed it for a moment, but the guards were too close.

"Will you walk with me?" I asked. "I would like to look out at the city."

We made our way along the corridor, the torches lighting our way, and out onto the open space that overlooked the forum. Fire flickered in some of the temples, and a few people moved between them: priests, servants, thieves.

Sorley kept a hand on my back: a friend supporting an infirm man, nothing more. I looked out at the hills beyond, at the glow of distant lamps in windows, the barest outline of buildings revealed by moonlight. From somewhere, the sound of a *cithar* drifted up to us.

"Mestrius—he wrote the lives of illustrious men, both of Casil and before—tells of a ruler who conquered a great city to the east," I said. "The night before it was lost to him, he heard, in the early hours, a procession of musicians, of voices and instruments."

"The god who had protected him, departing. I remember Perras reading that." His hand moved on my back. "Your god has not left you, *mo gràhadh*."

"Perhaps not," I said. "But Casil is lost to me. I will not come back, Sorley. I am too old to make the journey again."

I heard footsteps below us, and the notes of the *cithar*. A bat swooped, and another. "You never went to the libraries," Sorley said.

"No." A breeze caught at my hair; cold, carrying the bite of autumn. "Gwenna wants me to stay at Wall's End as her advisor."

"Will you?"

"How do I say no? Had I not refused the succession, she would not be *Principe* at eighteen. I have had seventeen years as *Comiádh*. It is time I remembered my other commitments."

He took a breath. "What does Lena say?"

"That it suits her. It is where she would have gone when we returned, regardless."

"Druise will insist on guarding Gwenna."

"Yes." I turned, resting a hand on his arm. "The *Ti'ach* is not far for a good horseman, Sorley." Another bat swept by, its high chittering faintly audible.

"Earlier," he said, "when I went to see the Empress, Alekos was there too. He asked me if I would ensure Bjørn knew of his request; he was concerned his men would not reach the north before the river froze.

"I told him I would: I would ride to the trading port and seek word of him, and if necessary I would go further. I will be gone for some weeks, once we reach home."

"And then?"

"Then I will go to Dun Ceànnar and ask Ruar to make me Linrathe's envoy to Ésparias again. I am sure the *Principe* can be persuaded to write to him with the same request."

"Your appointment to the *Ti'ach* is for life," I reminded him, controlling the rising hope.

"I am the head of the council. Rules can be changed. And Ésparias needs music taught in its schools."

I offered my arms, not trusting myself now to speak. He stepped into them, his head against my shoulder. My hand found the nape of his neck, holding him close, his hands tight on my back. I looked over his shoulder at the city beyond. The sacrifice to be made, the god taking his due. I had made my choice long before.

A cloud obscured the moon. The city faded. A light flickered, rose, died. One note sounded, and another, before the music ceased.

⌘⌘⌘⌘⌘

The baths, in the early hours of the morning, were deserted. Only when Apulo and I were leaving did three men come in. "Prince Cillian," Timor of Qipërta said. "Have I heard correctly? A sudden death in Ésparias, and your daughter now *Principe*?"

"You have." Apulo had done his work well. "We sail for home tomorrow."

He hesitated. "Go in," he said to the other two men. "I will join you shortly." He indicated a small room off to one side of the baths. "May we talk?"

"You know of course that Decanius is dead," he said, once we were alone. "If you are leaving, then where do our negotiations stand?"

"I imagine they will continue," I said. "The Empress will appoint someone. Might I suggest you should be present at any meetings, or perhaps represent Qipërta yourself?"

"I will," he said. "I was wrong, perhaps, to leave it to Decanius. He said—" He eyed me.

"That I was duplicitous, and not to be trusted?"

"Something like that." He tugged at an ear. "The reduction in copper tariff wasn't a bad offer."

"Don't admit it," I told him. "Argue for adjusted shipping rates, too." Gwenna had suggested that, to prolong the negotiations.

He nodded. "I will. A safe voyage home, Prince Cillian. May I ask—?"

"My daughter must establish herself as *Principe*. The marriage is still possible, but not for at least a year. The young Emperor may choose not to wait. Farewell, Prince Timor. I wish you success in your negotiations."

I was stopped twice more for questions on the walk back to our rooms. I gave the same neutral answers. Privately, I was almost sure now Gwenna would not marry Alekos. Were we allowed to leave Casil without a betrothal made, then I would be certain.

Breakfast awaited me, but neither Colm nor Gwenna and Lynthe were present. Gwenna's absence didn't surprise me; my son's did. I had expected him to be impatiently awaiting our decision.

"Gnaius has restrained him, I imagine," Lena said, when I voiced my thought. We'd talked last night, reaching the same conclusion Gwenna had: it was safer for her if he stayed with Gnaius. Perhaps safer for Colm, too. There had been tears, and not only Lena's.

"Gwenna should lead the conversation," I said.

"Practice?"

"Exactly." She nodded, a trace of sorrow still in her eyes. Colm would be a man when next we saw him. When next Lena saw him; I wondered if I ever would.

Gwenna joined us a few minutes later, dressed in her best tunic, her hair up to show her ruby earrings. "Did you sleep?" Lena asked her.

"Eventually."

I excused myself, going to the bedroom to change. Lena had things to tell Gwenna. When I was dressed, Apulo opened the chest to give me my pendant. "No," I told him. "Just the ring." I had worn it only once, at the formal dinner.

I slipped my father's ring onto the middle finger of my right hand, the eagle so badly worn it could barely be made out, no longer useful as a seal.

Casyn had given it to me. The ring of office brought to Gwenna was its replacement.

When I returned to the sitting room, Colm was there. I took my seat. "Are we ready?"

"I am," Colm said.

"Gwenna?"

"I want to hear what you would choose to do, and why," she told her brother. An approach used with older students at the *Ti'acha*. Colm would know how to answer.

"I want to stay," Colm said, "and this is why. There is always danger. People die of disease and accidents. Your ship could sink, on the way home."

He glanced at me. "On the voyage here, *Athàir*, we talked about the steam pigeon. Do you remember?" He paused, gathering his thoughts. "You knew about it from books. But it was invented here, or rather Heræcria. Medicine is the same. New things are tried here, studied, debated. I learned more in a few weeks with Gnaius than all my time at the *Ti'ach na Iorlath*." He looked from me to his mother, and then to Gwenna. "If I learn here, I can bring so much back to Ésparias. Can I please stay?"

"I have one other question," Gwenna said. "What happens to your dog?"

He blinked. "Let Constyn keep him," he said. "He'll need a friend, now his father's dead."

Colm's joy at being told he could stay was palpable; hugs bestowed on all three of us, rare from my self-contained son. When he slid his arms around my neck, I pulled him close, kissing his hair. "Remember Catilius's words," I said.

"Be a good man. I am trying to be."

Lena kept him in her arms longer, then took him aside for whatever words she needed to say. Gwenna frowned at me. "You're not wearing your pendant."

"I should wear no sigil that suggests I outrank you now." I held out my hand, palm down. "The Emperors' ring is enough."

She touched it. "Was it made here in Casil?"

"Perhaps," I told her. "We can never know. Gwenna, before we leave, will you give Colm the smaller pendant? You can have the one that was mine." He might need it, one day, as proof of who he was.

"Of course."

Colm came to stand before me. "May I go now, *Athàir*?" Behind him, Lena nodded her assent.

"But be here in the morning," she said. "We sail in the afternoon."

"Lynthe will take you to Gnaius." I told him. The palace guard would have done it, but I wanted no attention brought to my son. Decanius had been powerful.

"Before you go, Gwenna," Sorley said, approaching us, "may I speak to you?" He'd been out on the balcony, breakfasting with Druisius, giving us some time together. "It won't take long."

Chapter 54

~PRINCIPE~

I FOLLOWED SORLEY OUT ONTO THE BALCONY. Druise had gone. "Send the guards further away," he said, in the voice he used to a recalcitrant student. I gave the order, and they retreated.

"Gwenna, why are you so distant with Druise?"

"I—" I didn't have an answer, not one I could give voice to. I shook my head, mute in the face of Sorley's anger.

He swore, almost under his breath. "I watched him fall in love with you when you were a few minutes old," he said. "Druise would give his life for you. He came too close, a day ago, and he's in pain, and angry with himself over trusting the guard. Doubting his own judgment, and you're not helping. He thinks you don't have confidence in him now."

"He stabbed an incapacitated man." And I saw his face as he did. "Yet you took responsibility, knowing no one would blame you," Sorley said.

"I don't like what he did. It doesn't mean I don't love him, or want him punished." Tears pricked. I blinked them away; I couldn't go to the Empress with red eyes.

"Gwenna." Sorley's voice was gentler now. "Four years ago, he killed the Marai man who had surrendered. You asked me why."

"Because he had tried to kill me."

"And for that he had to die, even though he didn't know who you were. Decanius didn't have that excuse. So Druise killed him. Why is this different?"

"Because he shouldn't have needed to," I said, searching for reasons. "I went to my room alone. It was stupid, and it could have cost Druise his life. How do I forgive myself for that?"

Sorley sighed. "You both made mistakes. Talk to him, Gwenna. Ask his forgiveness. Do you think for a moment he could withhold it?"

"No. But—"

"But what, Gwenna? Is there more to this?" The edge had returned to Sorley's voice. I thought of what I had seen in Druise's eyes for that brief moment: satisfaction, but more than that, something I didn't want to give a name to. *Know the man.* I had believed I did.

"Decanius wanted Druise executed for desertion, didn't he?" I said in a rush. "When I was a baby?"

Sorley leant against the balcony wall. "The year you were born. Did you think that's why Druise killed him? For *revenge*?"

"I—" I stopped, seeing the look of incredulity on Sorley's face.

"Revenge would mean Druise actually thought—or cared—about what happened in the past. Except as a source of information, he doesn't. *Accept what fate brings you* could have been written for him."

You are wrong, I thought. You weren't at the baths to see the anguish Bernikë's parting words caused him. Spaces and secrets: did everyone have them?

I looked at the man beside me, thinking again of the day Druise had punched the sailor, and the muffled cry that had come from their cabin later. Different secrets. But not, some intuition told me, separate.

Not for me to know. I pursed my lips, making my smile apologetic. "My father says Druise is a better stoic than he. I'm so sorry, Sorley."

"Not me you have to say that to."

"Where is he?"

"Gone to talk to the guard captain about the arrangements for transport to the ship. You can find him later." He ran a hand over his pale beard. "Gods, I have just chastised the *Principe* of Ésparias, which I have no right at all to do. Will you forgive that?"

I blinked back the tears that had risen again. "You have as much right as any of my parents. I expect much worse from Druise."

Sorley grinned. "And you'll probably get it. Now go; even a *Principe* should not keep an Empress waiting."

Guarded, walking at my father's pace, our passage to the Empress's rooms did not go unobserved. I tried to be neither regal nor embarrassed, copying my father. He succeeded. I wasn't sure I did.

Eudekia sat in a chair, high backed, elaborately carved, not quite a throne. Beside her, Alekos occupied a similar seat. I steadied my father before I knelt. One knee now, my father had told me before we'd left, not both.

"Be welcome to our presence, *Principe* of Ésparias," the Empress said. As he had the first night, Alekos rose to take my hand as I stood.

"*Principe*." He kissed its back. "I am sorry you will be leaving us."

"With your permission, Empress," I said. "I am needed at home."

"You have it," she said, and then she smiled. "Although you will be missed, *Principe*, both you and your father. Sit, please." Chairs had been set out for us. We were alone: no servants, and the guards were on the other side of the doors.

"You sail tomorrow?"

"On the afternoon tide," my father said.

"You go home to unrest. A faction who does not believe a woman should lead." How did she know? I glanced at my father; he was unsurprised. He had told her, I thought.

"I wonder what they think of me?" Eudekia mused. "Although that is soon of no matter. It is unfortunate you could not stay for Alekos's investiture."

"As much as I would have liked Gwenna to be present," the Prince said, "I disagree. Her absence will convince the other princesses I have made no choice, do you not think?"

"You are likely right," his mother said. "So Qipërta will remain hopeful."

"Who will advise you on that situation, Empress?" my father asked.

"Bruccius. Other *magistera*. The senior officers who remain in the city." Faint surprise in her voice, I thought.

"Perhaps . . . " My father hesitated. "Have you given thought to why Decanius wanted Gwenna dead, Empress?"

"She stood in the way of his plans for his half-sister."

"But we had let it be known the negotiations were not proceeding well, and indeed likely to fail. Were not his actions drastic, in that case?"

"You are suggesting he knew it was a lie?" Alekos said. He inclined his head to me. "Because it is, *Principe*. I remain hopeful, although of course the situation is different now. You will need more time." Relief spread inside me. He was maintaining the ruse.

"I am," my father said. "In which case, I must ask how he knew. You may wish to be cautious of your advisors, Empress. Consider where you give your trust carefully."

Something Alekos had said . . . "Did Bruccius teach Faolyn, while he was here?"

"He did."

"Does he have a son serving in Ésparias?"

"I believe so," the Empress said. "Why?"

I told her of the spilled oil, our belief it had been meant for me, and of the young captain who had expressed a disinterested concern. She brushed a knuckle along her lips, thoughtful, analysing.

"The observation needs consideration. My thanks, *Principe*, Prince Cillian." The message was clear; no more was to be said. "*Principe*, is there anything you need; any help we can give you?"

"Some information, if you will." I spoke briskly. "Will you be recalling troops from Ésparias in the spring?"

"It is too early to tell," Alekos said. "Much depends on when the men from Varsland arrive."

"What instructions are you sending to your governor?"

"To be ready to send half the troops."

"Casilani? Or Casilani and Ésparian?"

"Both," Eudekia said. "If needed."

I had one last question, this one not at my mother's prompting. *Empires rose and fell*, Catilius reminded us. "Will they be returning?"

The Empress smiled. "Only the gods know, *Principe*. It is my hope. I can give you no other assurance. There may be no war at all."

So many possibilities, all of which I needed to consider. I nodded, accepting her words. Alekos rose. "*Principe*, may I speak to you privately for a moment?"

I walked with him to the far end of the room. "I wanted to apologize," he said quietly. "I should have spoken to you yesterday, after the inquest. How are you feeling?"

"I'm fine," I said. "I can't waste thought on a man who died because he was trying to kill me. I have larger things to concern myself with now."

"As I do. Gwenna, two questions. May we write to each other, Emperor to *Principe*? As our parents have? I would value your thoughts."

"Of course," I said. That too would help maintain the ruse. "And the second question?"

A faint colour rose in his cheeks. "I have no time to think about this," he said. "Tell me who I should marry."

"I can't," I said, keeping back my laugh. "But I'll say this. If you want to begin your reign with peace and stability, marry Sahira. If you want a companion to discuss your plans with, who will give you reasoned argument and a decent game of *xache*, consider Rosale." She would be a friend.

He smiled. I gave him my hand to kiss, as I would, were we courting. He kept his fingers on mine as we walked back to where our parents waited. "I must leave you now," he said. "Farewell, *Principe*. Farewell, Prince Cillian. I hope we will meet here again next year."

He had played his part perfectly. If the price of my father's freedom lay in accepting Alekos, I had nothing to worry about. The Prince would decide, at some time not too far in the future, that he would not wait for me. His decision, not mine.

"Sit, *Principe*," the Empress directed. "I have things to say."

Beside me, my father's hands rested on the silver eagle which topped his cane. He regarded the Empress, a tiny smile playing on his lips. I saw the connection between them, the long attachment, something more than friendship and less than love. They understand each other, I thought.

"You," she said to my father, "are teaching treason."

Cold fear gripped my spine. No, I thought. No. Please.

"I am not," my father said, untroubled. "I teach nothing more than the wisdom of Catilius and Annaeus, and others of their school. No different than what the learned men of Casil teach here, Empress."

"'Look back over the past, at the empires that rose and fell, and predict the future,'" she quoted. "What future do you ask your pupils to foresee?"

"Perhaps that is a question for my daughter, who was also my student."

"Then tell me, *Principe*. If war is Casil's fate, and Ésparias is left to its own defences, what will you do?"

What will you choose to do, and why?

"What I must, Empress," I replied, "to maintain a peace among the lands of the west. The ties between Linrathe and Ésparias are strong, ties of blood now, not just treaty. My own grandmother was Linrathan, you will recall." She would know this; I was revealing no secrets.

"And Varsland? A people who like war, and with whom you have only an imposed peace. A parallel with the Boranoi, I might add."

"Their king is an ally. If Prince Bjørn brings the younger men, restless for glory, east to support Casil, that threat is lessened." And we had the coastal forts now, although not in Linrathe. Something to discuss with Ruar?

"Lessened, but not removed."

"They asked for schools, for *Ti'acha* to be set up in their land. They are learning the wisdom of Casil and Heræcria, Empress, and their traders come east. They have more to think about than war and conquest now."

She raised an eyebrow. "I thought the same of my husband's people; it appears I was wrong." Her tone told me not to comment. "Sometimes a marriage alliance is not enough to prevent dreams of conquest and glory. Power matters to men, *Principe.* Do not forget that."

"I will not, Empress," I said. Her eyes softened.

"It is no easy thing for a young woman to lead a country, as well I know," she said. "Especially alone, with only advisors—who may or may not be trusted—to confide in."

"My daughter will not be alone," my father said. "I will be with her, and her mother, among other trusted advisors."

"Will you?" I said, surprise making me speak. Eudekia laughed.

"You had not told your daughter? That was cruel, Cillian."

"I thought her mother had," he admitted. "But I am clearly mistaken. We will be, Gwenna. All of us."

All. Sorley. How? A question for later. Relief washed through me, for myself, for my father. But Eudekia wasn't done.

"My son tells me he will wait a year."

"It may not be enough," I said.

"Be clear on one thing," she said, and now this was the Empress speaking, "As long as Ésparias is a province of my Empire, I—we—will tolerate no marriage with Varsland. I do not trust them, and we cannot afford that mistake twice. Weave your web of alliances against the future, the contingency plan for the day the Eastern Empire fails, for that is what all good leaders do. I will not call it treason, only forethought. But we have our limits, *Principe*, and you and your father must know it."

"I have," I said, "no intention of, and no interest in, a marriage alliance with Varsland, Empress. Not for myself. I will not rule out other avenues."

She nodded. "Nor should you. Varsland is better as an ally than an enemy, but marriage can be too close a tie." She held out a hand. I knelt to kiss it.

"I wish you safe travels, *Principe.*" Her eyes went to my father, still seated. "I wonder—" She hesitated, Eudekia again, not the Empress. "Cillian, would you indulge me?"

He smiled, the rare smile that lit his face. "You wish to be defeated?"

"I won the last game," she said.

"I remember it as a draw, or perhaps unfinished."

"Unfinished," she said. "You may be right."

I left them to the game, walking out from the palace's corridors onto the roof overlooking the forum. Behind me, I heard the footsteps of my guard.

My father was safe. We would go home to Ésparias, and Alekos would marry Rosale, or Dalphe, or maybe even Sahira, in time. He would not wait for the young *Principe* consolidating her position amidst unrest in her distant land. Something would be asked of me in time: the price deferred, not forgiven.

Ésparias. I saw the moorland and the sea, the sweep of the grasslands, the tamed and tilled fields. The villages spreading into towns; connected by the roads the Casilani had built, but still with space between them, distance. *You are a symbol,* my father had said, *a reminder that Ésparias is more than a province of Casil; that we have a history of our own.* It would be my life's work, and my successors, to ensure that was not forgotten. A promise to my land and my people.

Ruar had used those words, on a day in late summer; a parting in the courtyard of the *Ti'ach.* His eyes were as blue as the summer sky, and under my hand his muscles had been firm; a young man, still. He understood duty and leadership, and his succession was secured. A child born to us would be my heir.

I turned. The guard stepped aside to allow me back into the corridor, his back straight and his weapons gleaming, as befitted my rank. I was the *Principe* of Ésparias, and somewhere, Lynthe was waiting.

Ephēmeros

Fair the first buds after winter.
Fair the curl of new leaf
Opening; sweet scent of spring.
All pass in their time.
Where is there reason for grief?
Fair the green field of grain.
Fair the swelling berry
Ripening; rich scent of summer
All pass in their season.
Time does not tarry.
Fair the hanging fruit.
Fair the golden harvest
Gathered; deep scent of autumn.
All pass as they must
Before winter darkness.
Where is her laughter?
Where is her touch; the bright eyes,
The golden hair;
Her scent as sweet as spring's bloom?
Passed before time; life only lent.
Waste like winter obscures the world.
My heart laments.
Wind scatters blossom, seed; leaves fall
To ground undiscovered.
And like unto them is my child.

-found among the papers of Cillian of Ésparias after his death.

Author's Note

Writing a book is supposed to be a lonely endeavour, but in my experience, it's been tempered by the support of friends and writing groups and family, over coffee and lunches, meetings formal and informal, long walks and drives. Writing a book during a pandemic was a different experience: as I write this, it's been eighteen months since I've seen most of my scattered family, or my friends.

My heartfelt gratitude goes to two people I've never actually (yet) met, but without whom *Empire's Heir* might not be finished, and certainly wouldn't be the book it is: my friends from Twitter, Karen Heenan and Bjørn Larssen. For the hours and hours of messaging back and forth about plot and characters and structure, reading early versions of scenes, making suggestions, reading the first draft – and for making me laugh, thank you. I really doubt I could have done it without you.

To Margaret Courtney (Brook Allen) sincere thanks for pointing me toward a wonderful personal tour guide for Rome, Silvia Prosperi at *A Friend in Rome.* I hope the care and attention Silvia gave in showing me 4th century Rome is reflected in my representation of Casil, especially in the Imperial Palace, the Bassanian Baths, and in the marketplace where Druisius' brother Marius runs his family's business.

My beta readers, Terrence Thomas, Katie Thorpe, and Alistair Tosh all bring different skills and viewpoints, which is exactly what an author needs. I may not incorporate every one of your ideas, but I do consider them carefully, and your time and care and consideration is very much appreciated.

Thanks too to Tony O'Brien, my cover designer, for always finding a way to translate my vision into reality.

To the readers who have told me on social media and face-to-face that they are waiting impatiently for this book: I hope you are not disappointed. If, in the first half of chapter 53, you perceived an echo of Leonard Cohen and Sharon Robinson's haunting song *Alexandra Leaving*, itself a reworking of C.P. Cavafy's *The God Abandons Antony*, well, you are not wrong. (If you don't know it, search YouTube for the Sharon Robinson version.)

Finally, because 'last is a signal honour', there is my husband, Brian Rennie, who listens, argues, provides plot, reads, makes suggestions, tells me when I'm wrong, and makes me laugh. The line from the day we climbed Dunadd together, the moment when history and story and landscape became inseparable in my mind, to these books hasn't been a straight one, and you've been there for that entire wandering journey. You must know I love you.

Guelph, July 2021

www.ingramcontent.com/pod-product-compliance
Lightning Source LLC
Chambersburg PA
CBHW020230110726
47898CB00004B/1223